WEDDING CAKE MURDER

Hannah watched the timer tick off the minutes. What was taking Michelle so long? She should be back here so that she could start preparing the cookie sheets.

Hannah turned to look at the walk-in cooler door. It was open and she could see Michelle standing there, just staring at something.

"Michelle?" she called out, but her sister didn't react.

On legs that shook slightly, Hannah walked across the floor to the cooler door. She took a deep breath, stepped inside and peered over her sister's shoulder.

Alain Duquesne was on the floor of the cooler, splayed out on his back. A big piece of Hannah's Double Rainbow Swirl Wedding Cake was partially smashed next to his body, and the knife he'd used to cut her cake was buried up to the hilt in his chest . . .

Books by Joanne Fluke

Hannah Swensen Mysteries

CHOCOLATE CHIP COOKIE MURDER
STRAWBERRY SHORTCAKE MURDER
BLUEBERRY MUFFIN MURDER
LEMON MERINGUE PIE MURDER
FUDGE CUPCAKE MURDER
SUGAR COOKIE MURDER
PEACH COBBLER MURDER
CHERRY CHEESECAKE MURDER
KEY LIME PIE MURDER
CANDY CANE MURDER
CARROT CAKE MURDER
CREAM PUFF MURDER
PLUM PUDDING MURDER
APPLE TURNOVER MURDER
DEVIL'S FOOD CAKE MURDER
GINGERBREAD COOKIE MURDER
CINNAMON ROLL MURDER
RED VELVET CUPCAKE MURDER
BLACKBERRY PIE MURDER
DOUBLE FUDGE BROWNIE MURDER
WEDDING CAKE MURDER
CHRISTMAS CARAMEL MURDER
BANANA CREAM PIE MURDER
JOANNE FLUKE'S LAKE EDEN COOKBOOK

Suspense Novels

VIDEO KILL
WINTER CHILL
DEAD GIVEAWAY
THE OTHER CHILD
COLD JUDGMENT
FATAL IDENTITY
FINAL APPEAL
VENGEANCE IS MINE
EYES
WICKED
DEADLY MEMORIES

Published by Kensington Publishing Corporation

WEDDING CAKE MURDER

JOANNE FLUKE

KENSINGTON BOOKS
www.kensingtonbooks.com

KENSINGTON BOOKS are published by

Kensington Publishing Corp.
119 West 40th Street
New York, NY 10018

All Kensington titles, imprints and distributed lines are avail-
able at special quantity discounts for bulk purchases for sales
promotion, premiums, fund-raising, educational or institutional
use. Special book excerpts or customized printings can also be
created to fit specific needs. For details, write or phone the
office of the Kensington Special Sales Manager: Kensington
Publishing Corp., 119 West 40th Street, New York, NY, 10018.
Attn. Special Sales Department. Phone: 1-800-221-2647.

Library of Congress Card Catalogue Number: 2015951110

ISBN-13: 978-1-61773-218-8
ISBN-10: 1-61773-218-4
First Kensington Hardcover Edition: March 2016
First Kensington Mass Market Edition: February 2017

eISBN-13: 978-1-61773-217-1
eISBN-10: 1-61773-217-6
First Kensington Electronic Edition: March 2016

10 9 8 7 6 5 4 3 2 1

Printed in the United States of America

This book is for Anne Elizabeth, my lovely
and talented writer friend,
who's married to a SEAL *(the Navy kind)*.

Acknowledgments

Big hugs to the kids and the grandkids.
Having such a wonderful family is a real blessing.

Thank you to my friends and neighbors: Mel & Kurt, Anne Elizabeth & Carl, Dee Appleton, Lyn & Bill, Lu, Gina and her family, Adrienne, Jay, Bob, R.T. Jordan, Laura Levine, Dr. Bob & Sue, Danny, Mark B., Angelique, Mark & Mandy at Faux Library, Daryl and her staff at Groves Accountancy, Gene and Ron at SDSA, and everyone at Boston Private Bank.

Thanks to Brad, Stephanie, Eric, Nancey, Bruce, Alison, Cameron, Barbara, Gabriel, Lisa, Toby, and everyone at the Hallmark Movies & Mysteries Channel who gave us the *Murder She Baked* Hannah Swensen movies. What fun to see Hannah on TV!

Thank you to my Minnesota friends: Lois & Neal, Bev & Jim, Lois & Jack, Val, Ruthann, Lowell, Dorothy & Sister Sue, Mary & Jim, Pat and Gary at Once Upon a Crime Bookstore, and Tim Hedges.

Hugs to my multi-talented friend and Editor-in-Chief, John Scognamiglio.

Thanks to all the wonderful folks at Kensington Publishing who keep Hannah sleuthing and baking up a storm.

Thanks to Meg Ruley and the staff at the Jane Rotrosen Agency for their constant support and their wise advice. Go Barracudas!

Thanks to Hiro Kimura, my wonderful cover artist for the incredible wedding cake on this book cover! There are designs and decorations all over the book jacket, and I especially love his drawings of Moishe!

Thank you to Lou Malcangi at Kensington Publishing, for designing all of Hannah's deliciously stunning covers.

Thanks to John at *Placed4Success.com* for Hannah's movie and TV placements, and for always being there for me.

Thanks to Rudy at *Z'Kana Studios* for editing and compiling snippets from my televised interviews and baking segments, for maintaining my website at **www.JoanneFluke.com** and for giving support to Hannah's social media.

Big thanks to Kathy Allen for the final testing of Hannah's recipes.

Hugs to Judy Q. for helping with Hannah's e-mail at **Gr8Clues@JoanneFluke.com** and searching for answers to research questions.

Grateful hugs to my super friend Trudi Nash for going on book tours with me, for keeping me comfy and cossetted, and for coming up with new and innovative recipes for us to try.
If Trudi's oven ever breaks, Hannah's sunk!

Thanks to the Honey Moon Sweets Bakery in Tempe, Arizona, for baking the fabulous wedding cake we'll serve at the launch party for *Wedding Cake Murder* at the Poisoned Pen Bookstore in Phoenix.

And thanks to food stylist and
media guide extraordinaire Lois Brown
for her friendship and her talented assistance.

Special thanks to my publicist, Vida Engstrand,
for all she does.

Thank you to Nancy and Heiti for all sorts of wonderful
recipes, and for giving me permission to use their names in
Hannah's books.

Hugs to the Double Ds, Fern, Leah, and everyone on Team
Swensen who helps to keep Hannah's Facebook presence
alive and well.

Thank you to Dr. Rahhal, Dr. and Cathy Line, Dr. Wallen,
Dr. Koslowski, Drs. Ashley and Lee, and Dr. Niemeyer
(who reminds me of Doc Knight) for putting up with my
pesky Hannah-book-related medical and dental questions.
Norman and Doc Knight would be lost without you!

Grateful thanks to all of the Hannah fans who share
their favorite family recipes with me, post on
Facebook, watch the Hannah movies, and
devour each and every book.
I hope you find *Wedding Cake Murder*
particularly delicious!

Chapter One

"No, it's not the wedding I dreamed of, but it *is* the wedding I want!" Hannah Swensen's hands shook slightly as she replaced her cup of coffee in the bone china saucer. She'd been so startled by Grandma Knudson's question that a few drops had sloshed out of her cup and landed in its matching saucer. The matriarch of Holy Redeemer Lutheran Church was known for being outspoken, but Hannah hadn't expected to be grilled about her upcoming nuptials when Grandma Knudson had called her at The Cookie Jar, Hannah's coffee shop and bakery, and invited her to the parsonage for coffee.

"Everyone's talking, you know," Grandma Knudson confided, leaning forward in her chair. "No one can understand why they haven't been invited to the wedding. I told them you preferred a small, intimate family affair, but they feel left out. And almost everyone from my Bible study group asked me if there was something wrong."

"Wrong?" Hannah repeated, not certain what Grandma Knudson meant.

"Yes. People always think that there's something wrong when a wedding takes place behind closed doors. Weddings aren't supposed to be private. They're supposed to be joyous celebrations."

"I *am* joyous! I mean, *joyful*. And so is Ross. I just thought it might be easier for everyone if we didn't have a big public display."

"Because of Norman and Mike?"

"Well . . . yes. That's part of the reason. This is rather sudden, and they haven't had time to get used to the idea that Ross and I are getting married. I thought it would be . . ." Hannah paused, trying to think of another word, but only one came to mind. "I thought it would be *easier* for them this way," she finished.

Grandma Knudson was silent as she stared at Hannah, and that made Hannah want to explain. "You know . . ." she continued. "If I'd invited everyone to a huge wedding and reception, it would be almost like . . . like . . ."

The older woman let her struggle for a moment, and then she gave a nod. "Like rubbing their noses in it?"

"Yes! I mean, not exactly. But some people might think that that's what I was doing."

"Perhaps," Grandma Knudson conceded. "Tell me about Ross. Did he think that a small, private wedding was a good idea?"

"I . . . actually . . ." Hannah paused and took a deep breath. "Ross and I didn't really talk about that. He just told me that anything I wanted to do about the wedding would be fine with him."

"I see. Did you at least meet with Mike and Norman and talk to them about what you'd decided?"

"No. I wanted to spare their feelings. I thought it might be too painful for them to discuss it."

"You mean you thought it might be too painful for *you* to discuss it, don't you?" Grandma Knudson corrected her bluntly.

Hannah sighed heavily. She had to be truthful. "Perhaps you're right," she admitted, and made a move to pick up her cup and saucer rather than meet the older woman's eyes. "I guess I really wasn't thinking clearly, and I certainly didn't think that a small wedding would cause all this fuss. I just wanted to get married before I had to leave for the Food Channel *Dessert Chef Competition*. I thought that Ross could go with me and it would be our honeymoon."

"I see. And the competition is in three weeks?"

"That's right." Hannah managed to take a sip of her coffee and then she put it back down on the table again. Why was Grandma Knudson asking all these questions? There must be a reason. As Hannah sat there, trying to think of why Grandma Knudson was giving her the third degree, the light dawned. "Mother!" Hannah said with a sigh.

"What did you say?"

"I said *Mother*. She put you up to this, didn't she? She wanted me to have a big wedding and I refused. So Mother came running to you to see if you could convince me to change my mind! Isn't Mother the reason you invited me here for coffee?"

"She's part of the reason. But the other part is that I wanted you to taste my lemon pie. It's the easiest pie I've ever made. All you need is a lemon, sugar, butter, and eggs. You put everything in a blender, pour it into one of those fancy frozen piecrusts Florence carries down at the Red Owl, and bake it. But you haven't even sampled it yet."

Hannah looked down at the dessert plate resting next to her cup and saucer. Grandma Knudson's pie did look delicious. "Is that crème fraiche on the top?"

"Yes. It's your crème fraiche, the one you use on your strawberry shortcake. And if you don't want to go to the bother of making that, you can use vanilla ice cream or sweetened whipped cream. Taste it, Hannah. I want your opinion."

Hannah picked up her fork and took a bite. And then she took another bite. "It's delicious," she said. "It has exactly the right amount of tartness to balance the sweetness."

"I'm glad you like it, but let's get back to Mike and Norman. You're not getting off the hot seat so easily. Your mother's very upset, you know. People have been stopping her on the street and asking when your wedding invitations will arrive."

"Did she tell them that it was a small, private wedding?"

Grandma Knudson shook her head. "No. She was too embarrassed. You know as well as I do what people think when you get married so fast in a small, private ceremony."

"They think I'm . . . ?" There was no way Hannah could finish her question. She was too shocked.

"Of course they think that. It's usually the case, especially with a first marriage like yours. There's even a betting pool that Hal McDermott set up down at the café for the date the baby will be born."

Hannah's mouth dropped open and she shut it quickly. And then she gave a rueful laugh. "What happens to the betting pool if there's no baby? Because there isn't!"

"Good question. My guess is that Hal gets to keep the proceeds, and that's not right. I think I'll have Bob and Claire go down there and convince him to give all that money to the local charities. That would serve people right for betting on something like that!"

"Do you think Hal will agree to give the money to charity?"

"He'll have to. Betting pools are illegal in Winnetka County, and Hal knows it. So is playing poker for money behind that curtain of his in the back room of the café. He'll knuckle under. You don't have to worry about that. And if he doesn't, Bob will give a rousing sermon about gambling the next time Rose drags Hal to church."

Hannah couldn't help it. She laughed. Grandma Knudson always got what she wanted, and this would be no exception.

"That's better," Grandma Knudson commented. "It's good to hear you laugh. Now what are you going to do about Mike and Norman?"

"What do *you* think I should do? Invite them to be Ross's groomsmen at a huge church wedding?"

"I think that's *exactly* what you should do! Give Mike and Norman a chance to step up to the plate. As it stands right now, everyone's buzzing about the fact that their hearts are broken. If both of them are in the wedding party, it'll put all those wagging tongues to rest. Believe you me, they'll jump at the chance to do that!"

"Are you sure?"

"I'm positive." Grandma Knudson locked eyes with Hannah. "Neither one of those men enjoys being the butt of gossip, and both of them like Ross. Of course they're disappointed that you didn't choose one of them, but they'll do the right thing if you ask them."

Hannah thought about that for a moment. Norman and Mike *did* like Ross. The three men were friends. And she knew that Ross liked Mike and Norman. If she'd said she wanted a big wedding and asked Ross to choose two men to be groomsmen, he would probably have chosen Mike and Norman.

"Well?"

Grandma Knudson was waiting for an answer, and Hannah hedged a little. "You may be right, but I'll have to ask Ross what he thinks of the idea."

"I did that this morning. I called Ross at work and he said it was fine with him if that was what you wanted. And Mike and Norman are definitely on board. I double-checked with them right afterwards. And both of them told me that they'll accept if you ask them."

"You called Mike and Norman, too?"

"Of course I did. I wanted to make sure this would work."

Hannah gave a little groan. Railroaded. She'd been railroaded, but Grandma Knudson had a point she couldn't ignore. If everyone in town was gossiping about her and Hal had even set up a betting pool, she had to do something to turn things around. And then she remembered what Grandma Knudson had said. "You said you double-checked with Mike and Norman this morning?"

"Yes."

"If you *double*-checked, that means you or someone else had checked with them *before* this morning. Was that someone you?"

Grandma Knudson looked slightly flustered. "Actually . . . no."

With a burst of lightning clarity, Hannah saw the whole picture. Her eyes narrowed and she faced the matriarch of the church squarely. "*Mother* checked with them before you did. Is that right?"

Grandma Knudson sighed. "Yes, but she didn't want you to know that it was her idea."

"That figures," Hannah said with a sigh.

"Your mother is an expert when it comes to gossip," Grandma Knudson attempted to explain, "but she was afraid you'd reject her plan out of hand if she was the one to suggest it. That's why she asked me to talk to you about it. And I did. Your mother, Andrea, and Michelle are already working out the details of your wedding."

"They're planning my wedding without me?"

"Yes, but you know how long wedding plans take. Delores and the girls have everything organized, but nothing's been firmed up yet. All they need is for you to give them the go-ahead."

Hannah was silent. She wasn't quite ready to cave in yet.

"Your mother said to tell you that she knows you're busy at The Cookie Jar and you have to be in New York for the dessert competition very soon. She's absolutely certain that everything will be ready so that you can get married, have a reception at the Lake Eden Inn, and leave for New York the next morning."

"Mother can pull off a big wedding in less than three weeks?"

"Yes. And you don't have to do any wedding planning. Your sisters and Delores are completely prepared to arrange everything."

Again, Hannah was silent. She didn't like the idea of turning everything over to her mother and sisters, but it seemed like the only reasonable option since she'd made such a mess of it on her own.

"Delores said to tell you that there are only two things you have to do," Grandma Knudson spoke again. "The first thing is to choose your wedding dress. Your mother has already consulted with Claire at Beau Monde, and Claire has ordered more than a half-dozen gowns for your approval. When they come in, Claire will let you know so that you can run next door to try them on. All you have to do is choose the one you want to wear and Claire will do any alterations you might need."

Hannah gave a slight smile. At least they were letting her choose her own wedding gown! And it was true that she didn't have time to organize a big wedding. The nightmare of trying to arrange Delores's wedding was still fresh in her mind. There was no way she wanted to get involved in a morass like that again, but she was the bride and it was a bit disconcerting not to be involved in any of the planning. "What's the second thing they want me to do?" she asked.

"Show up at the church on time."

Hannah's sarcastic nature kicked in, and the question popped out of her mouth before she could exercise restraint. "Do they want me to show up with or without Ross?"

Grandma Knudson burst into laughter. "With Ross. Not even your mother could accomplish a wedding without a groom." The older woman reached out to take Hannah's hand. "Are you all right with this plan, Hannah? If you're not, we can try to come up with something else that'll work."

Grandma Knudson was waiting for an answer and Hannah took a deep breath. "Yes, I'm all right with it as long as Ross and I can get married before the Food Channel competition. Do you think that's possible?"

"Your mother assured me that it was."

Hannah gave a reluctant nod. "All right then. I'll do it, if you'll do something for me."

"What's that?"

"I'd like a second piece of your lemon pie, and I'd also like to have the recipe. It's the best non-meringue lemon pie I've ever tasted!"

EASY LEMON PIE

Preheat oven to 350 degrees F., rack in the middle position.

Note from Grandma Knudson: I got this recipe from my friend, Lois Brown, who lives in Phoenix, AZ. She has a lemon tree in her backyard so she always has lemons to make this pie.

    Hannah's 1ˢᵗ Note: You can make this recipe in a food processor or a blender. We use a food processor down at The Cookie Jar.

    1 frozen 9-inch piecrust *(or one you've made yourself)*
    1 whole medium-size lemon
    ½ cup butter *(1 stick, 4 ounces, ¼ pound)*
    1 cup white *(granulated)* sugar
    4 large eggs

Sweetened whipped cream to put on top of
    your pie before serving

If you used a frozen pie crust, take it out of the package and set it on a cookie sheet with sides while you make the filling for the pie.

If you made your own piecrust, roll it out, put it in a 9-inch pie pan, cut it to fit the pie pan, and crimp the edges so it looks nice. Then set it on a cookie sheet with sides to wait for its filling.

Cut the tough ends off your lemon. Cut it in half and then cut one half into 4 slices. *(The slices should be round, like wagon wheels.)*

Cut the other half-lemon into 4 similar slices to make 8 slices in all.

Examine the slices and pick out any seeds. Throw the seeds away.

Place all 8 seedless slices in a blender *(or a food processor)*.

Turn on the blender or food processor and process the lemon slices until they are mush. *(This is not a regular cooking term, but I bet you know what I mean!)*

Melt the half-cup of butter in the microwave or on the stovetop. *(If you'd rather do it in the microwave, this should take about 50 seconds on HIGH.)*

Pour the melted butter over the lemon mush in the blender.

Add the cup of white sugar.

Crack open the 4 eggs and add them one by one.

Turn on the blender or food processor and blend everything until it is a homogenous mush. *(Another non-regulation cooking term.)*

Pour the lemon mixture into the crust.

Bake your Easy Lemon Pie at 350 degrees F. for 40 minutes or until the mixture turns solid and the top is brown.

Take your pie out of the oven and cool it on a cold stove burner or a wire rack. Once it is cool, cover it with foil or plastic wrap and refrigerate it until you're ready to serve.

Hannah's 2nd Note: I like to use my Crème Fraiche on this pie. Here's the recipe just in case you don't have it handy:

HANNAH'S WHIPPED CRÈME FRAICHE

(This will hold for several hours. Make it ahead of time and refrigerate it.)

2 cups heavy whipping cream
½ cup white *(granulated)* sugar
½ cup sour cream *(you can substitute unflavored yogurt, but it won't hold as well and you'll have to do it at the last minute)*
½ cup brown sugar *(to sprinkle on top after you cut your pie into pieces)*

Whip the cream with the white sugar until it holds a firm peak. Test for this by shutting off the mixer, and "dotting" the surface with your spatula. Once you have firm peaks, gently fold in the sour cream. You can do this by hand or by using the slowest speed on the mixer.

Transfer the mixture to a covered bowl and store it in the refrigerator until you are ready to serve your Easy Lemon Pie.

To serve your pie, cut it into 6 generous pieces or 8 smaller slices and put each slice on a pretty dessert plate.

Top each slice with a generous dollop or two of Hannah's Whipped Crème Fraiche.

Sprinkle the top of the Whipped Crème Fraiche with brown sugar.

Hannah's 3rd Note: If you want to get really fancy, cut a paper-thin slice of lemon, dip it in granulated sugar, and put it on top of each slice of pie.

Chapter Two

Hannah breathed a deep sigh of relief as she hurried in the back door of The Cookie Jar and sat down on a stool at the stainless steel work island. She'd been manipulated by two master manipulators, but she couldn't be angry with either one of them. If everything Grandma Knudson had told her was correct, she had to change her small, intimate wedding plans and endure a huge church wedding and a reception with all the bells and whistles. Delores, Andrea, and Michelle would plan an elaborate affair, but there was no other recourse. And thankfully, there was nothing for her to do except choose her wedding gown and show up for the ceremony.

One quick cup of coffee later and Hannah was on her feet, mixing up sugar cookie dough. She was just getting ready to mix in a cup of chopped pecans when Lisa Herman Beeseman, Hannah's young partner, rushed through the swinging restaurant-style door that separated the coffee shop from the kitchen.

"There's a phone call for you, Hannah," Lisa announced breathlessly. "It's somebody named Eric, and he said he was from the Food Channel. I think it's about the *Dessert Chef Competition*."

Hannah handed the wooden spoon to Lisa and gestured

toward the bowl. "Will you stir in those pecans while I take the call? I'm making a variation of sugar cookies with maple flavoring and pecans."

"Sure. No problem. Aunt Nancy and Michelle have got everything covered out in the coffee shop."

Lisa began to stir, and Hannah headed for the phone on the kitchen wall. She flipped to a blank page in the short-hand notebook she kept on the counter, picked up a pen, and grabbed the receiver. "This is Hannah."

"Hi, Hannah. It's Eric Connelly from the Food Channel. We're in a little time crunch here and we had to move the *Dessert Chef Competition* up a week and a half. Can you clear the decks back there and be here on October tenth instead of October twentieth?"

"Oh!" Hannah was so flustered, it took her a moment to think of something intelligent to say. "Yes. Of course I can."

"Good. And I'm telling all four contestants that we've added a new wrinkle to the contest."

He seemed to be waiting for her to respond, and Hannah gave a little nod she knew he couldn't see. "What's the new wrinkle? Or is that something we'll find out when we get there?"

Eric laughed, a nice deep laugh that ended in a chuckle. "It's no secret. We just thought it would be more interesting if we went off-location for most of the episodes. We'll start here in our home studio, but the winner that night will have the hometown advantage from then on."

"Hometown advantage?"

"Yes. If you win, the remainder of the contest moves to your hometown in Lake Eden, Minnesota."

Hannah glanced at the one industrial oven she owned and began to frown. "But . . . my place is rather small. I don't have room for four other chefs."

"I know that. Your sister sent in a photo of your kitchen when she entered you in the competition. I took care of that, Hannah. I checked with your friend Sally Laughlin at the

Lake Eden Inn, and she has enough room in her kitchen for four baking stations. That's only if you win the hometown challenge, of course. The other four contestants all have large restaurants in their home cities, so it's not a problem for them."

The frown remained on Hannah's face. "Doesn't that put me at a disadvantage?"

"Not at all. The Lake Eden Inn can hold as many people as the other four restaurants. If you win, it won't be a problem at all."

"Oh . . . good."

"We're all set then? I can send you the travel arrangements and you'll be here on the tenth?"

Hannah blinked twice, trying to clear her thoughts. "Yes. That'll be fine with . . . oh, no!"

"What was the *oh, no!* for?"

"My wedding! It's scheduled for Sunday, the eighteenth!"

"That's not a problem. The contest will be over by then. And . . ." Eric paused for a moment. "This is just off the top of my head, but maybe we can find a way to incorporate part of your wedding into the *Dessert Chef Competition*."

Hannah was genuinely puzzled. "How could you do that?"

"If you win the hometown challenge, we'll be in Lake Eden. And we might just stick around to film it. You're having a reception at a local place, aren't you?"

"Yes. At the Lake Eden Inn."

"Perfect! Let us think about that for a couple of days and see what we can come up with. This could really bump up the ratings. Everyone loves a wedding. And everyone will love you as a bride-to-be. You'll definitely have the viewer vote. That much is for sure."

"There's a popular vote in addition to the judges' decisions?"

"No, but that's what keeps people watching. And that's what we want . . . viewers."

"Oh, yes. Of course you do. Ratings are everything . . . right?"

"Right." Eric chuckled again. "All right, Hannah. It was nice talking to you. My secretary will get back to you in the next couple of days with the travel arrangements. I've got her working on it right now. You do know that you can bring an assistant chef with you for the competition, don't you?"

"Yes. It was in the letter I received that told me I was a contestant. There was also a copy of the rules."

"Do you know who your assistant will be?"

"Yes, I do. My assistant is Michelle Swensen. She's my youngest sister."

"Good. The audience enjoys getting to know our chefs' family members. Your sister isn't under eighteen, is she?"

"No, she turned twenty-one this past year."

"Good. The reason I asked is because we have to make special provisions for anyone under the age of eighteen on the set."

"I see," Hannah said, even though she didn't.

"Now that I think about it, your wedding will make a perfect ending to our competition. We were afraid we'd run short after one of the contestants dropped out for personal reasons. Is your sister one of the bridesmaids?"

"Yes, she is. And so is my other sister, Andrea."

"Wonderful! It was too late to add another new contestant so the more bodies we can film, the better."

Hannah winced slightly. *Bodies* obviously meant something different to Eric than it meant to her!

"Have you decided which desserts you'll be baking for the competition?"

"No, not yet."

"That's all right. You have some time. As long as you give us a list of the ingredients you'll need when you get to New York, it'll be fine."

Hannah came close to groaning out loud. She hadn't done

any preparation for the competition. "When do you need my list?"

"When you get off the plane in New York."

"All right. I'll have my list ready for you."

"Good. That's all then, Hannah. We'll send your itinerary and your plane reservations in the next few days. We're going to put you up at the Westin in the Theater District."

"That sounds wonderful," Hannah said, and she meant it. Michelle would be thrilled to be in New York's Theater District.

"We're all set then. Good luck in the competition, Hannah. I'm looking forward to meeting you and your sister."

"I'm looking forward to meeting you, too. Thank you, Eric."

Hannah said good-bye and hung up the phone. When she turned to face Lisa, there was a frown on her face. If she won the hometown challenge, they might show her wedding on television! Could Delores and her sisters get everything ready in time? And would the fact that the wedding might be televised throw Delores into a tizzy?

Lisa looked up from her stirring. When she saw Hannah's expression, she looked concerned. "What's the matter, Hannah?"

"It's the Food Channel competition. They moved up the date. I have to be in New York by the tenth!"

"But how about the wedding?"

"They said the competition would be over by then and my wedding can go on as planned. And they're thinking about televising it!"

"Oh boy! You'd better tell your mother right away! It may make a difference in what she plans."

"You're right." Hannah took a moment to think about that. "Actually . . . this might not be a bad thing. I'm sure Mother and Andrea will do a great job. And they can consult with me by phone if there's a problem when I'm in New York."

"How about Michelle?"

"She's going with me as my assistant, so she's off the wedding team. I wonder if Mother and Andrea can handle it alone. They may have bitten off more than they can chew."

"I doubt that. Your mother's a force. She knows how to get things done."

"That's true." Hannah thought of something else that Eric had told her and she sighed heavily. "Will you call your dad and Marge and ask them if they can handle the coffee shop for us while we have a meeting to plan what I'll bake for the contest?"

"I'll ask them right now. They're here at a table in the back. Dad will be really pleased. He loves to help out up front and so does Marge."

"Is your Aunt Nancy here today? I know she's been helping you out in front."

"She's here. She says it's a wonderful way to meet the people in Lake Eden, now that she's moved here."

"Good. I'll need you, Michelle, and Aunt Nancy to come back here for the meeting. And I'll text Mother and Andrea to come here right away. I have to decide which desserts to bake so that I can give the producer a list of the ingredients I'll need."

"Okay. I just filled the display cookie jars and made a fresh pot of coffee. That should hold them out front for at least an hour."

"Thanks, Lisa."

"You're welcome. Do you want me to make some white chocolate cocoa for us? I've got a new recipe that uses cinnamon and white chocolate chips."

"That sounds great. I have to talk to all of you, and we'll meet right here around the work island."

"Okay. But if this is about the baking contest, why do you need your mother and Andrea? Andrea doesn't bake anything except whippersnapper cookies, and your mother doesn't bake at all."

"I know, but both of them have tasted everything we've

ever baked in here. And if I don't invite them, I'll just have to explain everything all over again."

"That makes sense. And you need Aunt Nancy because she's such a good baker?"

"Exactly. Aunt Nancy has more recipes than anyone I know, and she may be able to suggest some desserts that haven't even occurred to me. I have to come up with some real winning recipes before I leave for the competition, and there's not that much time."

"How many desserts do you need?"

"I need one super dessert for the hometown challenge. That's on the first night. It has to be the best thing I've ever baked."

"What's the hometown challenge?"

"It's the only part of the competition that'll be held in New York. The winner of the challenge gets to move the rest of the competition to his or her restaurant."

"If you win, they'll move the contest *here*?" Lisa glanced around their kitchen in dismay. "But that's impossible, Hannah! We only have one oven!"

"That's exactly what I told the producer, but he was one step ahead of me. He called Sally at the Lake Eden Inn, and she agreed to hold the competition in her kitchen if I win the challenge."

"Well, that's a relief! I was wondering how we could fit all those contestants in here."

"It's not just the contestants. There'll be a New York film crew here, too. The Food Channel is going to be airing the whole competition live."

"How many will be in the film crew?"

Hannah shrugged. "I'm not sure, but it's bound to be a lot of people."

"Thank goodness for Sally's big kitchen! If we had to crowd everyone in here at The Cookie Jar, we'd have to knock out a wall and expand to include the whole block!"

Chapter Three

Hannah gave a relieved sigh as she glanced down at her shorthand notebook. "All right. I've got seven desserts to try. Which one do you think I should bake for the hometown challenge?"

"None of them."

Hannah, Lisa, and Michelle turned to stare at Aunt Nancy in confusion. "*None* of them?" Hannah repeated.

"That's right. The first night is really important. You'll need something that'll knock their socks off."

"You're absolutely right," Delores said, smiling at Aunt Nancy. "Hannah simply *has* to win the hometown challenge." She turned to Hannah. "Just think about the business it'll bring to Lake Eden if you win, dear. They'll be shopping in the stores. Claire's Beau Monde is every bit as classy as a New York boutique. And Claire is a real person, not at all snooty the way most of those pseudo-French salesladies are."

"That's true," Hannah conceded the point, "but they'll probably be staying at the Lake Eden Inn for the entire time they're here. They may not even come into town."

"They'll come into town," Andrea said, taking up the argument. "There's not much to do out at the Lake Eden Inn. It's way out on the other side of Eden Lake. You can't swim this time of year and winter hasn't really hit yet. There's not enough ice to go ice fishing or skating, and it's not the season for regular fishing. The lake's beautiful, but you can only take so many walks around the lake. And that means they'll be bored silly, especially since you said most of them are from big cities."

"That's right." Hannah looked down at her notes again. "They're from Chicago, New York, Los Angeles, and Atlanta. I'm the only one from a small town."

"Big cities have entertainment. The Lake Eden Inn is nice, don't get me wrong. You can sleep in a beautiful room, eat great food, and drink fine wine, but that's about it. You can't cross-country ski, or go on the snowmobile trails if there's no snow yet. And there's no snow right now."

"Andrea's right," Michelle said. "They're going to get bored out there by the lake. If we can figure out some way to provide transportation, they'll come into town at least a couple of times. I'm sure of it."

Delores put her cell phone down. There was a smug expression on her face as she turned to Hannah. "Ross agrees," she said. "I just texted him, and he said it was bound to bring business to Lake Eden. He said the film crew from the Food Channel works hard and they play hard, too. They'll come into town to go bowling, hang out at the Red Velvet Lounge at the Albion Hotel, and do some background shots of your hometown. They'll probably even interview some locals."

Hannah stared at her mother in shock. "You sent a text message to Ross before I even had time to tell him about it?"

"Well . . ." Delores equivocated for a moment and then she nodded. "Yes, I did. I had no idea you hadn't told Ross. He's your fiancé. Why didn't you tell him before you told us?"

There was no way that Hannah wanted to say that she hadn't even thought of it, so she simply sighed. "I didn't want to bother him at work. I was going to tell him tonight when I saw him for dinner. Really, Mother! It's not like we're joined at the hip."

"I see," Delores said, and everyone around the table, including Hannah, realized that the mother of the bride thought that her daughter was in the wrong.

Hannah turned to Andrea. "When you were engaged to Bill, would you have sent him a message telling him that the competition had been moved up before you told anyone else?"

Andrea looked down at the table. It was clear she didn't want to meet Hannah's eyes. "I don't know," she said.

"It's a moot point," Michelle pointed out. "They didn't have text messaging then."

"But they had phones," Hannah argued, zeroing in on Andrea again. "Would you have called Bill, even at work, if something like this had happened to you?"

"Uh . . . well . . ." Andrea paused and the expression on her face resembled that of a rabbit trapped by a much larger predator. "I'm really not sure, but . . . maybe?"

"Was that a question?" Hannah asked.

Andrea sighed again. And then she took a deep breath. "Yes, I would have called Bill right away. But . . . it's different for you, Hannah."

"What do you mean?"

"I mean . . . you're older. You're established. You're more . . . secure with yourself. You don't need the constant approval from Ross that I needed from Bill."

Hannah wasn't sure she liked what Andrea was implying, but she did understand. "You think I'm more capable of making my own decisions and I don't need a husband the way you needed Bill."

This time, it was definitely a statement and no one said a word. Except Andrea, who gave a nod and said, "Yes. That's it, Hannah. You're much more self-reliant than I was at nineteen."

"Okay," Hannah said, and reached out to pat her sister's hand. "I ought to be more self-sufficient. I'm more than ten years older than you were when you got married."

"And she wasn't even preg—" Michelle stopped short and shot a guilty glance at Delores. "Sorry."

"And I'm not either," Hannah said, glaring at her, and then the humor of the situation got to her and she smiled. "Sorry. Grandma Knudson hit me with the same thing this morning. I really didn't realize that people would think I was . . . you know." There was an uncomfortable silence, and then Hannah went on, "Grandma Knudson is going to make sure that all the money people bet on the birthdate of the nonexistent baby is given to charity."

"Good! It serves those people right!" Delores looked outraged. "I, for one, never thought for a minute that . . ."

"Of course we didn't!" Andrea jumped in. "It was just that it was so sudden and nobody expected it, and . . ."

"And you shocked the pants off everybody in Lake Eden," Michelle finished.

"Michelle!" Delores turned to give her the glance that all three of her daughters called *Mother's icy glare of death*.

"Well, she did," Michelle defended herself. "Nobody in Lake Eden ever thought she'd make up her mind. You know that, Mother."

Delores didn't bother to reply, but the flush on her cheeks, coming through under her makeup, was answer enough for Hannah.

"Back to the recipes," Lisa said, rescuing all of them from a difficult discussion. "What do you think Hannah should bake first, Aunt Nancy?"

"Patience, Lisa. I need more information from Hannah before I can answer that. Who are the judges, Hannah?"

"There are five of them." Hannah looked down at her notebook. "Jeremy Zales is the first one. He won some kind of prestigious award."

"The Golden Knife," Aunt Nancy said. "It's almost as important as the James Beard Award."

"Another judge is LaVonna Brach."

"She writes cookbooks," Aunt Nancy informed her. "They're the kind of little paperbacks you can find at grocery store checkout counters, and they're extremely popular. She's written over a hundred. It says so on the front cover."

"Are they any good?" Andrea asked her.

"Surprisingly, yes. Sometimes those little books are worthless, but I've followed some of her recipes and they work perfectly. I've been collecting her cookbooks for at least five years and I have two shelves of them in the bedroom. Heiti says I'd better stop collecting before I run out of wall space."

Lisa frowned slightly. "Haiti? Like the country?"

"That's how it's pronounced, but it's spelled differently. Heiti is an Estonian name. That's where his ancestors come from."

"But who is this Heiti?"

"He's a friend I met at church and he's building my bookshelves. Heiti's a fine carpenter. You'll have to come over to see them. He also restores classic cars and he's promised to fix the old Thunderbird in my garage."

"He lives around here?" Lisa looked a bit nervous about her aunt's *friend*.

"He does now. He moved here from Connecticut." Aunt Nancy addressed Hannah, and it was obvious that she wanted to change the subject. "Who's the third judge, Hannah?"

"The third judge is Helene Stone."

"I've never heard of her," Aunt Nancy said, turning to Michelle. "Can you find out more about her on that phone of yours?"

"I'm already Googling her." There was a brief pause, and then Michelle read the information on her screen. "Helene Stone is a well-known purveyor of gourmet ingredients. She has a small store in New York that carries exotic spices and imported vegetables and fruits."

"Who's the fourth judge?" Delores asked.

Hannah referred to her notebook again. "Christian Parker."

"I know who he is!" Andrea said with a smile. "He has

his own show on the Food Channel. He seems very nice, Hannah."

"You watch the Food Channel?" Hannah tried not to look as shocked as she felt. To put it nicely, Andrea was culinarily challenged. The closest she came to preparing a gourmet meal was when she made peanut butter and jelly sandwiches.

"Yes, I *do* watch the Food Channel. It's Tracey's favorite channel, and she loves Christian Parker's show. We watch every weekday when she gets home from school. It's our private mother-daughter alone time."

Hannah knew she shouldn't ask, but she had to know. "Have you learned anything about cooking?"

"Yes!" Andrea pointed to the foil-covered platter in the center of the counter. "That's where I got the idea for my newest whippersnapper cookies."

"Christian Parker made whippersnappers?" Delores asked.

"No, but what he said about chips made me want to try some whippersnappers that way."

"He's an excellent chef," Aunt Nancy said. "What did he say about chips?"

"He said to mix and match them in cookies. His example was peanut butter cookies with peanut butter chips, milk chocolate chips, and dark chocolate chips. Would you like to taste my Chips Galore Whippersnapper Cookies? I brought some with me."

"We would!" Delores answered for all of them, and Hannah was glad. So far, Andrea had only made one type of cookie, but everyone, including her husband, hoped that her experimentation with baking would spread out to include additional successful culinary efforts.

Lisa jumped up to fill their cups and fetch fresh napkins. Even though they'd already had two of Hannah's Molasses Crackles, there was always room to taste one more cookie.

"These are just great, Andrea," Hannah said after her first bite. "You chopped the chips up in little pieces."

"That was Christian Parker's idea. He said that if the chips are in smaller pieces, you get different flavors of chips in each bite."

"I really like these," Hannah said, reaching out to take another cookie from the platter to prove it. "They're good, Andrea. You'll give me the recipe, won't you?"

"Of course. And you'll use it here in The Cookie Jar?"

"We will. I think our customers will love these, especially the peanut butter and chocolate fanatics."

Andrea looked very happy. "So everybody likes them?"

Delores laughed. "I've eaten two already, and I'm about to go for my third. They're wonderful, dear."

"Yes, they are." Aunt Nancy took another cookie, and then she turned to Hannah. "Didn't you say there were five judges?"

"Yes. The fifth judge is Alain Duquesne. I don't know anything about him."

"I do," Andrea said. "He was a guest chef on Chef Christian's show and he was really picky. He didn't like the way Chef Christian sautéed all the vegetables together. He said that each vegetable should be sautéed separately to get the full flavors."

"He said that on someone else's show?" Aunt Nancy began to frown when Andrea nodded. "He's known for being very critical, but it wasn't even his show!"

"That's what Tracey said. She said the only reason he was there was because Chef Christian had invited him and it was wrong to criticize your host."

"That's very adult of her," Delores commented.

"It certainly is," Aunt Nancy agreed, and then she turned to Hannah again. "You've named all five judges. Which one is the head judge?"

"Alain Duquesne."

"That's a stroke of bad luck," Aunt Nancy said, wearing the same expression she would have worn if she'd tasted something unpleasant. "He's a nasty know-it-all. And his recipes aren't worth the powder to blow them up!"

Hannah burst into laughter. She couldn't help it. Aunt Nancy looked terribly irate. "Sorry. I've just never heard you be so disapproving of anyone before. And what you said about his recipes was really funny."

"Well, it's true. They're unnecessarily complicated, incredibly time-consuming, and the results don't warrant that amount of work. The man doesn't know what *shortcut* means! Of course he's got as many assistants as he wants to do all the prep work and clean up his mess."

"Do you know him personally?" Lisa asked, gazing at her aunt in something very close to awe.

"You could say that. He was born less than five miles from my parents' farm, and I went to school with him. Of course his name wasn't Alain Duquesne then. He changed it when he became an important celebrity chef."

"What was his name back then?" Michelle asked.

"Allen Duke. He was the youngest of three children and his mother babied him. He grew up thinking that he was better than anyone else."

Hannah was silent for a moment, and then she asked, "Did he have any favorite foods?"

"I see where you're headed, and it won't do you a parcel of good." Aunt Nancy shook her head. "Allen doesn't really like food. When he was in third grade, he brought a peanut butter sandwich and a thermos of milk to school every day for lunch. And he never tried to trade with any of the other kids whose mothers packed different sandwiches and home-baked cookies."

"He didn't have dessert?" Lisa looked shocked.

"Yes, he did. Allen always had a little bowl of Jell-O or butterscotch pudding, the kind you can buy ready-made in the grocery store. He was crazy about Jell-O and butterscotch pudding."

"He ate them every day?" Andrea asked, and Hannah could tell she was surprised.

"Almost every school day, or at least every day that I was in the lunchroom with him. And I'm willing to bet that he had Jell-O or butterscotch pudding for dessert on the weekends, too. My mother always said that Allen's mother wasn't much of a cook."

Hannah jotted that down. She wasn't sure if it would come in handy, but it was a piece of personal information about the head judge. "Is there anything else you remember about him?" she asked Aunt Nancy. "I really need an edge for the hometown challenge."

"I have that covered," Aunt Nancy declared, looking very proud of herself. "I think you should bake something that Chef Alain Duquesne loves, but something he never could bake successfully."

"What's that?"

"A white chocolate soufflé. He adores soufflés, and he's crazy about white chocolate. I saw him interviewed on television and he mentioned that it was the one dessert he had trouble baking."

"Aren't soufflés difficult to bake?" Lisa asked.

"Normally, yes. I tried to perfect a chocolate soufflé for years," Aunt Nancy admitted. "But then my friend Anne Elizabeth gave me a never-fail recipe." She turned to Hannah. "That's what you can bake for the hometown challenge."

"A chocolate soufflé?"

"Yes, but not just any chocolate. You should make yours white chocolate. Allen loves soufflés, and he's crazy about white chocolate. I'm convinced that'll bring you right back here to Lake Eden for the next Food Channel challenge."

"Perfect!" Delores told her. And then she turned to Hannah. "What's the next challenge, dear?"

Hannah glanced down at her notebook. "The cake challenge."

"Wonderful!" Aunt Nancy clapped her hands. "I've got that one covered, too. The Allen I knew in high school was a dyed-in-the-wool romantic. As a matter of fact, when we were older, he took me to the senior prom."

"So he was your high school boyfriend?" Delores asked.

"Oh, no. Not at all. Allen wasn't anyone's boyfriend. He had someone he spent time with, but that wasn't exactly a boyfriend-girlfriend relationship. Allen was too in love with himself to love anyone else."

"If you felt that way about him, why did you go to the prom with him?" Hannah asked.

"I wanted to go and I didn't have a date. And Allen wanted to go so that he could show off in a white tuxedo. No one had ever worn a white tuxedo to a prom before. And he wanted his date to wear the black dress and long black gloves that Audrey Hepburn wore in *Breakfast at Tiffany's* because it would complement his white tuxedo so well. Allen fancied himself as a trendsetter."

"Do you think he's still that way?" Lisa asked.

"Oh, yes. You can tell that by the food he creates. I wouldn't want to eat some of his meals, but they're very successful and trendy. That man can put together the most unusual ingredients and make people eat them and rave about it."

Delores began to frown. "I'd like to know more about that prom. Did Allen go shopping with you to help you choose your prom dress?"

"Yes, and no. He handed me a photo of Audrey Hepburn wearing the dress and he asked me if I could sew a dress just like it if he paid for the material. And since I'd always loved to sew and I was good at it, I said, 'Yes, of course I can. What size do you need?' And I still remember how he leaned back and looked at me critically. I got the feeling he could see right through my clothes, and it made me terribly uncomfortable. I was about to tell him to forget it, that I couldn't make a dress like that after all, when he said, 'You'll do if you wear your hair up like it is in the picture.

And I'll buy the gloves. Make the dress in your size.' And then he asked me to be his date for the prom."

"That's not exactly romantic!" Lisa looked dismayed.

"I knew that then. And I also knew that he thought of himself as a sophisticated and debonair man of the world. He didn't care who he took to the prom as long as she looked the way he wanted her to look. His date was just a prop to make him appear even more suave and urbane. But I wanted to go to the prom, and he was the class president, the most desirable date I could possibly have, so . . ." Aunt Nancy gave a little shrug. "I made the dress, put it on, and went to the prom with Allen Duke."

"Did you have a good time?" Andrea asked her.

"I had a great time! All the girls admired my dress, and their dates couldn't take their eyes off me. We were the most stunning couple there. Allen was a superb dancer, and we spent the whole night on the dance floor. When the prom was over, Allen took me home and then he went out on a late date with another girl he said wouldn't have looked good in the Audrey Hepburn dress."

Delores just stared at Aunt Nancy. It was the first time that Hannah had ever seen her mother speechless. It took Delores several seconds to recover and then she said, "How awful for you!"

"Not really. I knew that Allen was all show, and I wasn't interested in him anyway. And I knew from the start that he wasn't interested in me. On the whole, he was a perfect prom date."

"But prom dates are supposed to be romantic," Lisa objected. "How could he be a perfect date?"

"Allen *looked* romantic. I'm talking about movie-star romantic. I looked the part of the ingénue, and Allen looked the part of the handsome lover. And that's the reason I told you this story. Chef Alain Duquesne appreciates someone who looks the part." Aunt Nancy turned to Hannah. "Everyone at the Food Channel knows you're getting married right after the competition. And by the time you arrive in New York, the judges will know it, too. That's why I think you should bake a wedding cake for the cake challenge. And you should present it to the judges wearing your wedding veil. Allen will really appreciate that, and I can almost guarantee that he'll give you a perfect score so that you can win that challenge too!"

CHIPS GALORE
WHIPPERSNAPPER COOKIES

DO NOT preheat your oven quite yet—this cookie dough needs to chill before baking.

1 box *(approximately 18 ounces)* yellow cake mix, the kind that makes a 9-inch by 13-inch cake *(I used Duncan Hines—18.5 ounces net weight)*

1 large egg, beaten *(just whip it up in a glass with a fork)*

2 cups of Original Cool Whip, thawed *(measure this—a tub of Cool Whip contains a little over 3 cups and that's too much!)*

1 teaspoon vanilla extract

1 cup assorted chips, chopped into little pieces *(regular chocolate, white chocolate, milk chocolate, butterscotch, peanut butter, or whatever you have left over from other cookies you've baked)*

½ cup powdered *(confectioner's)* sugar *(you don't have to sift it unless it's got big lumps)*

Pour HALF of the dry cake mix into a large bowl.

Use a smaller bowl to mix the two cups of Cool Whip with the beaten egg and the vanilla extract. Stir gently with a rubber spatula until everything is combined.

Add the Cool Whip mixture to the cake mix in the large bowl. STIR VERY CAREFULLY with a wooden spoon or a rubber spatula. Stir only until everything is combined. You don't want to stir all the air from the Cool Whip.

Sprinkle the rest of the cake mix on top and gently fold it in with the rubber spatula. Again, keep as much air in the batter as possible. Air is what will make your cookies soft and have that melt-in-your-mouth quality.

Sprinkle the cup of chopped, mixed-flavor chips on top and gently fold the chips into the airy cookie mixture. *(You can easily chop the chips in a food processor by using the steel blade and processing them in an on-and-off motion.)*

Cover the bowl and chill this mixture for at least one hour in the refrigerator. It's a little too sticky to form into balls without chilling it first.

Hannah's 1st Note: Andrea sometimes mixes whippersnapper dough up before she goes to bed on Friday night and bakes her cookies with Tracey in the morning.

Hannah's 2nd Note: If you see our mother, please don't mention that I told you Andrea always gives Bethie a warm whippersnapper cookie for breakfast on Saturday mornings.

When your cookie dough has chilled and you're ready to bake, preheat your oven to 350 degrees F., and make sure the rack is in the middle position. DO NOT take your chilled cookie dough out of the refrigerator until after your oven has reached the proper temperature.

While your oven is preheating, prepare your cookie sheets by spraying them with Pam or another nonstick baking spray, or lining them with parchment paper.

Place the confectioner's sugar in a small, shallow bowl. You will be dropping cookie dough into this bowl to form dough balls and coating them with the powdered sugar.

When your oven is ready, take your dough out of the refrigerator. Using a teaspoon from your silverware drawer, drop the dough by rounded teaspoonful into the

bowl with the powdered sugar. Roll the dough around with your fingers to form powdered-sugar-coated cookie dough balls.

Andrea's 1st Note: This is easiest if you coat your fingers with powdered sugar first and then try to form the cookie dough into balls.

Place the coated cookie dough balls on your prepared cookie sheets, no more than 12 cookies on a standard-size sheet.

Hannah's 3rd Note: I've said this before, but it bears repeating. Work with only one cookie dough ball at a time. If you drop more than one in the bowl of powdered sugar, they'll stick together.

Andrea's 2nd Note: Make only as many cookie dough balls as you can bake at one time and then cover the dough and return it to the refrigerator. I have a double oven so I prepare 2 sheets of cookies at a time.

Bake your Chips Galore Whippersnapper Cookies at 350 degrees F., for 10 minutes and take them out of the oven. Let them cool on the cookie sheet for 2 minutes, and then move them to a wire rack to cool completely. *(This is a lot easier if you line your cookie sheets with parchment paper—then you don't need to*

lift the cookies one by one. All you have to do is grab one end of the parchment paper and pull it, cookies and all, onto the wire rack.)

Once the cookies are completely cool, store them between sheets of waxed paper in a cool, dry place. *(Your refrigerator is cool, but it's definitely not dry!)*

Yield: 3 to 4 dozen soft, chewy cookies, depending on cookie size.

Andrea's 3rd Note: Tracey and Bethie love these cookies. Bill says the guys down at the Winnetka County Sheriff's Station love them, too. His deputies are real cookie hounds!

Chapter Four

Hannah scrutinized the small group assembled around the workstation. Everyone there looked just as shocked as she was. "But . . . I'm not getting married until *after* the competition."

"Of course you're not." Aunt Nancy smiled at her. "It's just showbiz. And Allen, for one, appreciates showbiz. Didn't you say that the head judge's scores count double?"

"Yes. That's what it says in the rules."

"Then it's a perfectly good tactic. Just say that since they moved the competition up two weeks, you didn't have time to practice making your wedding cake and you wanted to try out your idea with them to see what they thought of your creation."

"That's brilliant, Nancy!" Delores exclaimed. "That'll put the judges in the position of helping Hannah with something other than winning the competition. And everyone wants to help with a wedding, especially since they all might be there."

"That makes sense," Michelle said. "It might give you an edge over the other contestants."

"But . . ." Hannah paused and gave a little frown. "Do you think that's fair?"

"It's fair," Andrea said without hesitation. "All the other contestants will be researching the judges and trying to figure out how to use that information to their advantage. You'll be able to do that too, but you'll also have the advantage of getting married. And no one else will have that." She turned to Aunt Nancy. "We're just lucky you're here to advise us."

"Thank you." Aunt Nancy looked pleased as she turned back to Hannah. "So what do you think? Do you want to bake a Double Rainbow Swirl Cake for your wedding?"

Hannah shrugged. "I don't know. I haven't even thought about that yet. What *is* a Double Rainbow Swirl Cake?"

"It's a recipe I used to bake for special occasions, and it includes one of Allen's favorite ingredients." Aunt Nancy paused to smile. The smile was impish with a touch of smug mixed in, and Hannah knew Aunt Nancy had thought of a recipe that might give her another advantage over the other contestants.

"My Double Rainbow Swirl Cake starts with white cake batter. You can use your favorite white cake recipe. You'll only bake two layers for the judges, but the cake should be quite heavy so that the layers don't topple when you stack them up for your actual wedding cake."

"And I'm volunteering right now to bake the actual cake for the wedding and decorate it," Lisa declared.

"I'll help you bake it," Aunt Nancy offered.

"Thank you," Hannah said gratefully. If the competition ended the day before she was married, she really wouldn't have time to bake her own wedding cake.

"What makes it a Double Rainbow Swirl Cake?" Michelle asked Aunt Nancy.

"It uses different flavors of Jell-O for the colors."

"Jell-O!" Andrea exclaimed, looking intrigued. "I make a poke cake that has two colors of Jell-O in it."

Hannah hid a smile. When she'd driven Andrea to the hospital to have Bethie, Andrea had admitted that she bought the cake, ready-made, at the Lake Eden Red Owl Grocery store and simply added the Jell-O.

"This cake uses Jell-O powder that's added to the cake batter," Aunt Nancy told them. "You use three colors of Jell-O in one layer and three colors of Jell-O in the other layer."

"It sounds intriguing," Delores said.

"It is, and it's also very pretty. The layers are stacked on top of each other and that means you could get all six colors and flavors in every slice."

"It sounds perfect." Hannah smiled at Aunt Nancy. "Thanks for being here. Your help is . . . well . . . invaluable."

"I'll taste the test cake," Delores offered.

"Thank you, Mother," Hannah said, and then she turned back to Aunt Nancy. "This is sounding better and better. What do you think I should do for the 'free-for-all'? It's the last challenge in the competition and . . ." she referred to her notes, "it consists of any baked or cooked dessert the contestant chooses to make."

"You'll have to think about that one," Delores said. "You make so many good desserts. There's always your great-grandmother's apple pie. Everyone's crazy about that."

"I know. It's a really good pie. But everybody's going to be going all out for that final challenge. Do you think it's special enough?"

"Maybe," Aunt Nancy said. "Do you use a top crust, or a French crumble?"

"Hannah makes it both ways and gives us a choice," Andrea told her. "I like the French crumble best."

"And I like the top crust with a slice of really sharp cheddar on the side," Michelle said.

Delores looked slightly embarrassed. "I usually have two pieces so I can taste them both. And I like vanilla ice cream on top of both of them."

"I like the French crumble with sweetened whipped cream," Lisa gave her preference.

"This is beginning to sound better and better," Hannah said. "I could do all the variations with the crusts and the toppings. I've never met anyone who didn't like apple pie."

Andrea looked thoughtful. "I think you should offer the judges nutmeg on top of the whipped cream. Chef Christian always says that freshly grated nutmeg is a gift from the gods."

"Good idea!" Hannah turned to smile at her. It seemed that Andrea had learned something from watching Christian Parker's show. Then she glanced up at the clock on the wall and came close to groaning out loud. It was a quarter to three and she'd asked Norman to meet her at three for coffee. She had to ask him if he'd be a groomsman at the wedding and she wasn't looking forward to the encounter. She liked Norman. Perhaps she even loved him. That wasn't it, at all. Even though they were friends, it was bound to be a very uncomfortable encounter.

Hannah shut her notebook with a snap. "Thanks so much for helping me. I couldn't do it without you. I think that's enough planning for today. Can we all meet here again tomorrow at two o'clock? Michelle and I will bake tonight and we should have some samples by then for you to critique."

Michelle waited until Delores and Andrea had left, and Lisa and Aunt Nancy had gone back out to the coffee shop. When they were alone, she turned to Hannah. "What's going on? I saw you glancing at the clock. Is Ross coming here?"

"No, he's going to come back to the condo for dinner at six, but then he has to go to Jordan High to cover the basketball game. The Gulls are playing the Browerville Tigers tonight."

"KCOW is going to televise high school basketball?"

"They are now. It was Ross's suggestion, and they decided to give it a try. Ross told them he was sure it would increase their viewers."

"I think he's right. Everyone in town supports the Gulls."

"I know. And even if people go to the game, they'll still record the coverage on KCOW and watch it again later."

"You said that Ross isn't getting to the condo until six?"

"That's right. All we have to do is make some corn muffins to go with the Green Tomatillo Stew we started in the crockpot this morning. He can stop by after the game to have coffee and dessert with us. That'll give us a chance to bake something."

"That sounds good to me. I'll make the corn muffins. I've got something I want to try anyway. But I still don't understand why you kept glancing at the clock if Ross wasn't coming here."

Hannah sighed. Michelle was like a dog with a bone once she honed in on something. "I kept my eye on the time because I asked Norman to meet me here at three. And I didn't want him to arrive when everyone was still here."

"You asked Norman to come here?"

"Yes. I need to talk to him."

"Oh, boy!" Michelle looked worried. "That might be very awkward for you. You haven't talked to Norman since you decided to marry Ross, have you?"

"No. I didn't know what to say."

"And now you do?"

"I know what I have to say. I have to invite Norman to be part of the wedding party."

"Oh, boy!" Michelle repeated. "You *did* ask Ross first, didn't you?"

"Actually . . . no, *I* didn't. Mother called Ross to ask him if he minded Norman and Mike being in the wedding party. And Ross said it was fine with him. He likes both of them."

"*Mother* called Ross?"

"That's right. And that's not all. Then Mother called both Norman and Mike to sound them out about doing it. Grandma Knudson told me about it this morning."

"This is really convoluted. Are you telling me that you knew nothing about it before this morning?"

"That's right."

"And you agreed to everything?"

"Yes. Grandma Knudson convinced me that it was the right thing to do."

"Wait a minute. If Mother already talked to Norman and he said he'd do it, why are *you* asking him?"

"Because it's the right thing to do," Hannah repeated. "I'm the bride. I ought to talk to Norman and Mike about it."

"Then they're both coming here at three?"

"No, just Norman. Mike said he'd be here at four."

"Mistake," Michelle said. "You should have invited them to come together. They would have kept each other in check. Separating them means that each of them can tell you exactly how they feel about the fact that you're marrying Ross. They wouldn't do that in front of each other."

"I know that, but I decided that this way would be fairer. Both of them are my friends . . . or at least they *were* my friends. I've been avoiding both of them, and that's wrong. I should give them a chance to say whatever they want to say to me."

"You're probably right, but that doesn't change the fact that you're a glutton for punishment. Do you want me to stay here with you to help?"

"Now *you're* being a glutton for punishment!" Hannah did her best to smile. "Thanks for the offer, but I have to see them alone. If they want privacy to give me a hard time, I'm going to give them the chance to do it. That way all of their feelings will be out in the open and we can put this whole thing behind us."

"You hope."

"Yes. I do."

"Okay, but I still say you're asking for it." Michelle headed for the door to the coffee shop, but she turned back before she pushed it open. "Cookies!"

"What?"

"You'll need cookies. I baked Chocolate Almond Crisps this morning, and I'll put some on a platter for you. Chocolate would be best in case one or both of them gets upset. You'd better have one, too. Doc doesn't think it works, but you might need a dose of chocolate endorphins."

"That's a good idea, Michelle."

"I know. And then I'll go out in the coffee shop and keep everyone else out of the kitchen while you talk to Norman. Just give me the high sign when he leaves. And I'll do the same thing when you talk to Mike."

"Thanks, Michelle."

"You're welcome. I just hope I don't come back in here and find you in a little puddle on the floor!"

CHOCOLATE ALMOND CRISPS

Preheat oven to 375 degrees F., rack in the middle position.

> 1 cup melted butter *(2 sticks, 8 ounces,
> $\frac{1}{2}$ pound)*
> 1 cup white *(granulated)* sugar
> 1 cup brown sugar *(pack it down in the cup
> when you measure it)*
> 1 teaspoon baking soda
> 1 teaspoon baking powder
> $\frac{1}{2}$ teaspoon salt
> 1 cup almond butter *(I used Jif brand)*
> 2 teaspoons vanilla
> 2 beaten eggs *(just whip them up in a glass
> with a fork)*
> 2 and $\frac{1}{2}$ cups all-purpose flour *(pack it down in
> the cup when you measure it)*
> 1 cup regular chocolate chips *(6-ounce net
> weight package or half a 12-ounce pack-
> age—I used Nestle)*

Microwave the butter in a microwave-safe mixing bowl to melt it. This should take about 90 seconds on HIGH.

Add the white sugar, brown sugar, baking soda, baking powder and salt. Mix until everything is combined.

Measure out one cup of almond butter.

Hannah's 1st Note: Spray the inside of the measuring cup with Pam or another nonstick cooking spray before you put in the almond butter to measure it. Then the almond butter won't stick to the sides and bottom of the measuring cup, and it will be easier to remove.

Add the almond butter to your bowl and mix it in. Continue mixing until the contents are thoroughly incorporated.

Mix in the vanilla and the beaten eggs. Continue to mix until the contents are completely combined.

Add the flour in half-cup increments, mixing after each addition. Continue mixing until the cookie batter is smooth.

If you used an electric mixer, scrape down the bowl, give it a final stir, and mix in the chocolate chips by hand.

Let your cookie dough rest in the bowl on the counter while you prepare your cookie sheets. Either spray

them with Pam or another nonstick cooking spray or line them with parchment paper.

Hannah's 2ⁿᵈ Note: If you use parchment paper, the cookies will be easier to remove after baking. Then all you have to do is pull the parchment paper, cookies and all, over onto a wire rack.

When your cookie sheets have been prepared, roll the cookie dough into one-inch balls with your hands. *(Lisa and I use a 2-teaspoon scoop to do this down at The Cookie Jar.)*

Hannah's 3ʳᵈ Note: If the dough is too sticky to roll into balls, chill it for a half-hour or so before you try again.

Place the dough balls on the cookie sheets, 12 dough balls to a standard-sized sheet.

Use the tines of a fork to make a crisscross pattern on top of each dough ball, flattening them a bit in the process, the way you would for peanut butter cookies.

Hannah's 4ᵗʰ Note: If the fork sticks, either spray the tines with Pam or another nonstick cooking spray, or dredge the fork in a little flour.

Bake your Chocolate Almond Crisps at 375 degrees F. for 8 to 10 minutes, or until the edges just begin to brown. *(Mine took 8 minutes.)*

Take your cookies out of the oven and let them sit on the cookie sheets for 2 minutes. Then use a metal spatula to transfer the cookies to a wire rack to cool completely.

Hannah's 5th Note: When Sally and Dick Laughlin host their Oktoberfest celebration at the Lake Eden Inn, I always help Sally bake these cookies for the guests. If you substitute white chocolate chips for the regular chocolate chips, the cookie tastes a lot like marzipan, which is a candy or almond paste that is a popular ingredient used in desserts, cakes, and cookies in Germany.

Yield: A batch of Chocolate Almond Crisps will make approximately 5 to 6 dozen delicious cookies.

Chapter
Five

When the door swung closed behind Michelle, Hannah wondered whether her sister was right and she'd made a mistake. But before she could decide, there was a knock on the back door. Norman was here.

Hannah walked to the door on legs that trembled slightly and pulled it open before she could change her mind. "Hi, Norman," she said, not meeting his eyes for fear she'd start to cry. "Sit down and I'll pour you a cup of coffee. There's a platter of Chocolate Almond Crisps on the workstation that Michelle baked this morning."

"Thanks, Hannah."

Norman sat down on a stool at the workstation. As she poured the coffee, Hannah sneaked a glance at Norman's face. He was far from relaxed, but he didn't look as miserable as Grandma Knudson had led her to believe. She began to feel slightly hopeful. Perhaps they could remain friends, after all.

She carried their coffee mugs to the stainless-steel table and set them down. Once she'd noticed that Norman had already taken a bite out of his first cookie, she took a deep breath and plunged in. "I have something to ask you, Norman."

"I know. Your mother told me. The answer is yes."

"Good!" Hannah gave him a relieved smile. Perhaps this wouldn't be as bad as she'd thought it might be. "Then it won't bother you to be in the wedding party?"

Norman just stared at her for what seemed like a full minute to Hannah. He looked positively incredulous.

"Of course it'll bother me! I love you, Hannah. You know that. And you're going to marry someone else. There's no way I can ever be happy about that! Everybody in Lake Eden thinks I'm suffering from a broken heart, and they're all dead right!"

Hannah gave an audible gulp, she was so surprised. She'd never heard Norman sound that vehement before. It was obvious that his emotions were running high and she'd have to tread very carefully.

"I know. Grandma Knudson told me. I should have said something to you earlier, talked everything out and maybe you'd feel better about it, but I just . . ."

"Maybe I'd feel better about it?" Norman repeated, interrupting her. "Maybe I'd feel *better* about it? I can't believe you said that! Are you living in a different universe, or something? There's no *better*, Hannah. The only *better* would be if you'd marry me!"

Hannah felt the tears well up in her eyes. Norman was furious with her. He'd probably never speak to her again. She'd lost him forever, and she didn't think she could bear that.

Tears began to roll down her cheeks. She simply couldn't help it. And then she felt his hand cover hers.

"I'm sorry, Hannah. I didn't intend to make you cry. It's just that I really thought you'd marry me someday. And now I know that you never will. It's eating at me like a cancer. It's just not worth getting up in the morning, or going to work, or anything now that I've lost you. Heartbroken is the wrong word. I'm in mourning for the death of my hopes and dreams for the future."

Hannah squeezed his hand. "I feel the same way, Norman.

I'm not sure I can bear it if I lose you. But I have to marry Ross. I love him so much that I don't think I can breathe without him in my life. But I love you, too!"

They sat there, clasped hands stretched across the counter, both miserable and grieving. And then Norman did something that shocked Hannah so much that her head snapped up from its bowed position. He laughed!

"It sounds like we're both in a h . . . h . . . heck of a fix," Norman choked out, and then he started to laugh hard again.

And despite the fact that Hannah felt a bit like the end of the world had arrived, she found herself joining in Norman's laughter. "Are we c . . . crazy?" she managed to gasp.

"Certi . . . certifiable," Norman said, forcing out the word between gales of laughter.

"They . . . they should lock us up in the funny farm," Hannah answered, beginning to wonder if she could ever stop laughing.

"So . . . what are we . . . going to do?" Norman asked.

"I don't . . . don't know. I can't . . . think. My stomach hurts . . . too much . . . from . . . laughing!"

"Are you guys all right?" Michelle stood in the doorway, staring at them. "We heard you laughing all the way in the coffee shop and I came to find out."

"We're fine," Norman said, still chuckling.

"Yes, we're . . . we're fine," Hannah echoed. "There's nothing to worry about, Michelle."

"Okay, then." Michelle didn't look convinced. "I'll go back in and tell Lisa. We were really concerned."

"I guess she was expecting the worst," Hannah said to Norman.

"It *was* the worst, but our senses of humor got the better of us. I'll be in the wedding party, Hannah, and I'll pretend to be happy for you. I know you weren't happy about it when I was going to marry Bev, but you were nice to her even though you didn't like her. This isn't the same situation. I *do* like Ross. I just don't like the idea of you marrying anyone but me."

"Ross likes you, too," Hannah said, and then she took another deep breath. I have to ask you this . . . do you think that we can still be friends?"

It took Norman a long time to respond. It was obvious that he was thinking it through. "I think so. I'm not completely sure, but I know I'm going to try." He took another deep breath and then he reached out for her hand again. "I love you, Hannah. I'll never stop loving you. If anything ever goes wrong and you need me, don't hesitate. You can always come to me."

"What do you mean, Norman? What could go wrong?"

"I don't know. Life is uncertain except for one thing. And that one thing is that I'll always be there for you. Please, Hannah. I want you to remember that."

"I'll remember," Hannah told him. "I promise, Norman."

The hands of the clock on the kitchen wall seemed to march forward in double time as Hannah filled several display jars for the coffee shop, mixed up a batch of Cherry Winks and baked them, put on a fresh pot of coffee, and prepared another plate of Chocolate Almond Crisps for Mike's arrival. Before she'd entirely recovered from Norman's visit, there was another knock on the kitchen door.

Hannah sighed. Mike was here. Why hadn't she scheduled his visit for tomorrow instead? Perhaps Michelle was right and she really was a glutton for punishment.

"Hi, Hannah," Mike said, stepping into the kitchen. "So who's my partner for the wedding party? Andrea, or Michelle?"

"Andrea." Hannah poured coffee for Mike and moved the plate of cookies on the counter between them. "I paired Norman with Michelle."

"How about Bill? Won't he feel left out?"

"No. He was worried that if both of you were in the wedding party, there might be some kind of emergency call at the sheriff's department and neither one of you could go."

"Good thinking." Mike took a cookie and bit into it. "These are good. What are they?"

"Chocolate Almond Crisps. Michelle made them this morning."

"From your recipe?"

"No, it's hers."

"Michelle's a good baker." Mike finished his first cookie and took a second. "You said Norman was paired with Michelle for the wedding. Is he okay with being in the wedding party?"

Hannah chose her words carefully. She wasn't about to describe Norman's reaction to her marriage with the man who had been Norman's rival for her affections. "I saw Norman earlier and he agreed to do it."

"But was he *okay* with it?"

It took Hannah a moment to answer. Again, she knew she had to choose her words carefully. "Norman said yes when I asked him. He said he likes Ross."

"So do I, but that doesn't mean I'm totally okay with you marrying him. It's just there's not much I can do about it except kidnap you and hold you hostage."

Hannah smiled. There was very little chance of that happening. "You can't do that," she pointed out. "Kidnapping's illegal and you're a cop."

"True. There's one thing I want you to promise me, though."

"What's that?" Hannah held her breath, waiting for Mike's answer. She hoped he'd ask her to promise something reasonably simple so that she could say yes.

"Promise me that if Ross ever does anything to hurt you in any way, you'll let me know right away."

"Mike!" Hannah was flabbergasted. "Ross would never hurt me!"

"Maybe not. But if he does, I want you to tell me right away. Will you do that, Hannah?"

"Yes, I promise," Hannah said. She was convinced that Ross would never hurt her. He loved her. He'd told her so, and he'd shown it in countless other ways.

"Just don't forget what you promised."

"I won't forget," Hannah said, but she was puzzled. What possible reason could Mike have for asking her to promise such a ridiculous thing? There was only one way to find out. She had to ask him. Hannah looked up, met his eyes, and asked, "Why did you ask me to make that promise? Do you have some reason to think that Ross might hurt me?"

Mike frowned slightly. "No. I don't have anything concrete, but there's something about him that's . . . I'm not sure how to say this, but there's something that's not quite right. It's a feeling I have."

"A suspicion?"

"Not exactly. It's not as strong as a suspicion. It's not even really a hunch, but it's something that makes me twitch."

"Is that the cop in you talking?"

"Maybe. All I know is that I've been a cop for a long time and I've developed some kind of a sixth sense about some people, a little prickling at the back of my mind. I get the feeling that something about Ross is a little off-center, but I don't know what it is."

Hannah felt very uncomfortable. Norman had asked her to come to him if Ross ever hurt her and she'd promised. And now Mike was talking about Ross, and it was clear he was worried that Ross wasn't the wonderful, honest, caring man that he truly was. What was going on in the minds of the two men she cared for so deeply?

Even with her mind racing through the possibilities at top speed, it took a few moments. Then Hannah understood, and it was all she could do not to smile. Both Norman and Mike were jealous. That was all it was, coupled with the fact that they didn't know Ross as well as she did. She'd gone to college with Ross, lived just down the hall from him, and spent hours socializing with Ross and his college girlfriend. She could point all that out, but she wasn't about to tell Mike that he was just jealous. Mike would simply deny it. She'd let him think that his cop's sense was working overtime. It was simpler that way.

"Can we still be friends, Mike?" Hannah asked him, reaching out to pat his hand.

"Sure."

"And you'll come over to see Ross and me?"

"You bet!" Mike gave her his most devilish smile. "You always make too much food, Hannah, and you're a great cook. Somebody's got to make sure you don't have to put away all those leftovers."

When Mike left, after finishing three cups of coffee and the whole plate of cookies, Hannah sat down at the workstation again. She was tired, bone tired, and she could hardly keep her eyes open. She hadn't slept well last night, and today had been riddled with tension-filled events. She wanted to drive home and fall into her bed to sleep for a week, but she couldn't leave work now. It was almost time to lock the street door to the coffee shop for the day and begin mixing tomorrow's cookie dough. She still had work to do before she could leave for the night.

Just thinking about what she'd done and what she had left to do was difficult when she was this tired. Hannah could hardly wait until this competition and this wedding were over. Then she could go back to her normal routine of going to work every morning, coming home to the condo, fixing dinner and relaxing at night, and going to sleep with Moishe, her feline roommate, purring on the pillow beside her. Only one thing would be different once she was married and it would be wonderful. Instead of saying good night to Ross, and then going to bed with only Moishe for company, she'd be spending all night and every night with the man she loved.

Contemplating that wonderful state of affairs relaxed her, and Hannah decided that she could take a quick five or ten minute nap right there at her workstation. A quick nap would energize her and get her through the rest of her day. She folded her arms on the stainless steel surface, lowered her head, and fell asleep despite the fact that she was uncomfortable in that position and the banks of fluorescent lights overhead were blazing brightly.

Chapter Six

"Wake up, Hannah. It's time to go home. I'll drive."

Hannah heard the voice. It was Michelle. But she was home. She was in bed sleeping and . . . no. This wasn't her comfortable bed. Hannah groaned as she sat up, blinking. She was in her kitchen at The Cookie Jar and Michelle was standing next to her. She'd been so tired, she'd fallen asleep at the workstation. "We can't leave yet, Michelle. We have to mix up the cookie dough for tomorrow."

"It's done. Aunt Nancy, Lisa, and I did it."

Hannah groaned again as she got to her feet. She was sore and stiff all over, but there was a job to be done. "I'll help you put the bowls in the cooler."

"That's done, too. I saw you sleeping and we closed early. There were only two ladies in the coffee shop, and we gave them coffee to go and a half-dozen cookies. Just get into your jacket, Hannah. It's a little past four-thirty, and you said Ross would be there at six."

"That's right. And we still have to make corn muffins."

"I told you before, I'll make the corn muffins. And we already made dessert. Aunt Nancy and I tried out a recipe for pineapple crisp that Lisa gave us. We can sample it tonight for dessert and see if we like it."

"Great!" Hannah gave her youngest sister an appreciative smile. "I don't know what I'd do without you."

"That's simple."

"It is?"

"Yes." Michelle grinned from ear to ear. "You'd overwork, do something stupid like tell Ross that you were too busy to marry him, and die a miserable death as a single woman before your time. Now let's go home so that you can take a little nap in a comfortable bed and I can save you from all that."

Her alarm clock went off and Hannah was immediately aware of a delectable aroma in the air. She was in bed in her own bedroom and Moishe was stretched out on the pillow beside her. All she really wanted to do was go back to sleep for another ten minutes, but one glance at the clock convinced her that she had just enough time to make herself presentable before Ross arrived.

Ten minutes later, Hannah had taken a quick, bracing shower, dressed in clean jeans and the semi-dressy tunic top she'd found in the Helping Hands thrift store. She slipped on moccasins, gave her unruly red hair a cursory brushing, and hurried down the hallway to the kitchen.

Michelle was just taking a pan of muffins out of the oven, and Hannah realized that the delectable aroma was coming from Michelle's newest creation.

"They smell heavenly," Hannah praised her. "The aroma was so wonderful, I realized that I was starving."

"Of course you're hungry. You didn't have lunch, did you?"

Hannah took a fast moment to review her day. "No, I didn't. But I did have Grandma Knudson's lemon pie, a couple of Andrea's whippersnapper cookies, and one Chocolate Almond Crisp."

"All that is sugar central. It gives you fast energy, but

when you crash, you really crash. You can eat a couple of crackers and pâté to tide you over until dinner."

"You made the muffins and put together a pâté since we got home? After working all day at The Cookie Jar?"

"Yes. Why are you surprised? You do it almost every day. I also made Nutmeg and Cinnamon Faux Crème Fraiche to go on top of our dessert."

"I could try that now with a little bit of the dessert," Hannah offered.

"No, you can't. The dessert is in the oven, warming. You'll have to wait, along with the rest of our company."

"The rest of our company? Who else is coming besides Ross?"

"Mike called. He'll be here at six-fifteen. And I called Norman to see if he'd like to join us. He said yes, and he promised to be here at the same time."

"Really?"

"Yes, really." Hannah knew she must have seemed surprised because Michelle hurried to explain. "I figured it was okay since you two seem to be back on your former footing." She paused slightly. "I was right, wasn't I?"

"You were. I'm glad Norman's coming, too."

"Then it'll be like old times. I hope you don't mind, but I told Mike to bring Lonnie."

"Good. Lonnie's always welcome, but I thought he was working the night shift."

"Not anymore. Mike pulled him off the night desk and put him on day shift. The new rookie's got the night shift now."

"Great," Hannah said with a smile. This should be a fun evening. She'd been a bit depressed when she'd fallen asleep, but now she'd regained most of her energy and she felt much better. Instead of dreading a late night with company, she found she was looking forward to the evening ahead. In addition to being a great sister and a wonderful cook, Michelle had the ability to snap her out of her doldrums.

"I'll set the table," Hannah offered, spreading some pâté

on a cracker and popping it into her mouth. She chewed, swallowed, and asked, "Is this Mike's Rainy Day Pâté?"

"Yes. You had some braunschweiger in the meat pan that was going to expire in a couple of days, and there was a jar of horseradish sauce. I figured I might as well use the meat before you had to throw it out."

"Good thinking."

Hannah prepared another cracker, ate it, and headed for the cupboard to get out the plates. She was smiling as she spread a clean tablecloth on the dining room table and arranged six place settings.

"Oh, no, you don't!" Michelle said from the kitchen. "No pâté for you! There's too much horseradish in it. I'll put a couple of salad shrimp in your bowl, but that's it."

Hannah heard the freezer door open, and then there was a sound of running water. Michelle was thawing the shrimp for Moishe. The next thing she heard was the clicking of kitty toenails on the floor as Moishe rushed over to his food bowl.

There was the sound of something rattling against the kitty krunchies in the bowl and then a soft yowl of appreciation. Moishe was obviously thanking Michelle for being so thoughtful. When Hannah gave him frozen salad shrimp, she simply took them out of the freezer and tossed them into his food bowl. Michelle was not only good to her, she was also good to Moishe!

Once the table was set, Michelle brought Hannah a glass of white wine and motioned toward the living room couch. "Sit down and relax, Hannah. Everything's under control in the kitchen, and all we have to do is dish up when everyone's ready to eat. Do you want to watch the Food Channel and see if they're advertising the contest?"

"That's a good idea." Hannah set her wine on the coffee table and took her customary place on the couch. For the hundredth or so time she wished she had a couch with built-in recliners, but there was no way she could afford the expense of a new couch. Perhaps, after they were married, they could save up for one. With two salaries coming in, the budget wouldn't be as tight as it was right now.

Michelle had turned on the television and switched to the Food Channel, but Hannah barely noticed. She took a sip of her wine and thought about a new couch and perhaps even new carpeting. She'd hated the old green carpet when she moved in, and she'd vowed to save the money to replace it, but something always came up that was of a higher priority. Perhaps she could finally replace the threadbare carpeting once they combined her monthly profits from The Cookie Jar with Ross's salary at KCOW-TV.

"Hannah! It's on!"

Michelle leaned over and tapped her on the arm, and Hannah was startled out of her dream of couches and carpets. Her photo was on the screen! "Where did they get that?" she gasped.

"From me. I took it with my phone while you were in the kitchen baking. I had to submit a photo with the application for the contest."

"Good heavens!" Hannah groaned, staring at her photo as the camera panned the line of photos. There were five in all and her photo was directly in the center. There was a smudge of flour on her nose and her apron, the one that said THE COOKIE JAR on the bib, was rumpled. Every single one of the other contestants had photos that had obviously been taken by professional photographers. They stood posing, smiling at the camera in spotless toques and wearing chef's jackets. A banner across the bottom of the screen read, DESSERT CHEF COMPETITION—LIVE COVERAGE, and gave the date of the first night's competition.

Hannah was given another second or two to stare at her photo and wish Michelle had asked Norman to take it, and then the row of photos changed to show the Food Channel cooking set, with Chef Christian Parker standing behind a counter filled with an array of ingredients.

Hannah was about to ask Michelle to turn up the volume,

hoping that they could pick up some helpful information about the judge by watching his show, when there was a knock at the door.

"They're here," Michelle said, picking up the remote control. "I'll set this show to record if you'll go to let them in."

"Deal," Hannah agreed, not wanting to tell Michelle that she'd never bothered to learn how to record a show. She opened the door and was surprised to see Ross standing there, all by himself. "Ross!"

"You were expecting somebody else?" Ross asked, but he didn't wait for her answer. He just pulled her into his arms and kissed her for long, breathless moments.

Hannah was smiling happily when he let her go and stepped inside. He greeted Michelle, gave Hannah another hug, and said, "You didn't answer my question."

Hannah looked at him blankly, still feeling the effects of his kiss. "What question?"

"When you acted surprised to see me, I asked you if you were expecting someone else."

"Oh. Yes. Yes, you did. And yes, we are. We invited Norman and Lonnie to dinner. That was after Mike called Michelle and invited himself."

"I should have guessed that Mike's food-dar would strike again," Ross said with a smile. "If there's any good food within a fifty-mile radius, Mike will find it."

Hannah searched his face. "But you don't mind that he's coming for dinner, do you?"

"Of course not. Mike is a friend. And you said that Norman is coming, too?" He waited until Hannah had nodded, and then he smiled. "Good. That must mean you asked both of them to be in the wedding party."

"I did. Mother said she'd called to ask and you said it was fine with you."

"That's right. I'm glad we're having a big wedding, Hannah. I felt a little like we were teenagers sneaking off to get married for fear our parents would stop us."

Hannah was surprised. "But you never said that to me!"

"You're right. I didn't. The only thing I said was that you could plan anything you wanted and it would be all right with me. And it would have been, Cookie. Really, it would have been. It's just that I like this way better. All our friends will be there, and we can have a real celebration. It's the only wedding I'll ever have, and I want it to be special for both of us."

"Oh, it will be with Mother at the helm! I just hope that we'll live through it."

Ross gave her a curious look. "What do you mean by that?"

"I mean that you can never tell what special surprises Mother might have in store for us. She may decide to have the Lake Eden Players do *Taming of the Shrew* with real shrews!"

Ross threw back his head and laughed. So did Hannah, and then Michelle joined in. "I wouldn't put it past her," Ross said. Then he turned back to Hannah. "Have you ever seen a real shrew? I'm not really sure exactly what a shrew looks like."

"It's a little like a mouse," Hannah explained. "As a matter of fact, it's sometimes called a shrew mouse. My dictionary describes it as a mole-like creature between three and four and a half inches long."

Michelle laughed. "That could cause real panic at a wedding reception. A lot of people are afraid of mice."

"Do you think we should have Sally set traps, just in case?" Ross asked her.

At first Hannah wasn't sure how to answer. She thought he was teasing her, but she wasn't entirely sure. Then she saw the twinkle in his eyes and she shook her head. "No, let's let the shrews run wild. Then you can film it and air the footage on KCOW. If Stephanie Bascomb lifts her skirts and climbs up on a table, it'll be an overnight sensation."

"Or even better, maybe you can get Mayor Bascomb cowering behind one of Sally's artificial trees in the dining room," Michelle suggested. "That ought to increase viewer numbers for KCOW."

"Mother's afraid of mice, too," Hannah pointed out. "Maybe we should take Moishe along to the reception. He's a very good mouser. I had to take him to Mother's house once, to catch a mouse in her spare bedroom."

Ross laughed. "Loose shrews and enough cats to catch them. That sounds like the beginning of a comedy to me. Now, who or what is going to catch the cats?"

"Dogs," Hannah answered. "Mother can gather up all the dogs on her block and drive them out to the reception."

"And who or what is going to catch the dogs?" Ross carried it further.

"Their owners," Michelle answered quickly. "They'll be there anyway. Everyone in Lake Eden is coming to your wedding and your reception."

"It's going to be that big?" Ross asked Hannah.

"I'm afraid so. Mother only knows one way to throw a party. She doesn't want to take the chance that she'll leave someone out and cause hurt feelings. So, to make sure that doesn't happen, she sends invitations to everyone she knows."

"And some she doesn't," Michelle added, flashing a grin at Hannah. "You should have seen Hannah's high school graduation party. There were kids there that none of us had ever seen before."

There was a knock on the door, and Ross reached out to give Hannah a quick hug. "Go ahead and do what you have to do in the kitchen. I'll greet the gang and let them in."

Just as soon as coats had been removed, hands had been washed, and wine and beer had been poured, Ross and Hannah, Lonnie and Michelle, and Norman and Mike took seats around Hannah's big dining room table. As they passed the pâté, conversation flowed. Norman had brought his cat,

Cuddles, to play with Moishe and the two cats were prowling around, exploring every room in the condo, looking for anything that might provide feline entertainment.

Hannah noticed that at first Norman seemed a bit tense, but then Ross began to tell him about the new remote control cameras he'd bought for the studio at KCOW, and Norman visibly relaxed.

"You're taping the basketball game tonight at the high school, aren't you?" Hannah asked Ross, even though she knew he'd already gone there to set up his equipment.

"Yes, but it's not taped, Hannah. We're doing a live feed." Ross turned to Norman. "I don't suppose you'd like to come and help out, would you?"

A broad smile spread across Norman's face. "Sure! I'll be glad to come."

"Then we'll leave together, right after dinner. I still have a couple of things I have to set up before the game."

"Fine by me," Norman agreed.

Michelle, who was sitting next to Hannah, gave her a gentle poke in the ribs. Hannah turned to look at her and Michelle raised her eyebrows.

"Let's dish up the stew," Hannah said, knowing exactly what her sister meant. Michelle wanted to talk to her alone in the kitchen.

They waited, leaning against the counter, until the conversation around the table began again. Then Michelle turned to Hannah. "Do you think that was a ruse to get Norman to leave when Ross did?"

"Oh! I didn't even think of that!" Hannah exclaimed, keeping her voice low so that no one around the table in the dining room could hear her. "Do you think that's what Ross was doing?"

"Could be. And if that's so, Ross is pretty darn sneaky!"

"Sneaky? I'm not sure I like that idea. I'd rather think that he just wanted a friend to go with him to the game, and he knows that Norman's interested in all kinds of photography." Hannah opened the cupboard and took out six bowls. "Come on, Michelle. I'll dish up the stew while you take your corn muffins out of the pan and put them in a basket. We also need a bowl of sour cream for anyone who wants a dollop on top of the stew, some of that hot salsa I picked up at the Red Owl, and the bottle of Slap Ya Mama hot sauce for Mike. You can carry all those to the table while I fill the bowls. And when you come back, you can start carrying in the bowls of stew. We've got four hungry men out there who want to be fed."

While Hannah finished dishing up the stew and Michelle carried bowls to the table, Hannah thought about what her youngest sister had said. It *was* rather flattering to think that Ross might be a bit jealous of Norman. She wished she could tell him that he didn't have any reason at all to be jealous, but if Ross wasn't being devious, she'd look very silly saying something like that to him. It would be wiser for her to say nothing and ignore the whole thing.

Once dinner was served, Hannah received wonderful compliments on her stew. Ross even said that it was a pity the Food Channel contest was limited to desserts. Michelle's Cheesy Chili Corn Muffins were also a big hit.

"Now for the dessert," Hannah said when everyone had eaten at least two bowls of stew and Mike had finished his third. "Michelle and I need your honest opinion. We're testing desserts to see which ones we ought to bake for the competition, and Michelle baked a pineapple crisp."

Lonnie grinned at Michelle. "If Shelly baked it, it's bound to be great. I don't even have to taste it to know that."

"Thanks, Lonnie." Michelle took time to smile at him, and then she said, "But what we really need is your honest criticism and any suggestions you have to make it taste even better."

Hannah nodded. "Michelle's right."

The two sisters cleared the table and carried in coffee. Then Michelle cut squares of her dessert while Hannah carried the bowl of Nutmeg and Cinnamon Faux Crème Fraiche to the table. "Just pass the bowl around and take as much as you want after we bring in your dessert. And please think about whether we should serve it to the judges with the topping already on it, or whether we should give the bowl to the judges and let them pass it to each other."

Less than five minutes later, everyone was munching happily and the consensus of opinion around the table was that Hannah should deliver the dessert plates to the judges and Michelle should follow in her wake with the bowl of topping so that the judges could taste the dessert without the topping, if they wished, and then take some of the topping and judge it separately.

"That'll give you two chances to come out on top," Norman pointed out. "One chance if they like it better without the topping and another chance if they prefer it with the topping."

"Good idea, Norman!" Ross said, patting him on the back.

"He's right," Mike agreed. "That'll cover all the bases."

Michelle turned to Hannah. "I think we should talk to Lisa and Aunt Nancy about running a series of taste tests at The Cookie Jar. We could tell whoever's there, and The Lake Eden Gossip Hotline would take care of the rest."

"That's a good idea, Michelle." Hannah paused and gave Mike her own version of his own devilish grin. "Who knows? It might bring in as much business as another Lake Eden murder!"

GREEN TOMATILLO STEW

Grease or spray the inside of a 5-quart slow cooker with Pam or another nonstick cooking spray.

Start this stew in the early morning of the day you wish to serve it for dinner.

The Ingredients:

> 2 medium onions, roughly chopped
> 2 pounds frozen chicken tenders *(I used Foster Farms)*
> 1 cup carrot nuggets *(I used a fresh pack, the kind of carrot nuggets that you might put in a school lunchbox)*
> 14-ounce package frozen tri-colored pepper strips *(I used C&W, which is made by Birds Eye)*
> 4 stalks celery, cut into 1/2-inch pieces
> 16-ounce bag of frozen pearl onions *(I used Birds Eye White Pearl Onions)*
> two 7-ounce by weight cans of Salsa verde sauce
> diced green chilies *(I used one can of Ortega Green Chilies 4-ounces by weight)*
> diced jalapenos *(I used one can of Ortega Diced Jalapenos 4-ounces by weight)*

Additional Ingredients:

You will add these ingredients 1 hour before you're ready to serve your Green Tomatillo Stew.

1 teaspoon garlic powder
1 teaspoon onion powder
two 7-ounce cans mushroom stems and pieces *(NOT drained!)*
14-ounce can of green tomatillos *(If your store doesn't carry these, use a 13-ounce can of chopped stewed regular tomatoes instead—it won't be the same, but it will be tasty)*
two .88-ounce packets of chicken gravy mix *(or turkey gravy mix—I used Schilling Chicken Gravy Mix)*

Hannah's 1st Note: You may notice that there is NO SALT in this recipe. This is not an omission. The gravy packets that are called for in the recipe are very salty. They will usually add enough salt to the recipe. If your family would like more salt, you may add it later, when you adjust the seasonings right before you serve it.

Place the chopped onions in the bottom of the slow cooker.

Lay the frozen chicken tenders on top of the onions.

Add the carrot nuggets.

Sprinkle the frozen pepper strips on top.

Put the celery on top of the pepper strips.

Place the pearl onions on top of the celery.

Open the cans of salsa verde sauce and pour them over the pearl onions.

Open the cans of diced green chilies and jalapenos. If there's any liquid, you can add that to your stew. Then sprinkle the chilies over the top of the salsa verde sauce.

Hannah's 2nd Note: CAUTION!!! If you use your fingers to sprinkle in the chilies, WASH YOUR HANDS IMMEDIATELY! If you touch your eyes without washing your hands, your eyes will burn and smart from the chilies.

Cover your slow cooker with the lid, plug it in, and cook it on LOW for at least 8 hours.

Hannah's 3rd Note: If you cook on LOW in a slow cooker, the time is not that critical. You'll need 8

hours of cooking time, but if you don't get back home for 9 or 10 hours, that's okay, too.

When you get home from work, give the contents of the slow cooker a good stir and then add the additional ingredients in this order:

Sprinkle the garlic powder over the top.

Sprinkle the onion powder over the top of the garlic powder.

Stir the contents of the crock again to mix in the ingredients you just added.

Add the two cans of mushrooms, liquid and all. Stir them in. Then add the green tomatillos.

Sprinkle in ONE packet of gravy mix and stir that in. Reserve the 2nd packet of powdered gravy mix for later, if you need it.

Put the lid on the crockpot, turn it up to HIGH, and let the contents cook for another hour.

Right before you're ready to serve, take off the lid of the slow cooker and taste the broth again. If it's not thick enough, stir in the 2nd packet of powdered gravy mix, put the lid on again, and let it cook for another 5 to 10 minutes.

Hannah's 4th Note: Some people like this stew with a dollop of sour cream with fresh salsa on top of the bowl. Have these bowl toppers handy on the table if your family likes them.

Hannah's 5th Note: If you invite Mike Kingston for dinner (or anyone else who likes things very spicy) make sure you have a bottle of Slap Ya Mama Hot Sauce on your table. If your guest is Mike, have a BIG bottle!

Serve the stew in bowls with a basket of hot crusty bread or Michelle's Spicy Cheesy Corn Muffins as an accompaniment.

Yield: 6 to 8 large servings, unless you invite Mike. Then you'd better prepare a second crockpot.

CHEESY CHILI CORN MUFFINS

Preheat oven to 375 degrees F., rack in the middle position.

- enough packages of corn muffin mix to make 18 muffins *(Michelle used 3 packages of Jiffy Corn Muffin Mix, the kind that makes 6 to 8 muffins per package—each package weighed 8.5 ounces.)*
- 2 large eggs, beaten *(just whip them up in a glass with a fork)*
- 14.15 ounce net weight can of creamed corn *(Michelle used Libby's Cream Style Sweet Corn)*
- 10 and ¾-ounce net weight can of <u>condensed</u> cheddar cheese soup *(Michelle used Campbell's)*
- one 4-ounce net weight can of diced green chilies *(Michelle used Ortega Diced Green Chilies)*
- 8 ounces shredded cheese to sprinkle on top of your muffins before baking *(Michelle used Kraft Mexican Style Four Cheese mixture of shredded cheeses— if you can't find that, a mixture of Monterey Jack and Cheddar will do just fine)*

Prepare your muffin pans by spraying the inside of the cups with Pam or another nonstick cooking spray, or lining them with double cupcake papers. You will need 2 regular-size muffin *(cupcake)* pans with 12 cups in each, or 2 jumbo muffin pans with 6 cups in each.

Pour the dry muffin mix into a large mixing bowl.

Add the beaten eggs, but let them sit on top of the muffin mix.

Add the creamed corn on top of the eggs, but again, don't mix it in.

Add the condensed cheddar cheese soup on top of the creamed corn. Don't mix quite yet.

Drain the can of diced green chilies and put them on top of the cheese soup.

Mix all the ingredients together. Continue to stir until everything is thoroughly incorporated.

Hannah's 1st note: There will be some lumps in the muffin batter from the chilies and the corn. That's perfectly fine. Just make sure there are no dry spots of muffin mix that haven't been stirred into the batter.

Using a large spoon, fill the muffin cups three-quarters full.

Hannah's 2nd note: If you're using the jumbo muffin cups, divide the batter equally to fill the 12 large cups. They may be a little more than three-quarters full, but that's all right. If you're using the regular-size muffin cups, you may not have enough batter to fill all the cups in both pans three-quarters full. That's okay. Just take out the cup-cake papers in the empty cups so that you can save them for future use.

Once your batter is in the muffin cups, sprinkle the tops of the cups with shredded cheese. This will melt and turn golden as you bake your Cheesy Chili Corn Muffins.

Bake the muffins at 375 degrees F. for 25 to 30 minutes if you're using the regular-size muffin pans, and 30 to 35 minutes if you're using the jumbo muffin pans.

When the time is up for the size of muffins you made, test your muffins with a cake tester, long tooth-pick, or thin wooden skewer by plunging it into the center of a muffin. If it comes out clean with no muffin batter clinging to it, your muffins are done. If it still has sticky batter on the tester, toothpick, or skewer,

return your pans to the oven for additional 5-minute increments until they test done.

Remove your muffins from the oven and let them cool in the muffin pans on wire racks or on cold stove burners for at least 10 minutes. Then turn the muffins out of the pans and cool them right side up on wire racks until they feel warm, not hot. Then line a basket with a napkin and place them inside to serve them.

Serve your muffins with plenty of soft butter. They're delicious!

Yield: Approximately 18 regular-size muffins or 12 jumbo muffins.

Michelle's Note: Despite the fact that Mike was there the night I first made these, there were two muffins left over. Hannah and I stored them in a sealed plastic bag in the refrigerator and heated them in the microwave to have for a snack. If there had been more leftover muffins, we would have sealed them in a freezer bag and frozen them to accompany another meal.

Chapter Seven

Mike and Lonnie left shortly after Ross and Norman. Once they were gone, Hannah and Michelle cleared the table, rinsed and stacked the dishes in the dishwasher, and tidied up the kitchen. When they were through, Hannah poured a glass of white wine. "Do you want a glass of wine?" she called out to Michelle.

"No, thanks. I'm going to turn in for the night. I want to get up early and try another recipe. Aunt Nancy gave me an idea today, and we'll have it for breakfast."

"What is it?"

"I'm not going to tell you because it doesn't have a name yet. It's just an idea."

"What's in it?"

"You'll find out in the morning. I'm just hoping it'll work."

Hannah smiled as she headed for her customary spot on the couch. The moment she sat down, Moishe jumped down from his perch on the back of the couch and settled in her lap.

"I thought you'd deserted me," Hannah said, scratching him behind the ears. "You spent the whole night begging scraps from the guys. If you keep that up, you'll have to go on a diet again."

"Rrrowwww!"

The yowl was definitely irate. Hannah knew him well enough to recognize the difference between contented and alarmed. He was looking up at her with wide, startled eyes, and Hannah gave him another pet to reassure him. "Just kidding," she said. "You're okay. And if you're not okay now, you will be when I go off to the Food Channel competition and you go to stay with Norman and Cuddles."

Hearing the name of Norman's cat, Moishe's favorite kitty friend, gave Moishe an expression that Hannah interpreted as a kitty smile. Moishe purred very loudly, and settled back down in her lap. Norman had offered to keep Moishe while she was in New York, even before Hannah had thought to ask him.

"I think Norman missed you the past couple of weeks," Hannah said. "What do you think?"

"Rrrow!"

"That's right. I'm glad you agree with me. You get two days to play with Cuddles and both of you can sleep in front of the fireplace in his bedroom."

"Rrrow!"

Hannah smiled. She knew full well that Cuddles and Moishe didn't sleep in front of the fireplace. They slept on feather pillows in Norman's bed. Norman had told her that.

Since Michelle had already gone to bed and Hannah didn't know how to access the show they'd recorded, she settled for watching the Food Channel live. They were showing a chef Hannah didn't recognize, and he was preparing shrimp scampi. Hannah watched intently. She'd never made shrimp scampi, and Ross might like it. He'd told her he loved anything with pasta, and he'd raved about how good her Fettuccine Porcini was when she'd made it for him.

Hannah turned up the volume so that she could hear the chef. She still couldn't hear the directions, and she turned it up even further. It took her a minute to realize that the reason she had to have the volume so high was because the cat on her lap was purring so loudly.

She glanced down at Moishe to find that he was staring intently at the screen, ears perked forward and tail twitching in excitement as the chef deveined the jumbo shrimp.

"So you like this episode, do you, Moishe?"

Moishe didn't turn his head to look up at her. He just kept watching the shrimp in the chef's hand and purring so hard, she could see his ears vibrate.

"Next we put the cleaned shrimp into the pan on the stove-top," the chef said, tumbling them in and picking up the sauté pan to shake it. As he did, the camera zoomed in on the pre-pared pasta and the sauce that was in a separate pan on the stove.

"Rrrrowww!" Moishe yowled, and Hannah could hear the outrage in his voice. He jumped down from her lap, headed directly to the television set, and leapt to the top of it.

"Moishe! What are you doing up there?" Hannah asked, not expecting an answer, but Moishe yowled again, this time a yowl that sounded plaintive.

"Relax. They'll show the shrimp again," Hannah told him. "Jump down and you can watch it from my lap."

But it seemed that her cat had other ideas, because he inched forward and draped himself over the front of the television set, hanging over with his head and his front legs so that he could look down at the screen.

Hannah stared at him and then she gave an amused chuckle. She'd seen Moishe do something like that only once before. The incident had taken place several years ago, when her cable company had previewed a new channel for dogs and cats. She'd turned to the channel and left it on to see if it amused Moishe. When she'd come home from work, she'd found him draped over the top of the television set, exactly the way he was now, batting at the screen. The picture on the screen had been a close-up of a large fish tank, and it had been perfectly obvious that Moishe had been trying to catch the fish.

"Are you going to try to snag one of those shrimp when

they show them again?" Hannah asked him. He just lifted his head to look at her, gave her a glance that she was sure meant *Don't bother me, lady!* and lowered his head so he could go back to watching the screen again.

Hannah wished that Ross were here so that she could show him what Moishe was doing, and at that very second, there was a soft knock at her door. She rushed to answer it, pulled open the door, and saw Ross standing there.

"Come in, but don't say a word," she whispered. "Just follow me to the couch and watch Moishe. He's about to attack the television set."

Ross looked every bit as surprised as a man could look, but he did exactly as she asked. He followed her to the couch, sat down quietly, and grinned as he saw Moishe draped over the top.

The chef on the screen was shaking the sauté pan with the shrimp again. As they watched, all three of them, he picked it up and carried it over to the dish with the pasta. Obviously, he'd combined the sauce with the pasta and tossed it while Hannah had answered the door. Now he was ready to finalize the dish by adding the shrimp to the pasta.

Moishe leaned over the screen so far, Hannah was afraid that her cat would fall to the floor. But he didn't, and that made her wonder if the scratches on the top of her television set were from previous shows that had excited him so much, he'd dug in his claws.

"Watch this," she whispered and glanced at Ross's face. He was grinning, and she could feel the couch shaking from his silent laughter.

When the first shrimp tumbled from the edge of the pan, Moishe gave a yowl and batted at it. The rest of the shrimp followed, and Moishe's paw moved so fast it looked as if he might punch a hole through the glass.

"I've never seen a cat do that!" Ross said, clearly shocked. "I don't know why he doesn't fall. He's leaning over so far that . . ."

"Uh-oh!" Hannah exclaimed, watching in fear as Moishe began to slip. She was just jumping up from the couch when it happened. Moishe took a nosedive from the top of the television console, but somehow he managed to twist his body so that he landed on his feet.

"Moishe! Did you hurt yourself?" Hannah gasped.

Moishe turned toward her with a startled expression that quickly turned to something she interpreted as nonchalant. Then he began to wash his face as if he'd planned the whole thing to amuse her.

"I think he's trying to tell you he's fine," Ross commented, pulling her back down on the couch. "And I also think he's trying to tell you that he's a little embarrassed by the fall."

Moishe glanced up at Ross, gave a welcoming yowl that Hannah thought could have meant, *You're right, but don't tell her*, and began to wash his face again.

"Looks like I got here just in time," Ross said, taking Hannah into his arms. "I need to talk to you, Cookie."

He sounded serious and Hannah looked up to try to read his expression. "What about?"

"The Food Channel competition. Why didn't you call to tell me that they changed the date?"

Hannah felt a sudden stab of guilt. "I'm sorry, Ross. I should have called you right away. Andrea told me that and she was right. It was just I . . . well . . . it never occurred to me to call you at work."

"But didn't you think I'd want to know?"

Hannah sighed and admitted defeat. "I didn't think. That's the problem. I'm over thirty, Ross, and I've never been married. I've always been alone, and I guess I'm just used to handling things on my own. It's a big change, but I really am sorry, and . . ." she stopped as she realized that tears were gathering in her eyes. "I . . . I'll do better. I promise I will."

"Oh, honey!" Ross hugged her tightly. "It's okay. I know

you've never been part of a couple and it takes some time to get used to it. Don't worry. We're not joined at the hip, or anything like that. The only thing it took was a little arranging."

"Arranging?"

"Yes. I didn't want to tell you until it was firm, but KCOW is sending me with you to New York. I'm going to film a special about your experience as a contestant in a national baking competition."

Hannah was so surprised, she stopped feeling guilty. Instead, she was flabbergasted. "You mean you're going with Michelle and me?"

"Not just me. P.K.'s going along, too. He's their best cameraman, and they want him to get the experience. He told me he met you?"

"Yes, he did." Hannah smiled. "He was the night engineer at KCOW then."

"He told me. He said he met you during the Hartland Flour Competition and he helped set up some outtakes for you to watch."

"Does he still wear a ponytail and an earring?"

"Not anymore."

"I really liked him, Ross. We got to talking and he told me that someday he wanted to direct."

"He still does. He also wants to make independent films, and I'm training him. That's why I'm taking him along with us to New York. He'll be my second cameraman, but he'll also be learning about producing independent segments."

"That's just wonderful! I'm so glad you'll be with me in New York, Ross. I didn't like the thought of leaving you right before the wedding."

Ross gave her a quick kiss. "Were you worried that I'd get cold feet?"

"No, it's not that. I just knew I'd be lonely without you." Hannah's answer generated another, much longer kiss.

Hannah was just wishing that they were already married and Ross could stay when she heard footsteps coming down the hallway.

"Oh! Sorry!" Michelle said, walking into the room and noticing Ross on the couch. "I didn't know you were here, Ross. I was coming out to make sure I turned off the oven after I warmed the dessert. I'll just check and go right back to bed."

"You don't have to do that," Ross said, smiling at her. "I have to leave in a couple of minutes anyway, and I'll see you both for breakfast." He paused and began to smile. "Say, Michelle . . . you don't happen to have any of that dessert left, do you?"

Michelle laughed. "As a matter of fact I do. I was thinking about having a piece myself. How about you, Hannah?"

Hannah smiled. "Have you ever heard me turn down dessert?"

"No!"

Both Michelle and Ross answered at once, and then all three of them laughed.

"If you cut it, I'll warm it in the microwave," Hannah offered. "It'll be a perfect midnight snack."

"But it's only eleven," Ross pointed out.

"That's okay," Hannah said. "At midnight I'll probably be dreaming about how good it was."

Chapter Eight

The recipe testing at The Cookie Jar had been a huge success. When Lisa had announced that the whole town of Lake Eden would be helping Hannah and that they could watch the New York segment on television, everyone came in to offer suggestions and critique a small sample of the dessert of the day. That sampling seemed to whet their appetites for more sweet treats, and Hannah and Lisa sold more cookies than they'd expected.

It was the morning of the day they were leaving for New York, and Hannah was sitting in the living room of her condo with Ross and Michelle, her suitcase at her feet. Norman had already picked up Moishe, who'd been so obviously excited at the prospect of going to play with Cuddles that he'd tugged on the leash attached to his harness while Norman had said good-bye and wished them success.

"Isn't it almost time to leave?" Hannah asked Ross, who glanced at his watch.

"Yes. The driver should be here any minute."

Immediately following his answer, there was a knock on Hannah's door.

"I'll get it," Ross said, jumping up and carrying Hannah's suitcase to the door. "Our car must be here."

Just as Ross had predicted, a uniformed driver stood

there waiting. Hannah recognized him as one of the drivers that Cyril Murphy used for his Shamrock Limousine Service.

Ross handed the driver two suitcases, which the driver took down the outside staircase. When he reappeared, Ross handed him the rest of their luggage and then he shut the door again and turned back to Hannah.

"Let's go, Cookie. The driver said he's pulling the limo around to the sidewalk so we don't have to walk down to the garage."

"Oh, good! But it's not a limo, is it? The Food Channel told me they were sending a van."

"They were, but now that I'm going along, I upgraded to a limo."

"KCOW sprang for a limo?" Hannah asked him, amazed that the radio and television station that had a reputation for being on a tight budget would go to those lengths to make them comfortable.

"KCOW allowed a certain amount for P.K. and me, and I picked up the rest." Ross walked to the couch and took her arm to help her up. "I wanted my bride-to-be and her sister to ride to the airport in comfort."

Hannah waited until they were in the limo and the driver had pulled out of her condo complex. Hannah leaned close to Ross. "Can you afford something like this on KCOW's salary?" she asked in a low voice.

"Don't worry about it, Hannah. It's tax deductible because I still have my status as an independent producer. Didn't I tell you that I transferred my bank account here to Lake Eden First Mercantile Bank? Doug Greerson handled it for me."

"But . . . isn't a limo a lot more expensive than a van?"

Ross laughed. "No, not if you compare the price to L.A. I can afford it. I didn't spend much money when I was living in California and I've made a lot of money since I moved here. We can afford a limo for such an important trip."

Hannah felt a warm glow. Ross had said *we*, instead of *I*.

That meant he was already thinking of them as a couple. She still didn't understand how someone could save money when they were wining and dining the Hollywood luminaries Ross had told her about, and he certainly couldn't be making a fortune working at KCOW-TV, but she wasn't about to question him further.

It took a moment, but then Hannah remembered the independent film Ross had made right here in Lake Eden and the Minneapolis television station that had offered to pay a fee if they could air it on their *Minnesota Movies* show. Ross had told her they wanted to feature it in the premiere of their new programming, and the deal with them must have gone through.

Hannah gave Ross a big smile. "This is wonderful, Ross. I feel like a rich woman, riding in such luxury. Thank you so much for thinking of it!"

"Only the best for the woman I love." Ross pulled her into his arms and kissed her soundly. "We're going to have a really good life, Hannah. I know we will."

"Yes," Hannah said, but something was niggling at the back of her mind. How much money was there? And would it run out if Ross continued to spend it on limos like this? But he had said it wasn't expensive compared to Los Angeles prices. And this *was* a once in a lifetime experience. She highly doubted that she'd ever be invited to be part of a national competition again. She really should relax, enjoy herself, and trust the man who would soon be her new husband.

The time passed quickly when you were riding in a limo and didn't have to worry about driving, or directions, or traffic. Cyril's driver was a thorough professional and he got them to the airport early. He idled at the curbside check-in, got a skycap to check them in, get their boarding passes, and load their luggage. After a brief moment with Ross, the driver drove away. Then they all walked into the airport.

"Let's get through security and then we'll go up to the Sky Lounge," Ross said, picking up Hannah's carry-on and his. P.K. did the same for Michelle and they headed off to security.

The lines were short and they were through in less than ten minutes. Ross led them down the hallway, through a door marked MEMBERS ONLY that required a key card, and checked them in with a man at a huge desk in front of an elevator. Then he took them around a corner to another, smaller elevator.

"We go up in this one," he told them, slipping his key card into the slot again. Before Hannah could even think to ask where this elevator went, the doors opened and Ross motioned them inside. He inserted his card in a slot near the front, the doors closed, and the elevator began to rise.

"There aren't any buttons on this elevator," Michelle said, staring at the blank panel where the buttons for the floors would have been in most elevators.

"That's because this is an express elevator that only goes to one place," Ross told her.

Almost before the words were out of his mouth, the elevator slowed to a stop and the door opened to reveal another desk with a man in a suit sitting behind it.

"Good morning, sir," the man greeted Ross, taking the card Ross handed to him. He scanned it in some sort of card reader and gave Ross a welcoming smile.

"Everything is ready for you, Mr. Barton. Please follow me."

Ross motioned them forward and they followed him to a lounge on the top floor of the airport where they took swivel chairs around a black onyx table. A smiling waitress arrived almost immediately to take their drink and breakfast orders from the menus on the table. Once she'd left, Hannah turned to Ross.

"There's no one else here," she commented.

"That's because it's early. It'll fill up in a couple of hours."

"We must have gotten here right after they opened," Michelle said.

"No." Ross shook his head. "They're open twenty-four hours a day for members."

"Does it cost a lot to belong to a club like this?" Hannah asked, hoping she didn't sound worried.

"It's worth it if you fly as much as I do . . . or as much as I used to do. Everything's free, including the drinks, and there are cubicles where you can stretch out and rest if your flight is delayed."

"What if you fall asleep?" P.K. asked.

"They wake you in time to catch your flight and they have their own private cart waiting to take you to the gate. You get full VIP service, and you don't have to wait in those uncomfortable chairs in the waiting area by the gate."

Their breakfast arrived and Hannah was momentarily distracted. She'd ordered smoked salmon with capers, cream cheese, and toast points. It was so artfully arranged and presented on a bone china plate. It was so attractive that it could have been used on a gourmet magazine cover.

"Gorgeous!" Michelle breathed, and Hannah glanced at her sister's plate. Michelle had ordered Eggs Benedict and again, the breakfast entrée was so beautifully arranged, it could have starred in a magazine photo. The food looked lovely in the Sky Lounge and the service left nothing to be desired. But how did their breakfast entrées taste?

There was only one way to find out and Hannah could hardly wait! She spread cream cheese on a toast point and sprinkled on some capers. She'd learned that from Delores. Capers tended to roll off if you put them on top of the salmon, but if you pressed them down into the layer of cream cheese, they stayed in place until you could eat them.

Breakfast was wonderful. It was clear that everyone loved it because there was total silence while they ate and every one of them finished every bite. Four cups of excellent coffee later, a pleasant-looking young woman wearing an airline uniform approached their table.

"Your flight is ready, Mr. Barton," she said, smiling at Ross.

"Thank you," Ross said, rising from his chair. Hannah and everyone else followed suit. It was obviously time to go.

"Please follow me," the young woman said, leading them to the elevator. And when they'd reached the ground floor, she escorted them past the front desk and led them to a motorized cart driven by a uniformed driver.

"Please be seated," she told them. "Your flight is waiting for you. We wish you a safe and pleasurable journey to New York."

Hannah was impressed and she glanced at Ross. He seemed to be taking the special treatment they'd received in stride. Of course, Ross had flown many more times than she had. Hannah's only flight, thus far, had been on the private jet that had carried her sisters, Doc, and Delores to Las Vegas.

Prepared to experience a letdown when she boarded a commercial flight, Hannah followed Ross as he led them to the Jetway. The long, carpeted section was completely deserted and she turned to him with a frown. "We're flying a commercial jet, aren't we?" she asked.

"Yes, we are. It's my favorite airline."

"Good, but where are all the other people?"

Ross turned to her with a smile. "They're on the plane already. The people in the Sky Lounge wait until boarding is complete. They board last so that they don't have to stand in line."

Hannah was a bit nervous as she walked up the ramp. She'd heard horror stories about commercial flights. Rose McDermott had flown home to see her parents at Christmas, and she'd told Hannah about being sandwiched in between a terribly overweight man and a lady who kept falling asleep and putting her head on Rose's shoulder. Rose had told her that when you flew coach, you had to be in the first group that boarded to get the good seats.

Hannah tapped Ross on the shoulder. "Aren't all the good seats taken?"

"Yes, but I'm a Sky Lounge member and they saved our seats for us. Don't worry, Cookie. You'll be very comfortable on the flight."

His promise was good enough for Hannah. Ross had been right about everything so far. She smiled and followed him to the end of the Jetway and entered the plane right behind him.

"Would you like the window or the aisle?" Ross asked her, gesturing toward the bulkhead seats on the right of the plane.

"The window please. But those aren't our seats. According to the diagram the Food Channel sent me, we're near the back of the plane."

"Not anymore. We have these two bulkhead seats and Michelle and P.K. have the ones right across the aisle from us."

Hannah was almost afraid to ask, but she did. "But weren't we supposed to be in coach?"

"Yes." Ross gave her a little hug. "I called the airline and upgraded all of us. I may not be flying much in the job I have now, and I figured I'd better use my frequent flyer points for something."

"Well . . . thank you!" Hannah said, stretching out in the wide, comfortable seat. At least Ross hadn't paid extra for this. "This is just wonderful, Ross."

Ross gestured at the stewardess who was coming down the aisle. "What would you like to drink? Whatever it is, you'll have to drink it fast. We're almost ready to take off."

"Coffee would be good, if you think I'll have time to drink it."

"You will. They just finished their head count and they still have to report to the gate."

"Something before we depart, Mr. Barton?" the stewardess asked him.

"Coffee please. Two cups would be good. One with cream and one black."

"Right away, sir." The stewardess smiled, and hurried to the galley to get their coffee. A moment later, she delivered it and helped Hannah pull out the little tray on the console between them. "Would you like a cookie to go with that, Miss Swensen?"

"No, thank you," Hannah said. "We just had breakfast."

Hannah tasted her coffee. Rose McDermott had told her that the coffee on planes was undrinkable, but this coffee was very good. She'd just finished drinking it when the stewardess came back to collect their cups.

"Are you nervous, Hannah?" Ross asked her.

"No. Should I be?"

"Not at all. I've flown on aircraft like this hundreds of times and they have a very good safety rating."

Hannah swallowed hard. She wished that Ross hadn't said that. It was almost like tempting fate. But she smiled as he took her hand. At that moment she knew that she'd go anywhere with him, even into a dangerous situation, as long as he never left her side.

Chapter Nine

"Wake up, Hannah. We're on approach."

Hannah opened her eyes and somehow managed to orient herself. Instead of working on a cooking stage at the Food Channel competition, she was sitting next to Ross on an airplane and he was smiling at her. She blinked several times in an attempt to shake herself out of the dream. She'd been dreaming that she was mixing up her Double Rainbow Swirl Cake and she'd spilled grape Jell-O powder all over Alain Duquesne.

Her mind still felt sluggish and heavy, like wet woolen snow pants after an afternoon of playing in the snow. "On approach?" she repeated Ross's words groggily. "What are we approaching?"

"The airport." Ross gestured toward the cup of coffee on the little pull-out tray between them. "I had the stewardess bring you a fresh cup. That should clear out the remnants of that dream you were having."

"How do you know about my dream?" Hannah asked, reaching for the cup of coffee.

"You said, *Don't be mad. I'll wash your shirt.*"

Hannah took a sip of coffee. "That fits. I was dreaming that I was baking our wedding cake and I spilled grape Jell-O powder all over the head judge." She took another sip of coffee and leaned back with a sigh. "I guess I'm more nervous about the competition than I thought I was."

"You'll be just fine, honey," Ross reassured her. "You have a big advantage over the other contestants."

"I do?" Hannah was surprised. "What's that?"

"They have big fancy restaurants and they're not used to baking anything alone. All of them have at least three other people to help them in their kitchens. You're used to working alone, or with just one other person. You're also more comfortable with a time limit. You're required to bake a certain number of cookies in a certain amount of time so they're ready when your coffee shop opens for business in the morning. Their restaurants don't open in the morning. The earliest any of them open is noon for the lunch crowd. And I'm willing to bet that most of their lunch desserts are things like ice cream, sherbet, cakes, and pies that are left over from the previous night."

Hannah was surprised at Ross's insights. "How do you know all that?"

"I looked at their menus online. Their lunch menus only had two or three desserts and most of them consisted of things their staff could assemble in the kitchen like fresh seasonal fruit over ice cream with a sauce or a liqueur."

"How about the dinner menus?"

"The desserts were more elaborate on those, but don't forget that they have all day to make them and more than one assistant. And they don't have to bake take-out orders, or delivery orders, or answer the phone, or serve coffee when the restaurant gets busy. They also close between lunch and dinner. They have only one job, and that's to make the desserts. They're prima donnas. You're a jack-of-all-trades *plus* a fantastic baker."

Hannah began to smile. "Thank you, Ross. I think you're right and I do have an advantage. I feel much better about the competition now."

* * *

In less than an hour, Hannah and Michelle stepped into their hotel room. Their luggage had already been delivered, and there were two luggage racks set up in the very places that Hannah would have chosen. She walked over to her suitcase and snapped it open to take out the extra copy of the recipes that she'd brought with her. She was still searching for the file of recipes when she heard Michelle give a low whistle.

"What?" she asked, turning around to look for her sister. But Michelle wasn't standing next to her luggage rack.

"Where are you?" Hannah called out.

"I'm out on the balcony. Come out here, Hannah. The view's incredible!"

Hannah left her luggage rack, which was in an alcove, and entered the main part of the room. "It's a suite!" she gasped, gazing around at the separate bedrooms, two of them, and another room that probably contained the bathroom. One peek inside the partially open door proved her theory correct. But it wasn't just an ordinary bathroom. It was a bathroom with two rooms, one containing the largest, most luxurious, innovative shower that she had ever seen, with multiple jets protruding from the walls and a built-in waterproof sound system for those who liked to shower to music.

"Just wait until you see this shower!" Hannah called out to her sister, rushing out the door, through the living room, and onto the cold balcony. But the balcony wasn't cold. The tile was warm on her feet, and Hannah's mouth opened in surprise a second time.

"It's heated," Michelle said, stating the obvious. "And it's covered, too, so the snow can't come in unless it's a blizzard. I can hardly wait to come out here at night! We could be perfectly comfortable, even on a cold night, sitting in those chairs and looking out at the city lights. This is the biggest and fanciest suite I've ever seen, even in the movies.

It's like our very own luxury apartment. I can't believe that the Food Channel gave us a suite like this!"

Hannah sighed and then she smiled. "I don't think that the Food Channel gave us this suite."

"What do you mean? You said they told you that they would provide our accommodations."

"And they probably did pay for a perfectly nice room. But I think Ross got an upgrade for us. That's what he did on the plane."

"The Food Channel didn't fly us here in first class?"

"No, they paid for two round-trip tickets in coach. Ross used his frequent flyer points to upgrade all of us to first class."

"Tell him thank you for me. The plane food was even good. One of my roommates told me that all I should eat on the plane was cheese and crackers because the food was so awful, but I had the tuna wrap and it was really great. What did you have? I was so busy talking to P.K., I didn't even notice."

"I didn't have anything. I slept all the way here. Ross had to wake me up when we got ready to land."

"You must have been tired."

"I was, but I'm not now. I *am* a little hungry, though. I brought some Soft Chewy Milk Chocolate Cookies with me. Would you like one?"

"I'd like one and then I'd like more. I love those cookies. They smell like summer afternoons on the front porch."

"You're right. They do. The only thing we're missing is the mosquitoes."

"I could live without those." Michelle followed Hannah back inside and waited until she found the cookies in her suitcase. "Shall we unpack and then take a walk to get a feel for the city?"

"Sounds good to me. Ross and P.K. are going to be busy all afternoon, getting their equipment in order. And the Food Channel car doesn't pick us up until six."

"That's for orientation, right?"

"That's what they told me. We have to sign a bunch of papers and then we get to walk around our cooking stage and examine the contents of the pantry. Tomorrow morning's our time to practice. The sheet the Food Channel representative gave me at the airport says our time slot is from ten to one."

"And the competition is at seven that night?"

"Yes, but we have to be there at six. And then we fly out the next afternoon to the hometown of whoever wins the hometown challenge."

"That'll be Lake Eden," Michelle said confidently. "Everybody said your Magic White Chocolate Soufflé is the best thing they've ever tasted."

"I just hope the judges agree."

"They will," Michelle said with a smile. "You'd better bring the recipe with us so we can check to see if they gave us everything we need to bake it."

"I've got it all ready to go." Hannah patted the file she'd placed on the desk. "Let's eat while we walk, Michelle. This suite is a little bit too fancy for me. I might get to expect luxury like this and that means I'll be really disillusioned when we get home and go back to living an ordinary life."

SOFT CHEWY MILK CHOCOLATE COOKIES

Preheat oven to 350 degrees F., rack in the middle position.

1 and ¼ cups white *(granulated)* sugar
1 cup softened, salted butter *(2 sticks, 8 ounces, ½ pound)*
2 large eggs
1 teaspoon baking soda
1 teaspoon baking powder
½ teaspoon salt
1 teaspoon cinnamon
¼ teaspoon cardamom
½ teaspoon nutmeg *(freshly grated is best)*
1 teaspoon vanilla extract
2 Tablespoons strongly brewed coffee *(you can use coffee left over from breakfast)*
½ cup molasses
½ cup light Karo syrup
½ cup golden raisins
4 cups quick cooking oats *(I used Quaker 1-minute)*
3 and ½ cups all-purpose flour *(pack it down in the cup when you measure it)*
1 cup milk chocolate chips *(I used Nestle)*

Place the sugar in the bowl of an electric mixer. (You can also mix up these cookies by hand, but it's easier and quicker with an electric mixer.)

Pour the softened butter on top of the sugar.

Mix the sugar and the butter until the mixture is smooth and creamy.

Mix in the eggs and beat until it is well incorporated and the mixture is light and fluffy.

Sprinkle in the baking soda, baking powder, and salt. Mix them in until they're incorporated.

Add the cinnamon, cardamom, nutmeg, vanilla extract, and coffee. Mix well.

Mix in the molasses, golden raisins, and the light Karo syrup. Beat until everything is combined.

Add the oats. Mix thoroughly.

Add the flour in half-cup increments, mixing after each addition.

Take the bowl out of the mixer, give it a final stir by hand, scrape down the sides to make sure that none of the yummy cookie batter sticks to the sides, and stir in the milk chocolate chips by hand.

Set the bowl aside on the counter while you prepare your cookie sheets.

Spray your cookie sheets with Pam or another non-stick cooking spray, or line them with parchment paper.

Hannah's 1ˢᵗ Note: I prefer to use parchment paper when I'm baking at home. The paper makes it much easier to remove the baked cookies from the baking sheet. All you have to do is leave an "ear" of paper at the top and the bottom so that you can pull the parchment paper, baked cookies and all, over to the wire racks to cool.

Drop your cookies by heaping large spoonfuls onto your prepared cookie sheets, no more than 9 large cookies to a standard-size sheet. Think double-sized cookies and you won't go wrong. *(Lisa and I use a 2-Tablespoon scoop, rounded with dough on top, to do this down at The Cookie Jar.)*

Bake your cookies at 350 degrees F., for 15 to 18 minutes, or until they are springy on top when touched lightly and quickly with a fingertip.

Let your Soft Chewy Milk Chocolate Cookies sit on the cookie sheets for at least 2 minutes.

Remove the cookies from the cookie sheets with a metal spatula *(or, if you used parchment paper, simply pull the whole sheet off)* to a wire rack to finish cooling.

Yield: 2 to 3 dozen large soft cookies that everyone will enjoy.

Hannah's 2nd Note: This recipe can be doubled, if you wish. You *will* probably wish, because otherwise there won't be enough cookies for the kids and their friends after you get through tasting them.

Chapter Ten

"**E**verything checks out, Hannah. We're ready."

Hannah adjusted her apron and turned to look at Michelle. Perhaps her sister was ready, but Hannah felt as if she were facing a final exam without ever going to any classes or reading the textbook.

"Relax. You'll be fine as soon as you begin baking," Michelle told her, slipping their recipes in the Plexiglas holders on the counter in front of each of them.

"But what if my soufflé doesn't rise? Then I won't win and I'll disappoint everyone in Lake Eden."

"It'll rise," Michelle reassured her. "Has Anne Elizabeth's recipe ever failed to rise?"

"No."

"Then there's no reason to think it might fail to rise tonight. How many times have you made it?"

"Over a dozen."

"Exactly my point. And it worked perfectly when you baked it at The Cookie Jar and perfectly during rehearsal this morning."

"You're right. I guess it's just stage fright. I'm really nervous, Michelle."

"So is everyone else. Just look at Brooke Jackman. She must have checked her ingredients twenty times."

"But she's an important dessert chef!"

"That's true, but she's still nervous. I talked to Loren Berringer this morning and he said that this was completely different from working in a restaurant."

Hannah glanced at one of the neighboring kitchen sets. "Thanks for trying to make me feel better, but I think you're wrong. Rodney Paloma doesn't look nervous."

"Take a second look. He's hanging on to that mixing bowl like a drowning man holding on to a raft." Michelle waited until Hannah had glanced at Rodney again. "Do you see what I mean?"

"Yes, I do. He's hanging on so hard, his knuckles are white. I think he's trying to pretend it's no big deal, but he's certainly not at ease."

"Rodney's got a good reason to be nervous. I read the Food Channel bio on him and it said that *Dessert Enthusiast* magazine listed him as one of the top twenty-five dessert chefs in the country. Rodney has to do well in the competition. His reputation's on the line."

Hannah wanted to ask what the Food Channel had written about her, but perhaps she was better off not knowing. She could always find out once this competition was over. "Is Gloria Berkeley nervous? I can't see her from here."

"Neither can I, but she's already passed behind us three times on her way to the ladies' room. Either she ate something that didn't agree with her, or she's nervous, too."

Hannah drew a deep steadying breath. "Maybe it's not very nice of me, but I feel a lot better knowing that I'm not the only one with a case of the jitters."

"Contestants? Places, please!" The producer's assistant stood near the apron of the stage with a clipboard in his hand. "If there's anybody who hasn't been miked, give me a shout. We'll do a sound check in a minute or two."

"It's almost show time," Michelle said, smiling at Hannah. "You look great in that apron."

"Thanks!" Hannah glanced down at her apron. It was sunshine yellow with an embroidered rendition of The Cookie Jar sign on the bib. Michelle was wearing one too, and there were two extras folded neatly on the shelf under the counter of their kitchen set, just in case they spilled something. Hannah had ordered a dozen in all, and she planned to give them to her mother, Andrea, Lisa, Aunt Nancy, Marge, and Jack for Christmas.

The other contestants were wearing chef's jackets with the name of their restaurant on the front. Hannah preferred aprons because they were what she always wore when she baked. Her feet were clad in tennis shoes and she was wearing a black blouse and black slacks. Michelle was similarly dressed, and although they didn't have the outfits that real restaurant chefs wore, Hannah thought they looked professional enough to satisfy the audience.

The other contestants weren't wearing tennis shoes, but they did have lace-up shoes with non-skid soles. That made sense in a restaurant kitchen, where spills on the floor could cause accidents. There was only one exception to sensible shoes, and that exception was Gloria Berkeley. She was wearing dress shoes with heels so high, Hannah wondered how she could possibly work in them.

Gloria was a fashion plate from head to toe. She was dressed like a fashion model who was playing the part of a chef. Her bright red chef's jacket complemented her blond hair and it was expertly tailored, leaving no doubt that her figure was perfect. Her matching skirt was short, and it twirled around her hips as she moved. When they'd first come in and Hannah had seen Gloria, she'd commented in an aside to Michelle, that she hoped Gloria wouldn't drop anything during the competition. Because, if she did, and if she bent over to pick it up, their show might receive an X-rating. Of course Hannah had been joking, but she did think that Gloria's outfit was entirely inappropriate for a baking competition.

"All right, contestants and assistants," the producer's assistant spoke again. "We're almost ready to begin. As we introduce you and you hear your names, do some bit of business with the ingredients on your workstation. Don't actually start to prepare up your entry, but rearrange an ingredient or pick up a spoon or a mixing bowl. Then look up at the camera and give us a smile."

"You pick up the package of chips and I'll move the bowl," Michelle coached Hannah. "We can put them back down where they were right after the camera moves on."

As Hannah watched, the judges filed out of the greenroom. She recognized Alain Duquesne and Christian Parker from the taped show that Andrea had shown her, and she also recognized Jeremy Zales as the chef who had made the shrimp dish that had tantalized Moishe. LaVonna Brach looked exactly like the photo that accompanied her Food Channel biography, and since there were only five judges, the stylishly dressed fifth judge had to be the exotic ingredient importer, Helene Stone.

"Aunt Nancy was right about Alain Duquesne being a ladies' man," Michelle whispered to Hannah. "He's staring at Gloria's skirt."

"So are Christian Parker and Jeremy Zales," Hannah pointed out.

"But they're not leering like Judge Duquesne is. Maybe we should have worn short skirts."

"Not me," Hannah whispered back. "I don't think it would have done me any good at all."

Michelle stifled a laugh, and Hannah realized that her sister had succeeded in relaxing her. She wasn't as nervous as she'd been several minutes ago. Maybe this would be all right after all. She would do her best and hope that it was good enough. And even if it wasn't, she'd know that she had given it her all.

Suddenly it was brighter than daylight as the stage lighting clicked on and the exhaust fans began to whirr. Hannah blinked once or twice, but then her eyes became accustomed to the light. She peered into the darkness beyond the stages for a glimpse of Ross and P.K. She could see shapes, but that was all. Nobody outside the stage area was discernable.

One by one, the judges were introduced. As the announcer called their names, each judge walked forward and took a chair at the judges' table. As the announcer began to announce the contestants, Hannah felt the butterflies in her stomach take flight. This happened every time she had to appear in front of an audience.

"Hannah Swensen from Lake Eden, Minnesota, and her assistant, Michelle Swensen," the announcer intoned. "Miss Swensen owns a bakery and coffee shop called The Cookie Jar."

Hannah reached for the bag of white chocolate chips and moved it slightly and Michelle grabbed the bowl and the wooden spoon. It was their great-grandmother Elsa's spoon and Hannah had brought it with them for luck. Just in time, Hannah remembered to smile and then the cameras moved on.

"Good job!" Michelle whispered. "You didn't look nervous at all."

"Appearances are deceiving," Hannah whispered back, replacing the chips.

All of the contestants listened attentively while the announcer read the rules. Of course they all knew the rules from previous readings and reminders, but it was for the audience's benefit. Then the announcer cued Alain Duquesne to start the timer on the judges' table. It was a two-sided clock that was clearly visible to both the audience and the contestants, and it would tick off the seconds and minutes of their time limit.

For one very brief and panicked moment, Hannah was frozen in place. And then her muscles relaxed and she began to move. Michelle used the stovetop on their U-shaped work station to cook the sauce that would be ladled into the individual soufflé cups that they would present to the judges. As Hannah preheated the oven, prepared the soufflé dishes, and began to assemble the ingredients, the butterflies in her stomach calmed down and decided to take a nap.

They baked exactly as they had practiced in their rehearsal and everything went according to plan. Hannah kept an eye on the clock. Soufflés were time critical and their soufflés had to be ready at exactly the right moment to present them to the judges.

The soufflés rose as planned. They were very close to ready when the time clock at the judges' table sounded a two-minute warning with a klaxon-like sound that was much louder than needed. Hannah removed the soufflé dishes from the oven, Michelle poured the sauce into a pitcher, and they were ready.

When their names were announced Hannah carried the soufflés to the judges' table, and Michelle followed her with the sauces and the cutlery they needed for their presentation.

"Soufflés?!" Alain Duquesne sounded astounded. "You took quite a risk, Miss Swensen. What would you have done if they'd fallen? Served them to us anyway and called them pancakes?"

Hannah and Michelle laughed dutifully, even though the head judge's joke wasn't that funny. But he was waiting for an answer and Hannah spoke.

"I've made these dozens of times, Chef Duquesne, and they've never fallen. It's a wonderful recipe."

"And I suppose you created it?" Jeremy Zales asked her.

"No, Chef Zales. It came from a friend, Aunt Nancy, and she received it from a friend of hers, Anne Elizabeth. I just modified it a bit by using white chocolate chips."

"How much flour is in this soufflé?" LaVonna Brach asked.

"None, Ms. Brach. I'm not a nutritionist and I don't have the background to make this claim, but I think that this soufflé may be a gluten-free dessert."

"It sounds like you're right, Miss Swensen," Christian Parker said.

"It's delicious," Helene Stone commented. "Have you ever tried it with powdered vanilla?"

"No, Ms. Stone. I don't have access to ingredients like that in Lake Eden, but I'll check with Florence at the Red Owl Grocery when I get home to see if she can special order it. It sounds like a wonderful idea."

"I do like the fact you gave us two individual bowls of sauce," Christian Parker said. "Is that the way you serve it at The Cookie Jar?"

"Yes. We give people a choice and let them ladle it on themselves. Some want to try both sauces, others prefer one or the other, and there are a few who don't want any sauce at all."

"You haven't said anything, Michelle," Alain Duquesne commented. "Are you going to let the other Miss Swensen do all the talking?"

Michelle laughed. "Hannah is my older sister. In the interest of family harmony, I usually don't interrupt her."

Chef Duquesne gave a loud laugh. For one brief moment, he lost his haughty manner and seemed like a person that Hannah might like. "I know exactly what you mean, Michelle. I was the same way with my older sister. She was a real . . ." he stopped himself and chuckled before he finished the sentence. "She was a real force, and there was no way I wanted to cross her."

Michelle smiled at him. "I do understand . . . even though Hannah's not that way at all. Usually."

Alain Duquesne laughed again and then he turned to the other judges. "Please enter your scores on the Swensen sisters' dessert." Then he addressed Hannah and Michelle again. "Thank you, ladies. You may go back to your cooking stage now."

"I think he was hitting on you!" Hannah whispered as she began to walk back to their stage.

"Not now," Michelle whispered back. "Smile and look pleased. The camera's still on us."

Both Hannah and Michelle smiled pleasantly as they walked back the way they had come. Then the giant screen above their heads went to a commercial for a new cooking show that was debuting on the Food Channel, and Hannah sighed heavily. "How do you think we did?"

"Good. They all seemed to like it. Now all we have to do is pack up our things and go back to the greenroom until the other contestants have presented their desserts."

"And then we come back for the reading of the scores," Hannah said, her hands shaking slightly as she placed the bowl she'd brought from The Cookie Jar in a box.

"That's right. We're through, and I'm glad we were first. Now we get to relax for at least twenty minutes before the finale."

Hannah felt like laughing, but she didn't. *Relax?* her mind queried. *How can I relax when everyone back home is counting on us to bring the rest of the competition back to Lake Eden?*

"How do you think we did?"

"I think we did great! I doubt any other contestant will try to bake anything as tricky as a soufflé."

"But mine isn't tricky."

"They know that now, but I think the judges were impressed. Chef Duquesne finished every bit of it, and Jeremy Zales only had one spoonful left. Come on, Hannah. Let's get off our cooking stage and go to the greenroom, where there are no cameras. I never thought I'd say it, but I'm tired of being onstage."

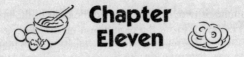

Chapter
Eleven

Hannah leaned back in the comfortable chair, and motioned toward the monitor in the greenroom. "Brooke Jackman's up now. Let's see how she does."

The two sisters watched as Brooke presented her strawberry mousse with marshmallow sauce, a rather odd combination to Hannah's way of thinking. She could understand strawberry sauce, vanilla or white chocolate sauce, or even another fruit sauce that didn't have a strong flavor, like kiwi, but she thought that a marshmallow sauce seemed a bit sweet and sticky to be served with a strawberry mousse.

One by one, the judges agreed that the mousse was excellent, but the sauce failed to complement the berry creation. Brooke left the judging table looking disappointed. But then, as soon as she realized that the camera was on her, she smiled. Hannah turned to Michelle.

"If Brooke comes in here, let's tell her that we want to taste her mousse after the contest is over for the night. And let's both tell her it's just as delicious as it looks."

"I'm in," Michelle said. "Brooke is really nice and I like her. It's a shame the judges weren't more complimentary."

"That's true, but they *are* judges. Their job is to rate us and criticize us. All the same, let's try to make Brooke feel better if we can."

In a minute or two, Brooke opened the door to the green-room and came in. From the expression on her face, it was clear she knew she hadn't won the hometown challenge. "Hi, guys," she said. "You looked good out there."

"Thanks," Hannah said. "So did you, Brooke."

"I stunk." Brooke gave a deep sigh as she sat down in one of the chairs. "They hated my mousse."

"No, they didn't," Hannah contradicted her. "They liked the mousse. They just didn't think the sauce complemented it enough."

Brooke thought about it for a minute. "You're right. I never should have asked anyone else for advice."

"What do you mean?" Michelle asked her.

"I mean, I should have stuck to what I'd planned in the first place."

Hannah's eyes narrowed. She remembered seeing Brooke talking to Gloria earlier and suspected what might have happened. "Was the person who advised you Gloria Berkeley?"

"Yes. She tasted my sauces and she said I should use the marshmallow sauce instead of the strawberry."

"That's what I thought. What reason did she give?"

"She said the marshmallow would be better because it was different and highly innovative." Brooke gave another sigh. "I know now that I was a fool for believing her. It was just that I was so nervous. And I really wanted someone else's opinion."

"Don't ask Gloria for advice again," Michelle warned her. "She doesn't want you to succeed. If you want to ask someone, ask Hannah or me. We'll give you an honest answer."

"Thanks!" Brooke looked very grateful. "Do you think I blew the whole competition tonight?"

Hannah shook her head. "Not at all. Tonight was only the first night. You have three more chances to impress the judges. I doubt that anyone will come in first every night."

"And don't forget that all our scores are tallied at the end,"

Michelle reminded her. "Everyone's nervous tonight and mistakes are bound to happen. I was listening to the judging and they didn't say anything negative about your mousse."

Brooke looked a bit more hopeful. "You're right. Chef Zales even said he liked it."

"Exactly." Hannah took up the effort to reassure Brooke. "Why don't you come up to our hotel room when we get back? We'll relax and have a glass of wine and some snacks on our balcony."

"Thanks! I'd love to, but . . . it's the end of October. Isn't it really cold on your balcony?"

"No, it's heated," Michelle explained. "Hannah's fiancé upgraded us to a really nice suite. You've got to see it, Brooke. It's the fanciest place I've ever been."

"Michelle is right, you've got to see it," Hannah said, smiling at Brooke.

"Are you . . . sure that you want me to come over?"

Brooke sounded very tentative and Hannah gave her a quick nod. "Absolutely. We'll be in the competition for another week. It'll be nice to have a friend who's in the same boat as we are. Bring your assistant too, if you like."

"Thanks, but her husband came with her on this trip. It'll be just me, if that's okay."

"That's fine," Hannah assured her.

Hannah, Michelle, and Brooke watched as the other contestants presented their entries. None of them fared particularly well. Chef Duquesne criticized Loren Berringer for a soggy pie shell on his cherry pie, and Rodney Paloma drew critical comments from Helene Stone for his meringue because it contained "beads" on top. Then it was Gloria Berkeley's turn, and all three of them leaned forward to see how the contestant who'd given Brooke bad advice would do.

Gloria's entry consisted of two little cakes for each judge, one vanilla and one chocolate. Her assistant had mixed up the cake batter, and all Gloria had done was ladle it into the pans.

While the mini cakes were baking, the assistant had made the two sauces, and Gloria hadn't really done anything at all except turn the cakes out when they were done.

"Frosting?" Michelle guessed.

Brooke shook her head. "It looks more like two different sauces."

"One's strawberry," Hannah said. "And the other is . . . uh-oh!"

"What?" Michelle asked her.

"I'm not positive, but . . ."

"I know what you're thinking, and I'm almost sure you're right," Brooke interrupted her, and Hannah noticed that she looked deeply troubled. "That's my marshmallow sauce! I noticed that the recipe was missing when I got back to the hotel this afternoon, but I didn't worry about it. I just thought I'd probably left it at my workstation and the people who came in to do the cleanup had thrown it away."

"Did you go down to the Food Channel building to check?" Michelle asked her.

"No. I brought my laptop and portable printer with me, and I just printed out another copy."

"Are you sure that Gloria's assistant made *your* marshmallow sauce?" Hannah asked, hoping that wasn't the case.

"I'm sure. I noticed that Gloria's assistant added hazelnut butter, and that's my secret ingredient."

"Are you going to say anything to the judges?" Michelle asked her.

"I don't think it'll do any good. She'd probably claim that it was her recipe in the first place and I took it from her!"

"Let's wait and see how she does in the judging," Michelle suggested. "One of the judges might notice that your marshmallow sauce and Gloria's marshmallow sauce taste the same."

"Maybe," Brooke answered, but she sounded doubtful.

They watched the monitor as Gloria walked forward and presented her dessert to the judges. The sauce was ladled on top of the cakes, strawberry on the vanilla cake, and marsh-mallow on the chocolate. The judges tasted the cakes and the sauces.

The critique of the cakes came first. The judges agreed that the cakes would have been quite ordinary without the sauces. And then they agreed that the two sauces were excellent. None of them seemed to realize that Brooke and Gloria had served the same marshmallow sauce. Chef Duquesne even commented that he liked Gloria's marshmallow sauce much better than Brooke's, and that it certainly complemented the cakes much better than it had complemented Brooke's mousse!

Hannah, Michelle, and Brooke watched the doorway to the greenroom as the other contestants finished their presentations and came in to wait to be called back for their scores. Gloria was the last one to enter the comfortable waiting area, and she took a seat on one of the couches next to Loren.

"You did just great, Gloria," Loren said, smiling at her. "I think we all ought to celebrate when we get back to the hotel, and meet up in the bar."

"Sorry, we have other plans," Hannah said, giving him a friendly smile. "But thank you for asking us, Loren."

"Can't make it tonight," Rodney said, giving Gloria a glance that could only be construed as suggestive.

"Same here," Gloria said, giving Rodney a sexy smile before she turned back to Loren. "I'm busy, too. Just wait until the contest moves to my restaurant in Atlanta. I'll show you all the hot places to go."

"That must mean you think you won," Hannah said to Gloria.

"Oh, I do. My dessert was better than any of the others, and I know Alain thought so, too."

Alain? Hannah's mind queried. Everyone else called him Chef Duquesne, or Judge Duquesne. By using his first name, Gloria had referred to him in a much more familiar manner. Either Gloria was guilty of wishful thinking, or she believed that she had an edge with the head judge.

"Do you know the head judge personally?" Hannah couldn't resist asking.

"Of course not. If I did, I'd have to disqualify myself. I only sat with him for one drink in the bar last night. After that, I went straight up to my room."

Alone? Hannah's mind prompted her, but she didn't ask. Instead, she asked another question. "You ran into Judge Duquesne in the bar and he bought you a drink?"

Gloria shook her head. "No. I already had a glass of wine. I was sitting there alone and he came in. He walked right over and sat down on the stool next to me. And then he ordered a drink. What could I do? I wasn't about to refuse to sit next to him. That would have been rude. So I finished my wine in a big hurry and went up to my room."

Alone? Hannah's mind repeated, but Hannah ignored it for the second time. And then, just as she was wishing for an interruption to this awkward conversation, the production assistant came into the greenroom.

"Please follow me, single file, and take your places at your cooking stages. The judges are ready to announce the scores."

Hannah's knees were trembling slightly as she followed the production assistant from the room. They were about to find out if Gloria's expectations had been correct. Hannah found herself hoping that Gloria would be disappointed and get what she deserved for stealing Brooke's marshmallow sauce recipe and then using it against her victim in the competition.

"Keep smiling no matter what happens," Michelle warned as they took their places at their workstation. And then Judge Duquesne began to read the scores, explaining that he would proceed from the lowest to the highest, and the name of the winner would be last.

"Chef Brooke Jackman," Judge Duquesne intoned. "Our judging panel agreed that your mousse was excellent. The sauce was also excellent, but it did not complement the flavor of the mousse."

Somehow Brooke and her assistant managed to keep smiling. Hannah wondered if she could have done the same if she were in Brooke's position. It showed remarkable aplomb, and Hannah was proud of Brooke for being such a good sport.

"Chef Loren Berringer. As we mentioned during the judging, your piecrust did not have the dry, flaky character that is desirable in a pie. The judging panel agreed that brushing the bottom and sides of your piecrust with egg white and prebaking it might not have worked with your filling. We suggest you look into the slip-and-slide method some chefs use with pies of this nature."

"Chef Rodney Paloma, your dessert was undeniably delicious, but that does not change the fact that your meringue had beaded. While I, personally, do not object to this slight imperfection, Ms. Stone's score reflected her displeasure with your meringue. If it is of any solace, I must tell you that I think the amber beading on a meringue is rather attractive and for that reason, I gave you a higher score."

Michelle reached out to squeeze Hannah's hand and Hannah realized that she'd been holding her breath. "Smile, no matter what happens," Michelle whispered.

"Chef . . ." Alain Duquesne began, and then he cleared his throat. Hannah shot her sister a startled glance. Chef Duquesne had called her "Miss" instead of "Chef" each time he'd addressed her. Could this possibly mean that . . . ?

"Chef Gloria Berkeley," the head judge continued. "You brought a faultless dessert to the judge's table. The only criticism that kept you from getting a perfect score is that you should have offered us a choice of sauces, the way Miss Hannah Swensen did. For that reason, your score was very close to a tie for the lead, but since there cannot be a tie in the hometown challenge, we unanimously declared Miss Hannah Swensen and her sister, Michelle Swensen, as the winning team."

He beckoned to Hannah and, with Michelle, she walked forward to the judges' table. Hannah felt as if she were in a dream as she was presented with a gold medal on a green ribbon. As she held it up for the cameras, Michelle didn't have to remind her to smile. She could feel herself grinning from ear to ear. They had won the hometown challenge and now the Food Channel Dessert Competition would be moving to Lake Eden, Minnesota. Hannah was so happy, she could barely contain her joy. She hadn't disappointed the people in her hometown, after all!

MAGIC WHITE CHOCOLATE SOUFFLÉ

Preheat oven to 425 degrees F., rack in the middle position.

> 6 large eggs *(straight out of the refrigerator)*
> 1 cup white *(granulated)* sugar
> 1 teaspoon vanilla extract
> 6 ounces *(by weight, not volume)* white choco-
>   late chips *(I used Ghirardelli)*
> ½ teaspoon salt *(salt brings out the full flavor
>   of the chocolate)*

Prepare 6 individual soufflé dishes by buttering the inside and sprinkling it with a coating of white granulated sugar.

Hannah's 1st Note: You may notice that this recipe uses chilled eggs. If your eggs are at room temperature, baking time may be a minute or two faster.

Place the individual soufflé dishes on a baking sheet with sides. A jelly roll pan is perfect for this.

Get out two mixing bowls, one large and one medium sized. Crack the eggs, one by one, and separate the yolks into the large bowl, and the whites into the medium-sized bowl.

Whisk the yolks in the large bowl until they are thoroughly mixed.

Add the cup of sugar to the large bowl and mix it thoroughly with the egg yolks.

Place the vanilla extract, white chocolate chips, and salt in a microwave-safe bowl.

Hannah's 2nd Note: Michelle and I use a half-quart Pyrex measuring cup to do this at The Cookie Jar.

Heat the contents of the microwave-safe bowl or measuring cup on HIGH for 60 seconds. Let the bowl sit in the microwave for another minute and then attempt to stir the contents smooth with a heat-resistant rubber spatula.

If you cannot stir the contents smooth and there are still lumps, return the white chocolate chip mixture to the microwave and heat on HIGH in 30-second increments, followed by a standing time of 1 minute, until you can stir the contents smooth.

Let the white chocolate, vanilla extract, and salt mixture sit on the counter to cool slightly.

Beat the egg whites in the medium-sized bowl with a hand mixer on HIGH until the whites form frothy,

soft peaks. Soft peaks are achieved if, when you remove the beaters from the egg whites, the peaks droop over a bit, but do not slide all the way back into the bowl. When you have frothy soft peaks, set the bowl with the egg whites aside on the counter.

Give the bowl with the melted white chocolate another stir and then SLOWLY pour the contents into the bowl with the egg yolk mixture, stirring constantly to make sure that the egg yolks don't cook and solidify from the heated white chocolate. Take your time with this. This step is critical.

When the melted white chocolate has been successfully added to the egg yolk mixture, pick up the bowl with the beaten egg whites.

Add several Tablespoons of the warm egg yolk and white chocolate mixture to the bowl of frothy egg whites. Fold the mixture in with a rubber spatula. This will temper the mixture.

Add the frothy egg whites to the rest of the egg yolk and white chocolate mixture in the large bowl, folding the egg whites in gently with a rubber spatula. Do not stir with a spoon. Your object is to fold in the egg whites and keep as much froth and air in the resulting mixture as you possibly can.

Divide the completed white chocolate soufflé mixture between the 6 individual soufflé dishes.

Hannah's 3rd Note: If you prefer, you can use a 2-quart glass bowl instead of the individual soufflé dishes. Simply butter the inside of the bowl and coat it with sugar.

Bake your individual soufflés at 425 degrees F. for 15 to 20 minutes. If you used the 2-quart glass bowl to hold your soufflé, bake it at 425 degrees F. for 25 to 35 minutes. Your soufflé is done when the top cracks open and a long wooden skewer or cake tester inserted in the center of the soufflé comes out clean.

Anne Elizabeth's Note: I prefer my soufflé gooey in the middle and will often scoop it out into individual bowls with a large serving spoon and serve it with sweetened whipped cream and berries.

To serve your soufflé, either do it as Anne Elizabeth does by scooping it into individual bowls at the table and adding sweetened whipped cream and berries, or put on another topping of your choice, or . . .

If you serve your soufflés in individual soufflé dishes, pull the soufflés apart in the middle with two forks at the table to expose the warm soft center. Then either spoon

on the topping yourself or let everyone pour as much sauce and/or berries as they wish on their soufflé.

Yield: 6 yummy individual soufflés or 6 helpings in dessert dishes. These are light, airy, and rich. It's a dessert that both adults and children will love.

VANILLA NUTMEG SAUCE

½ cup white *(granulated)* sugar
⅛ teaspoon salt
¼ teaspoon freshly ground nutmeg
⅓ cup flour *(not sifted)*
1 cup whole milk
1 cup heavy cream
⅓ additional cup of heavy cream
2 beaten eggs
2 teaspoons vanilla extract
1 ounce *(⅛ stick)* salted butter

Combine the sugar, salt, nutmeg, and flour in a saucepan off the heat. Stir well.

Gradually stir in the milk and ONE CUP ONLY of the heavy cream. Leave the remainder of the heavy cream *(⅓ cup)* on the counter to warm to room temperature. You will add that later, after your sauce has been cooked.

Blend the ingredients in the saucepan together off the heat.

Turn the burner on MEDIUM HIGH heat and cook the contents of the saucepan, stirring constantly until thickened. *(This takes about 10 minutes on my stovetop.)*

Remove the saucepan from the heat, but LEAVE THE BURNER ON.

Break the eggs into a small bowl and quickly beat them with a whisk until they're well mixed.

Stir several Tablespoons of the hot mixture into the bowl with the eggs. Whisk until it's incorporated.

SLOWLY pour the eggs into the saucepan with the hot mixture, whisking it all the while.

Return the saucepan to the heat and stir for 2 to 3 minutes until the mixture is very thick.

Remove the saucepan from the heat *(you can turn off the burner this time)*. Add the vanilla, stirring it in quickly.

Add the ounce of butter and stir it in until it's melted.

Let the mixture cool until it is slightly warmer than lukewarm. Then stir in the third cup of heavy cream. Pour the sauce into a pitcher so that you can serve it with your soufflé.

Yield: enough Vanilla Nutmeg Sauce to serve over 6 individual soufflés.

MILK CHOCOLATE SAUCE

1 cup whole milk
1 cup heavy cream
⅓ additional cup of heavy cream at room temperature
½ cup white *(granulated)* sugar
6 ounces *(by weight, not volume)* milk chocolate chips *(I used a 6-ounce package of Nestle Milk Chocolate Chips)*
2 large eggs beaten in a bowl
2 teaspoons vanilla extract
1 ounce *(⅛ stick)* salted butter

Combine the milk, ONE CUP ONLY of heavy cream, and sugar in a heavy saucepan off the heat. Let the additional third cup of heavy cream sit on the counter to warm to room temperature.

Heat the mixture over MEDIUM HIGH heat on the stove, stirring constantly until little whiffs of steam start to escape and you think it's about to boil.

Pull the saucepan from the heat, but don't turn off the burner. This next step will take only a moment or two.

Add the milk chocolate chips to the sweet milk and cream mixture, stirring them in until they're melted.

Give the beaten eggs a final stir and add approximately 2 Tablespoons of the chocolate mixture to the eggs, stirring it in quickly. *(This is called tempering and it's important—without it you could have scrambled eggs.)*

Off the heat, SLOWLY pour the egg mixture into the chocolate mixture in the saucepan, stirring all the while. When everything is incorporated, put the saucepan back on the heat.

Cook, stirring constantly, until the mixture comes to a full boil. *(This took about 3 minutes for me on my stove.)* Pull the saucepan off the heat and this time you can turn off the burner.

Quickly stir in the vanilla. Then stir in the butter and continue to stir until the butter is melted.

Let the mixture cool on the counter for five minutes and then stir in the one-third cup of heavy cream.

Pour the Milk Chocolate Sauce into a pitcher and serve it with your White Chocolate Soufflés.

Yield: Enough Milk Chocolate Sauce for 6 individual soufflés or one large soufflé.

Chapter Twelve

Hannah was so tired when she got off the plane, she could barely keep her eyes open. They'd stayed up late celebrating on their heated patio, and the stress of the first night's competition, coupled with the relief and euphoria she'd felt when Team Swensen had been declared the winner, had led to a night filled with both joyful and stressful dreams.

Now it was time to get off the plane, and Hannah stepped out into the aisle so that Ross could open the overhead bin and take out their carry-on luggage.

"Thank you for flying with us, Miss Swensen," the stewardess said when she beckoned Hannah toward the door. "Congratulations. I watched the competition and my husband and I were hoping you'd win."

For a moment Hannah was speechless. She hadn't realized that the stewardess had watched the *Dessert Chef Competition*.

"Thank you!" she said quickly to cover her surprise. "I'm really thrilled that the competition is coming to my hometown."

The stewardess leaned closer and lowered her voice so that it couldn't be overheard by the others standing in line behind Hannah. "My friend at the desk says there's a whole contingent of people from Lake Eden waiting for you at baggage claim with signs, and balloons, and bouquets of flowers. She said the baggage guy said there's even a squad of cheerleaders there from Jordan High in Lake Eden."

Hannah knew she must have looked shocked, because the stewardess laughed. "Don't worry. I told her to snag you when you and your party come down the Jetway. She'll show you another way out and someone will collect your baggage for you."

"That's . . . very thoughtful," Hannah said, wondering if they did this sort of thing often.

"No problem. We do it all the time with celebrities. Sometimes they want to avoid the fans and just get in their limo and go home."

"But I'm not a celebrity!"

"You are to them. And you were on national television. And you'll have even more fans if you win the entire competition. You might even get your own baking show and then you'll be a celebrity dessert chef."

"Oh my! I didn't even think of that!" Hannah drew a deep breath and let it out again. "Thank you for being so thoughtful about the other way out and everything, but the people that are waiting for me are probably family and friends. They're going to be really disappointed if I don't show up at the baggage claim carousel."

"You really *are* nice," the stewardess said, motioning Hannah toward the door of the plane. "Most celebrities don't want to be bothered."

"I heard that," Ross said, grinning as he handed her the smallest carry-on. "Eat it up, Hannah. You and Michelle deserve the acclaim. We'll be ready to shoot some really good footage."

As Hannah walked up the Jetway, she knew she was wearing a puzzled expression. She wasn't a celebrity . . . was she? She'd have to ask Ross later, when they were alone. He'd know, one way or the other. She really wasn't sure if she wanted to be a celebrity. She was perfectly happy being Michelle and Andrea's sister, Ross's bride-to-be, Moishe's human mommy, Delores Swensen's daughter, and owner of The Cookie Jar with her partner, Lisa. Anything other than that was an unknown position that she wasn't sure she wanted to explore.

"Welcome home, Hannah!" Mayor Bascomb was the first to greet her when they arrived at the baggage carousel.

Hannah put on her best smile, just as Ross had told her to do. "Thank you, Mayor Bascomb," she said in a clear voice. "I'll be so very glad to be back at home in Lake Eden again, and I know that Michelle feels the same way."

"I do! We're so excited about bringing the Food Channel *Dessert Chef Competition* home with us, Mayor Bascomb."

It was Hannah's turn to speak and she picked up right on cue. They'd rehearsed it while they were waiting for the cart to drive them down to baggage claim.

"I just know that everyone involved in the competition will love Lake Eden," Hannah said, hoping that she sounded sincere. She'd overheard Chef Duquesne refer to Lake Eden as a one-horse town that didn't even have a decent restaurant, and Gloria Berkeley had referred to Hannah's hometown as *Hayseed Central*, but she certainly didn't want to think of that now.

"Almost everyone in town will be coming to the competition," Mayor Bascomb said, turning toward the camera that was trained on him. "Chef Sally Laughlin put the tickets up for sale right after KCOW-TV aired their coverage and she told me that they were sold out within 10 minutes!" He turned to Hannah. "Everyone in town wants to see you win, Hannah. Can you give us a clue about what you'll be baking for your first entry?"

Ross and Michelle had prepared her for this question, and Hannah fielded it just the way they wanted her to. "It's a surprise, Mayor Bascomb, but I can tell you this . . ." Hannah paused for the required silent count of three, and then she continued. "It's something that Ross and I will be serving at our wedding reception."

"But that could be anything, Hannah."

Hannah gave the slightly impish smile that she'd practiced in front of the mirror in the ladies' room closest to the gate. "*I* know. And you'll know too . . . along with everyone else at the competition."

The Jordan High band was there and they played something that Hannah didn't recognize. Later, after they were in the limo on the way back to her condo, she'd ask Michelle if she knew what song it was. Then Mayor Bascomb gave a short speech which, in Hannah's opinion, could have been even shorter, to welcome them home.

All four of them, Hannah, Ross, Michelle, and P.K., gave collective sighs of relief as they climbed into the limo and the driver pulled away from the airport. That was when a most unwelcome thought occurred to Hannah and she turned to Ross with a question.

"You don't think there'll be another welcoming committee waiting for us at my condo . . . do you?"

Ross shook his head. "No one except Norman, Cuddles, Moishe, Mike, and Lonnie."

"I knew Norman would be there with Moishe and Cuddles. But why will Mike and Lonnie be there?"

"Because I called and asked them to keep out anyone who doesn't live in your complex. I didn't think you'd want to deal with another official welcoming committee." Ross paused and frowned slightly. "Was I wrong, Hannah?"

"Oh, no! You were absolutely right!" Hannah gave a big sigh of relief. It was wonderful to have the man she loved looking out for her. "Thank you, Ross," she added quickly. "That was very thoughtful of you."

Ross looked slightly embarrassed by her praise. "Actually, it wasn't my idea. Norman thought you wouldn't want to deal with any more obligations once you got home. He told me he thought you'd want to relax and get some sleep before tomorrow's practice session. As a matter of fact, he said he'd bring Chinese takeout for dinner."

"That's nice of him," Hannah said, hoping the takeout meal wouldn't turn into a dinner party.

"I can only stay long enough to help with your luggage," Ross told her. "P.K. and I have to go back to the station to start editing our footage from New York. KCOW is going to run my interviews with the contestants and judges right before the competition begins. Then we'll go to a live feed of the actual program from the Lake Eden Inn."

"Oh. Okay," Hannah responded, giving him a smile even though she wasn't sure if she was disappointed or relieved that she wouldn't be spending another late evening with Ross.

"You, or me?" Michelle asked as Hannah unlocked the door to her condo.

"Or me?" Ross added. "I'll drop these suitcases if you want me to do it."

"I'll do it," Hannah said, stepping back a foot or two. "I'm his mommy."

Michelle stood to the side and opened the door as Hannah braced herself. The moment the door opened, a ball of orange and white fur hurtled out to land squarely in Hannah's arms.

"Oof!" she said, involuntarily. And then she leaned down to rub her nose against Moishe's soft fur. "Were you a good boy while I was gone?"

"Rrrrow!"

Moishe looked up at her expectantly as she carried him to his favorite perch on the back of the living room couch, and she turned to head for the kitchen to get a few of his favorite salmon-flavored, fish-shaped kitty treats.

"He was very good," Norman said, handing her the canister before she could take a step. "And so was Cuddles."

Hannah glanced down at the middle couch cushion, the one that no one ever used unless they had a crowd of visitors. Cuddles was there, stretched out in comfort. Norman's cat was looking up at her expectantly and she was purring loudly.

Hannah shook some treats out of the canister and doled them out to the two cats. Then she turned back to Ross, who was standing in the doorway with the suitcases. "Just put them down anywhere, Ross. Michelle and I will move them later. Are you absolutely sure you don't want to stay for something to eat?"

"I want to, but I can't. P.K. and I have to put in at least another five or six hours to clean up that footage." He walked over and took Hannah in his arms. "Have a nice meal and then get some sleep. You have to really nail it tomorrow in front of the hometown crowd."

Hannah drew a deep breath. She hadn't been a bit anxious before Ross had spoken. Now, all the uncertainties came rushing back, flying into her mind on strong wings of doubt. Was it too theatrical to wear the circlet of pearls and the short veil that Andrea had picked up for her in the bridal shop at the Tri-County Mall? Would the judges think she was using her upcoming nuptials to gain an unfair advantage over the other contestants?

"Here. I'll put this back where it belongs," Norman said, taking the treat canister from Hannah's hand. "Go sit down, girls. The cats want to sit in your laps. I poured glasses of white wine for both of you. Your dinner is in the refrigerator and there's plenty of shrimp for Moishe and Cuddles. I'll be in the kitchen reheating our meal if you need me."

Hannah glanced at the coffee table in front of the couch. Two glasses of wine were waiting for them. Suddenly she felt much better and her anxiety actually started to abate as she gave Ross a hug, sent him on his way, and walked over to take her customary place.

"Nice!" she said, taking a sip of the wine. "I don't know much about wine, but I do know this isn't Chateau Screwtop from CostMart. What is it, Norman?"

"I don't remember, but I'll bring the bottle to the table so you can look at it when you and Michelle have your dinner. I called to ask Sally what to buy, and she recommended it."

"No wonder it's good!" Michelle said. "Sally and Dick really know their wines."

Hannah agreed. "Yes, they do, and so does Brooke. She was talking about the wine list at her brother's restaurant last night." Hannah stopped speaking as she remembered the curious way that Norman had worded his last comment. He'd said *when you and Michelle eat*, not *when we eat*. "Aren't you joining us for dinner, Norman?" she asked.

"I thought you'd be too tired for company," Norman said. "I was planning to take Cuddles home and fixing something for myself later."

"But that's ridiculous!" Hannah said immediately. "You're right about how tired I am. And it's true that I'm too tired for company, but you're not company. You're . . . well . . . you're *family*."

Norman looked a bit uncertain. "Are you sure, Hannah? I know you probably want to discuss tomorrow night's competition with Michelle. Are you sure I won't be in the way?"

"We're sure," Hannah turned to Michelle. "Aren't we, Michelle?"

"Yes, we're sure," Michelle agreed quickly. "Set three places, Norman. Cuddles is going to be very disappointed if she doesn't get at least three of those shrimp."

Chapter Thirteen

The conflagration of butterflies was raging in Hannah's stomach, causing a firestorm of nerve endings that made her feel as if she were teetering on the edge of a steep canyon with no way to save herself from tumbling into the abyss.

"Take a deep breath," Michelle coached her. "Do it right now."

Hannah took a deep breath. Perhaps it would help. The butterflies settled down a fraction, and that made her feel a bit better.

"Here." Michelle handed her a bottle of water. "Drink just a little. Then take another deep breath."

Hannah followed her youngest sister's instructions. What could it hurt? She was going to fall off the edge and into oblivion anyway.

"Much better," Michelle commented, smiling at her. "That particular shade of green didn't go with your lipstick at all."

It took Hannah a minute and then she laughed. "I was actually green?"

"You were. I've never seen anybody with stage fright that bad before. I thought you were going to pass out cold."

"I *felt* like I was going to pass out cold." Hannah took another deep breath and another swallow of water. "I'm a lot better now. Did you bring my veil?"

"It's on the second shelf down, right by your left hand."

"And the cake server?"

"It's right next to the veil. Don't worry, Hannah. Everything's here. I checked it twice to make sure."

Hannah gave a little sigh. "I suppose I have to wear the veil."

"That's right. You do. Lisa told me that if you didn't wear it, Aunt Nancy would have a cow."

Hannah smiled. And then she chuckled. And then she laughed. "Have a cow?" she asked.

"Yes. At least that what Aunt Nancy told Lisa. You'd better wear it, Hannah. If you don't, who knows what might happen!"

"Thanks, Michelle," Hannah said sincerely. "I'm not as nervous now."

"And you won't be nervous at all once you start to bake." Michelle glanced at her watch. "Let's arrange our bowls and pans, Hannah. It's almost time to introduce the judges and the contestants."

Michelle was right. Once the introductions were made and Alain Duquesne had started the clock, Hannah's nervousness disappeared in a blanketing cloud of activity. They'd rehearsed their cakes in Sally's kitchen early this morning, and everything had proceeded smoothly. Hannah wasn't sure if that was because she'd baked so often with Michelle, or because they'd rehearsed this cake more than five times. It really didn't matter in the giant scheme of things. They finished mixing the cake batter, coloring and flavoring it with the Jell-O powders, and were currently waiting for their oven timer to sound so that they could cool the cakes enough to frost them.

"The frosting's ready," Michelle said, carrying the bowl over to the center of their workstation. "Five more minutes before the cakes come out. Too bad we don't have a kitchen coffeepot. I could use a cup."

"We do," Hannah said, motioning toward the coffeepot

that was set up behind them. "I brought our kitchen percolator, and I just made a pot of church basement coffee."

"You brought that big pot just for us?" Michelle asked.

"No. I'm serving church basement coffee with my wedding cake. I think it'll be perfect to cut the sweetness."

"You're right. I wonder if they've ever heard of church basement coffee."

"I doubt it. It's hard to find percolators these days. Dad had a case of thirty-cup pots and another case of twelve-cup pots. I snagged them both before I sold the hardware store for Mother."

"Smart thinking! I'll get the coffee. Do you want a cup?"

"Yes, please. I need to keep my energy up for the judging."

"Do you think I should offer a cup to Brooke?"

"I really don't think we should disturb her right now. She looks a little frazzled. She told me last night that she was making three kinds of petit fours and she was afraid the time would expire before she'd frosted them all."

When Michelle brought the coffee for them, both sisters climbed up on the tall, counter-height stools that were provided for each contestant and assistant. They had just finished their coffee when the stove timer rang. The cakes were ready to come out of the oven, and they had to cool the layers and frost them before the end of the competition.

It took only five minutes to cool the cake layers in the micro-chiller. Then Hannah removed them from the pans and passed them to Michelle to frost.

It was obvious to Hannah that Michelle had been practicing her cake decorating skills with Lisa. Her sister worked quickly and confidently, spreading frosting between the layers and stacking them expertly. Once the layers were stacked, she frosted the outside of the cake and then the top.

"Time?" she asked Hannah.

"Twelve," Hannah said, glancing at the huge clock on the wall near the table where the judges were sitting.

"Plenty of time." Michelle picked up the pastry bag and proceeded to decorate the cake with a white-on-white scroll-work design that looked like fine lace, a copy of the pattern that was on Hannah's veil. She finished it with red roses around the layers and added a heart on the top.

"Done," she said, stepping back to turn her cake slowly around on the carousel plate to make sure the design was perfect. "Do you want me to carry it to the judging table?"

"Yes. I'll bring the tray with the coffee. It's beautiful, Michelle. Thank you for learning how to frost it."

"I had a great teacher. Lisa's really amazing with the pastry bag. Are you nervous about cutting it?"

"Only because I hate to spoil perfection. I'm really looking forward to cutting this cake. It's so pretty inside."

Hannah glanced at the clock again. They still had three minutes. "Are we good to go?" she asked.

"We're ready. I'll push the cart with the cake, the cake knife, the server, the forks, and the plates. All you have to do is put on your veil and bring the cart with the coffee."

Hannah felt silly as she clamped the veil on the top of her head. She felt as if she were making a spectacle of herself. But Aunt Nancy had been absolutely right, so far, and there was no reason to change the game plan at this late date.

When Hannah heard her name, she motioned to Michelle to deliver the cake. Then she pushed the cart with the coffee in her sister's wake. The cake was the star, after all. It should be the first thing the judges noticed.

"What have we here?" Chef Duquesne asked her, looking highly amused.

"It's a much smaller version of my wedding cake," Hannah explained. "I wanted something different, and I decided to serve a Double Rainbow Swirl Cake."

LaVonna Brach looked intrigued. "What's that?"

"It's a cake with all the colors of the rainbow inside. As you can see, it looks like a regular wedding cake from the outside."

"Except it's prettier than most," Christian Parker commented. "Most wedding cakes are over-decorated. This one is elegantly simple."

"But that's the whole idea!" Alain Duquesne told him. "The real decoration for Miss Swensen's wedding cake is her veil and what's inside the cake." He turned to Hannah. "Am I right?"

"You're right, Chef," Hannah told him.

"And you're wearing your wedding veil because you're going to cut the cake?" Jeremy Zales asked her.

"Yes, Chef."

"Hold on a second, Miss Swensen," Helene Stone said. "Is that coffee you have in that silver urn?"

"Yes, it is," Hannah answered quickly. "I thought it would be the perfect complement to the sweetness of the cake. Would you care for a cup?"

"Yes!"

Three of the judges spoke in unison and Hannah motioned to Michelle, who poured cups of Hannah's church basement coffee and passed the cream, sugar, and artificial sweetener.

"Oh. This coffee looks rather weak." Chef Duquesne looked highly disappointed.

"It's not weak, Chef Duquesne," Hannah told him. "It's church basement coffee and I used eggs and eggshells to clear the brew. Please taste it and see what you think of it."

Chef Duquesne picked up his cup and tasted the coffee. He took a second sip. "It has a good, robust flavor. How did you make it, Miss Swensen?"

"I made it in an old-fashioned percolator, but you can also use a pot on the stove, or even one of those antique blue enamel coffeepots on a campfire. If you make it on the stove or a campfire, you wait until the water boils and then you dump in three eggs mixed in with the ground coffee."

"Shells and all?" LaVonna Brach asked, looking surprised.

"Yes, shells and all. The shells and the eggs clear the

dark brown coffee color. You put the pot back on the heat, wait until it just starts to boil, pull it off, and douse it with a cup of icy cold water. Then you just strain it into cups."

"And how do you make your church basement coffee in a percolator?" Jeremy Zales asked her.

"That's a lot easier because you have a basket to hold the coffee grounds and the cracked eggs. All you really have to do is let it perk until the coffee is the right color and serve it."

"And do you serve coffee like this at your coffee shop?" Helene Stone asked her.

"Yes, every day. Many of my customers grew up on church basement coffee. They'd be disappointed if I served anything else."

"I agree that the coffee is superb," Chef Duquesne said. "But let's get to your wedding cake, Miss Swensen. Am I correct in assuming that you're going to cut your cake without your groom? Or is he here to help you?"

Hannah was so surprised at the question she was speechless for a moment, but then she answered quickly. "He's here, Chef Duquesne, but he's working behind one of the cameras. My fiancé, Ross Barton, is an independent producer for KCOW Television, our local station."

"Is there anyone who can take over for him so that he can help you cut your cake?" Chef Duquesne asked, his eyes searching the various cameramen stationed at strategic places near the cooking stages.

"I'll take over for him," someone called out, and Hannah recognized P.K.'s voice. "He'll be right there, Hannah."

Hannah knew she was probably blushing beet red as Ross came out of the darkness and took his place at her side. One glance at his face and she could tell that he was enjoying the unexpected appearance. Ross was laughing, and he gave her a little hug before he turned to Judge Duquesne.

"I've never cut a wedding cake before, Chef. Will it be all right if I deliver the plates to the judging panel?"

"Yes!" LaVonna Brach was laughing, too. "You don't

have to feed cake to each other the way you'll actually do at the wedding reception. I just want to taste Hannah's creation. If it's as good as her coffee, I'll be very impressed."

"I'm sure it will be," Ross said, giving her his most charming smile as Hannah cut the first slice and he delivered it to her. "Everything Hannah bakes is wonderful."

"And you are going to have a happy marriage if you keep on complimenting her that way," Helene Stone said, accepting her dessert plate and fork from Ross. "This is a beautiful cake." She looked up at Hannah. "Did you use food coloring?"

"No, I decided to use something that would give the cake the right colors, but also lend different flavors to those colors."

"Jell-O powder!" Chef Duquesne pronounced, tasting a bit of the green area. "I recognize the taste. That was brilliant, Miss Swensen."

"I saw you mixing the batter by hand," Jeremy Zales told her. "I noticed that you used butter, cream, and powdered sugar, but there was another ingredient that you added to your frosting."

"Yes, there was," Hannah answered. "It was white chocolate liqueur."

"Aha!" Christian Parker exclaimed. "I thought I recognized the underlying taste! That was an interesting choice, Miss Swensen."

Chef Duquesne nodded. "Yes, and it was a *good* choice. It doesn't overshadow the other flavors, but it adds another very pleasant dimension to the frosting."

"Thank you," Hannah said as the other judges began to praise her cake, describing it as innovative, surprising, and attractive on the plate. There were no negative comments and Hannah was delighted with their assessment.

"Would any of you care for a bit more coffee?" Michelle asked when she noticed that several of their coffee cups were empty.

"I would," Helene Stone said, draining the last swallow in her cup.

Several of the other judges agreed, and this time Ross carried the silver carafe over to fill the cups. Then he returned the carafe to the tray and gave Hannah a hug. "I'd better get back to work." He placed a kiss on Hannah's cheek and then he was gone.

"I think you made a very wise choice, Miss Swensen," Chef Duquesne said.

"Thank you," Hannah responded, even though she wasn't sure whether the head judge was approving her choice of husband or her choice of cake. Actually, she hoped it was both, but she'd have to wait for the reading of the scores to find out for sure.

DOUBLE RAINBOW SWIRL CAKE

Preheat oven to 325 degrees F., rack in the middle position.

1 and ½ cups softened butter *(3 sticks, 12 ounces, ¾ pound)*

2 cups white *(granulated)* sugar

4 large eggs

8-ounce package cream cheese *(I used Philadelphia cream cheese in the silver, brick-shaped package)*

8 ounces white chocolate chips *(I used half of an 11-ounce package of Ghirardelli white chocolate—it's about a cup and that's close enough for this cake)*

½ cup unflavored yogurt *(I used Mountain High)*

½ teaspoon salt

2 teaspoons baking powder

1 teaspoon vanilla extract

2 cups cake flour *(DO NOT SIFT—use it right out of the box—just scrape it out and swoop, leveling off the top with a table knife.)*

1 small package *(makes 4 half-cup servings)* raspberry Jell-O powder

1 small package *(makes 4 half-cup servings)*
  orange Jell-O powder
1 small package *(makes 4 half-cup servings)*
  lemon Jell-O powder
1 small package *(makes 4 half-cup servings)*
  lime Jell-O powder
1 small package *(makes 4 half-cup servings)*
  berry blue Jell-O powder
1 small package *(makes 4 half-cup servings)*
  grape Jell-O powder

Generously butter and flour two 9-inch round cake pans. *(Don't use Pam or any other nonstick cooking spray. Andrea says the Pam Baking Spray, the one with flour added, works just fine for her. But you can also butter the inside of the layer pans and sprinkle in flour to coat the bottom and the sides—that will work fine, too. Shake off any excess by thumping the bottom and sides of the pan and you're good to go.*

Personally, for a wedding cake, I don't want any browning on the top, bottom, or sides of the layer. The only way I know to prevent this is to line the layer pans with a circle of parchment paper in the bottom, and a strip of parchment paper around the sides that extends at least two-inches over the top of the pan. Once you've coated all the parchment paper

with Pam or another nonstick cooking spray, you've done all you could to prevent browning.

Beat the softened butter and white granulated sugar in the bowl of an electric mixer until it is light and fluffy. *(You can mix this cake by hand, but it takes some muscle.)*

Add the eggs, one at a time, and beat until they're light and fluffy. Make sure they're well mixed.

Soften the cream cheese in a microwave-safe container on HIGH for 1 minute. Let it sit in the microwave for 1 minute longer without heating.

Add the white chocolate chips, the half-cup unflavored yogurt, and the salt.

Heat the mixture you made on HIGH for 1 minute more and again, let it sit in the microwave for 1 minute. Then try to stir it smooth with a heat-resistant rubber spatula. If you can't stir it smooth, heat it in 30-second increments with 30 seconds of standing time until you *can* stir it smooth.

Add this to the contents of your mixing bowl. Beat until everything is thoroughly combined.

Add the baking powder and the vanilla extract. Mix until they're incorporated.

Add the cake flour one cup at a time, beating after each addition. Mix until the resulting batter has no lumps.

Divide the cake batter into 6 smaller bowls.

Hannah's 1st Note: This is easier if you first divide the batter evenly into 2 larger bowls and then divide each of those bowls into 3 smaller bowls. They do not have to be perfect. The cake batter police will not be knocking on your door to measure each bowl. Just do it as best you can.

Open the first Jell-O package and add 2 Tablespoons of the raspberry Jell-O powder to the batter in the bowl. Mix until it is thoroughly combined and the red color is deep and even.

Repeat with the next 5 Jell-O flavors, adding 2 Tablespoons of the orange Jell-O powder to the 2nd bowl, two Tablespoons of the lemon Jell-O powder to the 3rd bowl, 2 Tablespoons of the lime Jell-O powder to the 4th bowl, 2 Tablespoons of the berry blue Jell-O powder to the 5th bowl, and 2 Tablespoons of the grape Jell-O powder to the 6th bowl.

Hannah's 2nd Note: Lisa, Michelle and I prefer adding Jell-O powder rather than food coloring. The Jell-O powder gives a nice, intense color and it adds its own flavor to each bowl.

Seal up the packages of Jell-O that are left over and stick them in your pantry to use for the next Double Rainbow Swirl Cake you make.

To prepare your Double Rainbow Swirl Cake for baking, begin with the raspberry Jell-O bowl *(the red one)*. Use a soup spoon to transfer the batter into one of your cake pans in a puddle, leaving room for the other two colors.

Throw away the bowl if you used a paper bowl or rinse it out in the sink if you didn't.

Move on to the 2nd bowl flavored with lemon Jell-O *(the yellow one)*. Use a soup spoon to empty that bowl in a puddle next to the raspberry puddle.

Move on to the 3rd bowl, the orange one. Spoon out the batter in a puddle on the space that remains in your cake pan.

Here comes the fun part. Pick up your cake pan and stand at the counter near your sink. Hold the pan up about 4 inches from the surface and then drop it on the counter. This will "settle" the batter. *(I'm not really sure you have to do this, but it's fun!)*

Leave the cake pan on the counter and take a table knife from your silverware drawer. Insert the tip of your knife about 1-inch from the inside edge of your pan.

Run the knife around in a circle, dragging it against the bottom of the cake pan, but don't close the circle. Instead just jog up 2-inches or so to start another circle. You'll be making a spiral that ends in the center of your cake pan. Don't make too many circles. You don't want the cake batter to mix into the other colors too much. Three spirals is just about right for this size of cake pan.

Move on to the empty layer pan. Using the same technique, make puddles from the green, blue, and purple bowls. When you have your 3 colored puddles in the pan, drop the 2nd layer pan, "settle" it the same way you did with the 1st layer pan.

Use the rinsed table knife to repeat the swirling process with your 2nd layer pan.

Bake your layers at 325 degrees F. for 20 to 25 minutes, or until a cake tester or thin wooden skewer inserted one inch from the center of the pan comes out clean and the top is a light golden brown.

Remove from the oven and cool in the pans on a wire rack or on a cold stovetop burner for 20 minutes. Run a knife around the outside edge of the parchment paper to loosen the cakes. Then turn them out on a wire rack.

After the cakes are completely cool, it's time to frost your cake.

WHITE CHOCOLATE BUTTER CREAM FROSTING

(If you're a fan of frosting, double this recipe. Believe me, it won't be too much!)

> ½ cup *(1 stick, 8 ounces, ¼ pound)* salted butter, softened to room temperature
> ½ teaspoon salt
> ¼ cup *(4 Tablespoons)* white Crème d'Cacao *(I used Mr. Stacks)*
> 3 and ½ to 5 cups confectioner's *(powdered)* sugar *(don't pack it down when you measure it—just scoop it out and level it off on top—my frosting used the whole 4 cups of powdered sugar.)*

Hannah's 1st Note: If you're watching your salt intake, you can add less salt than is called for in the recipe. But remember that the reason the salt is there is because it cuts down on the sweetness of the frosting and enhances the flavor of the white chocolate.

Hannah's 2nd Note: If you don't want to use a liqueur in this frosting, you can substitute ¼ cup heavy cream for the white chocolate crème d'cacao.

If you do this, add 1 teaspoon vanilla extract to your frosting and call it Vanilla Buttercream Frosting.

Use an electric mixer to make this frosting. You can do it by hand, but you'll really have to stir fast and furious to get it to the creamy consistency you need.

Place the softened butter and the salt in the bowl of an electric mixer. Beat at HIGH speed until the butter is smooth and creamy.

Add 2 cups of the confectioner's sugar. Beat the resulting mixture until it is smooth and has no lumps.

Gradually add the white crème d'cacao, beating until the mixture is thoroughly combined.

Add another cup of confectioner's sugar. Beat until it is thoroughly incorporated.

Add another half-cup of confectioner's sugar and beat until everything is smooth and creamy.

If your frosting has reached a good spreading consistency, stop beating and proceed to frost your 2-layer cake. If it has not, you may add up to another cup and a half of powdered sugar.

Hannah's 3rd Note: This frosting is very forgiving. If you went a little overboard with the confec-

tioner's sugar and it's a bit too stiff, add a little more crème d'cacao or heavy cream. If your frosting is not stiff enough, add a bit more powdered sugar until it's just right. You may end up with extra frosting this way, but the kids will always appreciate frosting spread between 2 graham crackers, or even frosting spread on the unsalted side of a soda cracker.

To frost your cake, peel the parchment paper off the bottom of one layer and set it, bottom up, on the cake plate. *(If the top has risen too much and it wobbles on the plate, even the top with a sharp knife.)*

Put dabs of frosting on top of the 1st layer and spread it out evenly with a frosting knife.

Peel the paper off the bottom of the 2nd layer and place it, top side up, on top of the 1st layer. This time you don't care if it's risen a little. It will look pretty when you frost it.

Frost the sides of your cake next. When you've frosted the sides to your satisfaction, move on to the very top.

Put a generous dab of frosting in the center of the top. Then put dabs of frosting around it. Spread them

together to cover the whole top and your work of tasty art is finished!

Let the frosting dry for ten minutes or so. Then decorate your Double Rainbow Swirl Cake in any manner you choose. You can use colored frosting in a pastry bag, the little tubes of colored frostings you can buy at the grocery store, or you can stick colored candies on the top of your cake in a design you create. If you like, you can even sprinkle it with rings of multicolored decorating sugar, the kind you use on Christmas cookies. Whichever method you choose, the real surprise will come when you slice the cake and serve it to your guests!

Yield: 12 to 24 slices

Hannah's 4th Note: I looked this up online once and a bakery said you could get 24 slices from a 2-layer cake. I guess that's only if you don't invite Mike or Ross.

Chapter Fourteen

"I thought it went well," Michelle said when she got to the greenroom. "What do you think, Hannah?"

"I don't know. I thought so at the time, but now I'm not as sure. Rodney's cake with those candied violets on top looked really gorgeous. I've never seen anything like it before."

"Neither have I," Michelle admitted. "Did you see Brooke's cake?"

"No, but she's up right after this commercial. I hope she does better tonight. They were really tough on her in New York."

"And it was all Gloria's fault for telling her to use that marshmallow sauce."

The two sisters watched as Brooke wheeled her cake to the judging table. "It looks good," Michelle commented. "I like those peach slices on top."

"So do I. Fingers crossed that it tastes as good as it looks."

"You want her to win?" Michelle asked, and she looked surprised. "I thought you wanted to win the first night in Lake Eden."

"It's not that I don't *want* to win. It's just that I'd mind less if I lost to Brooke than I would if I lost to anyone else."

"Okay. I guess I can understand that."

The door to the greenroom opened and Loren rushed in. He was carrying a jacket on a hanger. "Hi, guys. I spilled powdered sugar all over my other jacket and I have to change before I'm up."

"You've got time," Hannah told him. "Brooke just wheeled in her cake. It looks really good."

Loren turned to look at the screen. "You're right. It *does* look good. I just hope Chef Duquesne gives her a better score than last time. He was really nasty to her."

"I know," Hannah said, "and it wasn't her fault. She got a piece of bad advice from Gloria."

"I know. Gloria told me. She was pretty proud of the fact she tried to sabotage Brooke and it worked."

"And you think Chef Duquesne is nasty?" Michelle asked in the most sarcastic tone Hannah had ever heard her youngest sister use.

"You're absolutely right, Michelle." Loren pulled off his stained chef's coat and put on a clean one. "Gloria's every bit as nasty. And that's probably why they hooked up last night. Nastiness must seek its own level. And as far as I'm concerned, they deserve each other."

Hannah exchanged glances with Michelle, and she knew that her youngest sister was thinking along the same lines as she was. If Gloria had wound up with Chef Duquesne last night, she might just win the competition tonight.

"Do you think it'll affect her scores?" Michelle asked the question that was on both of their minds.

"Probably. At least it sure can't hurt." Loren buttoned up the placket of his chef's jacket and turned for the door again. "Gotta run. I'm up right after Brooke finishes and I still have to put a couple more decorations on my cake."

"Good luck," Hannah said as he went out the door. And then, the minute he had closed it behind him, she said, under her breath, "And bad luck to Gloria. She deserves it."

* * *

"You won!" Michelle said, heading out to Hannah's cookie truck with their box of leftover ingredients.

"I didn't exactly win," Hannah reminded her. "I tied for first place with Rodney Paloma."

"Yes, but Gloria wasn't even in the running tonight. Doesn't that make you feel good?"

"Actually . . . yes!" Hannah admitted. "And Rodney's cake probably deserved to take first place instead of tying with my Double Rainbow Swirl Cake. It was absolutely beautiful, and I got to taste it after the competition was over. I wasn't sure how I'd like the taste of violets, but it was really good."

Michelle gave a little sigh. "I wish Brooke could have scored a bit higher."

"She didn't do that badly. She came in third. That's pretty good in a five-person competition."

"It's not that hot when there's a tie for first and second doesn't count. It means she took fourth and there's only five of us."

"But Gloria came in below Brooke. Brooke's got to feel good about that," Hannah said. And then she focused on the positive. "They said nice things about Brooke's cake, though. It's just that Chef Duquesne didn't think it was innovative enough."

"Aunt Nancy was right. He's a real snob."

"And Aunt Nancy was right about the Jell-O, too." Hannah gave a little smile.

"And also the fact that Chef Duquesne was impressed with appearances way back in high school. He liked the way the winning cakes looked, both yours and Rodney's. And from what Loren told us about Gloria last night, he still chooses his dates by the way they look."

"You're talking about Gloria," Hannah said, opening the driver's door of her cookie truck and sliding in behind the wheel.

"Right."

"But Gloria didn't win," Hannah pointed out, waiting until Michelle had climbed into the passenger's seat and buckled her seat belt.

"Neither did Aunt Nancy as far as her date with Allen Duke was concerned. He took her to the prom, danced with her, and then he dumped her at home so that he could go out with his girlfriend."

Hannah thought about that for a moment as she started the cookie truck and backed out of her parking spot. "That's interesting," she said at last, once they'd turned onto the access road and they were traveling toward the highway. "Chef Duquesne likes the right woman on his arm because it makes him look good, but he doesn't necessarily want to spend the whole time with her. Gloria looked good sitting next to him on a bar stool, and even though she spent the night with him, it had no effect on the score he gave her in the competition."

"Exactly." Michelle turned to smile at Hannah. "His obsession with appearances doesn't necessarily affect his professional judgment. He liked the way you looked as a bride. He thought that was the perfect way to present your wedding cake. But if your cake hadn't tasted as good as it looked, you would have dropped way down in the ratings."

"The way Gloria did?"

"Yes. He criticized her cakes for being too dry and not having enough flavor. But it was very clear he really liked the outfit she was wearing."

"Or *not* wearing!" Hannah said, referring to Gloria's extremely short skirt.

"Exactly right."

Both sisters sighed as Hannah drove up the on-ramp and onto the highway. It was almost eleven in the evening and there was very little traffic. Before either one of them had time to introduce a new topic of conversation, the lights of the Corner Tavern appeared in the distance.

"Hamburger and fries?" Hannah asked.

"I thought you'd never ask," Michelle answered with a laugh. "I started thinking about one of their double-doubles the minute I saw their sign."

Less than five minutes later, they were sitting in a booth at the back, sipping coffee and waiting for their food. Michelle yawned once and took another sip of coffee. "Tonight was exhausting."

"Yes, but the cookie competition will be better. You don't have to decorate those."

"True. I know Ross was busy, but did you get a chance to say good-bye to him before you left?"

"Yes. He's going to come over for breakfast early tomorrow morning before he goes to work. He said he'd be at the condo by six. I thought I'd make something easy, like pancakes."

"I'll make Breakfast Puffs," Michelle offered. "One of my roommates gave me a recipe from her mother, and I've been dying to try it. She said they're like doughnuts, except better."

"That sounds good." Hannah smiled at her. "But only if you're sure you don't mind getting up that early."

"I don't mind at all. Besides, you should sleep in tomorrow. I'll get you up in time to take a shower and get dressed before Ross comes over. And then we'll drive out to Sally's for our seven o'clock practice time."

"Seven o'clock?" Hannah was surprised. "But the kitchen will be crowded with staff if Sally's serving her breakfast buffet."

"I asked her about that, and she said she switched everything around so that all the contestants got time to practice. They're setting up an omelet station, a pancake station, and a waffle station in the dining room. And they're doing the cooking right there. She's having a table with pastry and muffins, a station for tea and coffee, and a carving station for ham and turkey. Dick's doing all kinds of sausages on their portable grill. Sally's locking the kitchen and drawing the curtains so that none of the contestants will be disturbed during their practice times."

"Are we the first contestants to practice?"

"Yes. Practice times run from seven in the morning to two in the afternoon. That's an hour to practice and a half hour to clean up."

"How about lunch? Won't Sally and her staff need to get into the kitchen to prepare that?"

Michelle shook her head. "She's serving sandwiches and soups for lunch. And there'll be a table for desserts. That's the way she planned it for practice days. On competition days, the kitchen will be open for business for breakfast and lunch, but dinner will be early, from four-thirty to six. And after the competition is over for the night, she'll serve a late supper to anyone who stays for it."

"That sounds like a lot of work for Sally and Dick."

"It is, but Sally says it'll be worth it as far as their business is concerned. While the film crew is here, they're going to film a series of commercials for the Lake Eden Inn, and the Food Channel is going to run them for a solid two months for free."

"National publicity." Hannah turned to smile at the waitress, who'd arrived with their burgers and fries.

"Anything else, Hannah?" the waitress asked.

"Not for me, thank you."

The waitress turned to Michelle. "How about you, Michelle?"

"Not right now, thanks. Maybe . . . dessert later?"

The waitress laughed. "Didn't you even get to taste that great-looking cake that Hannah baked?"

"Uh . . . actually, yes. But that was in rehearsal. It was really good."

"It looked good on TV. We had it on here, and I watched you two on my break. Congratulations!"

"Thank you," Hannah responded, and the waitress hurried off. "Mystery solved," she told Michelle.

"What mystery?"

"I was wondering how she knew our names when I couldn't remember ever meeting her before."

"You'd better get used to it," Michelle said, picking up her burger with both hands. "Maybe you're not classically trained like the other dessert chefs, but you're about to become a national celebrity around here."

BREAKFAST PUFFS

Preheat oven to 350 degrees F., rack in the middle position.

> 1 large egg
> 1 cup cream cheese, softened
> ¾ stick salted butter *(3 ounces)*
> ½ cup white *(granulated)* sugar
> 1 teaspoon baking powder
> ½ teaspoon baking soda
> ½ teaspoon salt
> ¼ teaspoon nutmeg *(freshly grated is best)*
> ½ cup cold milk
> 1 and ¼ cups flour *(pack it down in the cup when you measure it)*
> _____
> ¾ stick salted butter, melted *(3 ounces)*
> ½ cup white *(granulated)* sugar
> ½ teaspoon cinnamon

Spray the inside of a pan of 12 regular-size muffin cups with Pam or another nonstick cooking spray.

Beat the egg until it is light and fluffy.

Unwrap the cream cheese and the butter, and place both in a microwave-safe bowl.

Soften by heating the cream cheese and butter in the microwave on HIGH for 1 minute. Let the bowl sit in the microwave for another minute and then try to stir the mixture smooth. If you cannot stir it smooth, microwave in 30-second increments with 30-second standing times until you can stir it smooth.

Add the cream cheese and butter mixture to the beaten egg. Mix until everything is well combined.

Add the white sugar and mix it in.

With the mixer running on LOW speed, mix in the baking powder, baking soda, salt, and nutmeg until everything is thoroughly incorporated.

With the mixer still running on LOW speed, mix in half of the cold milk and half of the flour. Mix until well combined.

Add the rest of the milk and the rest of the flour. Mix thoroughly.

Pour the batter into the muffin cups, filling them ⅔ full.

Bake at 350 degrees F. for 20 to 25 minutes, or until the tops are golden brown and they have puffed up to fill the muffin cups.

When your Breakfast Puffs are approximately 5 minutes from done, place the second ¾ stick of

salted butter in a medium-size microwave-safe bowl. Melt it on HIGH for 30 seconds.

While the butter is melting, place the white sugar and cinnamon in a shallow bowl and mix them together with a fork.

Prepare a towel-lined basket to use for serving your Breakfast Puffs.

When your Breakfast Puffs are golden brown on top and the time is up, turn them out on a cookie sheet or a bread board, and dip them, one by one, into the melted butter. Immediately roll the puff in the sugar and cinnamon mixture and place it in the towel-lined basket you prepared for serving.

Repeat, working quickly, with one puff at a time, until all 12 puffs have been dipped in butter and rolled in the sugar and cinnamon mixture.

Serve immediately. They're best eaten hot.

Yield: 12 light and delicious Breakfast Puffs.

Hannah's Warning: If you invite Mike for breakfast and you don't have eggs, or sausage, or anything else to go with the puffs, you'd better make two or three pans.

Chapter Fifteen

"These Breakfast Puffs are great, Michelle!" Ross took another from the basket, broke it open, and spread on more salted butter. "My cholesterol level's probably through the roof, but I can't seem to stop eating them."

"That's because they're so good," Hannah told him, giving her sister a smile. "Would you like more coffee?"

"That would be great." Ross glanced at his watch. "I've got time for one more cup before I have to hightail it out to the station. P.K.'s meeting me at seven." He slipped his arm around Hannah and gave her a little hug. "Are you two rehearsing in Sally's kitchen this morning?"

Michelle pushed back her chair and stood up. "Yes. We're supposed to be there at seven. We drew names and I got the first slot."

"So that means the rest of your day is free?" Ross turned to Hannah to ask the question.

"Yes, and no. We'll be helping out at The Cookie Jar, but we also have to figure out how we're going to present our cookies to the judges."

"Present?" Ross looked a bit confused. "You're not going to pass a platter to the judges?"

"No. Everyone will do that, and Michelle and I want to

be different. I think we'll serve a coffee drink with our cookies."

"Something with a liqueur in it," Michelle explained. "There are all sorts of great dessert coffee drinks."

"We just have to choose which one goes best with the cookies," Hannah told him.

Ross smiled. "That's a good idea. Your cookies are special, but a coffee drink would make them even more special."

"That's what we thought. The judges liked it when we served coffee with our wedding cake," Hannah said.

"They *loved* it. Your coffee was a big hit with them. I've got a shot of Chef Duquesne drinking his third cup. And P.K. got some great footage of you cutting the cake. And that reminds me . . . the cookies you're baking aren't as colorful as the wedding cake, are they?"

Hannah shook her head. "No, they're not. That's one of the reasons why we want to pair them with a coffee drink."

"Excuse me a second," Michelle said, walking toward the kitchen door. "I'm just going to get my jacket. We've got to get on the road before we're late for our practice time."

Ross stood up and so did Hannah. He pulled her close to him and said, "You did great last night. I think you're going to be the grand winner, Cookie."

Hannah smiled. It was good that Ross had such faith in her, and there was no way she wanted to disappoint him. "I hope you're right," she told him, "but there are a lot of really good contestants and they've all been classically trained. I'm just a home baker."

"That may be true, but I think you're better than any of them."

"Thank you." Hannah hugged him, but then she pulled away to look up, into his face. "Will you be terribly disappointed in me if I'm not the grand winner?"

"Of course not!" Ross leaned down and kissed her. "I

love you, Hannah. Even if you don't win, you'll always be *my* grand prize."

Hannah was thoughtful as she zipped down the highway toward the Lake Eden Inn. "I think I'll bring a dozen of our practice cookies home so Ross can have them for breakfast tomorrow."

"Good idea."

"And I'll leave the rest of the dough in the walk-in cooler so Sally can use it for her lunch buffet."

"*Not* a good idea." Michelle shook her head. "Nobody should be able to taste what you're baking until after you present it to the judges."

"But I don't want to throw out the dough!"

"Of course not. You can take it home with you and put it in your freezer. And then you can use it at The Cookie Jar *after* you find out how it does in the competition."

"You're probably right." Hannah shivered and turned up the heater on her old Suburban. It was cold this morning, and it was starting to snow. It was definitely time to get out her winter parka. As she drove, huge, wet flakes of snow splattered against her windshield.

Michelle cleared her throat. "Look, Hannah . . . maybe I'm a little paranoid, but I don't think you should let anyone know which cookie you're baking until the actual night of the cookie challenge. That's why I don't want you to leave the dough in Sally's cooler. All the other contestants will have access to that cooler."

Hannah thought about that for a moment. "You're not paranoid," she said. "You're smart! This *is* a competition."

"That's right. And remember what happened to Brooke."

Hannah increased the speed of her windshield wipers to combat the blowing snow. "I should also be careful not to leave any copies of my recipes behind when we leave the kitchen."

"Right. Maybe we're going a little overboard, but I'd rather be safe than sorry. I think all of our recipes should be a secret until we bake them for the judges."

"Agreed." Hannah turned up the speed on her windshield wipers again. "It's snowing pretty hard, Michelle. I'm glad that Ross didn't have to go out on location today. He's spending the day at the studio, teaching P.K. how to edit the footage they shot last night."

"Are they coming over for dinner tonight?"

"Yes, but they're bringing takeout. Bertanelli's is close to the studio, and Ross said he'd pick up a couple of pizzas."

"So there's only the five of us?"

Hannah glanced over at Michelle. "Five? It's four, Michelle. You, me, Ross, and P.K."

"Not if Mike gets wind of it," Michelle said with a smile.

"You've got a point." Hannah braked cautiously as she came to the turnoff that led around the lake. "I'm glad we're almost there. The road's getting slippery. Maybe I should have taken the Food Channel's offer to let us stay at Sally's."

Michelle shook her head. "I think you did the right thing. You have the advantage of sleeping at home in your own bed, and you can practice in your home kitchen or in the kitchen at The Cookie Jar. Everybody else has to wait for their turn in Sally's kitchen."

"But there's five baking stations."

"That's true, but the producers don't want us all at the baking stations at once until the actual competition. Remember what happened to Brooke in New York?"

"Of course I do. But Brooke said she wasn't going to say anything about it to the judges."

"She probably didn't, but someone may have figured it out. And this does eliminate the possibility of cheating that way again." Michelle peered out at the snow stacking up on the roadway. "Do you think the weather will interfere with the competition tomorrow night?"

"I don't think so. The road will be plowed by then, and

Dick plows the parking lot and the turnaround in front of the inn. Besides, Minnesota drivers know how to deal with winter weather. This isn't exactly a blizzard, you know."

Michelle leaned back in her seat. "You're right. I'm just borrowing trouble. I probably need sleep. I kept waking up last night and I couldn't help thinking that something bad was going to happen."

"You had a premonition?" Hannah frowned slightly.

"No, it probably had something to do with the dill pickles I ate last night, right before I went to bed."

They traveled in silence for several moments, each thinking their own thoughts. Then the truck swerved sharply.

"Whoa!" Hannah squelched her urge to stomp on the brakes and steered out of the skid. The road around the lake was icy, and it felt colder than it had when they'd left her condo complex. Her headlights cut a bright yellow swath through the fog that had gathered around Eden Lake. "Are you all right?" she asked Michelle.

"I'm fine. You're a good driver, Hannah."

"Not *that* good. I should have realized that the road around the lake might be icy. It was only twenty degrees when we left the condo. That's pretty cold for this time of year, even in Minnesota."

Michelle shivered slightly in her light jacket. Then she leaned forward to peer down the tunnel that Hannah's headlights cut through the inky blackness. "It's really dark out here. I guess it's because there aren't any streetlights."

"And the fact that almost all of the lake cabins are dark and buttoned up for the winter."

"You're right. I forgot about that. I guess I'm used to Minneapolis. The sky never gets really dark like this. There's always a kind of perpetual glow."

"That's because of the ambient city lights. Just think about how many streetlights and neon signs are in a city that large. They reflect off the cloud cover." Hannah glanced over at her youngest sister and smiled. "Thanks for coming with me, Michelle. This would be a lonely drive all by my-self."

"When we get into Sally's kitchen, are we going to prac-tice everything from scratch so that we can check out the time?"

"Yes. Tomorrow's competition could get a little frantic since we only have an hour to mix up and bake our entry."

"I think I'm prepared for my part of it, but it couldn't hurt to set the timer and do a final run-through. Do you have the key Sally gave you?"

"I've got it." Hannah glanced down at her key ring. The key was there, right next to the one for her condo door. Sally had given every contestant a key to her kitchen. "I'd hate to let the audience down tomorrow night, especially in the cookie challenge."

"And I know you'd hate to let Ross down. I heard you ask him if he'd be disappointed if you didn't win."

Hannah couldn't keep from smiling, just remembering what Ross had said when she'd asked him. He'd called her *his* grand prize. She could hardly wait to marry Ross.

"Do you know that you smile every time anyone says Ross's name?"

Hannah thought about that for a moment. "No, but I guess it makes sense."

"I think it's sweet. I wonder if Ross smiles every time he hears your name."

"I don't know."

"Maybe we should put it to the test."

"No. Please don't," Hannah said quickly.

"Because you'll be disappointed if he doesn't smile?"

Hannah sighed. Michelle had a remarkable and some-times distressing talent for doing what their father had called *hitting the nail on the head*. Instead of answering, Hannah changed the subject. "You're not nervous about tomorrow night, are you?"

"Not at all. Of course, I'll have stage fright at the beginning. I always do. But that only makes me try harder to do everything perfectly. How about you?"

"I may be just a little nervous," Hannah admitted, making light of the fact that the horde of butterflies in her stomach always began to do a jig the moment the judges took their places and cameras began to roll. "I just hope that Aunt Nancy's right and the butterscotch in our cookies reminds Judge Duquesne of his childhood dessert."

There was a parking spot in front of the Lake Eden Inn and Hannah pulled in. "Ready?" she asked, turning to Michelle.

"I'm ready. Let's bake."

The lobby of the inn was deserted. The college student who usually worked from midnight until eight at the front desk was probably on break. Hannah gave a little wave at the security camera as they went by and mouthed the words, *Hi, Dick.* Dick would see her wave when he reviewed the footage.

There was a fire in the massive stone fireplace and Hannah stopped in front of it to warm her hands. Michelle did the same and they stood there for a moment, turning this way and that to warm up.

"I'll get my parka out tonight," Hannah said, leaving the fireplace reluctantly and leading the way down the hall.

"I didn't bring my parka with me on this trip," Michelle said. "I never dreamed it would get this cold."

"Don't tell Mother you don't have it. She'll call to remind you to bring it every time you say you're coming home."

It was a bit strange to walk down the empty hallways which were usually bustling with people during the day. Hannah cut through the dining room with its tables already draped with fresh white tablecloths and set for Sally's breakfast buffet. When Hannah arrived at the kitchen door, she pulled out her key and slid it into the lock. Then she turned the doorknob and opened the door. She flicked on the huge banks of fluorescent lights and the two sisters stepped inside the huge kitchen.

"It looks a lot bigger without anyone in here," Michelle said, looking around the huge empty space.

"I'll bet Sally feels this way every morning when she unlocks the door. I'll start the timer. You turn on the oven at our workstation. After that, we'll gather the ingredients."

With both of them working, it didn't take long for Hannah to carry the eggs, butter, sugars, baking soda, and salt to their workstation. Michelle was right behind her with the flour, and the chips. When all the ingredients were arranged in order, Hannah turned to her sister. "We'll do it exactly the way we did at The Cookie Jar. You run the mixer and I'll dump."

Michelle stationed herself at the industrial mixer and waited for Hannah to dump in the butter and the sugars. Once she'd mixed those until they were light and fluffy, she nodded to Hannah, who then added the eggs. Michelle turned the mixer up a notch and let it run while Hannah added more ingredients. Michelle scraped down the sides of the bowl, shut off the mixer, and looked back at Hannah. "Ready for dividing."

Michelle stepped back and Hannah scooped half of the dough out of the bowl and put it in a second bowl that fit their mixer. "Ready for the vanilla," she said.

As Michelle resumed her position and turned the mixer on low speed, Hannah dumped in the melted vanilla chips. Once that was thoroughly combined with the other ingredients, Michelle shut off the mixer, removed the bowl, and replaced it with the bowl that contained the second half of the cookie dough. "Ready for the butterscotch," she said.

Hannah poured in the melted butterscotch chips. Michelle mixed and Hannah stood back, watching. When both of them were satisfied with the outcome, Michelle removed the bowl from the mixer while Hannah prepared a lightly floured board.

"Ready to roll," Hannah said, dividing the half-batch of vanilla cookie dough into fourths and putting one of them on the board. Michelle quickly divided the contents of the second bowl, the one with butterscotch. Then she tore off a length of wax paper and set it on the counter next to the board. It would hold the four ropes of vanilla dough that Hannah was rolling.

Once the vanilla dough ropes were completed, Hannah began to roll the four butterscotch ropes. When that was done, there were four rolls of each flavor. Michelle tore off another length of wax paper and spread it out on the counter.

"I'm ready," Michelle said.

Together, the two sisters transferred four dough ropes, two of each flavor to the wax paper, with a vanilla and a butterscotch on the bottom and a butterscotch and a vanilla on the top, alternating the colors and flavors. Then Hannah rolled the four ropes together to form one thicker multi-flavored roll. Michelle wrapped the finished roll in the wax paper, twisted the ends to seal them, and they began the same process all over again with the last four dough ropes.

"Done," Hannah said after Michelle had wrapped the second large roll and placed both rolls on a cookie sheet. "Do you want to put them in the walk-in cooler, or shall I do it?"

"I'll do it. They might want to film a little interview with you at this point in the competition. I'll be right back."

Michelle headed off to the walk-in cooler with the two rolls of finished dough and Hannah glanced at the clock. She knew that chilling the two ropes of dough would take fifteen minutes in the coldest part of the walk-in cooler. She'd tested that in her own walk-in cooler at The Cookie Jar. The blast chiller would be quicker, but she preferred using the method she always used for cookie dough.

Hannah watched the timer tick off the minutes. What was taking Michelle so long? She should be back here so that she could start preparing the cookie sheets.

Two minutes ticked by and stretched into four. Hannah turned to look at the walk-in cooler door. It was open and she could see Michelle standing there, just staring at something.

"Michelle?" she called out, but her sister didn't react. Michelle just stood there like a statue, motionless and seemingly frozen in place. What in the world was wrong with . . . ?

"Oh, no!" Hannah breathed. The back of her neck was prickling and there was a cold, hollow feeling in the pit of her stomach. She was experiencing the reaction that Mike called Hannah's *slaydar*. He'd given an interview to the *Lake Eden Journal*, their local newspaper, and he'd explained that he used radar to locate speeders, but Hannah used her *slaydar* to find murder victims.

Hannah tried to convince herself that this time, it wasn't the case, but there was no denying that something was dreadfully wrong. She wished that she didn't have to walk over to the cooler and find out what was the matter, but she knew she had to do it.

"Michelle?" she called out again, hoping that it was something like a gallon of cream that had broken open and spilled all over the floor, or something that wasn't or hadn't ever been human. But even as she wished it, the back of her neck continued to prickle and the cold hollow feeling in her stomach intensified.

On legs that shook slightly, Hannah walked across the floor to the cooler door. She took a deep breath, stepped inside, and peered over her sister's shoulder to see what had rendered Michelle incapable of speech or movement.

Alain Duquesne was on the floor of the cooler, splayed out on his back like a Cornish game hen ready for the roasting pan. A big piece of Hannah's Double Rainbow Swirl Wedding Cake was partially smashed next to his body, and the knife he'd used to cut her cake was buried up to the hilt in his chest.

Hannah put her arms around Michelle. "I'm here," she said. "It's okay, Michelle."

The sound of Hannah's voice seemed to release Michelle from her frozen state and she drew a deep shuddering breath. "He . . . is . . . is he . . . dead?" she asked in a quavering voice that didn't sound at all like the confident young woman that she was.

"Oh, yes. At least I'm ninety-nine percent sure he is. Let me take you out to the workstation, Michelle. You should sit down. Then I'll call Mike."

"Was it . . . suicide?"

"I doubt it. It would be almost impossible to plunge a knife into your own chest and then fall to the floor on your back."

"Then . . . he was . . . murdered?"

"I believe so."

"It's awful!" Michelle gasped, and Hannah was relieved to hear that her sister's voice was a bit stronger.

"I know," Hannah said. She took Michelle's arm and pulled her away toward the door. "Come with me. I'll get you some water."

Once Michelle was seated on a stool at their workstation and Hannah had given her a glass of water, Michelle looked up at Hannah again. Tears were forming in her eyes. "It's awful!" she repeated.

"Yes, it is. It's always awful when someone is murdered."

"It's not *that*! We're baking Vanilla and Butterscotch Hopscotch Cookies because Aunt Nancy told us that Judge Duquesne loved butterscotch when he was a kid. And now he's dead and we've lost our advantage!"

Chapter Sixteen

"Oh, Hannah! Not again!"

Hannah gave a deep sigh. She hadn't really wanted to call Mike, but Michelle was in no shape to talk to him and someone had to do it.

"Yes, but this time Michelle was the one to discover the body."

"I'll bring Lonnie with me. He can calm her down before I interview her. You say you preserved the crime scene?"

"Yes. I shut the walk-in cooler door and we're here in the kitchen at our workstation. The kitchen door's locked and the next contestant isn't due to arrive here for another forty minutes."

"I'll call Dick and have him guard the kitchen door from the outside, just in case someone tries to get in."

"Okay."

"I probably don't have to say this, but don't go back inside the cooler."

Hannah shivered. "Don't worry. I won't."

"And don't touch anything else until I get there."

"Okay."

"Do you know if Michelle touched anything while she was in the cooler?"

"I don't think she did. She was still holding the cookie

sheet with our cookie dough on it when I went in the cooler to see what was keeping her so long."

"And she would have had to put the cookie sheet down to touch anything else?"

"Yes. She was just standing there like a statue, staring at . . . him. I led her out of the cooler and poured her a glass of water."

"Did you touch anything in the kitchen?"

"Of course we did. We mixed up the cookie dough we're making for the competition tomorrow night. Our finger-prints are all over."

"Hold on a second. Let me pull out of the parking lot. Lonnie and I are in the cruiser and we're on our way to you."

Hannah held on to the phone and waited. She heard the squad car accelerate and then there was the sound of a siren. Mike was on his way. Just knowing that made her feel much better.

"All right. We're on the highway and I've got you on speaker phone. Lonnie's taking notes for me. Did you notice anything unusual about the kitchen when you first walked in?"

"No. Everything was nice and clean, but it always is. And we were the first ones to come in this morning."

"Was the kitchen locked?"

"Yes, it was."

"Who let you in?"

"Nobody. Sally gave all the contestants and judges individual keys to the kitchen door."

"Did anyone else get keys?"

"I don't know. You'll have to ask Sally if . . ." Hannah gasped and stopped speaking in mid-thought.

"What?"

"When we came in, there were two wineglasses on the counter by the refrigerator. One was half full and the other was empty."

"Did you touch them?"

"No. We just went straight to our workstation, set the

countdown clock for an hour, and got right to work on our cookie dough."

"You said *two* wineglasses?"

"Yes. Chef Duquesne must have had someone with him in the kitchen."

"Perhaps. We'll have to check for prints. Tell me exactly what you and Michelle did when you entered the kitchen. Step by step, Hannah."

"Okay. I unlocked the kitchen door and turned on the lights."

"The lights were off?"

"Yes. There are dim night lights and those were on, but the big banks of fluorescents were off."

"All right. What did you do once you'd turned on the lights?"

"I waved at the . . ." Hannah stopped and gasped again. "Oh, Mike!"

"What?"

"There's a security camera in the kitchen! Sally asked Dick to install it the minute she learned the competition would be held at their restaurant. When we came in the first day, she told everyone it was there for their protection."

"Protection?"

"Yes. The Food Channel paid for added security to make sure that every contestant got the same length of practice time in the kitchen and the integrity of their ingredients were preserved."

Mike laughed. "In other words, no one could sneak into the kitchen in the dead of night and put salt in the sugar canister?"

"Something like that, I guess. But the important thing is that there's a security camera. You'll be able to find out who came into the kitchen with Chef Duquesne."

"Yes, if that person didn't know about the camera and didn't disable it in some way."

Hannah sighed. "You're right, of course. I'm just not

thinking clearly right now. I was just so happy about the way our practice time was going, and then Michelle found him, and . . . everything got . . . crazy here."

"I know that, Hannah. You're under a lot of pressure right now and it's getting to you. And the fact that your sister found Chef Duquesne's body must be almost worse than if you'd found it yourself."

"That's right!" Hannah was a bit shocked. She hadn't thought that Mike could be that perceptive. "How far away are you now?" she asked.

A scant second after she asked the question, there was a knock on the kitchen door and Hannah felt herself begin to panic. "Someone's here!" she told him.

"Yes. It's me. Let us in, Hannah."

Hannah's legs were trembling as she hurried to the door and opened it for Mike and Lonnie. "I'm so glad you're here!" she said, feeling almost giddy with relief. Now that she didn't have to be the strong older sister any longer, she could sit down on a stool and think about something, anything other than the celebrity chef who had been killed and how defenseless and pathetic he'd looked on the floor of the cooler. She had to think about something positive like how much she loved Ross, but that brought forth worries about the wedding itself and how she could manage to juggle her time so that she could do justice to the Food Channel competition, her wedding, her new husband, her business, her family, and the murder that she felt compelled to investigate.

Tears began to form in Hannah's eyes and she blinked them back. There was no reason to cry like a baby even though her tightly controlled world had gone into a tailspin. She would get everything done and nothing would be short-changed. That's what she'd done in the past, and there was no reason why she couldn't do it again.

Hannah looked down at the recipe in front of her on the counter. There were blotches of tears on the paper and the ink was beginning to smear. That was when she realized that tears were running down her cheeks, but before she could wipe them away with the back of her hand, someone handed her a tissue.

"Thanks, Mike," she said, managing a smile.

He sat down on the stool next to her and slipped an arm around her shoulders. "Things getting to you, Hannah?"

"I guess so."

"I can't blame you. There's a lot going on in your life right now. If there's anything I can do to help, let me know . . . okay?"

"Okay." Hannah looked up at him, but tears threatened to fall again and she quickly looked away. "Just a nervous reaction, I guess," she tried to explain.

"Sure. I understand. How about a cup of coffee from Sally's buffet? I'll go get some for both of us."

"Coffee would be good," Hannah said quickly. "I take mine . . ."

"I know how you take it," Mike cut off her explanation. "I'll bring a couple of Sally's cookies to go with it. They're not as good as yours, but they'll do."

Hannah felt herself smile as he walked toward the kitchen door. She felt better, a lot better, and more in control. If this emotional roller coaster that she seemed to be on was normal for people who were in love, she just hoped the ride would smooth out soon!

"Are you sure you're okay?" Hannah asked Michelle as she pulled up in front of their mother's house.

"I'm okay. And if I'm not, I will be as soon as I finish painting that last wall in the dining room. Andrea's showing the house tomorrow afternoon and I want everything to be perfect. Besides . . . I think the best thing I can do is to keep busy. That's what you always do, isn't it?"

"Yes. Yes, I do." Hannah did something quite uncharacteristic in her normally undemonstrative family. She reached out with both arms and gave her youngest sister a hug. "Come out to the condo the minute you finish."

"I will. What are *you* going to do when you get home?"

"Bake."

"Before you call Ross?"

"Yes. I need to calm down before I talk to him. If I call him right away, I'm afraid I'll start crying."

"And beg him to come home to you?"

Hannah gave a deep sigh. Michelle had done it again. She'd unerringly hit the nail right on the head. "Yes," she admitted. "I might do something like that."

"Are you going to bake the competition cookies again?"

Hannah shook her head. "No. That is, not exactly. I don't want to make them the way we did this morning. I want to change the recipe around and make it different somehow. It's just . . . wrong to do things the way we did them this morning."

"Because you didn't like the result?"

"That's right. If we do things exactly the way we did them this morning, it'll be too . . . evocative."

"Because it reminds you of what happened this morning?"

"Yes. And I don't want those memories hanging over my head when we bake tomorrow night for the judges."

"Good. Everything you said makes sense to me. I know I'd be more comfortable if we changed things around. One thing for sure . . . I don't want to step inside that walk-in cooler again!"

"Actually . . . now that I think about it . . . I'm not sure I'm entirely happy with the way the cookies looked. There wasn't enough color difference between the butterscotch part and the vanilla part."

"That's true, especially after your super-colorful wedding cake. The colors on the cookies were kind of blah."

"Right. Think about this for a minute, Michelle. Who's

the principal player here? The vanilla cookie, or the butter-scotch cookie?"

"The butterscotch, of course. The vanilla's very good, but it's just vanilla."

"Precisely. So why are we teaming the really good but-terscotch cookie with the good, but not spectacular, vanilla cookie?"

"I don't know. I don't think we should team them at all."

"Exactly what I was thinking." Hannah gave her a smile. "Let's make Butterscotch Sugar Cookies. If we do that, we'll have two advantages over the way we made them this morning."

"We won't have to roll the dough and assemble it, and we won't have to chill the rolls in the walk-in cooler?"

"Exactly. We'll save a ton of time, and that means we can make something else to go with the butterscotch cookies."

"Ice cream?"

"That's a good idea, but I've never made ice cream be-fore. Have you?"

"No."

"Ross and I were talking about it this morning and he thinks we should serve a coffee drink with the cookies."

"But not plain coffee, right?"

"Right. We've done that before, although it can't hurt to brew a pot and leave it behind at the judging table. They seemed to like that when we did it before."

"I've got it!" Michelle gasped, looking very excited. "White chocolate cocoa!"

"Like the white chocolate cocoa that Lisa makes?"

"Yes, but slightly different. Most coffee drinkers like mocha. And that's chocolate and coffee. Why can't we put white chocolate and coffee together and call it White Choco-late Mocha?"

Hannah thought about that for a moment. "There's no reason why we can't do that. Of course, we'll have to try it to make sure it works."

"That's easy. I'll make it tonight just as soon as I get back to your condo."

"And I'll go right home and make the Butterscotch Sugar Cookies. We can try them both together and see what we think."

"Okay. I'll be out as soon as I paint that wall. It shouldn't take me more than an hour."

"That's perfect. I should have some of the cookies baked by then since the dough doesn't need to chill."

"'Bye, Hannah. I love you."

"'Bye, Michelle. I love you, too."

There was a smile on Michelle's face as she turned to go into their mother's house. It was mirrored by the smile on Hannah's face as she drove away toward the freeway and the road home.

Hannah sat down on the couch in her living room and reached for the phone. Her first two pans of cookies were in the oven and she could hardly wait to sample them. She dialed Ross's cell phone number and sipped from her cup of coffee as she waited for him to answer.

"Hannah!"

Ross sounded surprised to hear from her, and Hannah smiled. At least this time, when something important had happened, she'd remembered to call him. "Yes, it's me. Are you busy?"

"I'm never too busy for you. Do you realize that this is the first time you've called me at work?"

"You're right. It is. I've got something serious to tell you, Ross."

"Is it about the wedding?"

"No."

"Then everything's okay with that?"

"Yes, it is. It's about Chef Duquesne."

"The head judge?"

"Yes. Michelle found him in Sally's walk-in cooler this morning when we went out to the Lake Eden Inn to practice. He was on the floor, dead."

"Poor Michelle! Is she okay?"

"I think so, but it was a shock. How did you feel about him, Ross?"

"I had no quarrel with him. He was fine with P.K. and me when we did our interview with him in New York. And he was nice to you when you baked our wedding cake. He was really too tough on some of the other contestants, though."

"How about the Food Channel film crew? Did they like him?"

"Not personally, but he made for a good show. If all the judges are nice, there's not much controversy. Duquesne provided controversy in spades."

"What was his personal life like?"

"I don't know. I only saw him once outside of the competition. He was in the bar when I walked through at the hotel in New York. It looked like he was trying to pick up one of the female . . ." Ross stopped and cleared his throat. "Wait a second. You wouldn't be asking me all this unless . . . was he *murdered*?"

"Doc hasn't made it official yet, but I'm pretty sure he was."

There was silence for a moment and then Ross sighed: "I can't say that I'm totally surprised. His comments to some of the contestants were a little out of line. I felt really sorry for Brooke Jackman that night in New York. He was really tough on her. And then, when you told me about what Gloria Berkeley did, I figured they deserved each other." Ross paused and cleared his throat. "Are you okay, Hannah? I can come home early if you need me."

"Thanks, but I'm okay." And, the moment she said it, she realized that she was. "Michelle will be here really soon. She just stopped off at Mother's house to paint a wall."

"Are you sure? I can ask for time off."

"No, you don't have to do that. Michelle and I will be fine. Just maybe . . . possibly . . . come here early tonight?"

"I'll see you at the condo at five. I love you, Hannah."

"I love you, too," Hannah said, and she was smiling as her kitchen timer began to ring and she hurried to take the first two pans of Butterscotch Sugar Cookies out of the oven.

BUTTERSCOTCH SUGAR COOKIES

Preheat oven to 325 degrees F., rack in the middle position.

2 cups salted butter *(4 sticks, 16 ounces, 1 pound)*
1 cup butterscotch chips *(I used Nestle Butter-scotch Chips)*
2 cups powdered *(confectioner's)* sugar *(pack it down in the cup when you measure it)*
1 cup white *(granulated)* sugar
2 large eggs
2 teaspoons vanilla extract
1 teaspoon baking soda
1 teaspoon cream of tartar *(critical!)*
1 teaspoon salt
4 and ¼ cups all-purpose flour *(not sifted— pack it down in the cup when you measure it)*

½ cup white sugar in a bowl for coating the cookie dough balls that you will make.

Melt the butter and butterscotch chips in a microwave-safe bowl by putting the chips on the bottom of the bowl and the butter on top of that. Heat for one minute on HIGH, let the bowl sit in the microwave for one minute, and then try to stir it smooth. If you can, you're done. If you can't, continue to heat in 30-second increments followed by a standing time of one minute, until you can stir the mixture smooth. *(You can also do this in a saucepan on the stovetop at LOW heat.)*

After you have stirred the mixture smooth, set it on the kitchen counter or on a cold burner to cool.

When the mixture has cooled to slightly above room temperature, pour it into a mixing bowl or the bowl of an electric mixer.

Add the powdered sugar and the white sugar. Beat until the mixture is smooth.

Add the eggs, one at a time, beating after each addition.

Mix in the vanilla extract. Make sure it's well combined.

Add the baking soda, cream of tartar, and salt. Mix until everything is thoroughly combined.

Add the flour in half-cup increments, mixing after each addition. You don't have to be precise—just divide your flour into roughly 4 parts. *(One very important reason for adding the flour in increments is so that the whole mountain of flour won't sit there on*

top of your bowl and erupt like a volcano all over your kitchen when you try to combine it with all the other ingredients.)

Once the dough has been thoroughly mixed, prepare your cookie sheets by spraying them with Pam or another nonstick cooking spray. Alternatively, you can line them with parchment paper.

Place a half-cup of white sugar in a shallow bowl.

Roll one-inch cookie dough balls with your fingers. *(You can also use a 2-teaspoon scooper to form the dough balls.)*

Dip the dough balls in the bowl with the sugar and roll them around until they're coated.

Hannah's 1st Note: Work with only two or three cookie dough balls at a time. If you put more than that in the sugar at a time, they may stick together.

Place the dough balls on the cookie sheet, 12 dough balls to a standard-size sheet.

Flatten the dough balls with the back of a metal spatula. This will make them bake evenly. If you leave them on the cookie sheet as dough balls, they will flatten out during the baking process, but the insides will be chewy instead of melt-in-your-mouth crispy.

Bake the Butterscotch Sugar Cookies at 325 degrees for 13 to 15 minutes. *(Mine took 14 minutes.)*

Yield: approximately 5 to 7 dozen chewy Butterscotch Sugar Cookies.

Lisa's Note: Herb says these cookies are like potato chips. You can't eat just one. They also hold up really well if you stick several in around the sides of a dish of vanilla or chocolate ice cream.

Chapter
Seventeen

Hannah had thought it was impossible, but the afternoon had flown by fast. When Michelle had arrived, they'd baked the rest of the Butterscotch Cookie Dough, had a quick cup of coffee, and baked some more. By the time they finished, they had over thirty dozen cookies to take to The Cookie Jar in the morning.

They were sitting on the couch, drinking tall glasses of lemonade when Hannah's phone rang and she reached out to answer it. "Hello. This is Hannah."

"Hi, Cookie."

It was Ross and Hannah began to smile. "Hi, Ross."

"I just called to tell you that I'm leaving the station now. I'll see you in about thirty minutes, okay?"

Hannah glanced at the clock on the end table. It was only four in the afternoon. "That's better than okay. That's wonderful."

Hannah knew that if she were a cat, she'd be purring as she said good-bye and hung up the phone. "Ross is on his way," she told Michelle.

"Good. Is there anything we have to do before he gets here?"

"Yes. I have to put on my dark green sweater and brush my hair."

"That's not all," Michelle said.

"What do you mean?"

"You have to wash your face. You've got flour on your nose and there might be some on your left cheek, too."

It took only ten minutes to wash her face, get into her favorite sweater, and brush her hair. When Hannah returned to the living room, Michelle had switched on the television set and she was watching the Food Channel.

"Nothing about Chef Duquesne yet," she reported.

"Good." Hannah picked up her lemonade and took a sip.

"I'm going to run in and take a quick shower," Michelle said, getting up and heading toward and guest bathroom.

Hannah did her best to relax. She felt a bit like a teenager going on her first date, experiencing a heady combination of nervous energy and extreme anticipation.

The next twenty minutes passed with the speed of a giant tortoise on tranquilizers, but at last there was a knock at her door. Moishe leaped down from her lap, Hannah leaped up from the couch, and both of them ran a foot race to the door. Hannah pulled it open, there were benefits in having opposable thumbs, and threw herself into Ross's arms. But it wasn't Ross!

"Mike!" she gasped. "Uh . . . sorry about that. I thought you were Ross. He's due here any minute."

"He's right behind me. He parked in your extra spot. I just left my cruiser at the side of the road." He gave her a big grin. "And you don't have to be sorry about hugging me. It's not like you haven't done it before."

For a moment, Hannah was speechless. "But . . ." she began to sputter.

"I know. You're engaged. Don't worry, Hannah. I'll never tell."

"You'll never tell what?" Ross asked, coming up the outside staircase.

Mike laughed. "I'll never tell you how Hannah thought I was you and threw herself in my arms."

"That's understandable," Ross said, arriving at the landing and giving Hannah a hug. "We look so much alike."

Hannah looked from Ross to Mike and then back to Ross again. Ross was a full four inches shorter than Mike, he had dark hair compared to Mike's reddish blond, and he had a sophisticated, man-of-the-world look about him, while Mike looked rugged and capable of stopping a fleeing felon by tackling him and rendering him helpless in two seconds flat.

"You're . . . you're kidding . . . right?"

"Yes, Cookie. I'm kidding." Ross turned to grin at Mike. "I guess we should have called her and told her that both of us were coming."

"That would have been slightly helpful," Hannah said, recovering her equilibrium. "It's just that I didn't expect to see Mike." She turned to him. "I thought you'd still be out in Sally's kitchen."

Mike shook his head. "We cleared it hours ago and the contestants are practicing. The crime scene techs got there fast, and so did the photographer. I told them it was top priority and they were in and out in less than two hours."

"Because of the Food Channel competition?"

"That's part of it."

Moishe made a soft sound of protest and Hannah looked down at him. He was sitting on his haunches staring up at Ross.

"Will you pick up Moishe, Ross. He's looking up at you pathetically."

Ross smiled and picked him up, scratching him behind the ears. "Come on, Mike," he said as he stepped inside the condo. "You've already been greeted a little too well by Hannah."

Mike laughed and followed Ross and Hannah inside. Hannah motioned toward the couch and asked them, "Drinks, anyone?"

"I'll take a beer if you've got it, but I can only have one. I have an active investigation going, and that means I'm on call."

"I'll join you in that one beer," Ross told Mike. Then he turned to Hannah. "Do you need me to run out for more beer?"

"No, I've got a twelve-pack in the refrigerator from the last dinner party. Cold Spring Export, if that's okay."

"My favorite," Mike said, which Hannah already knew.

"Fine with me," Ross agreed, heading for the kitchen. "Sit down, Hannah. I'll get the beer and pour you a glass of wine. You probably need to relax after the day you've had."

Hannah was about to tell Ross that she was relaxed, now that he was here, but she thought better of it. Perhaps it wouldn't be right to say that in front of Mike. Instead, she gave Ross a smile and said, "Thank you. That would be nice."

"Your guy is a real champ," Mike said, after Ross had left the living room. "Did you notice that big backpack he was wearing?"

"Yes. But why does that backpack make him a champ?"

"Because he's letting me watch all the footage they shot in New York and here in Lake Eden."

"So you can get a good grasp on the personality of the victim and how he interacted with everyone in the competition?"

Mike gave her a thumbs-up. "I knew you'd catch on right away. Do you mind if we watch it right here, Hannah?"

"I don't mind at all!" Hannah said quickly, since that gave her the opportunity to watch it, too.

"I figured that three pairs of eyes would be better than two."

"How about four pairs of eyes?" Hannah asked.

Mike raised his eyebrows. "You mean . . . Moishe?"

"No." Hannah laughed. "I mean Michelle. She's here, but she just went in to take a quick shower."

Mike looked thoughtful. "Maybe I should call Lonnie and tell him to get over here. We could all watch together."

"Sure. Lonnie's always welcome." Hannah gave a little laugh. "And since we seem to be having a footage-watching party, maybe you should call Norman, too."

"Great idea! I'll do that right away. Norman can stop at Bertanelli's on his way out here and pick up more pizza. P.K. is only bringing two. And Lonnie can stop at the Quick Stop and get some other snacks we can eat while we're watching."

Ross came back into the living room just in time to hear Mike's comment. "Do you want me to call P.K.? He might have some insights about Chef Duquesne. He was with me when I did all the interviews and he can tell you if he noticed anything unusual last night."

"How many people does that make?" Ross asked Hannah.

"You, me, Mike, Michelle, P.K., Lonnie, and Norman. That's seven . . . unless we count Moishe."

"I'd better go out to the car and get my flat screen monitor and my laptop. My flat screen is twice the size of your television set. I can rig it to play on all three screens, and then everyone will have a good view of one screen or another."

Mike jumped up. "Great idea. I'll help you carry things."

Hannah sat next to Ross on the couch, her steno notebook open in her lap and her pen in her hand.

"You're taking notes?" Ross asked her.

"Of course she is," Mike responded before Hannah could open her mouth. "Not only did Michelle find the victim, Chef Duquesne was actually nice to Hannah in the competition. That means she feels honor-bound to solve his murder."

Hannah locked eyes with Mike. Instead of the glare she expected, he looked amused. "You're right," Hannah said, giving him a little nod of acknowledgment. "I'll be happy to share my notes with you, if you want me to."

This comment earned a frown from Mike. "Thanks, but I'm taking my own notes. Since we're watching the same footage, I doubt that you'll catch anything that I miss. I'm used to analyzing evidence like this. You're not."

"Very true. You're the expert and I'm not." Hannah gave him a sweet and what she hoped was guileless smile.

"Knock it off, you two," Ross said, tightening his arm around Hannah's shoulders. "This isn't a competition. It's a murder investigation, and all that matters is that someone catches Chef Duquesne's killer."

"You're right," Mike said, surprising Hannah. "Sorry, Hannah. I didn't mean to get testy with you. Of course I'd like to go over your notes with you."

Hannah just smiled. Perhaps Mike's sudden change of heart had something to do with Ross's intervention, but she highly doubted that was the case. He'd probably realized that she might spot something he'd miss because she was familiar with the other contestants, their assistants, and the judges. And he wanted to know exactly what clues she might discover because of that knowledge. The Food Channel *Dessert Chef Competition* wasn't the only competition she had entered. Mike regarded her as his rival in the race to solve Chef Alain Duquesne's murder case.

"They loved the Butterscotch Sugar Cookies," Michelle said as soon as the door had closed behind Ross, Mike, Norman, Lonnie, and P.K.

"I know. Did you have one?"

"One?" Michelle gave a rueful laugh. "I had four, and my jeans are going to know it when I try to zip them up tomorrow morning."

"Stretch out on your back on the bed to do it," Hannah advised.

"Does that work?"

"Like a charm. I've been using that trick for years when I put on extra weight." Hannah switched gears. "Let's take a second to talk about the competition tomorrow night. We're serving the cookies, that's a given, but I thought the flavor of the White Chocolate Mocha was a little sweet with the butterscotch. What did you think?"

"I think you're right, but I have a solution. We can serve the same champagne cocktail that Sally served at Mother and Doc's wedding reception. That wasn't as sweet as the White Chocolate Mocha. But if we do that, we'll lose the benefit of coffee in the drink."

Hannah thought about that for a moment. "That's true, but we can serve the coffee *after* the champagne cocktail."

"Great idea!" Michelle said, smiling at Hannah.

"Thanks." Hannah yawned and rubbed her eyes. "I don't know about you, but I'm really tired. It's almost midnight and we have to be at the Lake Eden Inn at six-thirty to practice."

"That's more sleep than I usually get, but it's probably a good thing. Tomorrow's going to be a busy day with the practice so early in the morning and the competition at night. I'm almost sorry the producers gave us an extra practice session to make up for the one we didn't get to finish."

"Me too. I'm so tired, I can't keep my eyes open any longer." Hannah got to her feet. "I'll see you in the morning, Michelle. I'm too tired to talk about the footage tonight, but let's compare notes tomorrow. Ross isn't stopping by on his way to work in the morning, so all we have to do is make a pot of coffee and drink it on our way out to the lake. We can eat breakfast at the Corner Tavern on our way back from the practice session, and we'll talk about the footage then."

"That sounds good to me." Michelle looked around the living room as they headed for the hallway and the bedrooms beyond. "Where's Moishe? He didn't get out, did he?"

"No. He's on his pillow sleeping. He conked out about halfway through the footage."

"You mean when the last piece of pizza was gone?"

"That's exactly when. And I don't think that was a coincidence."

The two sisters parted ways near the end of the hallway. Michelle turned right to go into the guest room, and Hannah went straight into the master bedroom. Just as she'd told her sister, Moishe was stretched out on a feather pillow, but it wasn't *his* feather pillow.

"Not again," Hannah sighed, but she was smiling. She had bought a second expensive feather pillow, the exact duplicate of her pillow, to keep Moishe from stealing hers in the middle of the night. The two pillows were interchangeable, but he always stole her pillow anyway.

"Fine. I'll get yours later," she said, heading off to the master bath to take her shower before she went to bed, so she wouldn't have to shower in the morning.

Ten minutes later, Hannah had toweled dry and she was dressed in her oldest pair of flannel pajamas. They had been marked down to five dollars at CostMart and after one glance, Hannah had immediately known why. The pajamas sported the most hideous tartan design in bright yellow, screaming pink, and neon green that Hannah had ever seen.

"Note to self," she said after one glance in the mirror. "Do not take tartan pajamas on your honeymoon."

When Hannah reentered her bedroom, Moishe was still in the same, cat-run-over-by-a-snowplow position on her pillow. He was snoring softly, making little beeping noises that she found endearing. She watched him for a moment until her eyelids started to feel very heavy and then she carefully removed his pillow from his side of the bed, pulled hers, complete with snoring, sleeping cat on top, over to his side of the bed. She plunked his pillow down on her side, and crawled in under the covers. She was happy, she was in love, and she knew what she was baking for the competition tomorrow. Life was good in Lake Eden, Minnesota . . . if you didn't count the latest murder.

WHITE CHOCOLATE MOCHA

5 and ½ ounces white chocolate chips
   *(Michelle used half of an eleven-ounce net
   weight bag of Ghirardelli Classic White)*
½ teaspoon vanilla extract
2 and ½ cups whole milk
¼ teaspoon cinnamon
1 Tablespoon instant coffee granules **(Michelle
   used Taster's Choice)**
Sweetened whipped cream to garnish
Freshly grated nutmeg to sprinkle on top

Place the white chocolate chips, along with the vanilla extract, in a microwave-safe bowl on the counter.

Heat the milk and the cinnamon in a saucepan on the stove at MEDIUM LOW heat, stirring constantly, until it begins to steam and bubbles form around the edges of the saucepan. DO NOT LET IT BOIL!

Sprinkle the 1 Tablespoon of instant coffee granules over the top of the heated milk and stir them in. Make sure they are dissolved.

Pour the not-quite-boiling mixture over the white chocolate chips in the bowl. Stir once, and then cover it with a clean dish towel, a lid that'll fit it, or a piece

of heavy-duty foil tucked in around the edges of the bowl.

Let the bowl sit on the counter for 5 minutes.

Take off whatever you used for a lid and whisk briskly until the chips are melted and the mixture is smooth and creamy.

Hannah's 1st Note: If the chips haven't entirely melted, you can stick the bowl in the microwave and heat the contents on HIGH for 1 minute. Let it sit in the microwave for one more minute and then take out the bowl and attempt to stir it smooth. If that doesn't do it, heat it again for 30-second intervals followed by 30-second standing times, until you can stir it smooth.

Pour the White Chocolate Mocha into mugs and top with sweetened whipped cream sprinkled with freshly grated nutmeg.

Hannah's 2nd Note: If you like, you can serve this with a cinnamon stick in each mug for stirring. If you don't feel like making sweetened whipped cream, you can simply drop a handful of miniature marshmallows on top of each serving.

Michelle's Note: It was hot under the lights at the Food Channel competition so I didn't have any

trouble getting the white chocolate chips to melt, but Lisa told me that if she makes White Chocolate Mocha at home, she usually puts the white chocolate chips in her food processor and uses the steel blade to chop them up before she pours on the almost-boiling milk and coffee mixture. This takes less whisking than if you leave the chips whole.

Chapter Eighteen

"Perfect," Hannah said as they left Sally's kitchen and locked the door behind them. "We had plenty of time to do everything, Michelle."

"I know. It was a lot easier than making all those long ropes of cookie dough and combining them into rolls. And I think the cookies showcase better the way we're doing it now."

"This way, Michelle." Hannah guided her around the corner and knocked on Sally's office door. "I want to see if Sally's in yet."

The door opened immediately, almost as if Sally had been waiting for them to stop by, and there was a smile on Sally's face as she motioned them inside.

"I knew you'd stop by," she said, pouring each of them a cup of coffee from the pot she kept on a stand under the picture window that overlooked the kitchen. "You're doing it again, aren't you?"

Hannah nodded, but Michelle looked puzzled.

"Doing what?" Michelle asked Sally.

"Investigating," Hannah answered her sister. "Sally knows that I can't be hands-off when one of us is involved."

"You can forget about the *one of us* part," Sally told Hannah. "All you had to say is that you can't be hands-off."

"You're right," Hannah admitted. "We really need to figure out who killed him."

"Yes, and the sooner, the better," Sally agreed. "Every single one of my busboys is leery about going into the cooler. I watched them last night and no one wanted to be the first one in there."

"What did you do?" Michelle asked.

"I marched in the kitchen and went into the cooler. That shamed them into it, but I have to admit that it was kind of creepy just knowing that Chef Duquesne had been murdered in there. Then I had them bring me buckets of hot water and I scrubbed the floor with bleach."

Michelle shuddered. "You're a brave woman, Sally. I don't know if I could have gone in there again, especially alone."

"I just kept repeating what my father used to say when my mother would say she'd seen a ghost. He'd tell her, *The dead can't hurt the living*."

"And that helped you?" Hannah asked.

"Not really, but it didn't help my mother, either. I just kept telling myself that the killer wouldn't come back to the cooler to commit another murder with all the busboys and waiters standing around in the kitchen watching me." Sally paused and took a sip of her own coffee. "Anyway, you probably want to know my impressions of the judges and the contestants, and whether I saw anything pertaining to Chef Duquesne that I thought was unusual . . . right?"

"Exactly right!" Hannah praised her, taking her murder book from her purse and flipping to a fresh page. "Go ahead, Sally. Tell me anything that you think might help."

"Okay. I'm sure you already know that no one liked Chef Duquesne. The contestants thought he was overly critical and nasty when he commented on their entries. He did have an eye for the pretty women, though. One of my maids told me that he tried to get her to dry his back after a shower."

"When was that?" Michelle asked her.

"In the afternoon on the day he arrived. He called down for more towels and Rita went up to deliver them. She's the head of my housekeeping staff, and I asked her to take care of all requests from the contestants, their assistants, and the judges."

"And she's experienced at dealing with guests you think might cause problems?"

"Oh, yes. Rita's been with us from the beginning. She worked for us when we lived in the Cities and we brought her with us when we opened our inn."

Hannah sighed as she jotted a note. "We've heard that Chef Duquesne was a . . . womanizer. How about you, Sally? Did you see any behavior that could have been compromising?"

"I always see things that could be compromising. Dick and I run a hotel. Sometimes those things aren't really compromising and sometimes they are, but part of our job is to watch out for trouble and to keep our guests safe. Let's be a little clearer on this, Hannah. What would *you* call compromising?"

Hannah thought about that for a moment. "Let me put it this way . . . did you see any women leaving Chef Duquesne's room in the morning before anyone else got up?"

"No, nothing like that. The only women who went into his room left a lot earlier than that!"

"Who? And when?" Hannah asked, her pen poised over the page.

"Brooke Jackman. Rita saw her go into his room and come out less than ten minutes later. She tried to smile when she saw Rita in the hall, but Rita could tell she'd been crying."

"Anyone else?" Michelle asked.

"Well . . . there was a woman in the bar with him after the competition was over. They sat at a table, drinking."

"Who was it?"

"I don't know. I didn't recognize her. She wasn't a guest

in the hotel. I know that. And she wasn't part of a contestant team, either. As a matter of fact, she had her coat with her, a nice dark green wool with a fur collar. It was draped over the back of her chair. That tells me she came in for the competition and she planned to leave to go back home."

"What did she look like?" Michelle asked.

"She was a good-looking woman with brown hair and I'd say she was in her late forties or early fifties. She wasn't wearing much makeup, or if she was, it was very subtly done. The only thing I really noticed about her was the lovely double strand of multicolored pearls that she had around her neck. They were gorgeous against her white sweater."

Hannah wrote a note. "Thanks, Sally. That gives us something to go on. Did Chef Duquesne look like he was romantically interested in her?"

"He didn't look that way at first, but after a couple of drinks, he did."

"Was she drinking, too?"

"Nothing alcoholic. She ordered hot pink lemonade. We serve it in a mug with grated nutmeg on top. He caught me after they'd ordered their second round, slipped me a twenty, and asked me to put vodka in her lemonade."

Hannah's eyebrows shot up and Sally laughed. "Oh, don't worry. I didn't. If the lady had wanted vodka, she was the type who would have ordered it herself."

"Did you tell him you wouldn't do it?" Michelle asked.

"No. We try to avoid conflict in the bar. I just smiled, thanked him very much for the tip, and put the money in the cash register. Later on, Dick deducted the twenty dollars from his bar bill."

"Did the woman go up to Chef Duquesne's room with him?"

"Yes, after about an hour or two in the bar. It was a repeat of what happened with Brooke. Rita said that the woman came out of his room less than twenty minutes later."

"And she was crying, too?"

"No, but Rita said that she looked so upset, she practically ran down the hall to the elevator."

"I think we can all guess why the lady was upset when she left," Michelle said. "If Chef Duquesne thought she'd been drinking vodka in her lemonade, he might have assumed that she was smashed. And then, when he got her up to his room, he probably tried to hit on her."

"And it didn't work the way he thought it would because she was stone cold sober," Hannah added.

"I'm sure you're right," Sally agreed.

"What time did the woman leave his room?" Hannah asked.

"Eleven forty-five. I know because Rita said she had fifteen minutes of her shift to go and she gets off at midnight."

"Do you have a security camera in the bar?" Hannah asked, hoping to see an image of the woman.

"We've got one, but it's a dummy. People think it's real, but it's not. It's just like the one in the kitchen."

Hannah was surprised. "The one in the kitchen is a dummy, too?"

"Yes. The only camera that's fully operational is the one by the front door. That's why I knew that Rita was right about the time that the woman left."

"You've got her on camera?" Hannah felt her spirits rise.

"Yes, but only from the back. The camera catches them when they come in, not when they leave. And she had a scarf on her head. There's no way anyone could recognize her from that."

"What color was the scarf?" Michelle asked.

"I don't know. The surveillance camera shows everything in black and white and it's a pretty grainy picture. We're upgrading and putting in more cameras, but that won't happen until next month."

"So you didn't notice her scarf when her coat was on the chair in the bar?"

"Actually . . ." Sally looked very excited. "I did! I just forgot all about it. It was dark red and dark green in a checkerboard design. I remember thinking that I should get something like that to wear during the Christmas season."

"That's helpful, Sally," Hannah told her. "Thanks for the description. Ross made a copy of the footage from the competition and panned the audience a couple of times for their reactions to the judging. That footage is in color, and Michelle and I will fast-forward through it this afternoon to see if he caught the woman on camera. Brown hair, white sweater, and multicolored pearls . . . right?"

"And a dark green coat with a fur collar and the scarf Sally described," Michelle reminded her. "Maybe she hung up her coat when she came in, but there's always the possibility that she didn't."

"All right, girls. You've got everything I know." Sally got up from her chair. "Call if you need anything else, okay? And good luck in the competition tonight!"

"I think we'll be all right in the competition tonight," Hannah said, taking the on-ramp to the highway.

"So do I. And if those cookies we baked weren't in the back of the truck, I'd eat one right now. My stomach was growling like crazy when we were baking them. I had all I could do not to grab one when we packed them up to take home. The only thing that stopped me was I knew that if I had one, I'd eat two or three. And that would spoil my breakfast. We're still stopping at the Corner Tavern, aren't we?"

"Yes, we're stopping," Hannah told her, not mentioning that she'd sneaked two of the Butterscotch Sugar Cookies herself when Michelle wasn't looking.

"They look crowded," Michelle commented as they took the exit and pulled into the parking lot of the Corner Tavern.

"Yes, but it's a big place. They can probably find room for us."

"Look at that!" Michelle pointed to the parking spot in the front of the lot, very close to the entrance.

"I see it." Hannah circled and pulled into the convenient parking space. "Come on, Michelle. It was a late night last night, and tonight will be a long night, too. I need coffee."

"And protein," Michelle added. "If we can't get a table right away, let's see if we can order coffee and a side of bacon while we're waiting."

"Hi, Hannah!" Nona Prentiss greeted them after they'd hung their coats in the cloak room and entered the restaurant through the inner door. She was the owner's oldest daughter and, although she didn't work in her father's business on a regular basis, Nona always filled in at the hostess station when they were shorthanded.

"Hi, Nona," Hannah greeted her. "It's good to see you. You're really crowded this morning."

"Yes, we are. The hostess is taking a waitress shift and Dad called me in to help. He figures that everyone will come in for breakfast so they can hear the latest gossip about the murder."

"You're probably right," Hannah agreed, reaching out to pet Albert, the stuffed grizzly bear that was mounted right next to the hostess station. Albert had gotten a makeover from the taxidermist, and now he was holding up well. Everyone in Lake Eden had contributed money for the endeavor, since most of them had petted Albert when they were kids and they wanted their children to enjoy him as much as they had.

"Are you okay, Michelle?" Nona asked her. "I heard you were the one who found him in Sally's cooler."

"I'm okay," Michelle told her. "Right now, Hannah and I are just concentrating on getting ready for the competition tonight."

"You really did great at the last one! Everybody in here thinks you'll win again tonight. You two make a great team."

"Thank you. That's probably because Hannah taught me

how to bake and we've been baking together for fun for years."

Nona picked up two menus and smiled at them. "Just follow me. I'll show you to your table."

Hannah was surprised. "You have room for us in there?" she asked, gesturing toward the crowded interior of the restaurant.

"Of course we do. I'll take you in the back way so that people won't stop you and ask questions. Dad always saves one private table in the back, just in case someone really important comes in. And you two are the most important people in Lake Eden right now. Both of you are celebrities."

Hannah was puzzled as they followed Nona to a table. Were they celebrities because they'd done so well in the Food Channel competition? Or were they celebrities because Michelle had found another victim? Her inquiring mind wanted to know, but her cautious mind told her to leave well enough alone. It didn't really matter at the moment. Right now she was more concerned about drinking coffee and eating a great breakfast.

Nona led them to a secluded table shielded by an island of planters filled with large green plants that Hannah didn't recognize. "What kind of plants are those?" she asked Nona, pointing toward the lush, broad-leafed greenery.

"Plastic plants," Nona said with a perfectly deadpan expression.

Hannah and Michelle exchanged glances and then both of them burst into laughter.

"Dad was right," Nona said with a grin. "It gets to everyone the first time they hear it. I think they're supposed to be some kind of tropical thing that's really exotic and doesn't grow in Minnesota, but they *are* pretty special. If they get dirty, we just pull them out of the planter and put them in the industrial dishwasher. They come out as clean as a whistle and Dad just sticks them right back in the planter again."

"That sounds like the sort of plant I should have," Hannah said. "Lisa says that instead of a green thumb, I have the thumb of death when it comes to indoor plants."

"It's true," Michelle spoke up. "When I come to stay with Hannah, there's a dead philodendron on the ledge of the guest room window."

"That's not entirely true, Michelle," Hannah corrected her. "A couple of times, they've been dead African violets."

Nona was laughing as she walked back to her hostess station. Michelle waited until she was out of earshot and then she leaned toward Hannah. "I think I'd better call Lisa at The Cookie Jar and tell her to get ready for a big crowd. From what Nona said, everybody's going to want to know what happened when I found the body."

"You'll have to tell her about it so she can make up her story."

"Been there, done that. I called her this morning when you were getting dressed. Lisa's ready with the story, but she may not be ready for the size of the crowd."

After Lisa had been warned, and they'd ordered from the waitress, Hannah and Michelle took a moment to relax and look around the room. It was an oasis, peaceful and calm. But it seemed like only seconds had gone by, when their waitress came bustling back with their breakfast.

"That looks wonderful," Hannah said as their smiling waitress set her omelet down on the table in front of her.

"Our omelets are the best," the waitress told her, delivering Michelle's plate. "Your side of crispy bacon is coming right up, and I'll bring more coffee out in a bit. Is there anything else I can get for you right now?"

"No thanks. I think we're all set," Hannah told her.

"I guess I'm wrong," Michelle said when the waitress had gone back to the kitchen to get their bacon.

"About what?"

"About that local celebrity thing. I don't think she recognized you."

"That's a relief in a way. At least I don't have to wear a

smile when I don't feel like smiling, I don't have to put on gobs of makeup and have my hair done every day, and I don't have to think about everything I say before I say it just in case someone quotes me. I don't know how real celebrities handle being in the spotlight all the time. There's always someone taking photos and asking them for autographs. I'm just glad no one asks me to pose for pictures or sign anything."

"But you're going to sign the check, aren't you?" Michelle asked.

Hannah burst into laughter. "I would, but I brought cash."

That made Michelle laugh, too, and that was when the waitress came bustling back with their bacon. "Here you go," she said, setting the plate of bacon in the center of the table, and then refilling their coffee cups. "I really hate to disturb you at breakfast, but my mother made me promise that I'd get a photo with you two if you ever came in here for breakfast. And . . . she was kind of hoping for an autograph."

Hannah exchanged glances with Michelle, and she smiled her best smile. "If you can catch one of the other waitresses to take the photo, you can be in the picture, too."

"Thanks!" The waitress waved at another waitress who was passing close to their table. "Sherry? Can you come here a second?"

Hannah and Michelle listened as their waitress explained what she needed. Sherry agreed and they all posed together. The photos didn't take long, even though Sherry requested another photo for herself. Then Hannah and Michelle signed blank order forms for both waitresses and their mothers.

"Thanks so much," their waitress said, placing the autograph in her apron pocket. "My mother's going to love this. And wait until I tell her that you two are so nice, not anything like the contestant with Mayor Bascomb!"

Hannah and Michelle exchanged meaningful glances, and Michelle responded immediately. "Oh? When was that?"

"The night after the last competition. The mayor was

here with one of the competitors, and she turned me down flat when I asked for an autograph."

"Was it the blonde?" Hannah asked.

"Yes. She was really mad about something, and the mayor was trying to calm her down. It must have worked, because she started smiling when he ordered a bottle of champagne. All they had was one glass, and then they left."

Their waitress rushed off after thanking them again. Hannah and Michelle looked at each other and both sisters smiled, bemused, as they reached for their coffee cups at exactly the same time. Then Hannah looked down and her face assumed a more serious, *Let's get down to business* expression, as she reached into her saddlebag-size purse and drew out what Michelle and Andrea had referred to as her *murder book*. "Did you take notes on that footage we saw last night?" she asked.

"Of course. I've got them right here." Michelle picked up her cell phone and tapped it several times.

"You put them in a voice mail to yourself?" Hannah guessed.

"No, I used the note function and typed them in."

One by one, the two sisters went through their notes. Hannah had caught some things that Michelle hadn't noticed, and Michelle had noted several things that Hannah hadn't spotted.

"Okay," Hannah said, flipping to a clean page in her steno notebook. "Now that we've got a complete list, let's talk about what we've learned about the contestants and judges that we've met."

"The other judges didn't seem to like Chef Duquesne very much," Michelle said. "I saw LaVonna Brach roll her eyes several times when he said mean things about Brooke's strawberry mousse with the marshmallow sauce in New York. And Helene Stone leaned as far away from him as she could when he criticized the contestants, here in Lake Eden."

Hannah thought about that for a moment, and then her

mind offered a possible explanation. "Did it seem to you as if Judge Stone wanted to get out of camera range so that no one would associate her in any way with Chef Duquesne?"

"Yes. You could be right, Hannah. That could have been what she was trying to do. I was watching and it was subtle. There was nothing overt, not really. It's possible that it was completely unconscious on her part."

"I suppose that could be true," Hannah agreed. "I noticed something else about her, too. When Chef Duquesne handed her the coffee cup he'd refilled for her, she put her hand around the cup part, even though it must have been hot. I remember thinking that she must have preferred the discomfort over the possibility of touching his fingers on the handle."

"You're right! She *did* do that, and her reaction was a bit excessive. I wonder if something happened in the hotel in New York."

Hannah was puzzled. "What do you mean?"

"Remember when I ran back up to the room to get my copy of the recipe?"

"Yes. You went right after we ordered coffee and you said not to worry, that you'd be back in a flash."

"I was, but I did have to wait a few seconds for the elevator. I know because the elevator was up on the fourteenth floor. The elevator came straight down without stopping until it got to the eighth floor to pick me up. When the doors opened, Chef Duquesne and Helene Stone were inside."

"Is that important?"

"I'm not sure, but it's interesting because Helene Stone's room was on the sixth floor."

"How do you know that?"

"She was in line in front of us when we checked out of the hotel. I heard her give her room number."

"You're sure it was the sixth floor?"

"Positive. She had 626, and we had 826. I remember thinking that she was directly below us, two floors down."

"Did Chef Duquesne and Helene Stone do anything on

the elevator that gave you the impression they'd been together on his floor?"

"No. They were both staring directly ahead at the numbers on the display over the doors as the elevator went down
to the lobby. Neither one of them said a word."

"Did you get the impression that they were upset with
each other?"

"That's just it. I got absolutely no impression at all. They
didn't say anything and they didn't do anything. They just
stared up at the numbers as the elevator passed the floors
until we stopped at the lobby and we all got off."

"Do you think they recognized you as part of our team in
the competition?"

"I don't know. I wasn't dressed up or anything. And I
wasn't carrying anything that might have let them know that
I was your assistant, like an apron or a tote bag with our logo
on it. I was just in my usual jeans and sweatshirt and I could
have been anybody staying at the hotel."

Hannah flipped the page and jotted it down on a fresh
page. "It could mean nothing. Perhaps Helene Stone just
went up to his floor to ask him if he wanted to have breakfast with her."

"I don't think so. They didn't come into the restaurant
while we were there."

"Okay. Maybe it wasn't breakfast. They could have had
other business to discuss."

"That's possible, I guess. Do you want to hear what else I
discovered while I was watching the tapes?"

"Of course I do."

"One of the cameras panned the audience and caught
Mayor Bascomb looking very upset. It was when Chef Duquesne said Gloria Berkeley's cakes were ordinary."

"I saw that. Mayor Bascomb looked very perturbed. It
made me wonder whether our esteemed city leader had been
at it again."

Michelle shrugged. "Could be. I wouldn't put it past him. He's the type of husband that Stephanie can keep in line for a while, but the monetary pain of appeasing her with a new wardrobe and expensive jewelry fade into oblivion when he meets someone new and exciting."

"Nicely put!" Hannah thought about it for a moment. "I wonder if Gloria really *is* someone new. They hooked up pretty fast, considering that she was only here for two days. He might have known Gloria before she came here to Lake Eden for the competition."

"I guess that's possible. Judging from his past escapades, Gloria's exactly the type of woman he likes."

Hannah chuckled. "You mean a gorgeous blonde?"

"Exactly."

"And this one is also sneaky and underhanded," Hannah added.

"Exactly. Now all we have to do is figure out if we're right."

"That's easy," Michelle said with a smile. "We'll ask Mother and Andrea. They might not know how, but I bet they could find out. Andrea's got contacts and she's an expert at getting people to talk. And Mother can dig for dirt better than anyone else we know."

"That's not exactly a compliment," Hannah told her.

"Yes it is, but only if you want the whole truth."

"What else do you have?" Hannah asked her.

"Not much. The footage only gave me two new clues, but one of them may be important because of what our waitress said about Gloria and Mayor Bascomb. Do you remember when Rodney mentioned that Chef Duquesne tried to pick Gloria up in the bar of the hotel in New York?"

"Yes." Hannah thought about the ramifications of that for a moment. "I think I know where you're going. You're wondering if Gloria mentioned it to Mayor Bascomb. And *that's* the reason he looked so upset in the footage we saw."

"That's right. We already know that Mayor Bascomb

doesn't like someone else zeroing in on any woman he wants for himself."

"Let's take a break on that note, Michelle, and eat before our breakfast gets any colder," Hannah said, diving into her omelet. Michelle agreed, and for several minutes, the only sounds heard were small sighs of pure delight.

"This omelet is really good," Hannah commented after several bites. "I love the way the cheese melted all the way through and the bacon is nice and crispy."

"Mine is great too," Michelle agreed. "Be careful that you don't fill up on your omelet, though."

"Why? I didn't order anything else."

"I know you didn't, but you've still got a lot more to eat."

Hannah was puzzled. "What are you talking about, Michelle?"

"You just signed two autographs and posed for pictures with the waitresses. And you said that since you weren't a real celebrity, no one was going to ask you to pose for photos or sign autographs. That means I get to make you eat your words!"

Hannah laughed. "Can I at least have dessert first? They've got really great Chocolate Coffee Cake here."

"Okay, if I can have some." Michelle waved at their waitress. "But once we finish dessert and more coffee, you have to eat every consonant and vowel, and maybe even the punctuation."

"Okay, as long as it's not semicolons. I really don't like colons and semicolons."

"No colons, no semicolons," Michelle promised.

"Then it's a deal," Hannah agreed. "I just hope my words taste as good as the Chocolate Coffee Cake we're going to have first."

CHOCOLATE COFFEE CAKE

Preheat oven to 350 degrees F., rack in the middle position.

The Cake Batter:

> 1 cup salted butter, softened *(2 sticks, 8 ounces, ½ pound)*
> 1 and ¾ cups white *(granulated)* sugar
> 1 teaspoon salt
> 2 teaspoons vanilla extract
> 1 and ½ teaspoons baking powder
> 6 eggs
> 3 cups flour *(pack it down in the cup when you measure it)*

The Filling:

> 2 cups semi-sweet *(that's the regular kind)* chocolate chips *(I used a 12-ounce by weight bag of Nestle)*
> 2 teaspoons vanilla extract
> 1 ounce *(¼ stick)* salted butter
> ½ teaspoon cinnamon
> ¼ teaspoon nutmeg *(freshly grated is best)*

The Crumb Topping:

> ½ cup brown sugar *(tightly packed)*
> ⅓ cup all-purpose flour *(pack it down in the cup when you measure it)*
> ¼ cup salted butter, softened *(½ stick, 2 ounces, ⅛ pound)*

Spray the inside of a 9-inch by 13-inch rectangular cake pan with Pam or another nonstick cooking spray. You can also use nonstick <u>baking</u> spray, the kind with flour in it, if you prefer. If you don't have nonstick baking or cooking spray, you can grease the inside of the cake pan with butter and then flour it, but don't forget to knock out the excess flour.

Hannah's 1st Note: When I make this at home, I use my stand mixer for the cake batter. You can also do it by hand, but it takes some muscle.

Mix the cup of softened, salted butter with the white sugar until it's thoroughly blended and is nice and fluffy.

Add the salt, vanilla extract, and baking powder. Mix them in until they're thoroughly incorporated.

Add the eggs one by one, mixing after each addition.

Hannah's 2ⁿᵈ Note: If you add the eggs all at once, it's very difficult to mix them in. If you add them one at a time and mix in each egg after you add it, it's much easier.

Add the flour in one-cup increments, mixing thoroughly after each addition.

Hannah's 3ʳᵈ Note: DO NOT add the flour all at once and then try to mix it in. I did that once and had flour all over my kitchen floor. *(And then Moishe came in for a drink of water and tracked flour all over my condo. This is when I learned that most cats don't like to have their feet washed!)*

Spoon <u>half</u> of the batter in the cake pan and spread it out with a rubber spatula. Leave the rest of the batter in the bowl for later. *(You don't have to measure out exactly half of the dough. Just eyeball it. No one's ever going to complain if you're off by a quarter-cup or so.)*

Once half of the cake batter is in the pan, it's time to make the filling. Use another bowl for this.

Put <u>half</u> of a 12-ounce *(net weight)* bag of semisweet chocolate chips in a microwave-safe bowl. *(I usually use a 2-cup Pyrex measuring cup.)*

Add the 2 teaspoons of vanilla extract and the ounce of salted butter. Heat in the microwave on HIGH for 30 seconds. Let the mixture sit in the microwave for 1 minute, and then take it out and try to stir it smooth. If you can do this, you're done heating the chocolate mixture. If you can't do this, heat the chocolate mixture in 20-second intervals with one-minute standing times, until you can stir it smooth.

Set the chocolate mixture on the counter. Stir in the cinnamon and the nutmeg until they're well-incorporated.

Drizzle the chocolate mixture over the batter in the cake pan.

Sprinkle the rest of the chocolate chips *(approximately one cup)* over the batter as evenly as you can.

Hannah's 4th Note: There is a reason why you don't melt ALL the chips in the bag. It has to do with texture. The whole chips will soften during baking and the melted chips are almost like a chocolate sauce. This means that after your Chocolate Coffee Cake is baked, you'll have something that resembles chocolate sauce enhanced with cinnamon and nutmeg in the center with little soft nuggets of pure chocolate in each serving. It's just yummy!

Give the remaining cake batter another stir and then drop spoonfuls on top of the chocolate. Spread the batter out carefully with the rubber spatula.

Hannah's 5th Note: Don't worry if the cake batter doesn't cover the chocolate completely—the batter on top will fill in as it bakes and the crumb topping that you will make next will cover the rest.

To make the crumb topping, mix the brown sugar and the flour in a small bowl. *(I generally use a fork to do this.)*

Add the softened butter and mix until it's crumbly. *(You can also do this in a food processor with chilled butter and the steel blade.)*

Sprinkle the crumb topping over the pan as evenly as possible.

Bake your Chocolate Coffee Cake at 350 degrees F. for 45 to 60 minutes. To test for doneness, use a cake tester, a thin wooden skewer, or a long toothpick. Insert it one inch from the center of the pan and pull it out again. If it has chocolate on it, that's perfectly okay, but if it also has sticky unbaked dough clinging to it, your cake needs to bake at least another 5 or perhaps 10 minutes.

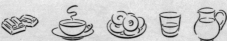

When your cake is done, remove it from the oven and let it cool in the pan on a wire rack.

Michelle's Note: I like this coffee cake slightly warm and I've discovered that if you cut it in square servings, you can reheat it in the microwave and it tastes like fresh-baked. It's really great for breakfast with a cup of strong hot coffee.

 # Chapter Nineteen

Hannah had just pulled into her parking spot in back of The Cookie Jar when her cell phone rang. She took it out of her purse to answer it and was surprised to hear Lisa's voice.

"Where are you?" Lisa asked.

"I'm here. I just pulled into my parking spot in back."

"Okay. Don't bother coming in," Lisa said. "Claire called to say that the wedding dresses she ordered for you came in this morning. She wants you to come over and try them on right away. Your mother and Andrea are already there waiting for you."

"My *mother* is there?"

"Of course she is. You didn't really think you could get away with trying on wedding gowns without your mother, did you?"

"I guess not."

"Go ahead then. It has to be done and you might as well get it over with. Take Michelle with you. They want her, too. Claire has to take her measurements for her bridesmaid dress."

"Are you busy?" Hannah asked her.

"We're packed. Even Stephanie Bascomb is here. In all her glory, of course."

"Stephanie got a new outfit?"

"And how! I heard her tell Becky Summers that she just bought several designer suits from Claire. And she's wearing a huge emerald ring. I told Herb, and he said that our mayor must have really done it this time! Hurry up, Hannah. They're waiting for you."

Hannah sighed in resignation. She had to do it. There was no other choice. "Okay, Lisa. Michelle's with me and she can lead the sacrificial lamb to slaughter."

"What was all *that* about?" Michelle asked when Hannah ended the call and slipped her phone back into her purse.

"Mother and Andrea are waiting for us at Beau Monde. The wedding gowns that Claire ordered came in this morning, and I have to try them on."

"Okay. Let's go then." Michelle opened the passenger door.

"Wait. Do you think I could get out of it if I sneaked into the kitchen and hid in the pantry?"

Michelle shook her head. "Not a chance. Mother would sniff you out. I tried hiding in my closet when I was a kid. Mother found me and spanked me. Just go over to Claire's and do it."

"That was Lisa's advice," Hannah said, accepting her fate as she got out of her cookie truck and shut the door behind her.

Hannah hesitated at the door to Claire's shop. She hated to try on dresses. There was something about standing in a little dressing room, even though Claire's dressing rooms were beautifully decorated and roomier than most, facing your worst figure faults in the mirror, and garbing your body in unfamiliar garments that could make you look more unattractive than you had before you put them on. She was still trying to think of some excuse, any excuse short of death, to save herself from the ordeal when she remembered what Lisa had told her about Stephanie Bascomb's new outfits and where she'd purchased them.

"Come on, Michelle!" Hannah urged her sister, yanking the door open and practically running inside.

Michelle grabbed Hannah's hand. "Hold on a minute. Tell me what changed your mind so fast. Just a second or two ago, you were heading for Claire's shop with the speed of an arthritic garden snail, and now you're acting like you can't wait to get inside."

"Murder changed my mind," Hannah said, leading the way to the inner door that opened into the dress shop itself. "I just remembered something Lisa told me on the phone. She said that Stephanie Bascomb is next door in the coffee shop, wearing an expensive new outfit she got right here from Claire. And Lisa also said that the outfit Stephanie was wearing wasn't the only one she'd bought over here."

"So you're going to see what Stephanie told Claire about the mayor's new affair?"

"That's the plan."

"Then you won't mind trying on wedding gowns?"

"I didn't say that, but I'll trade a half hour of my time, even if it means trying on new clothes, for information that'll help me solve a murder case!"

Five minutes later, after greeting her mother and Andrea, Hannah was sitting on a gold velvet settee, waiting for her torment to start. She'd accepted the offer of a cup of tea that she probably wouldn't drink, and followed Claire to the largest dressing room. Now she was waiting for Claire to return with the selections that had been chosen specifically for her.

Hannah picked up the tea, took a sip, and stared at her archenemy, the tall three-way mirror that showcased her less than perfect figure from many more angles than she wished to view.

"Here we are," Claire called out cheerily, opening the door

and hanging a half-dozen garments on the ornate hooks that protruded from the opposite wall. "I'll be right back."

Hannah gazed at the creation on the nearest hook and groaned softly. It was gorgeous, a fairytale wedding gown that was festooned with tiny pearls and expensive and intricate lace. Hannah had no doubt that it had been featured on the cover of *Vogue* or *Brides* magazine.

"I know," Claire said, catching Hannah's shocked expression as she came back with another armload of gowns. "I told your mother that you couldn't wear that gown, but . . ." Claire paused as Hannah burst into laughter. "What did I say that's so funny?"

"You said you *told* my mother," Hannah repeated. "You know better than that, Claire."

Claire smiled and looked slightly embarrassed. "Yes, I *do* know better. Nobody can tell your mother anything when it comes to fashion."

"Exactly. I'll try it on first. That'll prove to her that you were right."

"Do you need help with all those tiny buttons?" Claire asked, moving the gown to a closer hook.

"Probably, but there's something I'd like you to do for me first."

"What's that?"

"I need you to find my other glass slipper."

Claire burst into laughter. "You're right, Hannah. It *does* look like the gown Cinderella wore. Do you think your mother will admit that this gown is all wrong for you?"

"Never. But she might say that *I'm* all wrong for this gown."

Claire and Hannah shared conspiratorial smiles and then Claire left the dressing room, closing the door behind her. "Just call me when you're ready to button," she called out, her voice muffled through the door. "I'll be right here."

The moment Hannah took the wedding gown off the hanger, she knew she was in trouble. The skirt had so many layers of net between the silk underskirt and the lace and pearl overskirt that it could stand up on the dressing room floor by itself. There didn't seem to be any way she could pick it up and get it over her head by herself unless . . .

Hannah sighed as she eyed the gold velvet settee. She might be able to get into the skirt if she climbed up on the cushions and launched herself into the middle of it. But what if she missed? She might rip this obviously expensive dress.

"No," Hannah said aloud. The gown was probably worth more than she made at The Cookie Jar in a year, and there was no way she could afford to buy it if she damaged it. Actually, she couldn't afford to buy it anyway. She was only trying it on to prove that Delores had been wrong. Would her mother pay for an expensive, damaged wedding gown? Hannah thought about that for a moment. Yes, Delores might pay for it, but Hannah would never hear the end of it. There was no way she could take a risk like that! She hated to ask for help, but there was no other recourse.

"Claire? I can't do this by myself."

"I didn't think you could." Claire came in a split second later with a smile. "You need a dresser for this gown. Just stand over here by the settee and I'll slip it on over your head."

Hannah stood where Claire indicated, and Claire climbed up on the cushion with the dress and dropped it over Hannah's head. The dress whispered down past Hannah's upwardly stretched arms, and the silk lining slithered down into place. "Wow!" Hannah said, as the dress settled around her waist.

"It usually takes two dressers, but I've carried wedding gowns from day one, and I've gotten pretty good at doing it solo."

"You certainly have! How in the world does a bride get into a dress like this?"

"First of all, she doesn't get dressed in her bridal finery until she gets to the dressing room in the church."

"But why?"

"Because you can't get a skirt like this into a limo without crushing it. If a bride buys a dress from me, I warn her that at least two bridesmaids have to volunteer to help her dress. And then I teach the bridesmaids how to do it."

"It's not very comfortable," Hannah commented as Claire jumped down from the settee and began to button up the back of the gown.

"I know. Most brides who buy an elaborate gown like this don't care that much about comfort. They just want to look perfect for the wedding photos. Take a look, Hannah." Claire gestured toward the mirror. "You look really good, but it's definitely not your style."

"You're right. And with all this white lace, I could go snow blind. Let's go show this off and see what Mother says. And then let's get me out of it!"

In less time than it takes to eat a cookie, Hannah was back in the dressing room. "I told you," she said as Claire unbuttoned the dress.

"Yes, you did, and you nailed it. I thought I'd lose it when your mother said you weren't right for the dress." Claire unfastened the last button and tapped Hannah on the shoulder. "Raise your arms. I'm going to climb up and pull it right off."

Several moments later, the deed was done and Hannah gave a sigh of relief as Claire hung the gown back on its hanger. It was time to introduce a subject that was much more important than a wedding gown. "Lisa said that Stephanie Bascomb showed up next door in a new outfit. Do you know why she bought a new outfit?"

"A new *wardrobe*," Claire corrected her. "And yes, I can make an educated guess, especially since the mayor's newest girlfriend also has several new outfits."

"Stephanie made infidelity pay?"

"You could say that. And so did the mayor's newest girlfriend. He stopped by with his credit card this morning and told me to give Stephanie anything she wanted. And let me tell you, she wanted a lot!"

"Has this girlfriend been in here yet?"

"Not yet. He told me to keep his credit card because someone would be stopping in later on this afternoon. I'm supposed to make sure she gets a very nice good-bye gift."

"They broke up?"

"It sounded that way to me. Or if they didn't break up quite yet, he was planning to cut her loose really soon. Thanks to the mayor, this is going to be a big-ticket day for me."

"Will you tell me who it is when the mayor's new girl-friend comes in?"

"You don't have to wait that long. I already know who it is because he told me her name." Claire stopped speaking and started to smile. "To paraphrase your mother, *listen carefully because I never repeat gossip*."

"I'm listening."

"It's one of your fellow contestants, Gloria Berkeley. And her spending limit is a thousand dollars, but you didn't hear that from me, either." Claire paused and took a deep breath. "That's enough about our philandering mayor. Let's talk about something more pleasant. At least we have the Cinderella dress out of the way. Would you like to end your shopping ordeal early?"

"Of course I would! You know how I hate to try on cloth-ing."

"Then we'll bring out the best I have and knock their socks off with it."

Hannah watched as Claire placed one of the hangers on the first hook. "This is it," Claire said. "This is the one I think you should wear. Put on the long skirt, the shell top, and the tunic jacket that matches the skirt."

"Okay, but . . ."

"Just do it. We left them with a disappointing taste in their mouths. Now we're going to show them what Hannah Swensen should look like on her wedding day."

"Are you sure that we can . . . ?"

"Have I ever steered you wrong, Hannah?" Claire interrupted her.

"No, you never have. I'll do whatever you say I should do. And I'll send two dozen Lunchbox Cranberry Oatmeal Cookies over to you if you're right."

"It's a deal. Bob loves those cookies and so does Grandma Knudson."

The moment Claire had left the dressing room, Hannah reached for the hanger. This was the wedding dress that Claire had liked the best, a lovely cream-colored satin brocade with a raised design of lilacs in shades of green, violet, and a pink so pale, it gave new meaning to the term *pastel*. The barely visible colors and the sheen of the material created a palette that changed almost imperceptively with the light.

"Gorgeous!" Hannah breathed, slipping the top over her head and pulling it down. It was long, almost as long as her favorite tunic top. Then she reached out for the skirt and stared in confusion at the garments on the multiple hangers that had been nestled beneath the top she had donned.

"Hannah? Do you need help?" Claire opened the dressing room door a crack so that she could be heard clearly.

"Come in, Claire." Hannah walked over to open the door all the way and then she turned to gesture toward the other garments on the nestled hangers. "What is all this, anyway?"

"It's what the designer calls a *wardrobe*."

"Great, but what does that mean?"

"I'll show you." Claire walked over to the hanger and removed the first garment. "This is the skirt. It's floor length and it goes with that long shell top you're wearing. The designer calls this his evening dress. Put it on, Hannah. And then slip into this jacket. It's long enough to go over the tunic top."

Hannah did as Claire instructed and then she glanced in

the mirror. What she saw made her smile. "I really like this, Claire!"

"And so will they, especially if you thank your mother for choosing such a marvelous outfit for you."

"Mother *chose* this?"

"Of course not, but she'll never admit she didn't. Come on, Hannah. Let's go show them."

Hannah's knees were shaking slightly as they headed for the alcove where her family was waiting. Claire was absolutely right. She really wanted to wear this outfit for her wedding.

"Oh my!" Delores said, when Hannah approached. "That's gorgeous, dear!"

"It's perfect for the wedding," Michelle agreed, "especially since you love lilacs and we found a place with out-of-season lilacs for the wedding."

Andrea nodded. "You're right. It's perfect."

Hannah remembered Claire's advice just in time. "Thank you so much for choosing it, Mother. I absolutely *love* it!"

"You're welcome, dear," Delores said, never missing a beat. "I just knew it would be perfect for your wedding dress." She turned to smile at Claire. "You always have the best, Claire."

"Thank you," Claire responded graciously, studiously avoiding Hannah's eyes.

Delores turned to Andrea. "I just wish that you hadn't spilled red wine on my mother's wedding dress. I'm sure Hannah would have wanted to wear it."

Andrea put on her most contrite look. "I'm sorry, Mother. You know that I didn't do it. I don't drink red wine. It was Bill, and I couldn't get too angry at the man I was about to marry."

"I know, dear." Delores reached out to pat Andrea's hand. "It wasn't your fault. And you did take it straight to the cleaners. Actually . . . I'm glad they went out of business. They should have known how to remove a stain from red wine."

Hannah judiciously avoided Andrea's eyes. The red wine stain had been no accident. Andrea had admitted everything to her. Hannah was grateful to her sister, and she was sure that Michelle was, too. Perhaps she ought to team up with Michelle and make Andrea a special treat for saving them from family wedding gowns.

"We won't worry about that now," Delores said with a smile for Andrea. "It's water under the bridge, dear, and it probably wouldn't have fit Hannah anyway. My mother was petite, like you and Michelle. Hannah takes after your father's side and Grandmother Swensen . . ." She stopped and gave a little sigh. "They didn't have any money, you know. She probably made her wedding dress herself out of flour sacks and it fell apart years ago."

Hannah bristled slightly. She knew that, unlike her mother's family, her father's parents had lived on a tight budget. That hadn't mattered to her, or to Andrea, or to Michelle. All three of them had always loved their Swensen grandparents best.

Delores turned to Claire. "And now, our esteemed clothing adviser, we have to shop for Hannah's trousseau."

Claire smiled. "Actually, you don't. Just hold that thought and wait here. Hannah has several more outfits to show you."

Hannah waited until they got to the dressing room and the door was closed behind them. And then she turned to Claire with a frown. "What trousseau? I thought you said we'd be through if Mother liked this dress for the wedding."

"We *are* through." Claire reached down and flipped up the hem on the skirt that Hannah was wearing. Then she unzipped the bottom panel, helped Hannah out of her jacket, turned it inside out, and motioned for her to put it on again."

"It's reversible?" Hannah asked, even though she could clearly see that it was.

"That's the whole point of this ensemble. Take a look."

Hannah looked at her reflection in the mirror and she smiled. "Perfect," she said, realizing that now the jacket was the same green as the shell and the lilac leaves in the shortened skirt.

"We also have these." Claire held up a pair of green pants. "That's in case you'd rather wear a pantsuit. And then we have a lavender shell that goes with the patterned jacket and cream-colored pants. There are pants in pink and a pink tunic top, and another lavender jacket. If you count the variables, you have a whole wardrobe here, Hannah. And that's why the designer calls it his *wardrobe*."

LUNCHBOX CRANBERRY OATMEAL COOKIES

Do NOT preheat oven yet—this cookie dough needs to chill.

Hannah's 1st Note: Lisa and I use our stand mixer down at The Cookie Jar to mix up these cookies.

Lisa's Note: The reason we called these cookies Lunchbox Cranberry Oatmeal Cookies is that Herb just loves to take a couple of these to work in his lunchbox and eat them when he's driving around town in his cruiser, looking for parking violators.

1 and ½ cups Craisins *(I used regular unfla- vored Craisins, but any dried sweetened cranberries will work)*

1 cup cranberry juice

1 and ¼ cups white *(granulated)* sugar

1 teaspoon salt

1 and ½ teaspoons baking soda

2 teaspoons ground cinnamon

½ teaspoon nutmeg *(freshly grated is best)*

1 teaspoon orange zest *(that's just the colored part of the orange rind)*

1 cup white Karo syrup

2 beaten eggs *(just whip them up in a glass with a fork)*

1 cup *(2 sticks, 8 ounces, ½ pound)* salted butter, melted

2 Tablespoons *(⅛ cup)* reserved cranberry juice from the cup of cranberry juice above

4 cups quick-cooking oatmeal *(dry, right out of the package—I used Quaker's Quick-1 Minute)*

4 cups all-purpose flour *(don't sift, but don't pack it down either—scoop it out with your measuring cup and level it off with a table knife)*

1 cup chopped nuts *(I used walnuts)*

---

approximately ½ cup white *(granulated)* sugar for rolling the dough balls

Put the Craisins *(or other brand dried, sweetened cranberries)* in a microwave-safe bowl.

Pour the cup of cranberry juice over the top of the Craisins.

Heat the bowl in a microwave on HIGH for 90 seconds. Leave it in the microwave for 1 minute and then stir.

Set the bowl with the cranberries and juice on the counter. This will plump the Craisins.

Put the sugar in the bottom of the bowl of your mixer and turn it on LOW speed.

Add the salt, baking soda, cinnamon, nutmeg, and orange zest. Mix them in thoroughly.

Now add the cup of white Karo syrup. Keep the mixer running until everything is thoroughly blended.

Add the beaten eggs. Mix until they're well incorporated.

Melt the butter, either on the stovetop in a small saucepan, or in a microwave-safe bowl on HIGH 1 minute in the microwave. Let it sit in the microwave for another minute and then stir to see if it's melted. If it's not, give it another 20 seconds to finish melting it.

Add the melted butter to your bowl and mix it in.

Drain the Craisins with a strainer, but do not throw away the cranberry juice. Reserve 2 Tablespoons of cranberry juice *(⅛ cup)* to use in your cookie dough.

Add the 2 Tablespoons of reserved cranberry juice to your bowl and mix it in.

With your mixer running at LOW speed, add the oatmeal in one-cup increments, making sure to mix after each addition.

With the mixer still on LOW speed, add the flour in one-cup increments, making sure to mix after each addition.

Add the Craisins and mix them in.

Finally, add the chopped nuts and mix thoroughly.

Remove the bowl from the mixer, scrape down the sides, and give it a final stir by hand. This dough will be fairly stiff.

Cover the cookie dough with plastic wrap and put the mixer bowl in the refrigerator for at least an hour. *(Overnight is fine, too.)* This dough will be easier to work with if it's chilled.

When your dough is thoroughly chilled, preheat your oven to 375 degrees F., rack in the middle position.

Place the half-cup of white sugar in a shallow bowl. You'll use it to coat balls of cookie dough.

Prepare your cookie sheets by spraying them with Pam or another nonstick cooking spray, or lining them with parchment paper.

Roll the chilled dough in 2-inch balls with your fingers. *(That's approximately the size of a golf ball.)*

Roll the dough ball in the bowl of white sugar to coat it, and then place it on the cookie sheet, no more than 6 balls to a standard-size sheet.

Flatten the sugared cookie dough balls to a quarter-inch thickness with a wide metal spatula or with your impeccably clean palm.

Repeat the process of rolling dough balls, coating them with sugar, placing them on the cookie sheet, and flattening them. They should be 2 to 3 inches apart and a standard-size cookie sheet will hold 6 of these big, delicious cookies.

Bake at 375 degrees F. for 9 to 10 minutes or until slightly brown around the edges. *(Mine took the full 10 minutes.)*

Remove the cookies from the oven, leave them on the cookie sheet for a minute or so, and then remove them to a wire rack to cool completely.

Once the cookies are completely cool, you can store them in a tightly covered container or cookie jar.

Hannah's 2nd Note: If these cookies start to dry out before they're all eaten, drop a slice of apple or an orange or lemon peel into the bottom of the cookie jar to make them soft and chewy again.

Yield: 3 dozen large Lunchbox Cranberry Oatmeal Cookies.

Hannah's 3rd Note: If you want to make these cookies smaller, that's fine, too. If you decide to roll 1-inch cookie balls, they will bake from between 6 to 8 minutes. If you choose to do this, the yield will be double, from 5 to 6 dozen cookies.

Delores's Note: I'm really not fond of cranberries, but once Hannah made these cookies with dried blueberries for me. They were simply wonderful, despite the fact that there was no chocolate involved. I told her that she ought to leave out the fruit and try these cookies with chocolate chips someday. I even offered to taste-test them for her!

Chapter Twenty

The lovely lilac-print wardrobe was hers! Delores had insisted on paying for it, and Hannah had left it with Claire, who had promised to make the minor alterations that were needed. Both Hannah and Michelle were smiling as they walked across the parking lot to the back door of The Cookie Jar.

Hannah opened the door, they stepped inside the kitchen, and both of them spotted it at once. A dark green wool coat with a fur collar was hanging on one of the pegs on the wall by the door. There was a scarf draped over the peg, and it had a red and green checkerboard design!

"Our mystery woman," Hannah said, staring hard at the coat. "Nobody hangs their coat back here except Lisa, Marge, Jack, and Aunt Nancy."

"And Mother, Andrea, Tracey, Mike, Norman, Ross, and anyone else who comes in the back door with them."

"That's true, but I'm sure I've never seen this coat before. How about you?"

Michelle shook her head. "I know I haven't. It's pretty and I would have noticed it. Let's go see who's out front. It could belong to someone who came in the back way."

The two sisters pushed through the swinging door and entered the coffee shop. It was crowded with customers, and it took them a full five minutes to get to the front where Lisa was standing, because everyone wanted to wish them luck for the competition that evening. Finally they arrived at the cash register, where Lisa was ringing up sales.

"There's a green coat hanging in the kitchen. Do you know who hung it there?" Hannah asked her.

"Yes," Lisa said. "It's Aunt Nancy's new coat. Did you get my text?"

"No. My phone's been in my purse and I didn't hear it come in. What did you say?"

"I just wanted to tell you that Mayor Bascomb came in to join Stephanie. He had makeup on his cheek, but I could see the red skin right through it. Somebody slapped him really hard."

"Maybe Stephanie?" Hannah suggested.

"That would be my guess. But it's okay now. They stayed for my story and then they left."

"How did they react to the story?" Michelle asked her.

"Stephanie loved it, but the mayor looked a little green around the gills. I don't think he liked the way I described the murder scene."

"When is the next performance?" Hannah asked.

"At eleven. I do it on the hour and people start coming in twenty minutes or so before I start. See that table with Bonnie Surma, Donna Summers, Babs Dubinski, and Ava Schultz?"

"I see them."

"They've been here through two performances already and it looks like they're staying for a third. Dad said they just ordered more Chocolate-Covered Raisin Cookies." Lisa turned to Michelle. "Are you going to stay for a performance?"

"I don't think I'd better. You're too good, Lisa. I'm afraid it would be too much like finding him all over again and I don't want to go through that twice!"

"Michelle and I will go bake a few batches of cookies," Hannah told her. "From the size of the crowd in here, it looks like you'll need them. And Lisa?"

"Yes?"

"When you're through with your story, will you ask Aunt Nancy to come back to the kitchen? There's something I need to ask her."

"About the murder?"

"Yes," Hannah answered quite truthfully, and then she said something that could be taken in a multitude of ways. "It could really help that she knew the victim as well as she did."

Hannah and Michelle had just finished mixing up a batch of Peanut Butter Potato Chip Cookies when Aunt Nancy came into the kitchen. "Lisa said you wanted to see me?"

"Yes," Hannah answered. "Sit down and have a cup of coffee with us. I need to ask you some questions about Chef Duquesne."

Aunt Nancy sat down at the stainless steel work counter and accepted a cup of coffee from Michelle. "Thank you, Michelle," she said. "I'm so sorry you had to be the one to find him."

"So am I," Michelle replied. "Is that your green coat hanging by the back door?"

"Why yes it is."

"And that's the same one you wore the night of the baking competition?" Hannah asked her.

"Yes, I wore it that night. What is this about, girls?"

"It's about Chef Duquesne. We know you went up to his room with him on the night he was killed," Hannah said, going straight to the heart of the matter.

"Oh, dear! I was hoping no one would hear about that!"

"Tell us about it," Hannah prompted her.

"It was my own fault." Aunt Nancy looked very upset as she answered. "It was very foolish of me to go to his room. We were the only people in the bar, and Allen said we should go so that the bar could close. I was going to go home, but he invited me to his room. He told me that he had a suite with a living room and he could make coffee. He said he wanted to catch up with my life and tell me about his. And he wanted to hear all about the people we'd known in high school. And I *believed* him!"

"But that's not what he wanted?" Hannah asked, already knowing the answer.

"No! Not at all! I should have guessed that it wasn't the real reason. Allen never was interested in anyone except himself. But I guess I'm gullible. I always tend to think the best of people. I take what they say at face value until they prove otherwise."

"And he proved otherwise?" Hannah prompted her.

"He certainly did! He thought I'd come up to his room with him because I was interested in him as a man."

"He tried to hit on you?" Michelle asked.

Aunt Nancy's face turned pink. "Yes. It was terribly embarrassing. I told him that I wasn't interested in anything like that, grabbed my coat and scarf, and got out of there as quickly as I could. And the more I thought about it, the madder I got that he'd assumed I'd be willing to do something like that!" She stopped speaking, took a deep shaky breath, and looked up at Hannah and Michelle again. "How did you find out about it?"

"Rita, the housekeeper you saw in the hall that night, told Sally about it. Sally's her boss. And Sally told us this morning."

"You won't tell anyone else, will you?"

"No, we won't," Michelle promised for both of them. "It's nobody's business but yours."

"How about you?" Hannah asked her. "Have you told anyone else about it?"

"No one except Heiti. And I know he won't tell anyone."

Hannah and Michelle exchanged glances. "Heiti is the man who built your bookshelves?" Hannah asked.

"Yes. He could see that I was upset when I came home."

"You're . . . living with Heiti?"

Aunt Nancy gave a little laugh. "No, nothing like that.

Heiti has an apartment out near the highway. He was at my house, painting the decorative border under the living room ceiling. I asked him if he wanted to go to the competition with me, but he said he wanted to finish the stencils on the border."

"Stencils?" Michelle looked interested.

"Yes. Heiti does tole painting. He learned it as a hobby. He does a wonderful job and he's quite an artist. You can buy traditional border stencils at art stores, or you can make your own stencils. Heiti cuts his own stencils and they're just beautiful! He finished the border around my kitchen ceiling, all sorts of decorative kitchen utensils, and I liked it so much that I asked him to paint one in my living room, too."

"And he was still there when you got home?" Hannah led her back to the subject at hand.

"Yes. He'd just finished working and he was cleaning his brushes. Heiti saw right away that I was upset so he poured me a glass of sherry and asked me to sit down with him on the couch and tell him all about it."

"And you did?" Michelle asked.

"Yes. I was so upset, I had *two* glasses of sherry. And I never have more than one."

"Did Heiti have sherry, too?" Hannah asked.

"No, Heiti doesn't drink much. If we go out to dinner, he occasionally has a glass of beer, though."

"How about wine?" Michelle asked, and Hannah knew that she was also remembering the two wineglasses in Sally's kitchen.

"He doesn't care for it. As a matter of fact, he told me that he used to like red wine, but when he got older, it gave him a terrible headache right between his eyes. Don't they say that the tannins in red wine give some people headaches?"

"Yes, I've heard that." Hannah made a mental note to ask Mike if the police lab had found any fingerprints on the wineglasses. "This is really important, Aunt Nancy. Did you see anyone in the halls or the elevator when you left the inn?"

Aunt Nancy shook her head. "No one except that housekeeper. I was hoping she wouldn't stop me and ask any questions so I rushed to the elevator as fast as I could."

"You took the elevator straight down to the ground floor?"

"Yes, and I didn't see another soul on the way out! In fact, even the bar was closed when I passed by. I guess there might have been someone in there cleaning up, but I wasn't really looking. I just wanted to get out of there and go home as fast as I could."

"Where did you park?" Michelle asked her.

"In their parking lot. I was so angry with Allen, I hurried to my car and drove off."

"Were there any other cars in the lot?"

"Yes, but they'd been there for a while. There was a layer of snow on everyone's windshield. I know because I had to use my brush to clear mine off."

"Let's talk about when you got home," Hannah said. "You said Heiti could tell you were upset, so he poured you a glass of sherry and you talked about what had happened in Chef Duquesne's room. Is that right?"

"Yes. Heiti is a wonderful listener. He's totally nonjudgmental and he really cares about people. He's just a wonderful, talented, intelligent person."

Hannah drew a deep breath. She hated to ask the next question, but someone had to find out the extent of Aunt Nancy's relationship with Heiti and whether Heiti could have been so angry with Chef Duquesne's treatment of Aunt Nancy that he'd decided to take revenge. "It sounds like you're very fond of Heiti," she said with a smile.

"Oh, I am!"

"Are you fond enough of him that you think you could grow to love him?"

"Well, I don't know about that, but . . ." Aunt Nancy paused and then she nodded. "You're right, Hannah. I think, perhaps, that I *could* grow to love him. I look forward to spending time with him because he's such a remarkably fascinating man."

"Tell us about him," Michelle said.

"I'm not sure where to start. Heiti worked for years at an aerospace company as an engineer. He was their trouble-shooter. Sometimes they sent him to other aerospace companies as their expert. He was very well paid and he never married or had a family, so he saved most of his money and invested it. He did so well with his investments that he could afford to take early retirement when he was fifty."

"That's really wonderful!" Hannah said, wondering if she'd ever be able to retire. "What did he do then?"

"He moved back home to help his parents until they decided that they wanted to go into a senior living complex in Florida. He helped them sell their house and move there. And that's when Heiti decided that he wanted to do all the things he'd never had the time or the energy to do while he was working for the aerospace company."

"Things like tole painting?" Michelle asked.

"Yes. And designing gadgets to make people's lives easier. He's working on something right now, but he won't tell me what it is until he builds it and tests it to see if it'll work."

"He really sounds like an interesting man," Michelle commented.

"Yes, he does," Hannah added. "I can understand why you're so intrigued by him. And it sounds as if he enjoys spending time with you. Do you think that Heiti's interested in you romantically?"

As Hannah watched, Aunt Nancy's cheeks turned pink, and it took her a moment to respond. "I . . . I don't know, Hannah. He may be, although he's never said so to me." She paused again, and took a deep breath. "In a way, I hope he *is* interested in me romantically. Heiti would make a wonderful companion, and I think we could be very happy together."

"Did Heiti seem as upset as you were when you told him about what Chef Duquesne had done?" Hannah asked.

"Oh, yes! He was *very* upset! He said that somebody ought to teach that man the proper way to treat a lady like me, and . . ." Aunt Nancy stopped speaking in midsentence and her eyes widened. "Oh, dear!" she gasped. "Surely you don't think that *Heiti* could have driven out to the Lake Eden Inn and . . . and . . ."

Hannah knew that she was walking on eggshells. It was clear that Aunt Nancy was horrified by the notion that Heiti might have had anything to do with Chef Duquesne's murder. She had to reassure Aunt Nancy and keep her from alerting Heiti until after they had time to question him.

"Of course we don't think Heiti had anything to do with it," she said, reaching out to pat Aunt Nancy's shoulder. "I was just exploring the possibilities. He doesn't sound like a man who would do anything like that."

It was time to change the subject, and Hannah decided on another tack. "Did you know that Sally waited on you when you were in the bar?"

"No, but I remember what you said about the housekeeper telling her boss that I was upset when I left. Is Sally her boss?

"Yes, she is. Sally is also the head chef and co-owner of the Lake Eden Inn with her husband, Dick. Dick was behind the bar the night you were there."

"I liked Sally. She was nice. I didn't meet Dick because we sat at a table."

"Right. Now, let me tell you something that you may really like about Sally. Did you know that Chef Duquesne slipped a twenty-dollar bill to Sally after the second round of drinks and asked her to put vodka in your hot lemonade?"

Aunt Nancy looked completely shocked. "No!"

"Well, he did. And of course, Sally would never do that!"

"And Sally didn't put anything except hot lemonade in your drink," Michelle picked up that part of the story. "Sally would never do anything like that. She told us that you looked like the kind of lady who would have ordered vodka if you'd wanted it and she wasn't about to pour anything for you that you hadn't ordered yourself."

Aunt Nancy laughed. "Sally's right. I would have ordered it myself if I'd wanted it. And it's a good thing Sally's so honest. I don't drink very much and I had two more mugs of hot lemonade. I wouldn't have done what Allen wanted anyway, but I might have had trouble driving home!"

"Sally told us some other things," Hannah took over the conversation again. "It turns out that you weren't the only woman who was upset when she left Chef Duquesne's room."

"Oh, dear!"

"The other woman left right away, too," Michelle told her, not mentioning any names or the fact that Brooke had reportedly been in tears.

"Do you suspect her of killing Allen?" Aunt Nancy asked.

"No, but that's just the tip of the iceberg," Hannah told her. "There were also two women at the hotel in New York."

"Oh, my! It sounds as if you have your work cut out for you, Hannah." Aunt Nancy drew a deep breath. "Well, if I'm on that suspect list of yours, you can cross me off right now. You know that I didn't kill him." She turned to Michelle. "I've heard Lisa's story three times today, and she said that you found him in the walk-in cooler in the kitchen. That's true, isn't it?"

"It's true," Michelle said.

"Well, I saw that kitchen at the competition, but I've never been in there. And I've certainly never set foot in that cooler! Allen Duke, or Chef Duquesne, or whatever name he calls himself now, was very much alive when I left his room at eleven forty-five!"

"I have absolutely no doubt of that, Aunt Nancy," Hannah told her. "And I'm convinced that Heiti couldn't have had anything to do with it, either."

Aunt Nancy smiled. "I'm very glad to hear that! Is it because I told you how nice Heiti is?"

"No." Hannah gave a little smile. "Nice people can be capable of murder under extraordinary circumstances. I'm glad he's nice, but nice has nothing to do with why I no longer suspect him."

"What was it then?"

"The red wine. When Michelle and I unlocked Sally's kitchen door and went inside on the morning following Chef Duquesne's murder, we saw a bottle of red wine and two glasses sitting on the counter. And you told us that Heiti doesn't drink red wine."

Aunt Nancy looked delighted at this news. "I'm certainly glad that I mentioned that!"

"So am I," Hannah told her. "It cuts down on my suspect list, and there are a lot of suspects. It seems that no one liked Chef Duquesne and quite a few people had motives for wanting him dead."

When Aunt Nancy got up from her stool, she noticed the bowl on the counter with cookie dough. "What are you girls making?"

"Peanut Butter Potato Chip Cookies."

"Would you like me to help you bake those?"

"That would be nice," Hannah said.

"Heiti loves peanut butter," Aunt Nancy said as she helped them scoop out the cookie dough and place it on cookie sheets.

"Then you should take some home for him," Hannah said. "Is he still working at your house?"

"Yes, he'll be there until I get home. We'll have a bite to eat and then he's going to take me to the competition tonight."

"Good. We'll see you there," Hannah said, slipping the cookie sheets onto the racks in her industrial oven. "After these cookies cool, we'll bring them out front for you. Then we're going to try to get some rest before tonight. Feel free to pack up a dozen of them before they're all gone and take them with you for Heiti."

After Aunt Nancy had left the kitchen, Michelle turned to Hannah. "We're not going to rest, are we?"

"Probably not."

"Because we'll be too busy driving to Aunt Nancy's house to question Heiti, and trying to find out more about Mayor Bascomb and Gloria? And asking Andrea to see if she can get a copy of the police report?"

"And meeting with Mother at the hospital to get a copy of the autopsy report from Doc's files."

"And after all that, we'll go back to your place to rest up before the competition?"

"Not a chance," Hannah said. "Remember how Grandma Ingrid used to say *No rest for the wicked*?"

"I remember. It was her favorite phrase."

"Well, between the two of us, we must be very, very wicked."

PEANUT BUTTER POTATO CHIP COOKIES

Preheat oven to 350 degrees F., rack in the middle position.

The following recipe can be doubled if you wish. Do not, however, double the baking soda. Use one and a half teaspoons.

- 1 cup softened butter *(2 sticks, ¹/₂ pound, 8 ounces)*
- 2 cups white *(granulated)* sugar
- 3 Tablespoons molasses
- 2 teaspoons vanilla
- 1 teaspoon baking soda
- 2 beaten eggs *(just whip them up in a glass with a fork)*
- 2 cups crushed salted potato chips *(measure AFTER crushing) (I used regular thin un-flavored Lay's potato chips)*
- 2 and ¹/₂ cups all-purpose flour *(pack it down in the cup when you measure it)*
- 1 and ¹/₂ cups peanut butter chips *(I used Reese's, a 10-ounce by weight bag. I know that's close to 2 cups, but I like_lots_ of peanut butter chips in these cookies)*

Lisa's 1ˢᵗ Note: The butter in this recipe should be at room temperature unless you have an un-insulated kitchen and it's winter in Minnesota. In that case, you'd better soften it a little.

Hannah's 1ˢᵗ Note: 5 to 6 cups of whole potato chips will *crush down* into about 2 cups. Crush them by hand in a plastic bag, not with a food processor. They should be the size of coarse gravel when they're crushed.

Mix the softened butter with the white sugar and the molasses. Beat them until the mixture is light and fluffy, and the molasses is completely mixed in.

Add the vanilla and baking soda. Mix them in thoroughly.

Break the eggs into a glass and whip them up with a fork. Add them to your bowl and mix until they're thoroughly incorporated.

Put your potato chips in a closeable plastic bag. Seal it carefully *(you don't want crumbs all over your counter)* and place the bag on a flat surface. Get out your rolling pin and roll it over the bag, crushing the potato chips inside. Do this until the pieces resemble coarse gravel. *(If you crush them too much, you won't have any crunch—crunch is good in these cookies.)*

Measure out 2 cups of crushed potato chips and mix them into the dough in your bowl.

Add one cup of flour and mix it in.

Then add the second cup of flour and mix thoroughly.

Add the final half cup of flour and mix that in.

Measure out a cup and a half of peanut butter chips and add them to your cookie dough. If you're using an electric mixer, mix them in at the slowest speed. You can also take the bowl out of the mixer and stir in the chips by hand.

Let the dough sit on the counter while you prepare your cookie sheets.

Spray your cookie sheets with Pam or another non-stick cooking spray, or line them with parchment paper, leaving little "ears" at the top and bottom. That way, when your cookies are baked, you can pull the paper, baked cookies and all, over onto a wire rack to cool.

Drop the dough by rounded teaspoons onto your cookie sheets, 12 cookies on each standard-sized sheet.

Hannah's 2nd Note: I used a 2-teaspoon cookie scoop at The Cookie Jar. It's faster than doing it with a spoon.

Bake your Peanut Butter Potato Chip Cookies at 350 degrees F. for 10 to 12 minutes or until nicely browned. Then remove from the oven. *(Mine took 11 minutes.)*

Let the cookies cool for 2 minutes on the cookie sheet and then remove them with a metal spatula. Transfer them to a wire rack to finish cooling.

Yield: Approximately 5 dozen wonderfully chewy, salty and soft cookies that are sure to please everyone who tastes them.

Hannah's 3rd Note: DO NOT bake these for anyone with a peanut allergy!

Lisa's 2nd Note: These cookies travel well. If you want to send them to a friend, just stack them, roll them up like coins in foil, and cushion the cookie rolls between layers of Styrofoam peanuts, or bubble wrap.

Chapter Twenty-one

Andrea was their first stop after they left The Cookie Jar. Hannah and Michelle walked across the street to Lake Eden Realty and entered the small office. Andrea was sitting behind her desk, working on the computer. The bell inside the door tinkled as they entered and she looked up.

"Hi!" she said. "I was just about to call you two." She turned to Hannah. "You're investigating, aren't you?"

"Yes."

"That's what I thought, since Michelle found the body." Andrea swiveled in her chair to face Michelle. "I'm really sorry you had to go through that, Michelle. I remember how I felt when I found Max's body in the old barn."

"I'm okay now, but I don't want to go inside that cooler ever again!"

"I know that feeling," Hannah echoed their sentiments. "There are more than a few places in Lake Eden that I don't want to go. I have to force myself to do it, but it does get better with time."

"You're probably right," Andrea said. "What can I do for you two? I know you didn't come in just to say hello."

Hannah laughed. "You're right, of course. We were wondering if you could get . . ." She stopped speaking when Andrea pulled her center desk drawer open, took out a large manila envelope, and placed it on top of her desk. "Is that what I think it is?" she asked Andrea.

"Yes, I got it this morning while Bill was in the shower. There's a copy of the police lab report, the autopsy report, and the crime scene photos. It's a really good thing Bill takes long showers. It took me quite a while to copy everything."

"That's great, Andrea!" Hannah told her. "This will help a lot!"

Andrea looked very smug about getting Hannah something she needed. "Bill always brings a copy of the casework home with him. I just hope that he never catches on to what I'm doing."

"I'm almost sure he won't," Hannah said.

"Is there anything else I can do to help you?" Andrea asked.

Hannah noticed that her sister looked hopeful. Like Michelle, Andrea enjoyed being a part of Hannah's investigations. Hannah thought for a moment. "Actually . . . yes. We have to go to see Heiti. Would you like to come with us?"

"You want me to go to *Haiti* with you?" Andrea asked, looking shocked.

"Not the country, the person," Michelle explained. "It's spelled differently, but pronounced the same. Heiti is a man who's working at Aunt Nancy's house, building her bookcases."

Andrea gave a little laugh. "Oh! That's different. Is this man a suspect?"

"Yes, until I clear him," Hannah told her.

"Does he know you're coming to talk to him?"

"I don't think so. We didn't tell anyone where we were going when we left The Cookie Jar."

"What are you going to tell Heiti when you get there?" Andrea asked. "You don't really have any excuse for going to Aunt Nancy's house, do you, Hannah?"

"Not really. I'd planned to say that Aunt Nancy had told us about the wonderful bookcases that he was building and the beautiful tole painting border he'd painted in her kitchen and living room, and we'd dropped by to see it."

"That's pretty lame," Andrea said. "You need something a little more important than that. But don't worry, I've got the perfect excuse for going there. I sold Aunt Nancy the house and Al is doing this great promotion to increase our business. He's giving everyone who buys a house from us an insurance policy that covers the structure of the house and the major appliances. Lake Eden Realty pays for the first year. After that, the homeowner can choose to renew it and take over the premiums, or let it lapse."

"Does Aunt Nancy get that insurance policy?" Hannah asked, already guessing the answer.

"Yes. I was planning to drop by to give it to her anyway. I can say that I was going to just leave it under the doormat, but when I noticed that someone was inside the house, I decided to drop it off personally."

"That's a great idea!" Michelle complimented her.

"I know." Andrea looked very proud of herself for coming up with such a convincing story. "I'll make sure I notice the bookcases in the living room when I hand him the paperwork, and I'll tell him how great they look. And then I'll say that Aunt Nancy mentioned the painting he was doing and we all wanted to see it."

"Brilliant!" Hannah told her. "Do you have to get right back to the office when we're through at Aunt Nancy's?"

"No, I'm through working for the day. I was just killing time on the Internet, and there's no reason for me to go home. Grandma McCann is taking Bethie to an open house at Kiddie Korner so that she can meet the rest of the kids. That'll give Janice Cox and Sue Plotnik a chance to evaluate her to see if she's mature enough to enroll. Then they're going to pick up Tracey when school's over and they'll go out to the Tri-County Mall to look for Halloween costumes."

Michelle looked impressed. "You're really lucky to have Grandma McCann. She's so good with the kids."

"I know. I wouldn't be able to work at all if she hadn't agreed to live with us and be a part of our family. We could make it if I stayed home with the kids and all we had was Bill's salary, but we wouldn't be able to put much away for our retirement or Tracey and Bethie's college expenses."

Andrea stood up and grabbed an envelope from the outbox on her desk. "Okay. I've got Aunt Nancy's insurance policy. Doc Knight said the time of death was between midnight and three in the morning. Let's go find out if Heiti has an alibi for that."

"He's coming," Hannah said, hearing the sound of footsteps as someone approached Aunt Nancy's front door. A moment later, the door opened to reveal a tall, sandy-haired man in his late fifties. He was more handsome than Hannah had expected and there was a smile on his face.

"Yes?" the man inquired.

"Hello. I'm Andrea Todd," Andrea introduced herself. "I'm the real estate agent who sold this house to Nancy."

"Glad to meet you," the man said with a friendly smile. "My name is Heiti and I'm doing some work on the interior for Nancy. What can I do for you, Miss Todd?"

"Mrs. Todd," Andrea corrected him. "I just stopped by to drop off Nancy's insurance policy. It's something we provide for anyone who buys a house from Lake Eden Realty. Do you happen to know if Nancy's had any trouble with the structure or with any of the major appliances?"

"I don't think she has. At least she didn't mention it to me." He turned to Hannah and Michelle. "Are you two real estate agents, too?"

Hannah shook her head. "No, I'm Andrea's sister, Hannah Swensen, and this is our youngest sister, Michelle."

"The cookie lady!" Heiti reached out to shake her hand.

"Nancy talks about you all the time. She told me that you're a marvelous baker."

It was the perfect opening for Hannah and she took it. "And she told me that you're a wonderful carpenter and painter."

"She said you were building bookcases for her," Michelle said, once Heiti had taken her hand and greeted her with a similar handshake.

"That's right. Would you like to see my work?" Heiti asked, opening the door wider.

"We'd love to!" Andrea told him, stepping in.

Hannah and Michelle followed on Andrea's heels as Heiti led them into the kitchen and showed them the bookcases lining one wall.

The kitchen was exactly as Aunt Nancy had described it, a long, fairly narrow room with the appliances against one long wall, and bookcases against the other. The bookcases were finely crafted, and Hannah immediately wished she had them instead of the old plank and brick bookcases she'd built herself in her living room.

"They're beautiful," she commented, "and there are so many!"

Heiti laughed and it was clear that he was amused. His laugh was obviously genuine, and the sound of his laughter was musical in nature. Hannah felt herself smiling back at him, and she saw that Andrea and Michelle were also smiling. She began to understand how Aunt Nancy had become so fond of him. Heiti seemed like a man who loved life and found enjoyment in little things.

"Yes, there are many bookcases," Heiti told her, "but not enough to hold all of Nancy's books. Come with me, and I'll show you the others I built for her."

"Wait!" Andrea stared up at the border around the kitchen ceiling. "This is just incredible, Heiti! Did you paint it?"

"Yes. I finished it last week. This week, I've been working on the border in the living room."

"Aunt Nancy mentioned that," Hannah told him. "She

said she invited you to go to the competition with her, but you were painting the border in the living room and you wanted to finish it."

"That's true. Tole painting is a new hobby of mine and Nancy was kind enough to let me try my hand at it in her house."

"The border you painted in the kitchen is just wonderful," Michelle told him, "and I can hardly wait to see the one in the living room. Aunt Nancy said that you'd just finished and you were cleaning your brushes when she got home from the competition."

"She also said that you were very sympathetic when you heard about what had happened with Chef Duquesne," Hannah picked up where Michelle had stopped.

"Your aunt told you about *that*?"

"Yes, but she's not our aunt. We call her Aunt Nancy because she's my partner's aunt. It just seems to fit her. She's such a caring, kind-hearted person."

"She certainly is," Heiti agreed. "Did Nancy say how very upset she was?"

"Yes," Michelle replied. "She said you poured her a glass of sherry and asked her to tell you about it."

"She also said that you were a wonderful listener," Hannah repeated Aunt Nancy's words.

Andrea reached out to touch Heiti's arm. "We're very glad you comforted her. We're very fond of Aunt Nancy. And I know you must have been tired from working all day."

"It *was* a long day," Heiti admitted, "but I didn't want Nancy to come home to an empty house. And then, when she was so upset, I stayed for another couple of hours. I remember glancing at the alarm clock when I got home and went to bed, and it was close to three in the morning. And now you know how late I was here on the night Chef Duquesne was murdered."

Hannah knew she must have looked shocked. She thought

they'd been very clever, but Heiti had obviously caught on. "Sorry about that," she said, wincing slightly. "You see, I'm investigating . . ." Heiti held up his hand in a motion to stop and she did.

"Nancy mentioned that you investigated murders, and the moment you gave me your name, I knew that was why you were here. Perhaps I shouldn't have been so blunt, but . . ."

"That's all right," Hannah interrupted him. "If I'd known that you knew about that, I would have come right out and started to . . ."

"Grill me!" Heiti interrupted, breaking into his wonderfully contagious laugh again. "To be perfectly honest with you, Hannah, I wanted to drive out to the Lake Eden Inn to give that man a piece of my mind. But there was a very good reason why I couldn't do that."

"What was the reason?" Andrea asked him.

"I ran out of gas! I had to leave my car by the side of the highway and walk back to my apartment."

Hannah remembered the car that had been parked in Aunt Nancy's driveway. "But that's your car outside, isn't it?"

"Yes. One of my neighbors gave me a ride to the Quick Stop the next morning. He waited while I bought a gas can, filled it with gas, and then he took me back to my car. He waited until I poured in the gas and started my car before he drove off. I went straight to the Quick Stop to fill the tank. I can give you my neighbor's name if you want to substantiate what I told you."

"Thank you, but that's not necessary," Hannah said, not mentioning the fact that she was going to check his alibi with Sean and Don at the Quick Stop.

Once Heiti had walked them through the house and showed them all the improvements he'd made, he turned to Andrea. "This house is quite old, but it's very well built. It reminds me of the house my parents had. They knew how to build back then and they used good materials." He turned to address Hannah. "Nancy and I will be there to watch you tonight," Heiti said as he opened the door for them. "Which cookie are you baking?"

"Butterscotch Sugar Cookies," Hannah told him.

"They sound very good. I'll be looking forward to watching you tonight."

Chapter
Twenty-two

Of course they detoured past the Quick Stop on their way back to The Cookie Jar, and Hannah was glad to find out that Sean and Don remembered Heiti and confirmed his alibi. When they got back to The Cookie Jar, Hannah took one look through the front plate-glass window and stopped Michelle and Andrea from entering.

"It's the noon rush and Lisa's telling her story again. Let's go around to the back door and sit in the kitchen. Then Andrea can taste our cookies and tell us what she thinks of them."

The kitchen coffee pot was on and Michelle filled three cups while Hannah put the cookies on a plate. Then they sat down on the stools that surrounded the stainless-steel work island. But before any of them had even reached for a cookie, there was a knock at the back door.

"Mike?" Michelle guessed, motioning toward the plate of cookies. "He probably smelled them when he was driving by."

"Coming!" Hannah called out, getting up from her stool, but she took time to answer Michelle's question. "It's not Mike. He has a cop's knock. It's louder and more authoritative."

"Norman?" Andrea guessed.

"No. Norman has a nice, masculine knock, but it's not as

demanding as Mike's. It's probably Mother. Mother's knock is softer and more ladylike with an undertone of insistence."

"What's my knock like?" Andrea asked.

There was no way that Hannah was going to tell Andrea that her knock was exactly like their mother's knock. Perhaps Andrea would forget she'd asked, if she delayed her answer.

"I'll describe it later," Hannah said. "If I don't get this, Mother will be in a huff. And there's no way I want to open the door to Mother in a huff."

Hannah opened the door and found she was right. It was Delores. "Hello, Mother," she greeted her. "Come in and join us for coffee and cookies. We just got back here and we're about to sample the cookies that Michelle and I are baking tonight."

"Oh, good!" Delores said, as she saw them at the work island. "I'm glad all three of you are here."

Michelle jumped up to get their mother a cup of coffee, and Hannah waited until they were all seated again. "Why are you glad all three of us are here?"

"Because I brought you this!" Delores reached across the work table to give Hannah a white, official-looking envelope. "It's a copy of the autopsy report Doc sent to Bill."

"But I . . ." Andrea stopped speaking as Hannah gave her a look that said, *Don't steal Mother's thunder*!

"I know how you feel, Andrea," Hannah said quickly. "If there are any photos, we won't show them to you. Right, Mother?"

"Right." Delores turned to Andrea. "Don't worry, dear. We all know how squeamish you are about things like that."

"Thank you," Andrea said, quickly recovering her poise. "I really don't know how you do it, Mother."

"Do what, dear?" Delores asked her.

"Make copies of the autopsy photos."

"I'm married to a doctor," Delores explained. "I can't be delicate about things like that now."

"Good for you, Mother!" Hannah complimented her, remembering how their mother had refused to even discuss anything she termed *unpleasant* when they were growing up. "Overcoming something like that must have been very difficult."

"It was a necessity," Delores said. "There are certain requirements for doctors' wives, and I intend to fulfill them. And actually, dear, it isn't that difficult. Doc uses medical terms to describe these matters, and I never ask him what they mean. And as far as those awful autopsy photos are concerned, copying them was quite simple. I flipped them over on the color copier, pressed the button, slipped the copies into the envelope, and returned the photos to the autopsy report without ever actually looking at them."

"Very clever," Hannah commented, deliberately avoiding Andrea's eyes. That was exactly what Andrea had said she'd done when she'd first started scanning the police files in Bill's briefcase.

"Did Chef Duquesne die the way Hannah thought he did?" Michelle asked.

"Yes, but Doc found something else. He said that he found particles of foreign matter in Chef Duquesne's body."

Michelle looked interested. "But you didn't ask him what that meant because you didn't want to know in case it was something that might be too . . . uh . . . too . . ."

It was obvious that Michelle was searching for a word that wouldn't alienate their mother, and Hannah quickly provided it. "Something that might be too *graphic*? Right, Mother?"

"Exactly right, dear. But I know how important this investigation is to you, and I decided that I would set aside my sensibilities for the moment and find out exactly what Doc meant."

Hannah realized that she was holding her breath and she forced herself to breathe normally. Delores would tell them . . . eventually. But first she wanted to be praised for what she would probably describe as *going the extra mile for a greater cause*.

"Thank you, Mother," Hannah said, hoping that she sounded properly grateful.

"Yes, thank you, Mother." Michelle echoed Hannah's words. And then she added, "That was very selfless of you."

"Thank you. As you know, I'm happy to do anything I can for my daughters."

"Right. Get to the point, Mother. What did Doc tell you?" Andrea was clearly impatient, but after another warning glance from Hannah, she mitigated her words. "I hope that Doc's explanation wasn't too unpleasant for you to hear."

"Actually, it wasn't unpleasant at all," Delores answered. "I was expecting something much worse."

"Thank you for helping us, Mother," Michelle said. "We do appreciate it."

Delores paused to take another sip of coffee, and Hannah knew their mother was heightening the suspense. She also knew that Michelle had inherited her acting ability from their mother. If Lisa ever tired of telling murder stories at The Cookie Jar, Delores would be perfectly capable of taking over for her.

"Doc found fibers in Chef Duquesne's throat. He explained to me that this is not unusual. Most people aspirate their share of foreign material like animal dander, dust, various pollens, and small, airborne particles. Doc says that people don't even realize they're inhaling these particles and, usually, it doesn't bother them to the point where it makes them uncomfortable."

Almost in tandem, both Hannah and Michelle cleared their throats. Inhaling any amount of foreign matter was not a comforting thought. "So which airborne particles did Doc find?" Hannah managed to ask.

"He recovered some lint."

"Do you mean lint like the kind that's found in a clothes dryer?" Andrea asked.

"No, dear. This lint was from a dish towel. It was just a couple of minuscule threads. And Doc told me that a dish-towel was found on the floor of the walk-in cooler."

"Did Chef Duquesne carry it into the cooler with him?" Michelle asked.

"Perhaps he did. The police found it and sent it to their crime lab for analysis, but there didn't appear to be any blood spots or foreign material on it."

"Chef Duquesne was stabbed with the knife he was using to cut Hannah's wedding cake," Michelle recounted. "He could have carried the dish towel in there to wipe off the knife."

"That's possible, too," Delores agreed. "But that's not the interesting part."

Hannah leaned forward and attempted to curb her impatience. "Please tell us the interesting part, Mother."

"Of course, dear. But first, I have a little favor to ask of you, Hannah."

Delores smiled. It was a smug smile, the smile of some-one who knew an important secret that they didn't know. Hannah had the urge to grab her mother and shake the infor-mation out of her, but of course she didn't. Her mother had her over a barrel and there wasn't any way out of it. "What's the little favor, Mother?"

"I need you to write a short biography for your wedding page."

"*What* wedding page?"

"The one that Tracey and I started for you. It was her idea. She's very technologically-minded, you know, espe-cially for a second-grader. But then, I guess all the children are like that now."

"Who's going to look at this wedding page?" Hannah asked.

"All the guests we invited to the wedding. There's a sec-tion for your biography, and Ross's biography, and there's also a section for your gift registry. Ross has already agreed to write his biography for me."

Hannah sighed and caved in. It was the only way that Delores would tell them what Doc had discovered. "What sorts of things do you want me to write?"

"Just tell us how you met Ross and when he proposed to you, and when you accepted. That's about all. You'll do it, won't you, dear?"

"Yes, Mother. Now please tell us what . . ."

"There's one other thing, dear," Delores interrupted her.

Hannah rolled her eyes heavenward. Was there no end to this? "What's the other thing, Mother?"

"I need you to fill out your gift registry. All you have to do is go out to some of the stores in the Tri-County Mall and choose the things you'd like people to give you as wedding presents. Then Tracey and I will go out to the mall and sign you up at the stores you've chosen. That way, when someone chooses a gift from the list, the store will put a little tag on it saying it's already been purchased and you won't get a dozen toasters, or whatever."

"No!" Hannah was very firm. "I refuse to tell people what to give me for a gift and where to buy it. These are people from Lake Eden. If they want to give me a gift, they already know where to buy it. I run a business, Mother. I'm not going to choose one store over another store. That would be bad for my business. If I told people to go out to the mall for a toaster . . . and by the way, I don't *need* a toaster because I already *have* a perfectly good toaster . . . I'd be taking business away from Lake Eden Hardware. If you want to put something on that gift page for me, *you* have to choose it."

Delores looked completely shocked. "You want *me* to choose your wedding gifts?"

"Not exactly. It's fine if you suggest things, but please make it clear that you are the one who's suggesting. And I want you to put a line on that page that says something like, *Hannah says the best gift you can give her for her wedding is to come and celebrate this wonderful occasion with her.* Will you agree to those conditions, Mother?"

"Of course I will, dear! Everybody knows what a . . . generous and caring girl you are and they'll understand that you don't want to come right out and ask for anything. Besides, they'll have *my* suggestions to guide them."

What have you done?! Hannah's mind shouted, but she ignored it. She'd done what she had to do. "Now please tell us what Doc told you, Mother."

"Of course I will, dear. The interesting part is that Doc also recovered a small piece of hair lodged in Chef Duquesne's throat."

"He ate a piece of hair?" Michelle asked, looking thoroughly puzzled. "I don't see how that's possible, Mother. That hair couldn't have been in our cake. Both Hannah and I wore hairnets when we baked it for the competition."

"Doc doesn't believe it was in your cake, dear. He said that there may have been several final aspirations immediately before Chef Duquesne expired." Delores stopped and smiled. "He'd be so proud of me. I said that exactly the way he said it."

"Great," Hannah commented, trying her best to sound complimentary rather than sarcastic. Their mother was drawing this out every bit as much as Lisa had drawn out her story. "Did Doc say the hair belonged to Chef Duquesne?"

"He didn't think so. At least it didn't match the hair on the rest of his head. Doc took a sample from Chef Duquesne's head and compared it to the hair he found. He told me that he was no expert, but he was almost positive that the hair in his throat came from another source."

"Another person?" Andrea sounded fascinated.

"Yes. That's what he thought."

Andrea's eyes widened. "From the killer?"

"Perhaps. But Doc said it could also be from anyone who had used Sally's cooler in the past."

"So it doesn't really prove anything," Hannah said with a sigh.

"Maybe, and maybe not, but it *could* prove very helpful to you in your investigation!" Delores put on her *I-know-something-you-don't-know* expression again. "I saved the best part for last."

This time, Hannah couldn't help it. She groaned. Loudly. And then she quickly apologized. "Sorry. I have a touch of indigestion. It must have been something I had for lunch."

"Or something you *wish* Mother had given you to chew on," Michelle quipped in an undertone.

Hannah ignored her and managed to squelch the urge to burst into laughter. Michelle's comment was funny, but her mother's delay tactics were horribly frustrating. "Please tell us the best part, Mother," she said in a voice that only had the slightest hint of impatience. "All three of us are on pins and needles."

"Of course you are. This could be a crucial part of your investigation, Hannah."

Hannah felt her patience come very close to snapping. How much longer was her mother going to make her wait?! "What is it, Mother? Please tell me."

"Doc got a call from the lab early this morning. Remember when he did that DNA test for you and got the results so rapidly?"

Hannah nodded. She didn't trust herself to speak.

"Well . . . the owner of the lab, the same man Doc knew in medical school, told his techs to drop everything else and expedite the testing of the samples Doc gave him. His best tech compared the two samples and came to an early conclusion that there was the same very rare genetic marker in both samples."

"So both of the hairs were from Chef Duquesne?" Andrea asked with an expression that came close to mirroring both Hannah and Michelle's disappointment.

"No. That's just it. One sample was from Chef Duquesne.

But since the rare genetic marker was found in *both* samples, Doc's friend gave him a ballpark guess that if the hair found in Chef Duquesne's throat contained the same rare genetic marker, it must be from Chef Duquesne's immediate family."

Hannah took a moment to digest this. "I'm assuming this includes his parents and his siblings. How about his children?"

"Yes, they would be included. Do you know if he has any children?"

"His Food Channel biography didn't mention any," Michelle said, "but I'll do another search online."

Hannah turned to her mother again. "Does Mike know about this?"

"No, dear. Doc decided not to mention it until the conclusive results are in from the lab. That'll take another five days or so. It's just a hunch at this point, and Doc didn't want to risk sending the police on what might turn out to be a wild goose chase." She reached out to pat Hannah's hand. "Just put all this out of your mind for now and do a good job with your cookies tonight. You have a reputation for excellence to protect, and everyone in Lake Eden is counting on you."

"But no pressure, Hannah," Michelle said under her breath.

"I heard that!" Delores responded, turning to give Michelle the look that all three sisters had termed *Mother's drop dead look*.

"I'd better get back to work," Hannah said, rising to her feet.

Michelle caught Hannah's cue and she stood up, too. "I'll go tell Aunt Nancy that you want to see her on her break. She might know more about Chef Duquesne's relatives."

"And I'll take her place in the coffee shop," Andrea offered, also rising to her feet.

Hannah waited until both of her sisters had left the kitchen and then she turned to smile at her mother. "Thank you for telling me, Mother. And I promise to visit you in jail."

"What are you talking about?!!" Delores was clearly flabbergasted.

"It took you twenty minutes to tell me about the DNA. And you could have covered everything in two minutes or less."

Delores gave a little laugh. "That's not exactly a criminal offense, dear."

"Oh, yes it is." Hannah smiled, so that her mother would know that she was teasing. "While I was waiting for you to get to the point, I just about died of curiosity. And that means you're guilty of attempted murder!"

Chapter
Twenty-three

Hannah smiled as she sniffed the air. Her Angel Crunch Cookies were almost ready to come out of the oven and they smelled delicious. It was a new recipe she'd decided to try, a variation on an old recipe she'd been using for the past few years, and she was surprised she hadn't thought to try it before. The oven timer went off, and she walked over to peek in at the cookies. They were a lovely shade of golden brown, and she quickly pulled the pans from the oven and slipped them on the baker's racks to cool.

"Those cookies smell great!" Michelle complimented her. "What are they?"

"A meringue cookie made with brown sugar, vanilla, and ground pecans."

"They *sound* really good, too. When will they be cool enough to eat?"

"In five minutes or so. Then we can sample them to see if they're good enough to serve."

Hannah walked over to join Michelle at the stainless-steel work island. "Okay," she said. "Let's go over what we learned about Chef Duquesne's family."

Michelle pulled her cell phone out of her pocket and activated the notebook function while Hannah turned to the correct page in the steno pad.

"I'll go first," Michelle said. "Stop me if you want to add anything. Chef Duquesne has an older sister. She's married and she runs a fishing lodge with her husband in Canada. Aunt Nancy called her and she hasn't been back to the States since she attended her mother's funeral four years ago."

Hannah glanced down at her steno pad. "Chef Duquesne's father is still alive, but he's confined to a wheelchair. He lives in an assisted living place back east. Aunt Nancy talked to his nurse on the phone and he's too frail to travel. She needed some excuse for asking about him, so she told the nurse she wanted to send him some cookies."

"So we're going to ship some from these batches?" Michelle gestured toward the baker's rack.

"Yes, as long as Mike doesn't eat them all."

"Mike's coming here?"

"Probably. He usually checks in with me the day after a murder to find out if I've learned anything that he doesn't know."

"And to warn you to leave murder investigations to the professionals, like him," Michelle added with a laugh.

"That, too. He always manages to get here about the time a fresh batch of cookies is cool enough to eat."

"That's not difficult. You bake cookies all day long. There's always a fresh batch of cookies."

"True," Hannah admitted. "I guess it wouldn't really matter what time he came in."

Just then there was a knock at the door, and both Hannah and Michelle broke into laughter.

"Mike?" Michelle asked.

"Yes, that's Mike's knock. I'll put some cookies on a plate."

"Okay. I'll grab a couple, and then I'll go up front and make myself scarce. You're not going to tell him about the DNA, are you?"

"No. Doc will notify him when the results are conclusive.

Will you please go let him in, Michelle? I'll pour his coffee and get the cookies."

Less than five minutes later, Hannah was sitting across from Mike, watching him wolf down Angel Crunch Cookies. She'd eaten one, and she had to admit that they were really good, with a perfect balance between crunch and softness.

"Oh boy, these are good!" Mike said, reaching for the last one on the plate. "I think I could eat a dozen."

"You already have . . . and then some." The words were out of Hannah's mouth before she could call them back, so she smiled to take the sting out of her words. "Eat all you want, Mike. They're light and they're not all that big."

"Thanks. I will. They're new, aren't they?"

Hannah nodded. "I just baked them to try them out."

"Well, they're great!"

Mike looked down at the empty plate and then up at her. It didn't take a genius to get his unspoken message and Hannah got up to refill the plate. "Here you go," she said when she put it down in front of him.

"Thanks, Hannah." Mike took another cookie. "Will it do any good to tell you to stay out of my investigation into Chef Duquesne's death?"

"No."

"I didn't think so. Just remember, you had a close call last time. If you hadn't texted everyone when you did, you could have ended up dead."

"That's true," Hannah admitted.

"It's not that I resent you trying to help. It's just that I feel it's my duty as a sworn police officer to keep you safe. The last thing I want is to see you hurt. And if you keep doing things on your own, you *will* be hurt eventually." He sighed heavily. "I really don't know what to do with you, Hannah. You've never listened to me when I've warned you to stay out of it. Will you listen this time? I don't want to have to chase a killer and worry about you at the same time."

Hannah was touched by his concern, but she had to be truthful. "No, I probably won't listen."

"I didn't think so. You're a stubborn woman, Hannah. So . . . I might as well ask you, who do *you* think killed Chef Duquesne?"

"I don't know yet."

"You don't have any suspects?"

"Oh, I have suspects. Quite a few, as a matter of fact. I did have a prime suspect, but I already cleared him."

"Who?"

"Is it important? It involves some rather sensitive information."

"It's important, Hannah."

"If you agree to keep it confidential and not put it in any police report or mention it to anyone else, I'll tell you."

Mike thought about that for a minute. Then he nodded. "Agreed, as long as I'm convinced that you cleared the suspect."

"Fair enough." Hannah took a deep breath and told Mike about Aunt Nancy's encounter with Alain Duquesne and what had happened in his room.

"But Dick saw her on the security camera at the front door as she left?" Mike asked.

"That's right. Aunt Nancy was never a suspect. It was Heiti. He was there at her house when she got home, and she told him what Chef Duquesne did to her."

"Who's Heiti?"

"He's the man who built her new bookshelves, and he's helping her fix up the house."

"So Heiti is Aunt Nancy's boyfriend?"

Hannah hesitated. "I'm really not sure what to call him. *Boyfriend* seems a little juvenile when they're both over fifty. But yes, they really like each other and I think it might develop into something more than that."

"Okay. So you thought that Heiti might have gone out there to confront Chef Duquesne and it got out of hand?"

"It seemed possible. Heiti's very fond of Aunt Nancy. But he couldn't have done it."

"Okay. I'll bite. Just how do you know that?"

"For one thing, Heiti doesn't drink red wine. It gives him a headache. And I'm sure you had the two wineglasses you found in the kitchen tested at the police lab."

"I did and you're right. They both contained red wine, but the one that was empty had been wiped clean of finger-prints. There's no way to prove who used that glass."

Hannah smiled. She now knew that there had been no fingerprints on the empty glass, and that meant it had be-longed to the killer. "There's something else, too. Heiti lives about a mile from Aunt Nancy's house and he ran out of gas on his way home. He left his car by the side of the road and walked the rest of the way to his apartment. The next morning, his neighbor gave him a ride to the Quick Stop, where he bought a gas can. The neighbor took him back to his car and waited until Heiti poured in the gas and got it started. Then Heiti drove straight to the Quick Stop and filled his gas tank all the way."

"Did you simply take his word for that?"

"No, of course not. I checked with Ron and Sean. They said Heiti bought a gas can and when he drove back to the Quick Stop, his car took a full tank of gas."

"All that's good, Hannah, but he could have run out of gas on his way home from killing Chef Duquesne."

"Heiti didn't go out to the inn. Or if he was lying and he did drive out there and run out of gas on his way back, he still couldn't have killed Chef Duquesne."

"Why's that?"

"Because Heiti didn't go inside the inn. I called Dick to check. Dick went over the security tape and no one came in after Aunt Nancy left. There was no activity at all at the front entrance until Michelle and I came in for our practice time in the kitchen this morning."

"Okay. You did everything right, Hannah."

"Thank you. So you're not going to talk to Heiti?"

"I didn't say that. I'm definitely going to talk to Heiti."

"But why?"

Mike smiled the devilish smile that always made Hannah feel slightly weak in the knees. "Didn't you say that Heiti built custom bookcases for Aunt Nancy?"

"Yes, but what does that have to do with anything?"

"I need a carpenter to build a bookcase in my office at the station."

ANGEL CRUNCH COOKIES

Preheat oven to 275 degrees F., rack in the middle position.

(That's two hundred seventy-five degrees F.)

> 3 egg whites *(save the yolks in the refrigerator to add to scrambled eggs)*
> ¼ teaspoon cream of tartar
> ½ teaspoon vanilla extract
> ¼ teaspoon salt
> 1 cup brown sugar *(pack it down in the cup when you measure it)*
> 2 Tablespoons flour *(that's ⅛ cup)*
> ½ cup finely chopped pecans *(measure AFTER chopping)*
>
> 3 to 4 dozen candied pecan halves OR 3 to 4 dozen Maraschino cherry halves to place on top of your cookies before baking.

Before you do anything else, separate the egg whites from the yolks. Place the egg whites in the bowl of your mixer so that they will warm to room temperature. Egg whites at room temperature yield more volume and whip easier than cold egg whites.

Place the egg yolks in a Tupperware container with a cover. Store the yolks in the refrigerator to add to your scrambled eggs the next morning. *(My mother always said that there's nothing like a little extra protein for breakfast to give you a head start to the day. I once tried to convince her that cookies had extra protein, but it didn't work.)*

Hannah's 1ˢᵗ Note: I always use a stand mixer when I make these cookies. It's a lot easier than whisking egg whites by hand in a copper bowl.

Prepare your baking sheets by lining them with parchment paper *(works best)* or brown parcel-wrapping paper *(also works, but parchment is preferable)*. Spray the paper with Pam or another non-stick cooking spray and dust it lightly with flour. You can also use baking spray, which is cooking spray mixed with flour.

Beat the egg whites with the cream of tartar, vanilla, and salt until they are stiff enough to hold a soft peak. Add the cup of brown sugar gradually, sprinkling it in with your impeccably clean fingers by quarter cups and beating hard for ten seconds or so after each sprinkling.

Take the bowl out of the mixer.

In another bowl, mix the flour with the ground nuts. Sprinkle them on top of the whipped egg whites and

fold them in with a rubber spatula, keeping as much air in the mixture as you possibly can.

Drop mounds of dough by heaping Tablespoons onto your prepared cookie sheets. If you place 4 mounds in a row and you have 4 rows, you'll end up with 16 cookies per sheet. These cookies do not spread out very much as they bake.

Hannah's 2nd Note: I use a Tablespoon from my silverware drawer to drop the mounds on the baking sheets. A cookie scooper doesn't work very well for this.

Place one candied pecan or a half Maraschino cherry *(rounded side up)* in the center of each mound. Push the pecan halves or half cherries down a bit, but leave them clearly visible.

Bake your Angel Crunch Cookies at 275 degrees F. for approximately 40 minutes, or until the meringue part of the cookie is slightly golden and dry to the touch.

Cool your cookies on the paper-lined cookie sheets by pulling the paper, cookies and all, over to a wire rack. When the cookies are completely cool, peel them carefully from the paper and store them in an air-

tight container in a dry place. *(A cupboard shelf is fine, just NOT the refrigerator!)*

Yield: 3 to 4 dozen sweet and crunchy meringue cookies that are as light as air and that everyone will love to eat.

Chapter
Twenty-four

When Mike left, Hannah mixed up a batch of Honey Drop Cookies. She was tired when she sat down on a stool at the workstation to wait for them to bake. As always, baking had helped to clarify her thoughts and she reached for her shorthand notebook, flipped to the suspect page, and was just beginning the process of deciding which suspect to interview next, when Michelle came through the swinging door from the coffee shop.

"Lisa's telling the story again," Michelle announced, "and I found out more from Aunt Nancy. She touched base with a couple of friends from her old hometown and she found out that Chef Duquesne's older brother is a career Navy man and he's an instructor at Annapolis Naval Academy. I called the academy and found out that he had an eight o'clock class the morning after Chef Duquesne was murdered. There's no way he could have flown to Minnesota from Maryland, killed his brother, and then flown back in time to teach that class."

"Good work, Michelle!" Hannah praised her. "I'll cross him off my suspect list."

"Who do you have left?"

"No one except Chef Duquesne's children, if he has any."

"And the unidentified suspect for an unknown motive," Michelle reminded her.

"Of course. That's a given in all murder investigations."

"Andrea and I took a few minutes to check online for other biographies of Chef Duquesne. Neither one of us found any mention of children."

Hannah thought about that for a moment. "I guess it's possible that Doc's friend at the DNA lab was wrong."

"He must have been, unless Chef Duquesne had children that no one knew about."

"He could have had a child that not even *he* knew about," Hannah suggested.

"I guess so, but that's really unlikely, isn't it?"

Hannah shrugged. "Given his background, it might not be as unlikely as you think!"

Michelle laughed. "You've got a point. According to what Aunt Nancy told us, he's been a womanizer all his life."

"That's right. Just think about it for a minute, Michelle. What if Allen Duke got some girl pregnant when he was in high school? If that happened, and the girl's parents didn't want her to marry Allen, they might have convinced her to leave town and live with a relative until the baby was born. Then she could have given it up for adoption."

"That's certainly possible. And sometimes parents who adopted really young children don't tell them that they're adopted."

There was a knock on the door and Michelle turned to Hannah. "Mother again?"

Hannah shook her head. "It's not Mother's knock. And it's not Norman's or Mike's either. I don't know this knock at all. I'd better go find out who it is."

Hannah hurried to the door and opened it. She stared at the man standing there in surprise, and then she laughed. "Ross! I didn't expect to see you before the competition! Come in and have a cup of coffee with us. And try out some of the new cookies I just baked."

"There's no way I'll turn down an invitation like that," Ross said, pulling her into his arms for a kiss. "Do you know you have flour on your nose?"

"No, but it makes sense. I've baked a lot of cookies to-day."

"Too bad it's not powdered sugar." Ross gave her a look that made the heat rise to her face, and Hannah knew she was blushing. Then he turned to Michelle. "Hi, Michelle. All ready to steal the show tonight?"

"I'm always ready to steal the show. They teach us how to do that in our beginning acting class. But tonight I'll let Hannah be the star. Those cookies of hers are phenomenal."

"All of Hannah's cookies are phenomenal."

The stove timer rang and Hannah motioned to Michelle. "Pour coffee for all three of us, will you please? I'll just take these cookies out of the oven and be with you in a minute."

The Honey Drop Cookies were the perfect color on top, golden brown. They smelled divine as Hannah took the pans out of the oven and set them on the baker's rack to cool. She didn't usually bake with honey. It was messy and it didn't keep as neatly as sugar in her pantry. But Aunt Nancy had promised that this recipe would work like a charm, and it certainly looked as if it had. Hannah could scarcely wait to taste them!

"Great aroma," Michelle commented as Hannah walked back to the work island and took a stool next to Ross. "They look really good, too."

"We'll find out in a couple of minutes." Hannah turned to Ross. "What brings you here?"

"I came by to see if there's anything I can do to help you. I'll be going out to Sally and Dick's in an hour or so, and I wondered if you wanted me to sound anyone out."

"About what?" Hannah was genuinely puzzled.

"About Chef Duquesne's murder. I can always do a background interview with anyone you choose."

"Great idea!" Hannah praised him. "Have you interviewed Helene Stone yet?"

"No. I was planning to do that this afternoon. I even asked her if she'd be free around four-thirty for a background interview."

Hannah gave Michelle a meaningful glance that said, *How about that? He must have read my mind.* And Michelle gave her a glance right back that said, *You're right. This is perfect. It means you don't have to confront a Food Channel judge before the competition tonight.*

"Was that sisterly telepathy?" Ross guessed, noticing the unspoken exchange.

"Yes. Tell him about the elevator in New York, Michelle. I'll go see if the Honey Drop Cookies are cool enough to taste."

Once Ross had learned about the suspicious incident on the elevator, he turned to Hannah. "So what do you want me to ask her?"

"See if you can think of a way to get her to tell you where she was and what she was doing on the night that Chef Duquesne was murdered. And if you can, see if she'll mention anything about her relationship with him, whether or not she thought he was a good chef, and what she thought of his comments at the judging table."

"Piece of cake," Ross said and then he gave Michelle an apologetic look. "Sorry if that brought back bad memories."

Michelle laughed. "Don't worry about it. Working on this case with Hannah has been really good for me. I'm not that sensitive about it anymore."

The cookies were still very warm, but Ross reached for one. "Good cookies!" he said after his first one. "I really like these, Hannah. The flavor is complex. I can taste the cinnamon and the honey, but . . . there's another flavor that's . . . I can't think of the best word to describe it."

"Deeper?" Hannah suggested. "A little darker, smokier, and more mysterious?"

"Yes, that's it! What is it?"

"Cardamom. I used the ground kind, but you can also buy the pods and grind the seeds yourself. It's a very powerful spice."

Michelle began to smile. "If you use too much, it's awful! I did that once when I made Great-Grandma Swensen's cardamom bread and nobody could eat it!"

"It reminds me of some other spices, but it's different," Ross said, taking another cookie from the plate. "It tastes a little like cinnamon, with a tiny bit of cloves thrown in." He turned to Michelle. "You mentioned your great-grandmother's cardamom bread. Does cardamom come from the Nordic countries?"

"Hannah?" Michelle threw the question to her.

"No, but they use a lot of it in baking sweets. It's also used in Indian cuisine, and it's often found in spice mixtures like curry. Then it's used as a savory in meat dishes."

"Where does it grow?" Ross asked, obviously curious.

"The biggest exporter of cardamom is Guatemala, but it's not indigenous there. A German planter imported it before the First World War. It's also grown in India, Pakistan, and other parts of Indonesia."

"And it's really expensive!" Michelle added.

"How expensive?" Ross asked her.

"I just bought a bottle of ground cardamom, and it cost me almost ten dollars at the grocery store."

Ross finished the last of his coffee and stood up. "Could I get a doggy bag for some of these cookies?" he asked them. "I might not have time to eat once I get ready and drive out to the lake."

"Only if you promise not to give some to a doggy," Michelle said, getting up from her stool to get one of their cookies-to-go bags.

"Okay. I guess I should have said a people bag."

"And please don't give any to a certain judge you're

going to interview," Hannah warned him. "She might like them better than what we're baking tonight."

Ross nodded. "I promise I won't share with her. And I promise I'll do my best to get the information you need."

"I know you will," Hannah said, rising from her stool and waiting while Michelle packaged the cookies so that she could walk Ross to the door.

"See you later, " Ross said, pulling her out the door and shutting it behind them. "I have to go back to the station after the competition tonight, but I'll stop by with my interview and we can go over it first. Would you like to go out to breakfast?"

"Yes, but let's save that for another morning. Michelle and I will make something for breakfast tomorrow."

"Sounds good to me. Do you have a practice session tomorrow morning?"

"Yes, but it's not until eight."

"Is six-thirty too early to come over?"

"It's perfect. I'll see you after the competition and again tomorrow morning."

Hannah made a move to go back inside, but Ross pulled her into his arms. "Not so fast, wife-to-be. I'm in desperate need of a kiss."

Hannah just had time for a brief laugh before Ross kissed her and she completely forgot what he'd just said. She also didn't notice that the afternoon had turned colder and a light snow was beginning to drift down from a sky that had turned from blue to leaden gray. She didn't notice, or think about a single thing until Ross released her and turned to open the door for her.

"Better go inside," he told her. "It's snowing."

"It is?" Hannah glanced up at the sky and blinked. "When did that happen?"

Ross grinned and gave her a gentle push inside. "Go get warm, Hannah. I'll see you at the competition tonight."

Hannah stood there in the warmth of the kitchen for a moment, and then she realized that Michelle was staring at her. "What?" she asked.

"Your hair's wet. Better go towel it off."

"Oh. Right."

"I'm never going to get married unless I look like you do right now."

Hannah blinked and shook her head to clear it. "You mean with wet hair?"

"No, I mean so much in love that you're in a daze. I wasn't sure at the very beginning, but now I am. You got the right guy, Hannah. Nobody you ever dated made you look this way before."

HONEY DROP COOKIES

DO NOT pre-heat the oven yet. This dough must chill before baking.

1 and ½ cups melted butter *(3 sticks, 12 ounces, ¾ pound)*

2 cups white *(granulated)* sugar

½ cup honey *(I used orange blossom honey)*

2 beaten eggs *(just whip them up in a glass with a fork)*

2 teaspoons baking soda

1 teaspoon salt

2 teaspoons cinnamon

½ teaspoon nutmeg *(freshly ground is best)*

¼ teaspoon cardamom *(if you don't have it, you can substitute more cinnamon for the cardamom)*

4 cups flour *(don't sift it—pack it down in the cup when you measure it)*

½ cup white sugar in a small bowl for rolling the dough balls

Melt the butter in a large microwave-safe bowl. Heat it on HIGH for 1 minute. Leave the bowl in the microwave for another minute and then check the but-

ter after to see it's melted. If it's not, give it more time, in 20-second increments, until it is.

Take the bowl out of the microwave and mix in the white sugar. Mix until it's all combined.

Add the honey to the bowl and mix it in. Mix until it's thoroughly incorporated.

Let the butter, sugar, and honey mixture sit on the counter to cool.

When the mixture in the bowl is not so hot it'll cook the eggs, add them to the large bowl and stir them in thoroughly. Be sure to mix until they're well combined.

Hannah's 1st Note: Lisa and I use a stand mixer to mix up this cookie dough down at The Cookie Jar. You can do it by hand at home, but using an electric mixer makes it a lot easier.

Sprinkle in the baking soda, salt, cinnamon, nutmeg, and cardamom. Mix until all of the ingredients are well combined.

Add the flour in one-cup increments, mixing after each addition.

Hannah's 2nd Note: You don't have to be painstakingly precise when you add the four cups of

flour. No one's going to know if one cup is a little bigger than the next one. Just make sure you mix after each addition of flour.

The dough will be quite stiff after you add the flour. This is exactly as it should be.

Cover the dough with plastic wrap and refrigerate it for at least two hours. *(Overnight is even better.)*

When you're ready to bake, take the cookie dough out of the refrigerator and let it sit, still covered with the plastic wrap, on your kitchen counter. It will need to warm just a bit so that you can work with it.

Preheat your oven to 350 degrees F., rack in the middle position.

While your oven is heating to the proper temperature, prepare your cookie sheets. You can either spray them with Pam or another nonstick cooking spray, or line them with parchment paper. *(The parchment paper is more expensive, but easier in the long run. If you use it, you can simply pull the paper over to the wire cooling rack, cookies and all.)*

Prepare a shallow bowl by filling it with a half cup of white sugar. This is what you'll use as a coating for the cookie dough balls you'll roll.

Take off the plastic wrap and roll the cookie dough into walnut-sized balls with your impeccably clean hands. Roll each dough ball in the bowl with the white sugar, one ball at a time, and place it on your prepared cookie sheet, 12 dough balls to a standard-sized sheet.

Press the dough balls down just a little so they won't roll off when you carry them to the oven.

Hannah's 3rd Note: If you form the dough into smaller dough balls, the cookies will be crispier. If you choose to do this, you'll have to reduce the baking time. If I roll smaller balls, I start checking the Honey Drop Cookies after 8 minutes in the oven.

Bake for 10 to 12 minutes or until they're nicely browned. The cookies will flatten out, all by themselves. Let them cool for 2 minutes on the cookie sheets and then move them to a wire rack to finish cooling.

Hannah's 4th Note: Honey Drop Cookies freeze well. Roll them up in foil, the same way you'd roll coins in a wrapper, put them in a freezer bag, and they'll be fine for 3 months or so.

Michelle's Note: When I make these at my rented house just off the Macalester campus, I put

the rolls in a box and write "FROZEN KIDNEYS
FOR HANNAH'S CAT" on the box. So far, none of
my roommates, every one of them a cookie hound,
has ever opened the box to see what's inside.

Yield: 8 to 10 dozen, depending on the size of your
dough balls, tasty, honey-infused, and delicious cookies.

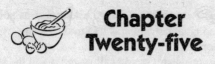

Chapter
Twenty-five

"Big smile," Michelle said, looking much more confident than Hannah felt at this point in the competition.

Hannah put on the biggest smile she could muster and made a mental note to ask Michelle how she had managed to speak without moving her lips. Did they teach ventriloquism in the acting class at Macalester College? Hannah doubted it, but she'd do her best to remember to ask the minute they were through presenting their cookies and had retired to the greenroom.

As she looked down at the plate Michelle had arranged, Hannah was pleased. Their Butterscotch Sugar Cookies looked wonderful, and so did the crystal dessert dishes Delores had given her. Hannah had filled them with the vanilla cream pudding she'd made. They'd discussed it on their way to the competition and both Hannah and Michelle had decided that their accompaniment for the cookies should be Emmy's Vanilla Custard, the recipe that Hannah had gotten from Lisa's late mother. It had been a difficult choice and they'd debated the virtues of Great-Grandma's Chocolate Pudding and Lisa's mother's vanilla custard, but they'd finally agreed that the rich chocolate taste of their great-grandmother's pudding might mask the mouth-watering scent and taste of their Butterscotch Sugar Cookies.

"The champagne is ready?" Hannah asked, just as soon as one of the Food Channel cameras had moved away from their baking station.

"I de-corked it, or whatever you call it, and it's in the silver bucket. You deliver the dessert and cookies. I'll take care of the champagne. I checked with Dick and he taught me how to fill the glasses so they don't foam over."

"Do you have a white napkin to use when you serve it?"

"I've got it. And Dick also taught me the correct way to wrap it around the champagne bottle."

"Don't forget to put the butterscotch liqueur in the bottom of the flutes before you pour in the champagne."

"I won't. Sally's going to be thrilled that we used the same champagne cocktail that she served at Doc and Mother's wedding reception. How about the coffee?"

"It's ready to go in the hot carafes." Hannah gestured toward the serving cart.

"And we're going to leave it there for the judges to help themselves after we serve the first cup?"

"Yes, exactly the way we did with the Double Rainbow Swirl Wedding Cake."

"I think that's a smart move on our part. Then nobody can accuse us of trying to get the judges smashed when we serve coffee, too."

Hannah turned away slightly to hide her grin from any wandering camera that might be panning across their workstation. "If I thought it would do any good, I would have told you to give each judge two or three glasses of champagne."

"Really?" Michelle asked.

Hannah could see that her sister was a bit shocked and she rushed to reassure her. "No, of course not. But I really want to win the cookie challenge."

"You will. Those Butterscotch Sugar Cookies are the best cookies I've ever tasted. Sally said she tasted a couple of every one of the practice cookies and ours were the best, hands down."

Hannah glanced at the judges. Now there were only four of them. To her relief, Helene Stone looked just as friendly as she'd been before. Ross must have done a good job interviewing her.

"Ross just waved at you," Michelle said, nudging her older sister.

"Thanks." Hannah smiled and waved back. She wished she could be as confident as Michelle seemed to be, but she was simply too nervous and the butterflies in her stomach had soared into the sky once again.

"Ready?" Michelle asked, as the announcer walked to center stage.

"As ready as I'll ever be," Hannah managed to say, a scant second before the camera focused on them.

"Miss Hannah Swensen and her assistant, Miss Michelle Swensen. You're up first, ladies. Please present your entry to the judges."

Hannah walked forward. Thank goodness she didn't have to pour the champagne! As nervous as she was right now, she'd probably spill it on one of the judges. She managed to keep the smile on her face, and her nervousness began to abate slightly as she pushed her serving cart toward the judging table. *I did my best, I did my best, I did my best*, she repeated her personal mantra for the night in her mind.

"What is this lovely creation?" Helene Stone asked when Hannah presented her with an antique crystal dessert dish containing Lisa's mother's favorite vanilla custard recipe. The dessert dish sat on a crystal plate and Butterscotch Sugar Cookies were arranged artfully around it.

"The dessert dish contains Emmy's Vanilla Custard. The recipe came from my partner's mother and it's the best vanilla custard I've ever tasted." Hannah turned to give Michelle a nod. They'd decided, on the drive to the competition, to take turns speaking.

"And the cookies are Butterscotch Sugar Cookies,"

Michelle continued smoothly. "They're Hannah's own creation."

"Champagne?" Jeremy Zales asked, accepting the flute Michelle had just poured for him.

"Yes," Hannah answered. "There's a half-ounce of DeKuyper Buttershots in the bottom. That's a butterscotch liqueur. The remainder of the flute is filled with domestic champagne. We used Korbel Brut tonight."

"Are you trying to influence us with champagne?" LaVonna Brach asked.

Michelle laughed. "Would it work?" she asked, clearly teasing the whole judging panel.

"It might, but I see a couple of coffee carafes," Christian Parker said. "Is that for us?"

"It is. We'll serve from the first carafe and we'll leave the second carafe with you so that you can have refills," Hannah told him. "Since we're in Minnesota and sweets are usually accompanied with a strong cup of coffee, we decided we'd better stand on Minnesota tradition and provide strong coffee for you."

"And we're glad you did," Jeremy Zales said, accepting a cup of coffee from Hannah. "Now let's see how well your cookies go with this vanilla custard."

The next few moments were filled with no comments, none at all. Hannah was beginning to get worried when LaVonna Brach put down her spoon and asked a question.

"Is there any butterscotch flavor in this pudding?"

"No," Hannah answered. "Michelle and I thought it would be too overwhelming and take away from the flavor of the cookies."

"And you were right," Christian Parker said.

"Agreed," Jeremy Zales offered his opinion. "As far as I'm concerned, the cookies are a stand-alone, but the vanilla custard is a very good accompaniment."

"Thank you, Miss Swensen and Miss Swensen," Helene Stone said, smiling at them. "Just as a matter of curiosity, have you ever thought about using cardamom in this vanilla custard?"

"Yes," Michelle answered. "We tried that, but both of us decided that the compelling flavor of the cardamom overshadowed the butterscotch in the cookies."

"And you were right," Christian Parker said again. "Cardamom is its own unique flavor." He turned to Helene Stone. "Wouldn't you agree, Helene?"

"I would," Helene Stone said, giving him a smile. "I just wanted to know if they'd tried it. The mark of a good dessert chef is to try new flavors and judge whether or not they enhance the original creation." She turned to face Hannah and Michelle. "Please leave your cookies. I'd like to have more later."

"Well, it's pretty clear that Helene Stone liked our cookies," Michelle said, once they'd finished straightening their workstation and were on their way to the greenroom. "At least it seemed that way to me. What do you think?"

"I agree. Of course, both of us could be wrong about that."

"I don't think so."

Hannah smiled at her youngest sister as she opened the door of the greenroom. It was deserted, and she breathed a sigh of relief. She didn't feel like making polite conversation with anyone else right now. Being the first to present their entry was a big advantage as far as she was concerned. It gave them a little breathing space before the other contestants presented their entries, straightened their workstations, and came to the greenroom.

"Brooke's up," Michelle announced, watching the large monitor on the wall in front of them. "Her cookies are really pretty."

"Good. I hope she does well," Hannah said, and she meant it.

"Do you think she did it?" Michelle asked.

The question was ambiguous, but was Michelle referring to Brooke's cookies, or something more ominous? Hannah thought she knew exactly what her sister was asking. But was it another case of sisterly telepathy, or was she reading more into the question than Michelle had meant when she'd asked it? There was only one way to find out, and Hannah turned to her sister. "Are you talking about Chef Duquesne's murder?"

"Of course. What did you think I was talking about?"

"Chef Duquesne's murder, but I didn't want to assume that without asking. No, I don't think she did it. I like Brooke. I don't *want* to think she did it."

"But you're planning to question her anyway?"

"Of course I am. I can't let my likes and dislikes get in the way of a murder investigation." Hannah glanced at the screen and smiled. "Look at the judges, Michelle. All four of them are smiling. That's a good sign for Brooke."

There was a close-up of Brooke's cookie platter, and Michelle glanced at Hannah. "Are those cookies deep fried?"

"Yes. Brooke used a rosette iron. Do you remember that metal, flower-shaped iron with a handle on the end that Great-Grandma Elsa used to make pretty cookies sprinkled with powdered sugar?"

"No. I guess I was too young to remember."

"I'll show you what it looks like when we get back to the condo. Great-Grandma Elsa gave me hers when she stopped making rosette cookies. I haven't seen those cookies in a long time. They're very fragile, and taking them off the rosette iron without breaking them is difficult."

"Do you think Brooke's cookies have a chance of winning?"

"I don't know, but I think they'll certainly place higher than her last entry."

"Because no one makes cookies like that anymore?"

"That would be part of it. But Brooke's cookies are unusual in another way. It looks to me as if they're chocolate. The dough is a lot darker than the recipe that Great-Grandma Elsa used. If they're chocolate, that's a real advantage. I've never seen a recipe for chocolate rosette cookies before."

"Brooke's going back to her station and she's smiling," Michelle commented. "I think she's pleased with what happened."

"And Jeremy Zales just took another cookie. That bodes well for Brooke."

Gloria Berkeley was up next, and Michelle turned up the volume on the monitor so that they could hear about her entry. After Gloria had finished describing her cookies, perfectly shaped rounds with colored bits of fruit on top, Michelle turned to Hannah. "LaVonna Brach just took a bite, and I don't think she looks impressed."

"Neither does Christian Parker. And look at Helene Stone. She put her cookie down after only one bite."

"Maybe she'll come in last this time," Michelle said. And then, when she noticed Hannah's expression, she began to explain. "I know it's not very nice of me, but I haven't liked Gloria ever since I found out about Brooke's marshmallow sauce."

The door to the greenroom opened and Brooke walked in. She was holding a plate with two cookies on it, and she was smiling. "I brought these for you," she said, setting the plate down on the coffee table in front of Hannah and Michelle.

"Thanks!" Michelle said, reaching for one of the cookies immediately. "They looked great on the monitor and they look even more delicious in real life."

"Chocolate!" Hannah exclaimed as she picked up the remaining cookie on the plate, took a bite, and confirmed her earlier speculation. "These are wonderful, Brooke! My great-grandmother used to make these, but she didn't make chocolate. She just used the recipe that came in the box with the rosette iron."

"That's a good recipe. It's the one I've always used in the

past. And the only reason these are chocolate is because of Loren."

"Loren Berringer?" Michelle asked.

"Yes. We were talking about the competition, and I told him I was going to make rosette cookies. Just like you, Loren knew what they were right away. He said his grandmother used to make them for Christmas. He told me he'd tried it once with his grandmother's rosette iron, but he could never get them off the iron without breaking them. And then he asked me what recipe I was using."

Hannah wiped her hands on one of the napkins Brooke had provided. The chocolate rosette cookies had been sprinkled with powdered sugar just like the vanilla ones that Great-Grandma Elsa had made. "What did you tell Loren?" she asked.

"I said I was using the recipe that came in the box, and I was a little worried about that. I mentioned that I wanted to make chocolate rosette cookies, but I wasn't sure how to do it."

"And he told you how to make them?" Michelle guessed.

"No. He said he didn't know either, but maybe we could figure it out. And we did! If I do well in the judging tonight, Loren is the one who deserves all the credit."

Hannah shook her head. "The two of you collaborated on the recipe. And Loren said he'd tried to make them, but he couldn't do it without breaking the cookies. It sounds like a joint effort to me."

"Me, too," Michelle said. And then she looked slightly worried. "You didn't tell the judges that, did you?"

"No. Loren told me not to say anything like that when the judges interviewed me, that as far as he was concerned, the idea for chocolate rosette cookies was mine since I was the one who'd made it work. He said that all he'd done was encourage me and that was what friends should do for each other."

Hannah exchanged glances with Michelle. Brooke had been much more animated than usual when she'd talked about Loren, and she looked much happier than she had earlier in the competition. It sounded as if there might be a bit more than simple friendship involved in Brooke and Loren's relationship. She gave a little nod to Michelle and got up to get herself a glass of water from the cooler at the far end of the greenroom.

"You like Loren, don't you?" Michelle asked Brooke.

Hannah turned slightly, so that she could see Brooke's face, and she saw the blush that began to color Brooke's cheeks. If Delores had written this scene in one of her Regency romance novels, she would have described it as a *telling blush*.

"Yes, I do," Brooke admitted. "He really helped me out."

"Loren seems like a really nice guy," Hannah said, walking back so that she could join the conversation. "He was very supportive when he helped you with the rosette cookies you made tonight."

"That's true, and he was also very supportive after . . ." Brooke stopped and took a deep breath. "I might as well tell you what happened. Maybe you can help me decide what I should do."

"We'd be happy to try," Hannah told her, and then she fell silent. It was a psychological tactic that had been used in one of the books Mike had given her to read. She glanced at Michelle, and Michelle gave her a slight nod to let her know that she'd realized what Hannah was doing.

There was a long silence. The only sound in the room was from the television monitor, and Hannah had deliberately turned down the volume.

The tension grew, and Hannah had almost come to the conclusion that the interviewing tactic she'd read about hadn't worked when Brooke gave a deep sigh.

"Alain Duquesne was my father," she said.

Chapter
Twenty-six

Both Hannah and Michelle were shocked speechless for another long moment. This was a development that neither one of them had expected. Brooke's statement had all the conversation-killing power of a bug bomb on a colony of ants.

Hannah was the first to recover. "Tell us about it," she said.

"I didn't know anything about it for years." Brooke's voice was shaky as she began to explain. "I always thought that my father was . . . my father. I had an older brother and a younger sister. There was no reason for me to doubt that it wasn't true. Honestly . . ." she stopped and cleared her throat. "You've got to believe me. I didn't know!"

"We believe you," Hannah reassured her. "How did you find out that Chef Duquesne was your father?"

"My mother told me. It was after my older brother entered my name in the *Dessert Chef Competition* and the Food Channel sent me a letter saying that they'd chosen me as one of the contestants. My mother was . . ." Brooke stopped speaking and took a deep, shuddering breath. "She was in the hospice ward at the hospital, and I thought . . . I thought it would make her happy. And instead it . . . it really upset her!"

"Oh, Brooke. I'm so sorry." Hannah moved over to give Brooke a hug. "But it really wasn't your fault. How could you have guessed that telling your mother about the competition would upset her?"

"That's true, but I still feel terrible about it. I would never have guessed that I had a different father. You see, my mother hadn't told anyone. My brother didn't know. My sister didn't know. And my mother said that she'd never told my father. None of us knew. She was the only one who knew, and she would have kept that secret forever if I hadn't been chosen as a contestant!"

Hannah gave Brooke another hug and moved back a bit. "What did your mother want you to do about all this?"

"She wanted me to make up some excuse to drop out of the competition. You see, it says right in the rules that relatives of the judges or the organizers are ineligible. And at the same time, she made me promise to keep her secret and never to tell my sister and brother that we had different fathers. She thought that if they knew, it would break up our family. And she said that when she was gone, the three of us would be the only family that was left and we would need each other."

"Did you try to drop out?" Michelle asked.

"Of course I did! It's what my mother wanted. I told my brother and sister that I was too nervous to be a contestant in a big competition like that, and I was sure that something bad would happen if I competed. And that would generate negative publicity for the restaurant."

"Your brother owns the restaurant?" Hannah asked, even though she remembered Brooke telling them that.

"Yes, and my sister and her husband helped him to finance it. I really thought I could convince them that I might hurt business if I stayed in the competition and they'd be happy to see me drop out."

"But they didn't see it that way?" Michelle asked.

"No. It was . . . just the opposite!"

Hannah could see that tears were gathering in Brooke's eyes so she quickly asked another question. "What did they say when you told them you wanted to drop out?"

"They were . . . very supportive. Too supportive. They said they had faith in me, that I was a good dessert chef. And then they told me that it didn't matter if I came in last, that it was a national competition and just being a contestant would increase business at the restaurant."

"Oh, boy!" Michelle shook her head. "That put you between a rock and a hard place."

"It did! And I couldn't tell them the real reason because I'd promised my mother I wouldn't."

"Have you heard from them since you've been here?" Michelle asked.

"Yes. They call me every night after the competition airs, and they give me a pep talk. And it turns out that they were right. Business at the restaurant has increased by sixty percent. They told me last night that they had to hire four new waitresses for the evening shift. And the bar business is way up because they record the competition and show it again, two hours later, in the lounge on the big-screen television."

"Let's talk about Chef Duquesne." Hannah brought the conversation around to the point where she could ask the questions that she needed Brooke to answer. "Why did you go to Chef Duquesne's room on the night he was killed?"

"You know about that?" Brooke looked astonished.

"Yes. The housekeeper saw you run back to your room, and she said you were crying."

"She's right. I had to tell someone why I had no business being in the competition. The lie I was living was just killing me. So I decided to ask Chef Duquesne for advice. I mean . . . he was my father, after all, and I thought he should know who I was."

"He didn't know before?"

Brooke shook her head. "My mother never told him. And I don't think he ever guessed, because she stopped working at the restaurant right after it happened between them. You see, my mother and my dad were having problems in their marriage and they separated. My mother went to live with my grandmother and Dad stayed in their apartment. My mother got a job at Chef Duquesne's restaurant as a dessert chef, and a second job as a fry cook at a truck stop. She told me that Grandma was living on a fixed income and she didn't want to be a financial burden on her, especially since Grandma was taking care of my brother while my mother worked."

"Your mother was working two full-time jobs?" Michelle asked.

"Yes. And helping Grandma take care of my brother when she was home. One night my mother was baking desserts for the next day at Chef Duquesne's restaurant when he came in. And he found her crying because she was so lonely and so tired. He asked her what was wrong and she told him, and she said that he was a good listener, and . . . well . . . you can guess the rest."

"So your mother had an affair with Chef Duquesne?" Hannah asked.

"No! She told me it was just that once. And she felt so guilty, she ended up calling my father and saying that she wanted to work things out with him. She packed up my brother and they went back home to my dad. They saw a marriage counselor, and they were doing great working things out when she found out that she was pregnant with me."

"That must have been a shock," Michelle commented.

"She said it was. She didn't know what to do. She wasn't sure whether Chef Duquesne was my father, or if my dad was my father. So she . . . she never mentioned it to Dad. They had a happy marriage, and they were together until the day he died."

"And your mother never told anyone about this?" Hannah asked.

"No one knew. She would have taken that secret to her grave if I hadn't told her about the *Dessert Chef Competi-*

tion. She said that she'd decided that a confession on her part wouldn't do anyone any good, but she had to speak up, now that I was a contestant."

"What did Chef Duquesne say when you told him?" Hannah asked, bringing them back to the point.

"He said that it was impossible, that he'd never had anything to do with my mother. He told me that he knew trouble when he saw it . . . and . . . he accused my mother of . . . of playing around with every man on his kitchen staff!"

"I'm so sorry." Hannah's heart went out to Brooke.

"But that's not all! When I started to cry and told him that my mother was dead, he wasn't sympathetic at all. And then he said that this was a first for him, that nobody had ever tried to shake him down for a higher score in any competition he'd judged by claiming to be his illegitimate child!"

Hannah knew the next part of the story. "So you ran out of his room, crying."

"Yes! I ran straight back to my room. And I double-locked the door, and I cried and cried. And then Loren heard me crying and knocked on my door."

"You told him what had happened with Chef Duquesne?"

"Yes! And he called room service, ordered a bottle of wine for me, and let me talk until I fell asleep. When I woke up in the middle of the night, Loren was there, curled up and sleeping on the little couch in my room. And he was still sleeping right there when I woke up the next morning."

"Loren's a good friend to have," Michelle said.

Brooke smiled. "Yes, he is. I was feeling so terribly alone and upset when I got back to my room. Thinking about it now, I really don't know what I would have done without Loren."

Hannah glanced at the monitor and smiled. "And speaking of Loren, there he is now. I'll turn up the volume. We were so busy talking, I guess we missed Gloria."

"Good!" Brooke said. "I didn't want to see her anyway."

She paused for a moment and then she smiled. "Look at Loren's cookies! They're just beautiful!"

Hannah and Michelle exchanged amused glances. Loren's cookies looked very good, golden brown on top and artfully arranged on a cobalt-blue platter that made them look even more golden and delicious. Handsome, yes. Good-looking, yes. But neither Hannah nor Michelle would have described them as *beautiful*. It seemed that their friend Brooke was now seeing one person in the world through rose-colored glasses, and only one emotion could cause a phenomenon like that to occur. Perhaps Brooke didn't know it yet, but they did. Brooke was definitely falling in love with Loren.

It was time for the judges to tally the scores and Hannah had to admit that she was more nervous than she'd been in any of the other challenges. Coming up with a good score in the cookie challenge was of paramount importance to her business.

"Smile," Michelle urged her, as the judges took their seats and the cameras began to pan the contestants.

Hannah smiled, hoping that her put-on smile didn't look like a grimace. This part of the program made her even more anxious than she'd been when she'd presented her cookies to the judges.

The announcer always started with the lowest scoring entry and worked his way up to the winner of the challenge. Hannah took a deep breath and held it. She didn't think she'd come in dead last, but anything could happen.

"In fifth place is Chef Gloria Berkeley," the announcer declared, and Hannah breathed a huge sigh of relief. She'd truly believed that her Butterscotch Sugar Cookies were just too good to come in last, but it was still a big relief. If she came in fourth, she wouldn't be happy, but she could live with herself. And if she came in third, in the center of the pack, she would be disappointed, but not devastated. Second would be better, a lot better. After all, every other contestant was a noted dessert chef and she was just a small-town baker. But if somehow luck smiled on her tonight and she came in first, she would be ecstatic!

"Our fourth-place winner is Chef Rodney Paloma."

The moment Rodney's name was announced, Michelle reached out to squeeze Hannah's hand. Their sisterly radar was at work again. If Gloria and Rodney had taken fifth place and fourth place, the top three were Hannah, Loren, and Brooke. Now she could relax slightly.

"The judges wanted me to tell you that the top three places were very difficult for them to decide. For this reason, they have reached a tie for first place in the cookie challenge. The third-place cookie was excellent and received top scores on appearance, consistency, and flavor. The judges did not feel, however, that it was as innovative as the top two cookies. For that reason, third place belongs to Chef Loren Berringer."

"This leaves a first-place tie between Chef Brooke Jackman with her unusual and innovative chocolate rosette cookies and Hannah Swensen with her incredible Butterscotch Sugar Cookies!"

Hannah heard the next announcement through a fog of happiness. The announcer was telling the audience that the next and final challenge of the competition would be a free-for-all challenge. The contestants were allowed to choose any dessert they wished to make and present it to the judges.

Hannah smiled and hugged Michelle. They'd won! And then Brooke came racing over to hug both of them. That was when Michelle must have glanced up just in time to see a cameraman getting a shot of all three of them because she said, "Smiles! Quick! Link arms!"

And they did exactly as Michelle instructed so the cameraman could get a good shot of all three of them celebrating their first-place win.

Chapter Twenty-seven

"**I**'m all set," Ross told them, sitting down with the remote control. "I think I've got something that'll help." He smiled as he started the taped interview. "What time did Doc say that Chef Duquesne was murdered?"

"Between midnight and three in the morning," Hannah answered. They were sitting on her couch, all four of them. Ross was seated on one end, Hannah was in the middle next to him with Moishe in her lap, and Michelle was on the other end of the couch. They were sipping tall glasses of lemonade, and Moishe was eating a salmon-flavored, fish-shaped kitty treat.

"Between midnight and three," Ross repeated. "Good! That's what I remembered. Well . . . this interview should help to give Judge Stone an alibi."

"She looks happy," Michelle said when Helene Stone appeared on the screen.

"She was happy and relaxed," Ross replied. "You'll see why when I fast-forward through the opening questions."

They watched the screen as the images sped by. Helene Stone moved only inches, but Ross had shot this footage in the lobby by the massive stone fireplace and the people in the background were moving at a speed that was humanly impossible under their own locomotion.

"Here we go," Ross said, stopping the forward motion and turning up the volume. "Just listen to this next part."

"Are you glad the competition is almost over?" Ross asked the next question of his interview subject.

"Actually, no," Helene replied with a smile. "My husband surprised me by flying in two nights ago, and it's beautiful and relaxing out here in the winter at this lovely inn. It's been almost like a second honeymoon for us."

"You said that he surprised you by coming here?" Ross followed up on her statement.

"Yes. I had no idea he was coming. He called me the afternoon of the cake challenge and told me he'd just landed at the airport, rented a car, and was about to drive here. He got here an hour before the competition was due to start. You probably saw him in the front row. Sally added a chair on the aisle for him."

"Tall with dark brown hair and wearing a blue blazer and grey pants?" Ross asked her.

"That's my husband. Both of us are staying for your wedding and the reception. I wish we could stay even longer, but we have to get back to New York the next day."

Ross paused the tape and turned to them. "What do you think? Does that take her name off your suspect list?"

It took Hannah a moment to reply, and when she did, she worded her reply carefully. Ross was so proud of himself for getting the information about Helene Stone's husband, and it was very helpful. "It's certainly a factor, Ross. And it does make her a less likely suspect. Now all I have to do is check to make sure that both of them stayed in their room during the time when Chef Duquesne was murdered."

"I'm way ahead of you," Ross said with a smile. "I spoke with Sally right after I finished the interview and she checked with her staff. The college kid at the desk said they sat in the lobby by the fireplace until almost midnight and then they went up to their room. He can see the elevator from the desk and they got on together. That elevator didn't come down again until some woman got off and rushed out the front door."

Hannah glanced at Michelle and knew they were both thinking the same thing. The woman had been Aunt Nancy.

"One or both of them could have come down the stairs," Hannah suggested.

"I asked about that, too. It's possible, but it's doubtful that one or both of them did that. You see, Helene's husband stopped at the bar right before Dick closed it for the night and ordered a bottle of champagne. Dick offered to bring it up to their room after he closed the bar, and they took him up on his offer. He said he delivered it at twelve-thirty, opened it for them, and poured two glasses. Sally had some hors d'oeuvres left in the walk-in cooler so he brought up some of those, too."

"And there was no one in the kitchen or the walk-in cooler at twelve-thirty?"

"No. And no one was in the hallway, either. Sally's housekeeper said she was almost positive they didn't leave their room. Her room is right across from theirs, and she's a light sleeper. The night maintenance guy was supposed to oil their door because it squeaked when it opened and shut, but he hadn't gotten around to it yet. She told Sally that she's sure she would have heard their door if it opened or closed during the night."

"You've convinced me!" Hannah said, giving Ross a little hug. "You did a super job following up on everything and I really appreciate it. I'll take Helene Stone off my suspect list. And thanks to you, I can now narrow the time of death by a half hour since Dick said there was no one in the kitchen and no one in the walk-in cooler when he got the hors d'oeuvres."

"One other thing," Ross said, "I remembered what you said about the bottle of red wine and the glasses on the kitchen counter when you went in the next morning. I asked Dick if he noticed them on the counter, and he said no, he doesn't usually go in the kitchen when no one's there, and he had to look around for a plate. He found a clean one on the kitchen counter and he's sure he would have noticed if there'd been an open bottle of wine and glasses."

"Interesting," Hannah said. "It took some time to open the bottle and pour two glasses."

"And Chef Duquesne's glass was half empty," Michelle pointed out. "That means he'd taken time to drink half a glass of wine."

"To *sip* half a glass of wine," Hannah corrected her. "I don't think Chef Duquesne would have tossed back a half a glass of red wine. It's just not in character for him."

"You're right," Ross said. "And that means we can tentatively shorten the time of death by another fifteen or twenty minutes."

"Right," Hannah agreed. "And Dick said he didn't meet anyone coming down from the second floor or anyone walking in the halls. That could add another five or ten minutes. Thanks to you, Ross, we can shorten Doc's time of death by a whole hour. And that means Chef Duquesne was killed between one and three in the morning."

Hannah smiled in her sleep. She was on a lovely beach with Ross and it was their honeymoon. The sun was warm, the gentle sea breeze caressed her skin, and she knew she'd never been this happy before in her life. She was with the man she loved. Her husband. And everything was so perfect, she had trouble believing that it was real.

They were relaxing together in a tropical paradise. Jamaica, Aruba, she wasn't sure exactly where, but it was delightful and she intended to enjoy every moment with her new husband. She was so happy and so relaxed that her eyes had fluttered closed, and now both of them were napping on the sparkling white sand of the beach.

The sun was so warm. The breeze held a hint of moisture

from the azure-blue sea. She sighed as she breathed in the unique and wonderful scent of the tropics. Cinnamon, rich and pungent. Nutmeg that added depth to the mixture. A hint of cardamom, a smidgen of allspice, perhaps even a trace of ginger to carry her away in her tropical dream.

The fruits on the breeze were redolent with a ripe and mouthwatering scent. So wonderful. So unusual. There were some she could not identify, a mystery of the island. But there was one scent in particular that was marvelously aromatic, tauntingly addictive, and both irresistible and awe-inspiring. It was a scent that made her want to jump up and search it out so that she could taste it.

Did her love smell it? Hannah reached out to touch his hand. It was warm, loving, and . . . furry!

"Moishe!" she exclaimed, opening her eyes to find him snuggled into the pillow beside her.

"Rrrowww!" Moishe yowled and jumped down to the floor. He raced across the bedroom rug and launched himself up to the top of her dresser where he stared at her accusingly.

"Sorry," Hannah apologized. "I didn't mean to scare you. I was dreaming about Ross and a tropical island, and he had fur on his hand."

Moishe was still staring. Obviously, her explanation hadn't registered with him. "I *said* I was sorry."

As she watched, Moishe gave the kitty equivalent of a shrug. He stared at her for a moment, and then he settled himself between the lamp and her hairbrush, and began to take his morning bath.

Hannah felt better, now that Moishe was purring. She gave a little sigh of relief and went on with her explanation. "You see, Ross and I were on a tropical beach and we fell asleep. I was smelling the most marvelous aroma and . . ." She aborted her explanation in mid-thought and sniffed the air again. The scent was still there!

"Michelle's baking," she stated the obvious to her feline

roommate. "And it smells incredibly wonderful. Let's go find out what it is."

Hannah reached for her slippers at the same time that Moishe jumped down from the dresser. She pulled on her slippers, he padded over to watch her put on her comfortable old robe, the one she'd found at the Helping Hands thrift store, and cat and cat-lover walked down the hallway and through the living room to the kitchen.

"What is it?" Hannah asked, almost causing Michelle, who was standing by the oven, to drop the pan she'd just taken from the interior.

"Blue Banana Muffins," Michelle told her, placing the muffin pan on the wire rack sitting on the counter. "I'm trying an experiment."

"Blue Bananas?"

"That's just the name I made up for them. It's like your Blue Apple Muffins. Bananas and blueberries with a streusel topping."

"It smells successful to me," Hannah said, taking a seat at her kitchen table. "The scent woke me up from a really great dream. I was napping on a beach on a tropical island with Ross on our honeymoon. The scent of your muffins is probably why I dreamed it in the first place."

"That sounds like a great dream. I'm sorry my muffins woke you up."

"That's okay. Who knows what could have come next? Hurricane, shark attack, whatever. I can hardly wait to taste one. They smell fantastic. Of course I'm a little too sleepy to judge anything right now."

"Here you go." Michelle poured a cup of coffee and set it down in front of Hannah.

Hannah took a sip of the strong, hot brew and smiled. "You're a lifesaver, Michelle."

"That's good, just as long as I don't have to save you from that hurricane or that shark."

Michelle poured a cup of coffee for herself and took the

chair across from Hannah. The two sisters sat in companionable silence for several minutes, sipping their coffee.

"You said your muffins were an experiment?" Hannah asked when she was capable of rational thought.

"Yes. I'm trying to use frozen bananas."

"Do you mean the chocolate-covered ones?"

"No. Just frozen bananas."

"Where do you buy frozen bananas?"

"You don't. You freeze them yourself. Suzi does it all the time."

It was too early to figure that out. Hannah got up, fetched the carafe of coffee, and brought it over to the table. She poured herself a second cup, took a sip, and turned to her youngest sister again. "Who's Suzi?"

"Jessie's mother. Jessie's one of my housemates at college and her mother lives in Phoenix. Jessie says Suzi's been freezing bananas for years."

"Overripe bananas?" Hannah asked, remembering an article she'd read.

"No. That's the beauty of it. Suzi buys bananas when they're on sale and she buys a lot of them. She chooses only bananas that are perfectly ripe. Then she peels them, puts them in freezer bags, and freezes them for up to six months. Maybe longer, but Suzi's never last that long!"

"Interesting." Hannah breathed in the scent again. "Are your muffins cool enough to eat?"

"Maybe not, but I'm willing to try one if you are."

"I'm willing. They smell really good!"

"They are. Jessie brought some from home the last time she went to visit her mother. They don't taste like regular banana muffins."

Hannah's mouth was watering as Michelle got up and returned with a muffin for each of them. "I think they're a lot better than any banana muffins I've ever tasted. Let's see what you think."

Hannah removed the cupcake paper and split the muffin

in half. She picked up one half, juggled it a bit from hand to hand, and then she took a bite. "Yummy!" she said after she'd swallowed. "They don't have that perfume-like smell that always reminds me of fruit gone bad."

"I know. That's what I've always noticed about banana bread and I tried to make it once with bananas that weren't overripe. That's when I discovered that you can't do it. The bananas won't mush up unless the peel has a lot of black spots."

"I know," Hannah said, taking another bite of her muffin. "I even tried to do it with a food processor, but the bananas wouldn't liquefy the way they're supposed to for banana bread or muffins."

"Well, these do. I think it's because they're peeled and then they're frozen. All you have to do is thaw them and they liquefy. And the taste is different."

"It certainly is!" Hannah was thoughtful as she took another bite. "Perfectly ripe frozen bananas would work for everything from muffins, to banana bread, to banana pudding."

"So you like these muffins?" Michelle asked.

"I love them! I like them so much that if there was a muffin challenge, we'd make them for the judges!"

BLUE BANANA MUFFINS

Preheat oven to 375 degrees F., rack in the middle position.

Before you begin: take 2 medium-sized frozen bananas out of the freezer. *(See the instructions at the bottom of recipe for freezing bananas.)* Remove them from the bag and put them in a bowl on the counter to thaw.

The Muffin Batter:

> ¾ cup melted butter *(1 and ½ sticks, 6 ounces)*
> 1 cup white *(granulated)* sugar
> 2 beaten eggs *(just whip them up in a glass with a fork)*
> 2 teaspoons baking powder
> ½ teaspoon salt
> ½ teaspoon cinnamon
> ¼ teaspoon nutmeg *(freshly grated is best)*
> ½ cup fresh or frozen blueberries *(no need to thaw if they're frozen)*
> 2 cups plus one Tablespoon all-purpose flour *(pack it down in the cup when you measure it)*
> ½ cup milk
> 1 cup thawed frozen banana

The Crumb Topping:

> ½ cup white *(granulated)* sugar
> ⅓ cup all-purpose flour *(pack it down in the cup when you measure it)*
> ¼ cup softened butter *(½ stick, 2 ounces)*

Grease the <u>bottoms only</u> of a 12-cup muffin pan *(or line the cups with double cupcake papers—that's what I do at The Cookie Jar.)*

Mix the melted butter with the sugar in the bowl of an electric mixer. Beat until they're thoroughly combined.

Add the eggs and beat on low until they're incorporated.

Sprinkle in the baking powder, salt, cinnamon, and nutmeg. Beat them in at LOW speed.

Put one Tablespoon of flour in a baggie with your cup of fresh or frozen blueberries. Shake it gently to coat the blueberries and leave them in the bag for now.

Add half of the remaining two cups of flour to your bowl and mix it in with half of the milk. Then add the rest of the flour and the rest of milk, and mix thoroughly.

Measure out one cup of the thawed frozen banana.

Add the cup of banana to your muffin batter. Stir it in thoroughly.

Hannah's 1st Note: If there's any banana left over, save it in a covered container in the refrigerator to add to pancakes in the morning. It may turn dark overnight, but that doesn't matter. The kids will love the taste, especially if you also add a few chocolate chips to your pancake batter when you put it in the frying pan!

Fold the frozen or fresh blueberries into your muffin batter. Mix gently so the blueberries will stay intact.

Fill the muffin tins three-quarters full and set them aside. If you have any batter left over, grease the bottom of a small tea-bread loaf pan and fill it with your remaining batter.

To make the Crumb Topping, mix the sugar and the flour in a small bowl. Add the softened butter and cut it in until it's crumbly. *(You can also do this in a food processor with chilled butter and the steel blade.)*

Fill the remaining space in the muffin cups with the crumb topping.

Bake your muffins in a 375 F. degree oven for 25 to 30 minutes. *(The tea-bread should bake about 10 minutes longer than the muffins.)*

When your muffins are baked, take them out of the oven and set the muffin pan on a wire rack to cool for at least 30 minutes. *(The muffins need to cool in the pan for easy removal.)* Then just tip them out of the cups and enjoy.

These are wonderful when they're slightly warm, but the banana and blueberry flavors will intensify if you store them in a covered container overnight.

Hannah's 2nd Note: To freeze bananas for baking or drinks, buy perfectly ripe bananas, peel them, cut them into 2 pieces and place the pieces into a closeable plastic sandwich bag. Bag all the bananas you want to freeze this way. When you have as many as you want, slip the sandwich bags into a large freezer bag and stick them in your freezer. Freeze them solid before using them, but they can be stored in your freezer for as long as 6 months.

To thaw frozen bananas, take out as many as you need, extract them from the sandwich bag and place the frozen pieces in a bowl on your counter.

Cover the bowl and let it warm for twenty to thirty minutes. Your bananas will turn to banana puree all by themselves without benefit of food processor or blender. Stir them up, measure out what you need, and use them for baking or for smoothies.

**Chapter
Twenty-eight**

It was their practice session before the final challenge, and they were working in Sally's kitchen. The stove timer rang, and Hannah removed both pies from the oven and set them on a rack to cool. Their section of the kitchen smelled so good, her mouth was watering.

"What do you think?" she asked Michelle. "The top crust pie, or the French crumble pie?"

"Both. Let's give the judges a little slice of both pies. It shows your versatility."

"Good idea. How about the toppings?" Hannah pointed to the tray Michelle had prepared with slices of sharp cheddar cheese, the vanilla ice cream that Michelle had made in the ice cream maker, and Hannah's Cinnamon Crème Fraiche.

"Serve all three on the tray and let them choose. Do you want to taste my ice cream?"

"You betcha!"

Michelle laughed and dished up a scoop for Hannah. She waited until Hannah had tasted it and then she asked, "Is it good enough?"

"I don't know. I'd have to eat at least a gallon to be sure." She waited until Michelle laughed and then she did, too. "It's wonderful, Michelle! And I wasn't kidding about eating more. I could sit down right here and eat the whole gallon."

"Then it's a go for the final challenge?"

"I think we've done the right thing, Michelle. Your ice cream is phenomenal and Mom's Apple Pie is the best pie I make."

"That's true, as long as you don't count your Lemon Meringue, or your Key Lime Pie, or any of the other pies you bake."

"Thanks, Michelle. How about coffee? Are we serving it tomorrow night?"

"I think we'd better. It's become almost a tradition with the judges. Let's pack our things in the truck and then see if Sally has anything left on her breakfast buffet. Maybe we'll run into someone we need to see."

Hannah smiled. "Like Loren, or Rodney. We haven't had a chance to talk to them. If we're lucky, they'll come down from their rooms at different times and we can catch them alone."

Michelle picked up the ice cream bowl and carried it to their designated freezer.

"Lock it after you put it in," Hannah reminded her. "I don't trust Gloria not to tamper with our ingredients."

"I agree, and I will. We have to interview her, too . . . don't we?"

"Yes. I need to know where Gloria was between one and three in the morning on the night that Chef Duquesne was murdered. And I need a timetable for Mayor Bascomb, too. That means I have four suspects left to interview and only three days to do it. Gloria, Loren, and Rodney will probably leave on Sunday for home."

"Then we'll save Mayor Bascomb for last," Michelle decided. "He's not going anywhere. Come on, Hannah. Let's hurry and load up those pies, then we'll come back for

Sally's buffet. Just looking at them is too much for me. I'm practically starving to death."

Hannah laughed. "After four Blue Banana Muffins?"

"Yes. I wonder if Sally's got waffles this morning. I could do with a couple of those. And maybe an omelet or eggs Benedict on the side. I really like Sally's hollandaise."

Hannah turned around to stare at her youngest sister. Michelle had a perfect figure and she ate every time she got hungry. The same was true of Andrea and Delores. It made Hannah wish that she'd inherited the same metabolism, or body type, or whatever it was that allowed her mother and sisters to eat anytime they wanted and still not gain an ounce.

"Uh-oh!" Michelle said as they walked into the dining room and surveyed Sally's breakfast buffet.

Hannah turned to her in surprise. "What's wrong?"

"Loren and Rodney. They're sitting together at that corner table. What are we going to do now?"

"We'll go with our original plan. I'll talk to Rodney and you'll talk to Loren. And then, when you're talking to Loren, notice something on his plate and say you didn't see whatever dish it was. Ask him where he got it and I'll bet he'll offer to show you."

"You're probably right. Loren seems like a gentleman. And when I get him alone, I'll be able to ask him if he spent the whole night with Brooke."

"Yes, if you can figure out how to do it."

"I already figured that out. All I have to do is ask him to alibi Brooke for the time of the murder and he'll say he was with her if he was."

"How are you going to know if he's protecting her, or telling the truth?"

"Easy. He'll be uncomfortable if he has to lie for Brooke. He'll do it, but it'll show on his face."

"Okay. That sounds like a plan to me. Do you think you can give me a few minutes alone with Rodney?"

"That's easy. Brooke just walked in with her assistant and they took a table near the front. I'll point that out to Loren and we'll walk over to say hello."

Their plan worked like a charm, and five minutes later, Hannah was alone with Rodney while Michelle and Loren went off to find Sally's corned beef hash. "Did you practice for tomorrow yet?" Hannah asked him.

"Not yet. I've got the kitchen from twelve to one-thirty. How about you?"

"Michelle and I just got through. I had to put things away in the cooler, though. Michelle hasn't been able to go in there since she found Chef Duquesne. It really bothers her."

"That's understandable. From what I heard, it can't have been a pretty sight."

"I guess the police aren't getting anywhere with their investigation. At least that's what I heard. Were you in the hotel when Chef Duquesne was murdered?"

"What time was that?"

"Between one and three in the morning."

"Actually . . . no. I was so excited about tying for first place with you in the cake challenge, I couldn't sleep. I went for a drive around the lake. You live in a pretty place, Hannah."

"Yes, I do. You ought to see the lake in the summer. It's just lovely. What time did you get back from your drive?"

Rodney stared at her for a moment. "Why all the questions? You don't suspect me of killing him, do you?"

"Of course not. Why would you? You took first place with that incredible cake of yours."

"True. He wasn't very nice to some of the other contestants, though. As I remember, Gloria really didn't do very well that night."

"You're right. I think she came in last. Relax, Rodney. The

only reason I asked about the time you got back is to find out if you saw anyone when you came in the front door."

"Oh. Okay. Well, for one thing, I didn't use the front door. I used the back door. I came in the back way because I was parked out there."

"But then you had to walk past the kitchen door."

"Right! I didn't even think about that! Of course I didn't know about Chef Duquesne then."

"What time did you leave, and what time did you come back? It could be important, Rodney."

"I can see that now. I didn't check my watch when I left, but I think I left a little before one. And I know I was gone for two or three hours. I stopped off at some little place for a drink. It was quite a ways away, and I think they were open until one in the morning. I got back here after three. I'm pretty sure of that. When I got to bed it was three-thirty and I remember thinking that if I got up in time to make Sally's breakfast buffet at ten in the morning, I'd get close to seven hours of sleep."

"Did you see anyone walking on your way out or when you came in?"

"No one at all. The lobby was deserted. The night guy at the desk must have been somewhere else. I didn't see anyone in the halls either."

"Thanks, Rodney," Hannah said, even though he'd been of very little help to her. "If you remember anything you didn't tell me about that night, will you let me know?"

"Sure thing. No problem." Rodney stood up and gave her a smile. "That's enough breakfast for me. I'm going to go up and read through my recipe again before my practice time in the kitchen."

After Rodney left, Hannah went back to the buffet line for more coffee and when she got back to her table, Michelle was there. "What did you find out?" she asked her youngest sister.

"Loren was with Brooke all night. He was a little embarrassed about telling me, but when I said she'd already told us, he was fine with it. He wasn't lying, Hannah. I'm convinced of it. How about Rodney?"

"He seemed sincere and his account of that night was reasonable."

"But you're not convinced."

Hannah shrugged. "Not really, but I'm never convinced that anything is completely true until I can identify the killer."

"That's fair. What do we do now?"

"We go back to The Cookie Jar and find out what Lisa and Aunt Nancy need us to bake. Then we'll check in with Andrea and Mother to see if they found out anything about Mayor Bascomb. After that . . . I don't know."

"Do we have anything to do for the competition tomorrow night?"

Hannah considered it, and then she shook her head. "No, not really. We did fine in practice today and I think we're ready."

"Great! By the way, did Mother tell you that she invited all of us for dinner at the penthouse tonight?"

"Oh, no!" Hannah groaned. "I'm sorry, Michelle . . . I really don't think that I'm up for . . ."

"Just listen for a second," Michelle interrupted what was sure to be a refusal. "I already talked to Ross and it's fine with him. Mother wants both Moishe and Cuddles to come. We're going to eat outside under the dome, and she thought they'd like to play in the garden. Andrea and Bill are coming. Grandma McCann is taking Tracey and Bethie to a movie. And Mike, Lonnie, Norman, and Ross are going to meet us at Mother's. What do you say, Hannah? Doesn't it sound like a nice, relaxing evening?"

Hannah thought about that for a minute. "Yes, it does . . . if it were anywhere else but Mother's place."

"What's wrong with Mother's place? It's beautiful, and she's got a swimming pool and a Jacuzzi."

"I know. There's just one thing, Michelle. I'd like to know if Mother is making her Hawaiian Pot Roast, or her EZ Lasagna."

"Neither one. Mother's not cooking tonight. Doc's picking up pizzas and salads at Bertanelli's on his way home from the hospital."

"In that case, it's a deal!" Hannah said, smiling at her sister. "Let's take our apple pies with us and we can all have dessert."

The sky was just beginning to darken when Michelle, Andrea, and Hannah climbed into the hot tub. A partially empty bottle of white wine sat in a cooler on the lip of the Jacuzzi, and all three Swensen sisters were holding one of their mother's new non-breakable wineglasses.

"These are nice," Hannah said, sinking down in the bubbles and smiling.

"Yes, they are," Andrea agreed. "Mother told me she got a whole assortment of non-breakable glasses for the pool and Jacuzzi. She said she knocked one down from the lip of the pool and it didn't even scratch."

"Speaking of things that got knocked down," Hannah said to Andrea, "did you manage to find out anything about Mayor Bascomb?"

Andrea laughed. "Yes, I did. Stephanie got him good this time. I saw that new ring he bought her, and it must have cost a fortune! I really didn't find out much more about the mayor, although I did uncover some things about Gloria."

"What things?" Hannah moved a little closer.

"Gloria was back in her room at Sally and Dick's at eleven-thirty that night. I went out there for lunch yesterday and I talked to one of the waitresses in the bar. She said that Gloria called down to order a bottle of champagne and the waitress logged in the time."

"Do you think Gloria had Mayor Bascomb with her in her room?" Michelle asked.

"No. I questioned the waitress about that, and she said she took the bottle of champagne up there herself and no one was there except Gloria."

"Was she sure of that?" Hannah asked. "I wouldn't put it past Mayor Bascomb to hide in the bathroom or the closet until the waitress left."

"I asked her that. She said she noticed the bathroom door was wide open and so was the closet. There was no one else in the room. Not only that, the waitress brought up two glasses, and Gloria told her to take one back to the bar."

"Either our esteemed mayor struck out, or he's a fast worker." Michelle commented.

"I heard that, Michelle!" Delores walked over to the Jacuzzi. "That wasn't very polite, dear. But the information you received is correct, Andrea. Ricky-Ticky came home at twelve-thirty and he was reeking of perfume. That would lead me to believe that it was a rather rapid assignation."

"That's exactly what I said!"

"No, dear. That's what you *should* have said. I phrased it much more delicately."

"Hold on." Hannah knew she had to divert what might evolve into a mother-daughter skirmish. She turned to her mother. "How do you know what time Mayor Bascomb got home?"

"I invited Stephanie for tea in the garden this afternoon and she told me. We had a nice bottle of white wine, just like the one I opened for you girls, and your caviar pie."

"*You* made my caviar pie?" Hannah was thoroughly shocked. As far as Hannah knew, Delores had never used any of her recipes before.

"Yes, dear. I decided to try it because there's no cooking

or baking involved. And I must say that it turned out to be a smashing success."

"You mean that *Stephanie* got smashed," Michelle interpreted her mother's polite phrase.

"Yes, although I wouldn't have worded it quite that way, Michelle. Stephanie also mentioned that the mayor had lipstick on his shirt. She confronted him, of course. She's had enough of these encounters with her husband to recognize the signs. And he admitted everything and begged for her forgiveness."

"So she got a new wardrobe and expensive jewelry out of the mayor as an apology," Andrea stated the obvious.

"That's correct, dear. She did get a bit tiresome extolling the beauty of her new wardrobe and telling me about all of the new gems she had, but she finally left."

"I hope she wasn't driving!" Hannah said.

"No, dear. I told her that I'd take her home, that she'd been through an ordeal with her husband and it probably wasn't wise for her to drive all the way home."

"Good for you, Mother!" Michelle exclaimed. "Friends don't let friends drive drunk."

"Your sentiment is correct, dear. Stephanie was quite . . . wobbly on her feet, let us say. But of course, I couldn't blame her for that. Most people would be a bit impaired if they consumed four glasses of wine in less than an hour."

"You're one of the most devious people I know," Hannah said. "And *that's* a compliment!"

"Thank you, Hannah. I'll take it as such. Using a bottle of my best white wine did prove one thing. Given the time frame, Mayor Bascomb couldn't have possibly killed Chef Duquesne."

Hannah frowned slightly. "This is really helpful information, Mother, and I do appreciate it, but it doesn't entirely clear Mayor Bascomb. Andrea found out that Gloria called down for room service at eleven-thirty that night. And Mayor Bascomb wasn't in her room. The waitress who delivered the champagne will substantiate that. But Mayor Bascomb could have dropped Gloria off and then gone to the kitchen to kill Chef Duquesne."

"But I haven't told you everything yet!" Delores exclaimed. "Oh, dear! Perhaps I should have done that first." She gestured toward the stack of thick towels by the side of the hot tub and then crooked her finger at her daughters. "Come with me, girls. I have something to show you."

A bit reluctantly, Hannah climbed out of the Jacuzzi. Her skin was beginning to turn very pink and she knew she'd been under the jets of hot water long enough, but she wanted to stay there for the rest of her life, and not think of Chef Duquesne's murder at all. Unfortunately, she simply had to figure out who'd killed him. She needed to do it for Michelle, who'd found him, for Brooke, who was a suspect, and for herself, simply because she couldn't bear the thought of leaving a murder case unsolved.

The towels were warm, and Hannah snuggled into hers, wrapping it tightly around her body. Leave it to her mother to have the very best luxury towels that money could buy! She let Delores lead them all inside and down the hallway to the bedroom that she used for an office. And over to the window that looked out onto the city street.

One glance out the window and Hannah knew why Delores had brought them there. "City Hall!" she exclaimed. "Were you in here that night, Mother? And if you were, what did you see?"

"I saw Mayor Bascomb's car pull up at ten-thirty. And I saw it leave at eleven o' clock."

Hannah gave her youngest sister a look that said, *Don't make a comment right now. If you do, it'll take forever for Mother to tell us what she knows.*

Michelle must have caught her unspoken message, because she said nothing. Just as Hannah had hoped, Delores continued her story.

"As you can see, I have a great view of the mayor's office

from here. And although I can't see into his office from this floor, I can see when the lights go on and off, and when the curtains are pulled."

"You were looking out the window that night?" Andrea asked.

"Yes. I always look out that window when I'm searching my mind for a word or phrase I need for my books, or when I just want to rest my eyes. Doc was gone and I couldn't sleep, so I worked late. There was an emergency appendectomy at the hospital, and he went because he knew the patient. His new intern had only done the procedure a dozen or so times. I decided to finish a chapter in my newest book, and I was here, working on the computer."

"And you saw . . ." Hannah prompted.

"Ricky-Ticky's car pull up at ten-thirty. Then someone pulled the curtains in his office. I didn't see any more until the lights went out and Mayor Bascomb's car left at eleven o'clock."

"Speed racer," Michelle said, under her breath.

"Then his car came back at midnight," Delores continued, either not hearing Michelle's comment or deliberately refusing to acknowledge it. "He was in his office until twelve-fifteen, and then the curtains were opened, the lights went back out, and a few minutes later, he drove away."

"You're right, Mother. That clears him," Hannah said.

"I'm *really* sorry to hear that," Michelle said, giving a heartfelt sigh. "He was number one in my book."

"Michelle!" Delores looked shocked. "He's our mayor!"

Michelle shrugged. "I know, Mother. That's my problem. He's our mayor!"

Just then, the doorbell rang and Delores gestured toward the large bedroom at the side of the penthouse that her daughters had used for a changing room. "Go change out of your bathing suits, girls. Our guests are here and I want all three of you to enjoy the evening."

Chapter
Twenty-nine

The evening had been enjoyable and the night's sleep had been even more so. Hannah was energized and excited as they arrived at the Lake Eden Inn for the final night of the competition.

"Ready?" Michelle asked.

"I'm ready. I just hope we chose the right recipe."

"What's better than apple pie?" Michelle asked her.

"Absolutely nothing. It's a really good pie."

"And it's an American tradition. Not only that, we're pleasing everyone by making it two ways." Michelle smiled. "It's going to be wonderful, Hannah."

"The toppings are really good," Hannah said. "The judges are bound to like one of them, maybe all of them, but especially your ice cream. You make incredibly good ice cream, Michelle."

Michelle looked proud. "It *was* good, wasn't it?"

"I'll say! I got hungry in the middle of the night so I got up and had a bowlful."

Michelle laughed. "No wonder there was only half a container left! We had the rest on our pancakes this morning, you know."

"You added it to the batter?"

"No. I added the leftover pureed bananas to the batter. The ice cream was mixed in the whipped cream on top."

"No wonder it was so good! I just hope that the apple pie isn't too ordinary. Everyone else will probably make fancier desserts."

"Maybe, but that doesn't matter. You're right going with the apple pie, Hannah. Just wait and see."

It was time for the judging, and Hannah was a bundle of nerves.

"Smile," Michelle said, giving her a nudge with her elbow.

"I can't. My face is frozen."

"Then thaw it quick and freeze it again in a smile. The cameras are panning the cooking stages, and you look scared to death."

Somehow Hannah managed to change her panicked expression to a smile. She held it, fixed in place, until the camera moved on. "Will this never end?" she asked, not expecting an answer.

"It'll end and you'll win." Michelle sounded very sure of herself. "Just try to stay calm. The judges are getting ready to give the results to the announcer."

As they watched, the announcer took center stage. "I'll read the results from lowest to highest," he said. "In fifth place is Chef Gloria Berkeley."

There was applause from the audience as Gloria took the stage to receive her fifth place medal.

"In fourth place is Chef Brooke Jackman."

Hannah and Michelle applauded as Brooke came up to the announcer to receive her fourth place medal.

"In third place is Chef Loren Berringer," the announcer stated, and there was applause as Loren went forward to receive his third place medal.

"And now . . . an unprecedented event has occurred. Never

in the history of our Food Channel Chef competitions, have our judges had such a difficult decision. Although our top two contestants have tied for first place in tonight's challenge, only one of them can be crowned as Food Channel's Top Dessert Chef."

The audience was silent. Everyone seemed to be holding their collective breath, and Hannah realized that she was also not breathing.

"Would Chef Rodney Paloma's team and Miss Hannah Swensen's team please join me during our commercial break while the judges make a final tally of the scores?"

Michelle nudged Hannah. "Breathe!"

Hannah managed to draw a shocked breath as she turned to Michelle.

"Smile, Hannah! I did the math last night. I'm sure you won the grand prize."

"But . . ." Hannah took another breath. "Are you sure? You almost flunked algebra!"

"That was only because I was dating Doug Kreske, and I never bothered to study. Maybe I can't deal with imaginary numbers and quadratic equations, but I can add up scores. You're the winner, Hannah! I'll stake my whole bank account on it!"

"Then you must be overdrawn again," Hannah said with a laugh that served to relax her, and she wasn't quite as nervous as she'd been before.

Michelle pushed her forward. "Get up there, Hannah! Rodney's already hogging the spotlight."

Hannah walked up to join Rodney. The die was cast, the tally was done, what would be would be, and many other fatalistic phrases danced through her head while she waited for the results.

The announcer turned to the contestants to give them a smile. "We're back, folks!" And Helene Stone walked up to hand him the tally sheet for the grand prize.

"The judges have spoken," the announcer intoned. "The grand prize winner of the Food Channel *Dessert Chef Competition* is . . . Miss Hannah Swensen!"

It took Hannah a moment to react. She simply couldn't believe her good fortune. Her smile was still frozen in place as the audience applauded, and Rodney shook her hand.

"How does it feel to win the Food Channel *Dessert Chef Competition*?" the announcer asked her.

"I . . . I can't believe it!" Hannah told him. "I never expected to win. I'm not even a real chef!"

"You are now!" the announcer said, presenting her with the trophy. "Are you going to put this on the mantel at The Cookie Jar?"

Hannah couldn't help it. She laughed. And then she began to smile. "We don't have a mantel at The Cookie Jar," she said. "We don't even have a fireplace. But I'm going to put this wonderful trophy behind the counter in the center of our display jars of cookies."

"Are you going to take it with you on your honeymoon?" the announcer asked her.

"I might, but we're not going to have a honeymoon. We're going to take the weekend off, but both of us will be back at work on Monday morning."

"Oh, no you won't!" the announcer said, and there was a smile on his face. "We've cleared it with your groom's employer, and your partner and your sisters are going to make sure that The Cookie Jar runs smoothly while you and Ross go on your Food Channel honeymoon."

Hannah just stared at him. "Our . . . Food Channel honeymoon?"

"That's right, Hannah. Not only are we going to film your wedding and reception for our viewers, we're also going to send you on a ten-day honeymoon cruise to the Mexican Riviera, all expenses paid. What do you have to say about that?"

"I . . . I don't know what to say. Except . . . thank you!"

The camera moved away to show the judges, who were all smiling at her.

When the show was over, Hannah joined Michelle, who looked just as amazed as she was. "You didn't know about the honeymoon?" Hannah asked her.

"No! If I'd known, I would have told you. You did beautifully, Hannah. Everyone could see how surprised and happy you were."

Hannah smiled, but she knew she still wore the startled expression of a rookie pitcher who'd just managed to throw a no-hitter.

"How do you feel?" Michelle asked her.

"Grateful, happy, and . . . exhausted. Let's go home, Michelle. I think I'm on overload, and all I really want to do is go to bed and cuddle with Moishe until I go to sleep."

Of course that didn't happen, at least not right away. There was a television interview, a champagne celebration in Sally's dining room, and congratulations from the other contestants. Michelle and Ross sat on either side of her, fending off the questions that she couldn't handle, and gradually, very gradually, Hannah began to relax and actually enjoy all the fuss. There was only one little fly in the ointment, one pesky problem left unsolved. She still didn't know who had killed Chef Duquesne, and she desperately wanted to solve the case so that she could put it off her to-do list and truly enjoy her special Food Channel honeymoon with Ross.

It hit her with the force of a grand piano dropping from the top of a tall building. Ross liked red wine. Were they serving it on the tables at the wedding reception? Since she hadn't been part of the planning, she didn't know. She had to call her mother right away.

Delores answered the phone on the second ring. "I have a question, Mother," Hannah said. "Will there be red wine on the tables at the wedding reception?"

"Of course, dear. We'll have a bottle of red and a bottle of white for each table."

"Good!" Hannah breathed a sigh of relief. "I just remembered that Ross likes red wine. Do you know which wines you'll be serving?"

"No, dear. I left that up to Sally. She's an expert when it comes to wines."

"Okay. Thanks, Mother. I just thought I'd check."

"Just a minute, Hannah. Would you like me to get a special bottle of red wine for the bridal table? I could call Sally and ask her what she recommends."

"That's okay. I'll do it. I need to talk to her anyway. Thank you, Mother. I'll see you at the church."

"All right, dear. The girls are at the church right now with your wedding clothes. They're going to get everything arranged so all you'll have to do is get dressed and look beautiful."

"Fat chance!" Hannah said, and then she winced. "Sorry, Mother. The words just popped right out. What I meant was that I don't think anything could make me look beautiful, but I promise you that I'll look as good as I can."

"You'll be beautiful, dear. You're already beautiful, even though you don't seem to know it."

Tears sprang to Hannah's eyes. Her mother had never said anything like that to her before. "Thank you, Mother. I love you and I'll see you later."

The moment she'd hung up the phone, she reached for a tissue and dabbed at her eyes. Her mother was being unusually sweet, and Hannah wasn't quite sure how to deal with that. Instead of attempting to figure it out, she decided to run out to the Lake Eden Inn and ask Sally's advice about a truly special bottle of red wine for Ross. She had plenty of time to talk to Dick and Sally in person. Her wedding was at eight-thirty that evening, and it was only a few minutes past five in the afternoon. There was nothing, absolutely nothing she had to do to get ready. She'd already taken a shower, carefully protecting the elaborate hairstyle that Bertie had fashioned for her. That meant her hair was perfect and she needed to do nothing with it before the wedding. Her sisters had picked up her bridal gown, and she would go to the church to get dressed with their help. Right now, she was wearing clean jeans and her favorite sweatshirt, and she could stay in her comfortable clothing until it was time for Andrea and Michelle to help her put on her wedding finery. Staying here at the condo was boring. Moishe was already gone. Norman had picked him up earlier this afternoon so that he could run off some energy by racing around Norman's house with Cuddles.

Did she have everything she'd need for her wedding? Hannah glanced around her condo. She didn't need any extra clothing or toiletries. Her sisters had taken care of all that. And why in the world did she feel like crying as she took one last walk through the condo?

"Bridal nerves," Hannah said out loud. It was a simple case of anxiety before the wedding. She remembered how nervous her mother had gotten before her marriage to Doc. Delores had been a bundle of nerves, and it had taken chocolate to calm her. Even Doc, who wasn't convinced that the endorphins in chocolate made a difference, had agreed that if eating chocolate worked to make his bride-to-be less nervous, he was definitely in favor of doing it.

Hannah hurried to the kitchen, ripped the top off a bag of chocolate chips, shook out a handful, and popped them into her mouth. It was a bit too late to start counting calories. Today was her wedding day and she intended to enjoy it to the fullest.

Once a second handful of chocolate had been consumed, Hannah picked up her purse and headed for the door. It was time to go. Perhaps the chocolate would start to work on her drive to the Lake Eden Inn.

The air outside was crisp and it was scented with a mixture of pine and something vaguely flowery. It puzzled Hannah for a moment, and she paused at the landing on the outside staircase to try to identify it. She'd smelled this particular scent before, usually in the late afternoon. It was coming from the direction of the condo directly below hers, and this was the time that Sue Plotnik usually did her laundry.

"Dryer sheets!" Hannah exclaimed, identifying the scent. One glance at her neighbor's window, as she hurried down the staircase and passed by, told Hannah that she was right. The light was on in Sue's laundry room.

Hannah was smiling as she raced down the concrete steps to the underground garage and hurried to her cookie truck. She was right about the dryer sheets, this was her wedding day, and she was marrying the man she loved. Could anything be more perfect than that?

She drove out of the garage, out of her condo complex,

and down the access road to the highway. There was very little traffic on the roads, and Hannah felt her spirits soar as the miles clicked by on her odometer. It was a picture-perfect evening, warmer than anyone had the right to expect in late October in Minnesota, and the stars were just beginning to emerge in a darkening sky. There were no clouds. The starry night would be perfect. It made her wish for a skylight in her bedroom so that she could watch the stars with Ross and Moishe, but the attic that ran the length of the building made that dream impossible. That didn't matter in the giant scheme of things. All the rest of her dreams would come true tonight. And she could always go out on her tiny second-floor balcony, or stand on the landing by her door to watch the stars.

It didn't take long to get to the Lake Eden Inn, and by the time she got there, she knew the red wine she wanted. It was the very same Cabernet Sauvignon that Chef Duquesne had been drinking in the kitchen on the night he'd been killed. Thank goodness she wasn't superstitious, or ordering the same wine for the bridal table might have bothered her. Instead, it was quite the opposite. Chef Duquesne had been touted for his knowledge of vintage red wines in several magazines devoted to spirits. Any wine he'd chosen would have been the very best Dick and Sally had to offer.

Hannah pulled up in front of the Lake Eden Inn and found that the parking gods had smiled on her. There was a vacant spot just to the left of the door. She pulled in, shut off her cookie truck, locked it, and headed inside.

"Hi, Miss Swensen. What are *you* doing here?" the college student who manned the desk asked. "The wedding's still on, isn't it?"

Hannah laughed. "Yes, it's still on. I just made a quick trip out here to talk to Dick or Sally."

"Sally's upstairs getting ready for your wedding, but Dick's in the bar." The student paused and then he said, "Your hair looks nice."

Hannah's first instinct was to ask him if it usually *didn't* look nice, but she quickly squelched that impulse. "Thank you," she said, following her mother's advice for dealing with compliments and heading across the lobby in the direction of the bar.

The large room was crowded, but there was a stool at the bar and Hannah took it. There were two women she didn't know on either side of her and she presumed that they were new guests at the hotel. Some of the Food Channel guests had already left, and only the contestants, the judges, and the members of the film crew were staying on for another night. Everyone would leave the following morning, and Sally and Dick were hosting a convention at the new convention wing they'd built in a separate addition attached to the side of the existing hotel.

"Are you here for the Pretty Girl convention?" the lady on Hannah's left asked. She was a middle-aged woman who was dressed to look younger and she had bright pink streaks of color in her blond hair.

"Actually . . . no. I'm a local from Lake Eden. I just came out here to talk to the owners."

"Dick? The guy behind the bar?" the lady on Hannah's right asked. She was a tall, thin brunette who should not have been wearing the low-cut, tight-fitting top that she'd chosen for the evening. "He told us he was the owner."

"He is," Hannah said.

Just then Dick came over and did a double-take when he saw Hannah. "What are *you* doing here?"

"I came out to talk to you or Sally. And the college student at the desk told me that Sally was upstairs getting ready for the wedding, so I came in here to find you."

"That's right. What can I do for you, Hannah?"

Before Hannah could answer, the lady on her left spoke up. "Hannah? I knew I recognized you from somewhere! You won the Food Channel *Dessert Chef Competition*!"

"Guilty as charged," Hannah said, and both women laughed.

"And you're getting married tonight and they're going to televise it on the Food Channel," the lady on her right stated. And then she started to frown. "There's nothing wrong, is there, Hannah?"

"Not a thing. I just drove out here to ask a question about red wine for the wedding reception."

Since the ladies were listening, Hannah didn't want to mention the name of the wine that Chef Duquesne had consumed right before he'd been murdered, so she turned to Dick and rephrased the question she'd originally planned to ask. "What's the best red wine you carry? I want to have something special on the head table for Ross."

"Cabernet, Merlot, or Cabernet Sauvignon?" Dick asked her.

"Cabernet Sauvignon."

Dick sighed. "Sorry, Hannah. I don't have any of the really high-end Cab left. I had four bottles of 2008 Hourglass Estate Cabernet Sauvignon from Napa Valley. They lay it down for four years before they sell it, and I bought it for a hundred and ten a bottle. Now it sells for over a hundred and fifty. If I had any left, I'd give you a bottle for a wedding present."

"But you don't?"

"No, but I do have another Cab that's really very good. I'll put a bottle of that on your table."

"Thanks, Dick. I'm sure it'll be wonderful." Hannah felt her excitement build. She was almost sure that the wine in the crime scene photos had been the one from Hourglass Estate that he'd mentioned. "I'm curious, Dick. Who bought those expensive bottles of wine?"

"I sold three bottles to Chef Duquesne. Someone else ordered the fourth from room service."

"When did that fourth bottle sell?"

"Uh . . . night before last, maybe? Yes, that's it. It was the same night that . . ." he stopped short, glanced at the ladies who were clearly listening, and turned back to Hannah. "I get it," he told her. "Someone else took the room service order, but I can find out if it's important."

"It could be."

"Okay. It'll take a couple of minutes. Do you have time to wait?"

Hannah glanced at the time display on her phone. "I've got an hour before I have to get to the church."

"Good. Jackie comes on in ten minutes and then I'll get a break. I'll look it up for you during my break and tell you what I find. Then I have to go upstairs and get dressed for your wedding." He paused and looked at the empty bar space in front of Hannah. "Would you like a little liquid courage, Hannah? This is a big step for you."

"I know, but I don't need courage. I need some liquid that's not at all courageous. How about something nonalcoholic? Aunt Nancy said you have some really good pink lemonade, and I could use a glass of that."

"Done." Dick put ice in a glass and filled it from one of the spigots behind the bar. He added a sprig of mint and handed it to her. "Here you go. Pure pink lemonade. Cheers, Hannah."

"Cheers!" the two ladies said, raising their glasses as Hannah took her first sip.

"Thank you." Hannah smiled at them in acknowledgment. It had been a nice gesture.

"So tell us about your handsome groom," the blonde with the pink streaks said.

"Yes!" her fellow Pretty Girl conventioneer chimed in. "Is he as incredibly sexy as he looked that night on television?"

Hannah managed to keep the smile on her face, but she shot Dick a desperate glance. She couldn't leave. She needed the information that Dick would give her. But this was going to be a very long ten minutes!

Hannah was right. She made what she hoped was polite conversation for at least twenty-five minutes before Dick came back to the bar. He no longer had on his bar apron, and he tapped her on the shoulder. "Come with me, Hannah. I have something for you."

"Thanks, Dick." Hannah got up from her stool, said good-bye to the Pretty Girl conventioneers, and followed Dick to the lobby. When they got there he pointed to a couch in the far corner, away from anyone who could hear them, and Hannah took a seat.

"It was Rodney Paloma," Dick said.

"Rodney ordered that expensive wine from room service?"

"That's right. The call came in at midnight. According to room service records, Rodney answered the door himself and asked the girl who delivered it not to open it, but to leave the wine opener with him."

"And she did?"

"Yes. We don't usually do that, but she said he gave her a ten-dollar tip and she figured she could replace the corkscrew if he didn't return it and still keep at least half of the tip for herself."

"Smart girl," Hannah said.

"Yes. We tell our staff that the guest is always right, even if they're dead wrong. Lucy's very good at following the rules and she had this one covered. She went back to his room later and retrieved the opener. Rodney wasn't there and his bed hadn't been slept in. Lucy assumed that he'd taken the wine somewhere to drink it with friends."

"What time was this?" Hannah asked.

"A little after two in the morning. Lucy said she walked through the lobby on her way downstairs for her break, and Rodney wasn't there. She presumed that he must have taken the wine to someone else's room and he was still there."

It took a moment for the information Dick had given her to register in Hannah's mind. When it did, Hannah came close to gasping as the puzzle pieces twisted and turned, and then clicked into place. She gave Dick a smile. "Thanks, Dick. There's just one more thing. Is the back door you use for deliveries locked at night?"

"It's not locked, but it's automatically alarmed from seven at night until six in the morning."

"So if anyone uses it during those hours, the alarm goes off?"

"Yes, unless they know the code to disarm the alarm."

"How about the kitchen staff? Do they know the code?"

"No. We don't give it to them. When they leave for the night, they deposit any waste in the Dumpster in the hallway by the back door and the garbage service collects it every night."

"But doesn't someone have to wheel the Dumpster out to the parking lot?"

Dick shook his head. "The garbage service has the code. They load the Dumpsters in the parking lot first, and then they punch in the code and get the one in the hallway outside the kitchen."

"How many people have the code?"

"Only four. There's the garbage service, Sally, the maintenance man, and me. That's it."

"But how about the other delivery men? Don't they have it?"

"No. We don't get deliveries at night. They all come during the day when the alarm is off." Dick paused to smile at her. "Are you planning to open a restaurant, Hannah?"

"No!" Hannah was shocked. "Of course not, Dick. I'll leave that up to the professionals like you and Sally."

"Okay. If you're not planning to open a restaurant, all these questions must have something to do with Chef Duquesne's murder."

"They may," Hannah admitted, "but right now I'm just gathering information and hoping it'll all fall into place for me."

"It will. You're good at this, Hannah. And nobody's more eager than I am to get that killer behind bars. The fact that it happened out here is frightening. For all we know, the killer may still be here."

"That's a possibility," Hannah admitted.

Dick glanced at his watch. "Do you need anything else, Hannah?"

"Not right now. Thanks, Dick. Tell Sally I'll see her at the church. Grandma Knudson said she's planning to have coffee and cookies in the basement after the service, and then everyone will drive out here for the reception."

"We'll be ready. Happy wedding, Hannah."

"Thank you. Just one other thing, Dick. Rodney Paloma's still here, isn't he?"

"He's here. Rodney's not checking out until early tomorrow. All the contestants are coming to your wedding. And every one of them has baked a dessert for Sally's dessert table."

"Wonderful! You don't happen to know where Rodney is right now, do you?"

"Actually, I do. He went out for a walk by the lake and he ought to be back pretty soon. He said he was going to come in the back way so I told him about the automatic alarm on the door. He said he'd be back by the time it activated."

"Then he's coming in the back way?"

"Yes. And he said he's going straight in the kitchen to check on his coconut cream pies. He just baked them this afternoon and he wanted to make sure they were properly chilled in time for Sally to put them out on your dessert table."

Chapter Thirty-one

L uckily, she'd brought her key. Hannah sat in Sally's kit-chen, staring at the clock on the wall. The kitchen staff had gone and there was nothing to do but wait. They'd done all the prep work and they would come back at eight to start preparing the reception dinner, which would be served at ten in the evening.

She wished she could bake. It would help to pass the time. But Sally's kitchen was spotlessly clean, since the staff had readied it for the wedding reception. There was nothing to do but sit here and wait. She'd have to leave by seven-thirty at the latest to be at the church in time to get dressed for her wedding. Dick had told her that Rodney would be back before the automatic alarm activated on the back door at seven. There was plenty of time to catch him when he came into the kitchen to check his pie.

While she was waiting, Hannah reviewed what she knew about the murder case. The suspects who had strong motives were already eliminated. Every one of them had an alibi. And the genetic marker on the hair Doc had found hadn't turned out to be the important clue, now that Brooke had re-vealed that she was Chef Duquesne's daughter. When they'd met with Loren at the breakfast buffet, he'd given Brooke an alibi.

Hannah was out of both motives and suspects. That meant no one with an ax to grind was left, at least no one that Hannah had discovered. There was only one thing that made her slightly suspicious, one thing that didn't fit the pattern. That was why she'd stayed to talk to Rodney.

Although she really couldn't think of a possible motive, Hannah knew that Rodney had lied to her about going for a drive on the night that Chef Duquesne was murdered and coming back in through the door. Rodney didn't have the code to the door. Why had he bothered to lie about something like that to her? It was almost as if he had tried to provide himself with an alibi, and he wasn't even on her suspect list!

Hannah drew the murder book from her purse and reviewed the list. Everyone on it had an alibi for the time of the murder. There was only one name remaining and that wasn't even a real person. As always, when she wrote notes to herself on a murder case, she added that mythical suspect. It was *Unidentified Suspect with an Unknown Motive*.

Hannah glanced at the clock. It was almost time to do something to shake things up. She'd done everything according to the guidelines in Mike's detective manuals. She'd eliminated all the reasonable suspects who could have had a motive for killing Chef Duquesne. And since that hadn't shown any positive results, she'd decided to think outside the box, to concentrate on someone previously unsuspected who had done something that appeared to be totally unnecessary to provide himself with an alibi. This was why she was sitting in Sally's kitchen at the Lake Eden Inn, watching the minutes tick by on the eve of her wedding, and waiting for Rodney Paloma.

"Hannah!" Rodney came in the kitchen door and stopped short when he saw Hannah. "I thought you were getting married!"

"I am." Hannah glanced at the clock. It was one minute

before seven, and she had thirty minutes to clear this up with Rodney. "Why did you lie to me?"

"Lie to you?" Rodney looked genuinely confused. "About what?"

"About going for a drive on the night that Chef Duquesne was murdered. You didn't go for a drive at all, and you certainly didn't come in the back way. The reason you got back to your room so late was because you killed him!"

Mistake! Hannah's mind shouted. Rodney was staring at her with narrowed eyes, and Hannah felt chills run up and down her spine. His eyes were trained on her like a bird of prey that had just spotted a field mouse, and they were as cold and hard as lumps of coal in the belly of a mine shaft. Hannah moved back a step, involuntarily, and shivered in dread.

"He did not deserve to live!" Rodney said, and his words were icy as his eyes.

"What did he do to you?" Hannah asked, terribly afraid, but desperately attempting to maintain a conversational tone. "I agree that he was not a nice man." And all the while she spoke, her mind was racing and her eyes scanned the room for something she could use to defend herself.

"Not nice? Not *nice*?!" Rodney gave a snort of derision. "He was the very essence of evil. He didn't care how many lives he ruined by his own self-indulgence. He killed my mother!"

"He killed your mother?" Hannah hoped she sounded reasonable, even though she was afraid that Rodney had slipped from the brink of sanity into the abyss of madness. "How did he do that?"

"She tried so hard to please him, and every time she tried, he told her she just wasn't good enough. If he'd thought she wasn't good enough, he should have fired her. At least then she would have had a chance to start over in some place that she was appreciated. But he didn't do that. He wanted to control her like a puppet master. He wanted to pull the strings and watch her jump."

"Your mother worked for Chef Duquesne?"

"She worked for the *devil*!" Rodney paused to take a breath. "He was the devil incarnate! And she couldn't quit because of me. She was alone, and her paycheck was the only thing that kept us alive. It was just enough so we couldn't get welfare and so little that we fell behind every month. We scrimped and saved, but we just kept falling further and further behind. But the bills kept piling up until there was no way out, but I never knew! I was just a boy and she kept it from me. She did it to *protect* me! She was living in hell, and I never knew it!"

"You said Chef Duquesne killed your mother?" Hannah asked, hoping that the memory of that sad time would distract him enough so that he wouldn't notice that she was exploring the shelves under the counter. Using her fingers and feeling around for something that she could use to keep him from turning on her. There was no doubt in Hannah's mind that he would try to kill her. He was telling her why he'd committed murder. After he finished, he couldn't let her live to tell anyone else.

"I was just a kid," Rodney repeated. "I didn't know she was sick. I thought she was just tired," Rodney said. "She was always working, every minute of every day while I was in school. She'd leave food for me and she taught me how to fix it in the toaster oven she'd found in a thrift store. But there were nights when she didn't get home from the restaurant until I'd gone to bed."

As Rodney told the story, Hannah took a chance and pulled out a bowl that was filled with something. She could hear it slosh. It was covered with plastic wrap and she carefully inched off a bit from the edge. Then she dipped her finger into the bowl and rubbed it against her palm. It was slick and smooth, lightly viscous, and that meant it was some kind of oil. It must be premeasured for something that Sally was planning to make for the wedding reception.

"I remember how thin she was. When she held me, her arms were bony. I noticed, but I didn't notice, not really. Do you understand?"

"I understand," Hannah responded quickly. This was a good sign. He was no longer just telling a story. He was interacting with her now. "Did Chef Duquesne know that she was sick?"

"If he did, he didn't care. He just made her work longer and longer and told her that what she baked wasn't any good. I could hear her crying in the night."

Hannah's heart went out to Rodney, and she had to remind herself that he was a dangerous killer. If she let sympathy get in the way of her determination to stay alive, she'd never walk down the aisle in her beautiful wedding gown. She'd never hear Reverend Bob pronounce them man and wife, never dance with Ross at their wedding reception, and never see the man she loved again!

New determination filled her. Hannah lifted the bowl and held it in one hand. It was heavy, but that was all to the good. She wasn't quite sure how she would use it, but somehow she would.

"One night she baked a cake," Rodney went on, plagued by his memories of the past. "She was very excited about it and she even copied the recipe for me. It was something that she'd been practicing after work at the restaurant every night. She told me that he was bound to like it and to praise her for her work when he tasted it. When he did, she'd ask him for a raise and he'd give it to her because he'd be so impressed with her cake."

Suddenly it all came together and Hannah knew what had driven Rodney Paloma to murder. "The candied violet cake," she said.

"Yes. Very smart, Hannah. But tonight you were too smart

for your own good. I would have been gone tomorrow and no one would ever have figured it out."

"But you *won* that night! We tied for first place. Chef Duquesne must have liked your mother's cake."

"Oh, he did! But that was only a partial vindication. It was for me because I made her cake. And it was for her because he had to admit that it was superlative. But he *still* had to answer for the fact that he had killed her!"

"Yes," Hannah said, taking a deep breath. "I can see that."

"Of course you can." Rodney dismissed it. "I ordered a special bottle of wine, one that I knew he liked, and I found him right here in the kitchen. I opened the wine and poured it, and then I said I had a toast to make. And I toasted my mother and told him that it was her cake!"

"What did he say?" Hannah asked as she inched off a little more of the plastic wrap. Over half of the circumference of the bowl was now exposed.

"He said that it was his cake in the first place and he'd spent months trying to teach her to bake it. And the only reason he'd hired her in the first place was because I was his child. And he'd thought that he could get some use out of supporting us, but she was too dumb to learn anything."

"And that's when you killed him?" Hannah asked, her fingers scrabbling at the edge of the plastic wrap. Another few inches released their hold on the lip of the bowl and almost all of the oil was now exposed.

"I didn't kill him then. I wasn't planning to kill him, even after he said that about my mother. He grabbed a knife, told me to follow him, and led me to the walk-in cooler. He said he'd show me what he thought of my cake."

"But he cut a piece of mine, instead of yours!" The oil sloshed slightly as the rest of the plastic wrap came loose. Hannah dropped it on the floor and readied herself for what was about to come. "I understand why you did it now, Rodney."

"What else could I do when he stuffed a bite of *your* cake in his mouth and swallowed? And then he said I was a lousy baker, just like my mother. He told me my cake was pretty, but it had no taste, just like my mother. And that's when I picked up the knife and stabbed him for my mother!"

"He really was a devil," Hannah said, hoping that she could buy just a bit more time. But that was when Rodney picked up a knife and moved toward her.

Everything happened very fast, so fast that she had trouble believing how rapidly she moved. Hannah threw the bowl of oil in his path, pivoted on her feet, and raced toward the kitchen door. She heard him fall heavily, but a split second later, she was out of the kitchen and in the back hallway. She pulled the back door open and the alarm sounded, just as she'd expected. She ran out and saw a garbage truck parked by the back door.

The driver of the truck was moving one of the Dumpsters from the back wall so that he could get behind it and wheel it to the truck. Hannah didn't hesitate. She dashed up the ramp and into the trailer of the truck. He'd already loaded several Dumpsters, and Hannah lifted the lid of the closest one. She scrambled inside and closed the lid just as Rodney ran out the door, looking for her.

"Hey, fella! What are you doing out here?" the driver called to Rodney. "You set off the alarm."

"Sorry!" Rodney answered. "I just came out for some air. I didn't realize that would happen."

"No sweat. I'll take care of it."

Hannah lifted the lid of the Dumpster just enough so that she could see what was happening. Rodney followed as the driver punched in the code, the alarm stopped ringing and they both stepped inside. Then the driver retrieved the Dumpster from the hallway, said goodbye to Rodney and shut the door behind him, wheeled the Dumpster outside, and reset the alarm.

She was safe! Rodney was back inside and there was no way he could get out this way again without setting off the alarm. Hannah was about to raise the lid on the Dumpster when the cargo door at the back of the truck slid down all the way. She heard the ramp rumble back into place below the door, and she wasn't sure whether she was relieved or frightened. Rodney couldn't get to her now, but where would the driver be taking her?

"Help!" she called out, but the driver must not have heard her because the cargo door remained closed and the engine turned over with a roar. She was trapped in the truck, and she had to get out of the Dumpster and bang on the wall that connected the back of the truck with the cab where the driver was sitting.

Hannah raised the lid of the container and attempted to climb out, but every time she thought she'd be successful, the contents of the Dumpster shifted and she sank back down again. It was squishy on the bottom and she really didn't want to think about why that might be. She was stuck and she could feel that the driver was picking up speed.

She heard a car horn honk, and the truck lurched to the left. There were several other honks and the noise of traffic passing the truck. She was on the freeway in the garbage truck. Where was the driver taking her?!

Chapter
Thirty-two

Hannah felt a moment of pure panic before her rational mind took over. The driver was taking her to the dump, of course. All she could do was hope that it was a local dump and she'd be there soon.

What time was it? It had been almost seven when Rodney had come into the kitchen. And her wedding would start at eight-thirty. What would happen if she wasn't there? Would they wait for her? She had to find out the time!

That was when she felt it, the weight on her shoulder. It was her purse! Somehow, she'd grabbed her purse in her mad flight to get away from Rodney.

Hannah used both hands to rummage around in her purse. Her cell phone was in there somewhere. All she had to do was find it and she could call the sheriff's station.

It took several anxious minutes, but at last she grasped it. It was right where it should be, in the inside pocket at the back of her purse. Her panic was slowing her brain. She had to think clearly if she wanted to get out of this Dumpster and marry Ross.

Did the garbage truck have a compacter? Would the driver use it? There was another brief moment of panic, and then Hannah sighed loudly. Of course the driver wouldn't use a compacter, even if he'd had one. This garbage truck was like a moving truck. It didn't have a trash compacter. And even if the driver's truck had contained a compacter, he wouldn't have used it. Dumpsters were expensive. You might dump out the trash and put it through a compacter, but you would never compact the Dumpster itself.

Hannah wiped her hands on her sweatshirt and felt for the buttons on her phone. It was off and she had to turn it on. But it wouldn't turn on! There was something wrong! Had she forgotten to charge it again?!

The moment she thought of it, she knew it was true. So much had been on her mind with the murder, and the competition, and her wedding that she hadn't even considered charging her phone. What could she do now? She was cut off from the world and stuck in this Dumpster inside a truck that was going to some location that only the driver knew.

She had to think and she had to think clearly. Tracey had taught her how to use her smartphone. And Tracey had said that there was a way to get an extra charge out of the battery by pressing a certain sequence of key numbers. The numbers were different for some carriers and some phones, but Tracey had given her the sequence of numbers that would work on her particular phone.

First, she had to think of the numbers and the sequence. And then she had to decide who to call. The sheriff's station would be the logical choice under any other circumstances, but Delores had invited all of the deputies to the wedding. There would be only a skeleton staff on duty, and in the worst case scenario, they'd be dealing with other calls and she would be put on hold!

"Think. You've got to think clearly." Hannah said the words out loud, hoping they'd sink in more rapidly that way. She'd be better off calling an individual deputy, one that put duty ahead of anything else and who wouldn't turn off his or her phone.

Mike. The moment Hannah thought of it, she knew she was right. Mike was a cop through and through. Even during the ceremony, he'd have his cell phone in his pocket. It would be set on vibrate so that it didn't disturb anyone else, but he'd check it if he got a call.

Now all she needed was the sequence of numbers and the name of the garbage service. She'd seen the name on the side of the Dumpster. It was something starting with an A. She was sure of that. And it was someone's name, a name that had reminded her of a professor she'd had in college. History. That was it. Alquist. Professor Alquist. That was the professor's name, but the garbage service's name was something slightly different. Alquin. That was it. Alquin Trash Removal.

That was when something wonderful happened. Hannah's mind kicked into high gear. She remembered the sequence of numbers, punched them in, and heard a most welcome dial tone. Then she hit the speed-dialing number for Mike and she heard his phone begin to ring.

"Kingston here," Mike answered and Hannah gave a little sob of relief. She had to be fast. She had to be thorough. She had very little time to give Mike all of the information he needed.

"It's Hannah. I'm in an Alquin Trash Removal truck that left the Lake Eden Inn ten minutes or so ago. Rodney Paloma tried to kill me. Pick him up. He murdered Chef Du . . ."

The dial tone sounded again and then her phone went dark. Hannah gave a little sob and sent up a silent prayer that Mike would act fast.

"Where *is* she?" Delores asked. "You don't suppose she fell asleep, do you?"

"No, Mother." Andrea took a deep breath and prayed for patience. Since she was right here in church, perhaps her prayer would be answered. They'd been trying to calm their mother down for almost an hour, and she'd asked this and other questions countless times before.

Michelle reached out to pat their mother's hand. "I called the condo five times, Mother. There's no answer. And Doc contacted the hospital, just in case she'd been in an accident."

"And Bill checked with the sheriff's station." Andrea began to go through the list of calls everyone had made. "Michelle and I called everyone we knew who isn't already here, and no one's heard from her."

"Eat this, dear," Grandma Knudson said, handing Delores a chocolate bar that she'd run back to the parsonage to get. "It'll help to calm your nerves."

"*Nothing* will calm my nerves at this point!" Delores insisted, but she opened the candy and took a bite.

Just then, Lisa's cell phone rang and she glanced at the display. "It's Herb. He sent me a text. He says he located Hannah's cookie truck in front of the Lake Eden Inn. He's going inside to look for her."

The five women exchanged bewildered glances, and then Grandma Knudson asked, "What is she doing out there?"

Delores, who'd jumped to her feet when Lisa had told them about Herb's text message, sat down heavily in her chair. "I just knew something like this would happen! My baby's been kidnapped and we haven't even held the wedding yet!"

"Have they heard from her?" Ross asked, not pausing as he paced the floor of Reverend Bob's office.

Norman shook his head. "Not yet."

"How about Mike? Have they heard from him?"

"No, not a word."

Ross swallowed hard. "You don't suppose that . . ." he paused, unable to go on with his unwelcome train of thought.

"Absolutely not." Norman was very definite. "Don't even think it, Ross. If Hannah had second thoughts about marrying you, she'd march right in the door of the church and tell you."

Ross smiled. "You're right, she would. It's just that I feel so . . . so . . . I don't even know how to describe it."

"Helpless?"

"Yes! I'm stuck here just waiting. She could be in trouble and maybe there's something I should be doing."

"The only thing you can do right now is try to relax. She'll show up. It's just a matter of time. Hannah wants to marry you. She loves you, Ross. She told me that. This wedding will start a little late, that's all. And it's only eight-fifteen."

Hannah raised the lid and let it bang back down again. She'd been doing this for the past few miles, but the driver didn't seem to hear her. It was probably because he had the radio in his cab turned up to full volume. It was tuned to a country-western station that played classic songs, and Hannah had listened to a man sing a plea to his girlfriend to send him the pillow she dreamed on, a woman who'd sung about her lost love and her broken heart, and several singers who'd lamented everything from cheating husbands to divorce, suicide, and accidental death. Right now, the subject was lonely nights and someone was wailing about it. Hannah just wished the next song would be something soft enough so that the driver could hear the lid on her Dumpster clanging shut. If he did, he might pull over to the side of the road, get out of his truck, and open the back to see what was making so much noise.

She banged the lid on the Dumpster until her arm was tired and then she stopped. It was no use. The radio was just too loud. And then she heard it, a siren coming up behind them. Could it be Mike? It just *had* to be Mike!

The Dumpster rolled as the driver pulled over to the side of the highway. Hannah's foot slipped, and she fell against something wet and gloppy. Somehow she managed to stand up again and raise the lid on the Dumpster just in time to see the back of the truck start to open.

"There she is! I told you she was back here. I'll get her out."

"No way, Officer." The driver put his hand on Mike's arm. "Looks like you're all dressed up for a wedding or something, and it's nasty in there. I got on my work clothes. I'll get her out. How did she get in there anyway?"

"She was hiding from a killer," Mike answered as the driver lowered the ramp and climbed into the truck.

"Figures. That's the only thing that would get me into something like this." The driver opened the lid of the Dumpster all the way and braced it open. "Give me your arms, lady. I'll lift you out."

It took three tries, but the driver was strong and he managed to lift her high enough so that she could climb out. He helped her down, and then he went to the back of the truck and came back to hand her a large orange garbage bag. "Better sit on this," he told her. "Drape it right over the seat so you don't get the officer's car seat dirty."

"Thank you," Hannah said and made a move to hug him, but she noticed that unidentified goop was clinging to her clothing and she gave him a grateful smile instead.

Mike shook his head as he walked her to the cruiser. "Use that bag, okay? The car wash will never get my seat clean if you don't."

"Did you get Rodney?" she asked as she lined the passenger seat with the plastic garbage bag and sat down.

"Yes. He was waiting at the dump for you and he had a knife. Lonnie and Rick rushed him and took him into custody."

Hannah reached for her seat belt, but a gesture from Mike stopped her. "You'll never hear me say this again, but don't use the seat belt. The car wash will never get that clean, either. I'm going to have to take your statement later, but I'll wait until the wedding's over."

"What time is it?"

"It's almost nine, but we're only about fifteen minutes away. Don't worry. They'll wait another half hour at least, and we'll be at the church before then as long as this constitutes an emergency. Does it?"

For a moment, Hannah was puzzled and then she understood. Mike could use his siren, but only in an emergency. "Yes, it's definitely an emergency. It could even prevent another murder."

"Another murder?"

"Yes. If I miss my own wedding, Mother will kill me."

Mike laughed and, siren blaring and pedal to the floor, they sped down the freeway toward Lake Eden. Hannah took a deep breath and let it out in a shuddering sigh. Mike knew she'd been kidding about the attempted murder. Perhaps her mother wouldn't have actually killed her, but she would have made Hannah feel guilty for the rest of her life.

"Hannah?"

"What is it, Mike?"

"Will you promise me that you'll stop all this investigating once you're married?"

Hannah stared at him in shock. "I was just about killed by a man with a knife, I had to dive into a Dumpster to save myself, and you're trying to extort that kind of a promise from me?"

"Yes. Will you?"

"No!"

Mike sighed. "I didn't think so, but it was worth a try." He paused for a moment. "Hannah?"

"Yes, Mike."

"What's that in your hair?"

"I don't know. What does it look like?"

"It's red and it's thick, and it looks kind of sticky."

"Oh," Hannah said. "I'm not sure what it is, but I really hope it's spaghetti sauce."

They got to Lake Eden in less than fifteen minutes, just

as Mike had predicted. Mike took the corner by the rectory at a speed that was definitely unsafe, and squealed to a stop in front of the church. "Stay there," he told her. "I'll get your door."

Mike ran around to open her door and Hannah clambered out. "Get inside!" he told her. "I'll park in the back and come in that way."

Hannah didn't need any further urging. She raced up the steps of the church, intent on getting inside as quickly as she could.

As she barged through the doors, she heard several of the ushers gasp, but she didn't stop in her headlong rush down the aisle. "I'm here!" she called out, heading straight for the front of the church. And that was when she saw the cameras.

Every single one of the Food Channel cameras was trained on her, documenting her dash into the church. No one said a word and Hannah stopped as she approached the front, as if there were some sort of invisible barrier. "Sorry I'm late," she said as she faced the bank of cameras. "I was catching a killer."

There was perfect silence in the crowded church for a few brief seconds, and then Grandma Knudson rose to her feet. "Relax," she said, addressing the congregation. "That's our Hannah for you!" And the moment she said it everyone, including the members of the Food Channel film crew, burst out into laughter.

"I'm sorry I'm late," Hannah apologized, "but Chef Duquesne's killer tried to attack me and I had to hide from him in a Dumpster, and then the garbage truck came, and . . ."

"Not now, Hannah," Grandma Knudson interrupted her. "Claire? Take Hannah to the parsonage and get her into the shower, clothes and all. I don't even want to think about what's in her hair." She turned to Hannah. "Go, Hannah. Your sisters will bring you your wedding gown."

As Hannah meekly followed Claire to the side door of the

church, she heard Grandma Knudson address the congregation again. "Come with me, everyone. We're going down to the basement for refreshments before the wedding ceremony, instead of after. We'll drink coffee and eat cookies while Hannah gets herself presentable. I made plenty of cookies and that's good. From the looks of Hannah's hair, it's going to take a while."

In less than fifteen minutes, Hannah was squeaky clean. She'd dropped her clothes in a garbage bag, and they were now agitating in Grandma Knudson's washer.

Hannah had just dressed in the lovely underclothes that Claire had chosen for her to wear, and she was sitting in a chair in front of Claire's dressing table while Andrea applied her makeup and Michelle blow-dried her hair.

"What time is it?" she asked.

"Relax," Claire said. "We're almost through. And before you even think to ask, I called and told Sally's assistant chef that the wedding was delayed, and we wouldn't be out there until ten-thirty. He said not to worry, that everything would hold, so you can put that right out of your mind. And I called Bob on his cell and he promised me that he'd keep the wedding service short and sweet."

"Thank you," Hannah said, grateful that she had such a good friend and such loving sisters. "Do you think everyone's terribly mad at me?"

"Not at all," Claire said. "You just gave everyone the most exciting wedding they've ever attended."

Michelle laughed. "That's right. The Lake Eden Gossip Hotline is going to have something to talk about for months to come."

Hannah looked up at Andrea. "How about Mother? Is she terribly angry with me?"

"I'm sure she's not," Andrea answered. "She's probably the center of attention at the church right now, and you know how Mother loves to be the center of . . ."

"What's wrong?" Hannah asked her sister, who was staring out the window toward the church.

"It's Mother. She just came out the side door of the church and she's on her way over here."

"Where's my Hannah?" Delores called out, the moment she came in the back door.

"In here," Claire called out. Then she turned to Hannah. "She certainly doesn't sound mad. She sounds . . . like a mother who's been worried about her daughter."

Delores burst into the room and rushed over to Hannah. "Oh my!" she exclaimed. "You look just perfect, Hannah!"

"I had a little help," Hannah told her, smiling at Claire and her sisters. "I'm almost ready, Mother."

"Good! I'll help Grandma Knudson round up everyone and get them back in the pews." Delores took a step toward the door, but she turned back to give Hannah a kiss on the cheek. "That's from Ross. He told me to say he loves you so much, he can't see straight."

"That's so sweet!" Claire gushed.

"And this is from me." Delores bent down to kiss the top of Hannah's head. "I love you, Hannah. If your sisters weren't here, I'd tell you that you were always my favorite."

All three Swensen sisters burst into laughter. Delores laughed too, but Claire looked completely puzzled.

"What's so funny?" she asked.

"Mother told each of us that we were her favorite," Hannah explained. "She knew we'd end up comparing notes and we'd get a good laugh out of it."

"That's true," Delores admitted. "But when I said it to each of you, I meant it. All three of you are my favorites." She stopped, grabbed a tissue from the box on Claire's dresser, and dabbed at her eyes. "I'd better get back to the church before I ruin my makeup. Weddings always make me cry."

As Hannah took Doc Knight's arm and walked down the aisle, a phenomenon happened, something that had never occurred in the one-hundred and twenty-six-year history of the Holy Redeemer Lutheran Church. Heads swiveled to look at the bride, smiles appeared on every face, and the congregation broke into spontaneous applause.

Hannah smiled at everyone there, and then her eyes swept up to the altar, where her sisters, the bridesmaids, were standing on the bride's side, and Ross, Norman, and Mike were standing on the groom's side. She was here, she was ready, and as the traditional wedding march swelled in volume from the organ, she basked in the warmth of Ross's smile. He loved her. She loved him. This was the perfect day for her perfect wedding.

The church and everyone in it were covered with a golden glow of happiness for Hannah as Doc Knight escorted her down the aisle and presented her to her groom. Hannah and Ross took their places in the center, and Reverend Bob began the wedding service.

The service was short and sweet, just as Reverend Bob had promised, and much sooner than usual, the bridal couple was ready to speak their vows.

"Do you, Ross Jeffrey Barton, take this woman to be your lawfully wedded wife, to have and to hold, to love and to cherish, from this day forward until death do you part?"

"I do," Ross said, smiling at Hannah.

"And do you, Hannah Louise Swensen, take this man to be your lawfully wedded husband, to have and to hold, to love and to cherish, from this day forward until death do you part?"

Hannah felt a chill run through her body. It had almost

happened. Death had almost parted them. She'd almost died before their wedding!

Images ran through Hannah's mind at the speed of light. If the bowl of oil hadn't been under the counter in Sally's kitchen, and if Rodney hadn't slipped on the oil and fallen, and if the driver hadn't been right there loading the Dumpsters, and if she hadn't hoisted herself up and tumbled in, she would be dead right now and parted from Ross forever.

And then her eyes found Mike and she realized that he'd guessed what was running through her head. He was giving her the okay sign with his thumb and his index finger curled together in a circle. And then he winked and she winked back. They exchanged a look that meant complete understanding. Hannah turned and looked up at the man she loved and gave him a radiant smile.

"I do," she said, in a loud, clear voice.

Wedding Cake Murder
Recipe Index

Baking Conversion Chart

These conversions are approximate, but they'll work just fine for Hannah Swensen's recipes.

VOLUME

U.S.	Metric
½ teaspoon	2 milliliters
1 teaspoon	5 milliliters
1 tablespoon	15 milliliters
¼ cup	50 milliliters
⅓ cup	75 milliliters
½ cup	125 milliliters
¾ cup	175 milliliters
1 cup	¼ liter

WEIGHT

U.S.	Metric
1 ounce	28 grams
1 pound	454 grams

OVEN TEMPERATURE

Degrees Fahrenheit	Degrees Centigrade	British (Regulo) Gas Mark
325 degrees F.	165 degrees C.	3
350 degrees F.	175 degrees C.	4
375 degrees F.	190 degrees C.	5

Note: Hannah's rectangular sheet cake pan, 9 inches by 13 inches, is approximately 23 centimeters by 32.5 centimeters.

New York Times Bestselling Author
Joanne Fluke
and
Hannah Swensen
invite you to an exclusive sneak peek
of Hannah's Wedding Reception!

The reception was every bit as wonderful as Hannah had thought it would be. Dinner had been absolutely delicious, and the red wine that Dick had chosen for their table was excellent, according to Ross, Bill, and Doc Knight. Hannah knew she'd thanked her mother and sisters at least four times already, but she smiled at her mother, who was sitting next to Doc, and thanked her again.

When the coffee had been served, Hannah and Ross had cut their beautifully decorated Double Rainbow Swirl Wedding Cake. Sally and her staff had served it, and toasts had been made to the bride and groom. Then Hannah had invited everyone to visit Sally's dessert buffet while carafes of hot coffee were placed on each table for those who wanted more than one cup.

Hannah and Ross had visited the dessert table first, and Hannah was glad to see that Rodney's pies were not on display. Sally had pulled her aside and confessed that she'd thrown them out because she didn't want anything to remind Hannah of the man who'd almost prevented this joyous celebration from taking place.

Hannah was just indulging her sweet tooth with one of Brooke's superb Lemon Cheesecake Stack Cookies and a slice of Loren's incredible Peach Cheesecake when she noticed that Norman wasn't sitting at their table. And now that she thought about it, she hadn't seen him at Sally's dessert buffet, either. "Did Norman leave before dessert?" she asked Ross, beginning to worry a bit about whether something had happened to one of the cats.

"No, Cookie. He's around here somewhere," Ross told her. "I saw him talking to his mother and Earl near the dessert buffet. Maybe he went over to their table to have dessert with them."

Hannah began to relax again. She'd been borrowing trouble on this, the most wonderful night of her life. Once she'd recovered her equilibrium, she'd begun to enjoy the evening. It had been a dream wedding, a perfect meal at this beautiful reception, and most important of all, her hair was clean!

At the moment, the band that her mother had hired was playing softly in the background. Hannah noticed that they had changed from a medley of familiar standards to songs that were undeniably romantic. She recognized the strains of "Some Enchanted Evening," and she smiled. It had been an enchanted evening for her, at least for the past two hours. She gave a little chuckle under her breath and turned to the man she loved, her new husband, and told him, "I'm just glad the band's not playing country-western music!"

Ross reached out to squeeze her hand. "Don't you like country-western?"

Mike, who was sitting next to Ross, burst into laughter. "Not after Hannah's ride in the trash truck. The driver had his radio on so loud, he couldn't hear her calling out for help and banging the lid on her Dumpster."

Ross released her hand and put his arm around her instead. He gave her a hug and then he smiled at her. "It's funny now, but I don't even want to think about what could have happened if Mike hadn't chased down that driver before he got to the dump."

"Neither do I," Hannah admitted, leaning up against his side.

"Ladies and gentlemen!" Dick spoke into the microphone the singer would use when the band began to play dance music. "Could I have your attention please?"

It was more of a directive than a request, and everyone quieted down and turned toward him.

"Sally and I have a surprise for Hannah," Dick told them. "Is Norman back yet?"

"I'm here," Norman called out from the doorway.

"Sally and I know that there's an important member of Hannah's family that wasn't present at her wedding."

Hannah was completely puzzled. She'd already said hello to her cousins and their families. There was no relative missing that she could remember.

"We wanted this celebration to be complete," Dick continued, "so we decided to bring this family member here to be part of the celebration." He turned to smile at Hannah and Ross. "Ross? Would you like to do the honors?"

"I'd love to!" Ross stood up, gave Hannah a kiss. Then he walked to the door where Norman was standing.

She knew she'd never been so surprised in her life! Hannah's mouth fell open, just like it did in Saturday morning cartoons, and a huge, delighted smile spread over her face. "You didn't!" she exclaimed as Ross picked up an orange and white furry bundle, and walked back to the head table.

"Moishe! You're here!" Hannah felt tears come to her eyes as Moishe began to purr loudly. She hooked his leash to the leg of the table, and gave him a scratch behind his ears. This was the best surprise present anyone had ever given to her!

"You'll probably want these." Sally came over with a dish of jumbo shrimp. "I'm sure he's hungry from racing around Norman's house with Cuddles."

"Rrrrrow!"

Moishe yowled loudly as Hannah picked up a shrimp. And as Hannah fed it to the most important feline member of her family, she knew that this moment was perfect and that she would remember it for the rest of her life.

PEACH CHEESECAKE

Preheat oven to 350 degrees F., rack in the middle position.

For The Fruit:

> 1 can peach pie filling *(I used Comstock)*

Place the unopened can of pie filling in the refrigerator to chill while you make the cheesecake and bake it.

For The Crust:

> 2 cups vanilla wafer cookie crumbs *(measure AFTER crushing)*
> ¾ stick melted salted butter *(6 Tablespoons, 3 ounces)*
> 1 teaspoon almond extract

Pour the melted butter and almond extract over the cookie crumbs. Mix with a fork until they're evenly moistened.

Cut a circle of parchment paper *(or wax paper)* to fit inside the bottom of a 9-inch Springform pan. Spray the

pan with Pam or another nonstick cooking spray, set the paper circle in place, and spray with Pam again.

Dump the moistened cookie crumbs in the pan and press them down over the paper circle and one inch up the sides. Stick the pan in the freezer for 15 to 30 minutes while you prepare the rest of the cheesecake.

For The Baked Topping:

> 2 cups sour cream *(I used Knudson)*
> ½ cup white *(granulated)* sugar
> 1 teaspoon vanilla

Mix the sour cream, sugar, and vanilla together in a small bowl. Cover and refrigerate.

For The Cheesecake Batter:

> 1 cup white *(granulated)* sugar
> 3 eight-ounce packages cream cheese at room
> temperature *(total 24 ounces—the brick
> kind, not the whipped kind)*
> 1 cup mayonnaise
> 4 eggs
> 2 cups white chocolate chips *(I used
> Ghirardelli eleven-ounce net weight bag)*
> 2 teaspoons vanilla

Place the sugar in the bowl of an electric mixer. Add the blocks of cream cheese and the mayonnaise, and whip it up at medium speed until it's smooth.

Add the eggs, one at a time, beating after each addition.

Melt the white chocolate chips in a microwave-safe bowl for 2 minutes. *(Chips may retain their shape, so stir to see if they're melted—if not, microwave in 15-second increments until you can stir them smooth.)*

Cool the melted white chocolate for a minute or two and then mix it into the batter gradually at slow speed. *(Don't add the melted chips too fast, or you may cook the eggs!)*

Scrape down the bowl and add the vanilla, mixing it in thoroughly.

Take your crust out of the freezer and set it on a pan with sides to catch any drips.

Pour the batter on top of the chilled crust.

Bake your Peach Cheesecake at 350 degrees F. for 55 to 60 minutes. Remove the pan from the oven, but DON'T SHUT OFF THE OVEN.

Starting in the center, spoon the sour cream topping over the top of the cheesecake, spreading it out to within a half-inch of the rim.

Return the pan to the oven and bake for an additional 5 minutes.

Cool the cheesecake in the pan on a wire rack. When the pan is cool enough to pick up with your bare hands, place it in the refrigerator and chill it, uncovered, for at least 8 hours.

To serve, run a knife around the inside rim of the pan, release the Springform catch, and lift off the rim. Place a piece of waxed paper on a flat plate and tip it upside down over the top of your cheesecake. Invert the cheesecake so that it rests on the paper.

Carefully pry off the bottom of the Springform pan and remove the paper from the bottom crust.

Invert a serving platter over the bottom crust of your cheesecake. Flip the cheesecake right side up, take off the top plate, and remove the waxed paper.

Open the can of peach pie filling and spread it over the sour cream topping on your cheesecake. You can drizzle a little down the sides if you wish.

LEMON CHEESECAKE STACK COOKIES

Preheat oven to 350 degrees F., rack in the center position.

   24 vanilla wafer cookies
   2 eight-ounce packages softened cream cheese
   ¾ cup white *(granulated)* sugar
   2 eggs
   1 Tablespoon lemon juice
   1 teaspoon vanilla
   24 cupcake liners *(48 if you're like me and you like to use double papers)*
   1 can lemon pie filling, chilled *(I used Comstock)*

Brooke's 1ˢᵗ Note: I got this recipe from Michelle and she told me that it was one of Hannah's favorites. Hannah uses brick cream cheese, the kind that comes in a rectangular package. Don't use whipped cream cheese unless you want to experiment—whipped cream cheese, or low-fat, or Neufchatel might work, but Hannah's never tried it and she doesn't know that for sure.

Brooke's 2ⁿᵈ Note: Hannah has Florence at the Red Owl Grocery order lemon pie filling, but you can also make your own or follow the directions on a package of Jell-O Lemon Pudding and Pie Filling, the kind that makes enough for one pie.

Line two muffin pans *(the kind of pan that makes 12 muffins each)* with paper cupcake liners. Put one vanilla wafer cookie in the bottom of each cupcake paper, flat side down.

Chill the unopened can of lemon pie filling in the refrigerator while you make the cheesecake part of the cookies.

You can do all of this by hand, but it's easier with an electric mixer on low to medium speed:

Mix the softened cream cheese with the white sugar until it's thoroughly blended. Add the eggs one at a time, beating after each addition. Then mix in the lemon juice and vanilla, and beat until light and fluffy.

Spoon the cheesecake batter into the muffin tins, dividing it as equally as you can. When you're through, each cupcake paper should be between half and two-thirds full. *(They're going to look skimpy, but they'll be fine once they're baked and you put on the lemon topping.)*

Bake at 350 degrees F. for 15 to 20 minutes, or until the top has set and has a satin finish. *(The center may sink a bit, but that's okay—the topping will cover that.)*

Cool the Lemon Cheesecake Stack Cookies in the pans on wire racks.

When the cheesecake part is cool, open the can of lemon pie filling and divide it equally among the 24 cupcake papers.

Refrigerate in the muffin tins for at least 4 hours before serving. *(Overnight is fine, too.)* Then take the Lemon Cheesecake Stack Cookies out of the tins, carefully remove the cupcake papers, and place them on a platter for an elegant dessert at a reception or any party where finger food is served.

Brooke's 3rd Note: Right after I took off the cupcake papers and placed these on a platter, I put half of a Maraschino cherry, rounded side up, in the very center of each one. They looked really pretty for Hannah's wedding reception.

Yield: 24 servings

A romantic ten-day cruise is the perfect start to bakery owner Hannah Swensen's marriage. However, with a murder mystery heating up in Lake Eden, Minnesota, it seems the newlywed's homecoming won't be as sweet as she anticipated . . .

After an extravagant honeymoon, Hannah's eager to settle down in Lake Eden and turn domestic daydreams into reality. But when her mother's neighbor is discovered murdered in the condo downstairs, reality becomes a nightmarish investigation. Victoria Bascomb, once a renowned stage actress, was active in the theater community during her brief appearance in town . . . and made throngs of enemies along the way. Did a random intruder murder the woman as police claim, or was a deadlier scheme at play? As Hannah peels through countless suspects and some new troubles of her own, solving this crime—and living to tell about it—might prove trickier than mixing up the ultimate banana cream pie . . .

Please turn the page for an exciting sneak peek of Joann Fluke's newest Hannah Swensen mystery BANANA CREAM PIE MURDER coming soon wherever print and e-books are sold!

Chapter One

Delores Swensen typed THE END and gave a smile of satisfaction as she leaned back in her desk chair. She'd finished the manuscript for her newest Regency romance novel. She was just about to get up and open the bottle of Perrier Jouet she'd been saving for this occasion when she heard a loud crack and she fell to the floor backwards.

For one stunned moment, she stared up at the ceiling in her office in disbelief, unable to move or make a sound. She blinked several times and moved her head tentatively. Nothing hurt. She was still alive. But what had happened? And why had she fallen over backwards?

When the obvious solution occurred to her, Delores started to giggle. The loud crack had sounded when the cushioned seat of her desk chair had sheared off from its base. It was something Doc had warned her would happen someday if she didn't get around to replacing it. And she hadn't. And it had. And here she was on her back, her body effectively swaddled by soft, stuffed leather, barely able to move a muscle.

As she realized that she was in the same position as a turtle flipped over on its back, Delores began to laugh even harder. It was a good thing no one was here to see her! She must look ridiculous. That meant she *had* to figure out some way to get up before Doc came home. If he saw her like this, she'd never hear the end of it. And she wouldn't put it past him to take a photo of her stuck in the chair, on her back, and show it to everyone at the hospital.

Unsure of exactly how to extricate herself, Delores braced her hands on the cushioned arms of the chair and pushed. This didn't work the way she'd thought it, but it *did* work. Instead of moving her body backwards, her action pushed the chair forward. The part of her body that Doc referred to as her gluteus maximus was now several inches away from the seat of the chair, far enough for her to bend her legs, hook her heels on the edge of the chair seat and push it even farther away.

She was getting there! Delores pushed with her heels again and the chair slid several more inches away. By repeating this motion and squirming on her back at the same time, she somehow managed to free herself from her cushioned prison and roll over on hands and knees. She got to her feet by grasping the edge of her desk and pulling herself upright. When she was in a standing position, Delores gave a sigh of relief and promised herself that she'd buy a new desk chair in the morning.

Now that she was on her feet again and none the worse for wear, she decided that celebratory champagne was a necessity. She took the prized bottle from the dorm refrigerator Doc had insisted she install in her office, and opened it with a soft pop. Loud pops were for movie scenes. She'd learned to remove the cork slowly so that not even a drop would escape.

Delores set the open bottle on the desk and went to close the window. She liked fresh air and she always opened it when she worked in the office. She was about to close it when she heard a blood-curdling scream from the floor below.

For a moment Delores just stood there, a shocked expression on her face. Then she glanced at the clock and realized it was a few minutes past eight in the evening. The scream must have come from one of Tori's acting students.

The luxury condo immediately below the penthouse Doc had given her as a wedding present was owned by Victoria Bascomb, Mayor Bascomb's sister. Tori, as she preferred to be called, had been a famous Broadway actress. She'd recently retired and moved to Lake Eden to be closer to the only family she had left, her brother Richard. Unable to completely divorce herself from the life she loved, Tori had volunteered to direct their local theater group, to teach drama at Jordan High, and to give private acting lessons to any Lake Edenite who aspired to take the theater world by storm. If not the richest, Tori Bascomb was undeniably the most famous person in town. Just yesterday, Tori had told Delores that she had won the lifetime achievement award from STAG, the Stage and Theater Actors Guild and she would receive her award, a gold statuette that resembled a male deer, at a nationally televised award ceremony soon.

Delores gave a little laugh. How silly she'd been to forget that Tori gave acting lessons in her home studio! The scream she'd heard was obviously part of an acting lesson. Smiling a bit at her foolishness, Delores reached out again, intending to close and lock the window, but a loud cry made her pause in mid-motion.

"No!" a female voice screamed. "Don't! Please don't!"

Whoever the aspiring actress was, she was very good! Delores began to push the window closed when she heard a sound unlike any other. A gunshot. That was a gunshot! She was sure of it!

The gunshot was followed by a second gunshot, and then a crash from the floor below. Something was wrong! No acting student could be that realistic. This was really happening!

Delores didn't think. She just reacted. She raced for the doorway that led to the back stairway that had been used by hotel employees before the Albion Hotel had been converted into luxury condos. The old stairway had been completely refurbished and accessible exclusively to the penthouse residents.

When Delores arrived at the landing of the floor below, she unlocked the door and rushed out into the narrow lobby that separated the two condos on the floor below the penthouse. She raced to Tori's door and only then did the need for caution cross her mind.

Delores stood there, the key Tori had given her in her hand, and listened. All was quiet inside Tori's condo, no sounds at all. If what she'd heard had been an acting lesson, Tori should be speaking to the would-be actress, critiquing the scene she'd just performed.

As Delores continued to listen for sounds, she considered her options. She'd look very foolish if she unlocked the door and stepped inside to find that Tori and her student were perfectly fine. On the other hand, she could be walking into danger if what she'd heard was a real murder and the intruder was still there. If she called the police before she went in, they'd advise her to wait until they got there. But what if someone needed immediate medical attention?

Delores hesitated for another moment or two and then she decided to knock. She might feel foolish if Tori came to the door and said that everything was fine, but it couldn't hurt to check. She raised her hand and knocked sharply three times.

There was no answer and she heard no rushing footfalls as the intruder hurried to a hiding place. There were no sounds from inside at all. Delores hesitated for another moment and then she made a decision. She reached into her pocket, pulled out her cell phone, and dialed the emergency number for the Winnetka County Sheriff's Station.

"Sheriff's station. Detective Kingston speaking."

Delores took a deep breath. She'd been hoping to contact her son-in-law, Bill Todd, but instead she'd gotten Mike. He was a by-the-book cop and he'd tell her to stay outside the door and wait for him to get there.

"Mike. It's Delores," she said, thinking fast. "Stay on the line, will you, please? I heard a sound from Tori Bascomb's condo and I'm going in to make sure everything's all right."

"Delores. I want you to wait until . . ."

Delores unlocked the door with one hand and pushed it open. Then, holding the phone away from her ear so she wouldn't hear Mike's objections, she glanced around Tori's living room. Nothing was out of place, no overturned chairs, no strangers lurking in corners, no sign of anything unusual. But the scream she'd heard hadn't come from the living room. It had come from the room directly below her office and that was the room that Tori had converted into her acting studio.

Delores moved toward the studio silently, holding the phone in her left hand. It was still sputtering and squawking, but she ignored it. As she prepared to open the door, she spotted a piece of artwork on a table in the hallway. It was made of a heavy metal, probably silver, and it resembled a thin but curvaceous lady holding her arms aloft. Delores grabbed it. It was just as heavy as it looked and it would serve as a weapon if the occasion warranted.

The door to the studio was slightly open and Delores peeked in. The focus of the room was the U-shaped couch facing a low platform handcrafted of cherry wood. The platform was one step high and ran the length of the opposite wall, forming a stage for Tori's would-be actors and actresses. The couch served as Tori's throne. It was where she sat to observe her students. Delores had sat there one afternoon and she knew it was made of baby-soft, butterscotch-colored leather. A fur throw was draped over the back of the couch. Delores hadn't asked Tori which particular animals had given their lives to create the fur throw, but she suspected that it had been very expensive and was probably made from Russian sable.

The scene that presented itself did not look threatening, so Delores stepped into the studio. The indirect lighting that covered the ceiling bathed the studio in a soft glow. Delores glanced at the round coffee table in front of the couch and drew in her breath sharply. A bottle of champagne was nestled in a silver wine bucket next to the table and a crystal flute filled with champagne sat on the table next to a distinctive bakery box that Delores immediately recognized. It was a bakery box from The Cookie Jar, the bakery and coffee shop that her eldest daughter owned. The lid was open and Delores could tell that it contained one of Hannah's Banana Cream Pies. It was Tori's favorite pie and she'd told Delores that she often served it when she had guests.

The flute filled with champagne was interesting. Clouds of tiny bubbles were rising to the surface and that meant it had been poured quite recently. Delores knew, through personal experience, that the bubbles slowed and eventually stopped as time passed.

Two crystal dessert plates were stacked on the coffee table, along with two silver dessert forks. It was obvious that Tori had been expecting a guest.

Delores set the phone down on the couch and stared at the coffee table. The puzzle it presented was similar to the homework that her daughters had brought home from kindergarten, a photocopied sheet of paper with a picture drawn in detail. The caption had been *What is wrong with this picture?* Something was wrong with Tori's coffee table. What was it?

The answer occurred to Delores almost immediately. Tori had set out two dessert plates and two dessert forks, but only one flute of champagne. That was a puzzling omission. Delores knew that Tori loved champagne and judging by the label that was peeking out of the ice bucket, this was very good champagne. Did this mean that Tori was imbibing, but her anticipated guest was not? Or had Tori filled her champagne glass and carried it away to drink someplace else in the condo? And that question was followed by an even more important question. Where *was* Tori?

Delores was dimly aware that hissing and crackling sounds were coming from her phone. Mike was still talking to her, but his words were undecipherable, muffled by the fact she'd placed her cell phone down on the cushions of the couch. Delores ignored it and glanced around the studio again. Her gaze reached the floor near the back of the couch and halted, focusing on that area. The white plush wall-to-wall carpet looked wet. Something had been spilled there.

Delores moved toward the wet carpet. She rounded the corner of the couch and stopped, reaching out to steady herself as she saw a sight that she knew would haunt her dreams for years to come. Tori was sprawled on the rug, a sticky red stain on one of the beautiful silk caftans she wore on evenings that she worked at home.

The stain on the caftan glistened in the light from the tiny bulbs in the ceiling. Delores shuddered as she saw the crystal champagne flute tipped on its side on the floor, its expensive contents now permanently embedded in the plush white fibers. Thank goodness the blood hadn't gotten on the carpet! That could have permanently ruined it. She'd have to give Tori the name of a good carpet cleaning firm so that they could remove the champagne stain.

"Ohhhh!" Delores gave a cry that ended in a sob. Tori wouldn't need the name of a carpet cleaner. Tori would never need anything again. Tori was dead! Her friend was dead!

Tears began to fall from her eyes, but Delores couldn't seem to look away. Her friend's eyes seemed fixed on the ceiling and her mouth was slightly open, as if she were protesting the cruel twist of fate that had befallen her.

"It's okay, Delores. We're here."

The sound of a calm male voice released Delores from her horrid fixation and she managed to turn to face the sound. It *was* Mike, and he had brought *Lonnie with him.*

They had both come to help her. She wanted to thank them, but she couldn't seem to find the words.

"Lonnie's going to take you back upstairs and stay with you until Michelle comes."

"Michelle's still here?" Delores recovered enough to ask about her youngest daughter. "I thought she was going back to college tonight."

"She was, but she decided to stay until Hannah and Ross get back. I'll be up later to take your statement."

As Lonnie took her arm, Delores began to shake. It was as if she had been hit with a blast of icy winter wind. She leaned heavily on Lonnie's arm as he led her from the room, from the awful sight of the friend she'd never see again, the friend who wouldn't come over for coffee in the morning, the downstairs neighbor who would no longer sit by the pool under the climate-controlled dome in Delores and Doc's penthouse garden, and chat about her career on the stage. She would never collect her lifetime achievement award and hear the applause of her peers. Victoria Bascomb's stellar life had ended and Delores was overwhelmed with grief and sadness.

As she entered the penthouse on Lonnie's arm and sank onto the soft cushions of the couch, another emotion began to grow in her mind. It replaced the heaviness of her sadness, at least for the moment. That emotion was anger, anger that her friend had died in such a senseless manner. How dare someone come into Tori's home and hurt her!

As Delores sat there waiting for Michelle to arrive, she was filled with a fiery resolve. She had to tell Hannah that Tori had been murdered. The moment that Michelle arrived, they had to try to reach Hannah. They needed her and she had to help them. Her eldest daughter would know where to start and what to do. Hannah had to come home to Lake Eden immediately so that they could find Tori's killer and make him pay for the horrible crime he had committed!